Adopted Son

By Dominic Peloso

The Invisible College Press

Arlington, VA

Publisher's Note:
This is a work of fiction. Names, characters, places, and incidents are either the product of the author's imagination or are used fictitiously, and any resemblance to actual persons living or dead, events, alien viruses, or locales is entirely coincidental.

Print Edition ISBN: 978-1-931468-26-8
Electronic Edition ISBN: 978-1-931468-76-3
Cover Painting by Julie Peloso
Cover Design by Paul Mossinger
Second Printing

The Invisible College Press, LLC
P.O. Box 209
Woodbridge VA 22194-0209
http://www.invispress.com
Please send question and comments to:
editor@invispress.com

Prologue

Tyler Memorial Hospital, Tyler, TX

"Push!"

Lorraine strained her stomach muscles. Her heart pounded, her feet struggled against the stirrups. "Push!" the doctor yelled again, louder this time. Tom looked down at his wife and rubbed his hand softly across her hair. Sweat poured down Lorraine's face. She breathed, in out in out, it didn't help. The doctor said that this would be a difficult birth owing to the baby's size, but she hadn't expected so much pain. The Lamaze lessons were useless. She was about to rip apart.

"Just a little more honey," said Tom quietly, trying to sound reassuring. He wished that he could make it better somehow, help things along, but all he could do was stand there and squeeze Lorraine's hand. With childbirth, men are just impotent bystanders.

"I see the head," said the doctor, all crouched down beneath Lorraine like a catcher waiting for a pitch. "Give me one more big push Lorraine, just one more." The doctor had his hands on the baby's bald skull. Lorraine let out a moan. The doctor guided the newborn out of the birth canal. Tom heard a tiny cough, then another, then a child's cry. He was a father at last. A nurse dropped a tool on the floor. It clattered loudly as Tom rushed over to see his child for the first time.

The doctor looked down at the small bloody creature he cradled in his arms. The most apparent thing that you could see wrong was the color. The child's skin wasn't the traditional peachy-pink, but instead a cold, dull gray. Its head was big, far larger than normal. The rest of its body seemed thin and underdeveloped in comparison. The thing looked up at him with its two large, insect-like, black eyes. A cry came from its tiny mouth– familiar sounding at first, but it grew more and more inhuman the longer you listened to it. "Let me see, let me see," Lorraine called, still in a bit of a stupor from the drugs and the strain. Tom looked over the doctor's shoulder and got his first glimpse of his child as it reached out and squeezed the doctor's thumb with its tiny hand.

"What the hell is that?" exclaimed Tom.

Book 1: Birth

Six months earlier, in Mercury, NV

Ray Johnston walked past the rows of empty newspaper boxes that line the path to the cafeteria. It was early morning in the secret city and the air was fresh and clean. He lit a cigarette and crossed the parking lot, his steps falling heavily against the worn asphalt. Under his arm was a package– an orange diplomatic pouch, with the seal still intact. Ray wasn't normally a man to worry. He had spent almost twenty years of his life on the inside. He had seen all sorts of bizarre and dangerous things. He had come across everything from ricin-filled darts hidden in umbrellas to blueprints for matchbook-sized nuclear weapons, but nothing scared him as much as the thing in the pouch. He had spent twenty years as a spook, moving closer and closer to the inner circle, having more and more secrets revealed to him. He had always been ready to accept what they had told him. He had always been able to conceive of how all the schemes, all the betrayals, all the gadgets had been put together. Nothing they had revealed to him had truly surprised him. That was before his introduction to the Majestic-12 project. Now nothing made sense, especially the thing in the pouch.

But Johnston was a company man, and he wouldn't let a little thing like abject terror stop him from doing what needed to be done. He couldn't let his feelings show on his face. He had gotten so used to that attitude that his bravado came naturally. He spit out the remains of his cigarette and moved purposefully towards his car, parked near the dormitory. He walked past the dreary, yellow-shingled buildings that make up the secret city of Mercury, Nevada. Outdated signs hand-painted in 1950s style letters warned him to look out for radiological safety and to report all suspicious activity. He walked past the rusted spools of wire and the dilapidated Mobile Radiation Lab van. Mercury was a dinosaur, a last pathetic remnant of the Cold War. It was built in the 1950s as part of the Nevada Test Site, and it was used to house the thousands of workers that spent the later half of the Twentieth Century making bigger and bigger holes in the Nevada desert with nuclear bombs. After the U.S. stopped testing, there wasn't much use for all the miners, geologists, and other workers, so they all left the secret city. It was mostly abandoned now. Just a few scientists scattered about, doing research on the environment, and of course the black projects. Johnston got in his car and turned on the ignition. He turned the air conditioner up to full. It would soon be very hot here in the desert.

The Nevada Test Site is larger than Rhode Island and was built to maintain secrets. They lie scattered out there, in the barren Nevada desert. Johnston drove north on the main road. As you pass over the initial ridge into the central valley, you can see small buildings, dirt roads leading to nowhere, esoteric arrays of pipes and wires. Johnston ignores them as he drives. What goes on in those buildings? Who works there? Those questions are not easily answered. Each place has its own secrets and its own cadre of workers. None of them know what the others are doing. That is the point of the site. It provides the isolation, the secrecy, the privacy that these groups need to accomplish their mission. The question of whether or not the missions are in the public interest never occurs to Johnston. He knows that they are. He's a company man.

An hour's drive north of Mercury is a mesa. You can recognize it easily; it's the only flat-topped mountain around. Beyond that mesa lies Johnston's destination. In the prospector days of the old west it was named Groom Lake. Today it is known by the more generic title: Area 51.

Tyler Memorial Hospital, Tyler, TX. Six months after Ray Johnston's drive to Groom Lake.

Tom Miller sits in the waiting room of the sterile, white hospital. He sits uncomfortably and erect, hands in his lap. He looks like he's not really sure that he's supposed to be here. Up and down the hall, people come and go on seemingly urgent missions. The cacophonous noise of dozens of voices combined with the clattering of equipment fills the air. A television hangs in the corner of the waiting room. The drone of an old sitcom was intermittently drowned out by a siren or an announcement over the PA system. Tom wasn't really listening. He was waiting for news. It had been over two hours already and still nothing. Tom's gaze remained fixed on the swiveling door that led to the operating rooms. Men dressed in green scrubs kept coming and going, coming and going, but not his wife's doctor. He was nowhere to be found. He was still in there, trying to figure out what happened, what went wrong. Tom pulled off his dirty baseball cap and dropped it in the chair next to him. He put his face in his hands in a combination of despair and fatigue. He and Lorraine had been trying for so long to have a child, to give a grandson to his father. And now this happens.

"Mr. Miller?" Tom looked up from his seat. His wife's doctor was standing over him. "Mr. Miller we've examined your son. The good news is that he seems to be internally healthy. His heartbeat is strong and he is alert. That bodes well for the future." The doctor sat down next to him. A second doctor came and joined them on the couch. "I've called in a specialist." He looked over to the second doctor.

"Mr. Miller, I'm Doctor Robbins. I'm a pediatric surgeon. I've looked at your child." He held out his hand.

"What's going on doctor? What the hell happened? What is that monster?" Tom was desperate for answers. No one had told him anything.

"It's not a monster Mr. Miller, it's your son. It is a baby boy. You've got to be strong for him. He's going to have a rough time ahead, if he even survives at all."

Tom was a simple man. He had some corn fields on the outskirts of town. He knew the land, he knew how to drive a tractor. He wasn't ready to deal with a problem like this. He wasn't sure that he would have the internal strength to handle the responsibility. He wasn't even sure what was going on.

"Mr. Miller, your son has severe birth defects. He is underweight, and his skull is much larger than it should be. There is also some major problems with his eyes. I doubt that he will ever be able to see very clearly."

"Is he going to die?" asked Tom sheepishly.

"Well," replied Dr. Thomas, "The prognosis looks good for now. As I said, he seems to be eating and alert. He seems to have a strong heartbeat, and he seems to be functioning quite normally. It doesn't look like there is any neurological damage at this point. We can't be sure that there won't be any long term developmental consequences though."

"What happened? What went wrong?"

"I don't think that we will ever know the answer to that Mr. Miller. It might be radiation exposure, it might be pesticides, it might be just some rare genetic deformity. We will be doing some tests, but we won't have the answers for a while." The doctor flipped through the charts. "According to this, neither parent has any genetic disposition to the major things we check for. Of course we can't rule out anything at this point."

"Just before she got pregnant, Lorraine had a little cold. We both got sick." Tom was stretching for answers.

"No Mr. Miller" Dr. Thomas said knowingly, "Colds don't cause birth defects. It must have been something else."

"What happens now doctor?"

"Well, we'll keep him here for a while," replied Dr. Robbins. "We'll run some tests and try to determine what exactly happened. I have to warn you, although the child appears to be healthy right now, we have no idea how he'll develop. He's likely to have problems with his internal organs since his chest cavity seems to be undersized. Plus, judging by his skin color, his blood isn't moving oxygen as efficiently, he seems rather anemic."

Dr. Thomas continued, "You can see him if you'd like. He's with your wife right now. We thought that it would be best to allow them to bond a little while they can. That child is going to probably going to spend a lot of his life in institutions like this."

The two doctors rose to their feet and helped Mr. Miller up. His muscles were sore from sitting on the couch for so long. The doctors led him down the hallway to the rooms for new mothers and their babies. As he passed each door, he glanced inside and saw happy little families. Mothers, with hair still disheveled from labor, cradling their infants in brightly colored blankets. Doting fathers sitting by the bedside, playing cootchie-coo with their bundles of joy. Tom wondered to himself about his child. It was a freak. How could he deal with that? What would he tell his friends? This was a great shame on him. All those things he wanted would never come to pass. The kid wouldn't be the star quarterback of the football team. They'd never go on their first deer hunt. He wouldn't be able to pass on to his offspring his love of the land and knowledge of how to make things grow. He was saddled with a freak. This was going to screw up his entire life. Was it worthwhile trying to have another kid? Maybe that one would be normal. Maybe he could send this one away, to a home for freaks or whatever. Maybe try from scratch. Maybe that would be the best for it. He couldn't give it the care it needed. He wasn't sure that he could feel for this deformed thing. He wasn't sure that he could love it in a way that a kid needed to be loved. On a subconscious level he began to doubt his own wife. What was wrong with her that she could bear such a hideous thing? There must be something defective about her womb. Or maybe it was him. He looked down at his pants as he walked. Was he defective in some way? Was there something wrong with his genes? He was less of a man, incapable of propagating the species properly. Was this some punishment from God for some unrecognized sin? Tom was not a particularly religious man, but he found himself asking his creator why this terrible burden had been laid on him.

He walked through the door of Lorraine's room, still looking blank, hat twisted up in his hands. Most of his attention was directed inwards, and he didn't have the energy to project expression. She was lying in the bed, hair all a mess, cradling their little boy in her arms. She looked as gorgeous as the day he first met her. Tom moved closer, hesitantly, not sure what to expect, not sure what to feel. The little hairless thing in the blanket looked up at him with its big black eyes and cooed softly. "Isn't he beautiful?" said a sobbing Lorraine. Tom leaned over to get a closer look. It wasn't that bad really. He moved his hand to touch the child's head but pulled back instinctively when the boy fidgeted. It would take some getting used to. He tried again. The forehead was warm and soft. Tom could feel the life flowing through it. The young boy reached his tiny hand out and wrapped its impossibly long, slender fingers around Tom's thumb. A tear welled up in his eye. He tried to hold it back, after all, men don't cry.

Outside the room, down the hall, another man was meeting his son for the first time. He shouted loudly over and over again, "I'm a father! I'm a father!" The Millers could hear the anonymous man quite clearly. They could tell the joy in his voice as he celebrated the miracle of creation. Tom stood silent over his progeny.

That same day, in an unmarked building in Groom Lake, NV

"I'd like to welcome you all to the annual status meeting of Project Beachcomber." The general continued with his opening remarks. Ray Johnston sat stiffly in his seat. He wasn't a "suit guy" and having to spend the afternoon with a silk noose tied around his neck made him uncomfortable. He looked about the room, scanning the crowd. There were a lot more people here than usual, many new faces. The project was expanding. To Ray, that implied that there was more serious interest at higher levels. Someone up there was listening. As the general droned on, Ray nodded and bobbed his head in a half-sleep. He didn't have the proper temperament for meetings. He was more action oriented.

"Since we have so many new faces here, I thought that I would begin with a little history," said the general. Unlike Ray, Brigadier General Dumphries was a "suit guy." That was how he made it as far as he did in the Air Force. Meeting after meeting in sharply-pressed, blue, polyester suits, looking good and being punctual. It was the clean, crisp look of his uniform that got him that first star. It was his crisp, clean look that made him appear to be the ideal candidate for such a high-security assignment. He was getting quite pudgy around the waist. His PT scores were pretty poor, even for a general. However, his attention to detail, regulation, and following orders to the letter had always caught the eye of superiors. His evaluations were always exemplary, even if most of his accomplishments were simply dull reports that were shelved and never read. Such is the life of an intelligence officer.

"Project Bluefly was started during the Cold War. Our original mission was to search out and recover film canisters from spy satellites. Back in the old days, there wasn't digital transmission of images, so the only way to get photos back to earth was to drop them from orbit. Of course, they didn't always land where they were supposed to land. The Soviets knew what was going on, and they were trying just as hard to recover our canisters as we were, those things were valuable. The U.S. government couldn't publicize the fact that these canisters were landing all over small town America because we didn't want to admit that we were spying on anyone. It was all hush-hush stuff back then. So we sent out our boys to investigate any reports of 'strange things'– stuff falling from the sky, alien artifacts, whatever. It was from our efforts, and the Ruskies, that led to the myths about 'men in black.'" To emphasize the point, General Dumphries made the little "quote" sign with his hands when he said "men in black."

"Of course, once we started broadcasting analog data from our satellites the number of canisters that dropped to earth declined rapidly." There was some scattered giggling. "The problem was though, that it didn't go to zero. We were getting ready to shut Bluefly down, but we kept getting reports of stuff falling from the sky. We kept checking it out. Sometimes it was Russian film canisters, but even those stopped falling after a while. The rest of the stuff was unknown– strange metals, pieces of things, who knows what. Not all of it could be identified by the science boys. Instead of shutting Bluefly down, the President gave us a new mission, to seek out and find any anomalous objects that we could and to try to identify them. We were renamed Beachcomber to allow the government to declassify the Bluefly documents without admitting that the mission was ongoing, and we were moved into the Majestik-12 security compartment. And that brings us here today for our annual meeting." The general cleared his throat. "I can see that we've got all the usual suspects here today, so if everybody has had their donuts and bagels, I'll introduce our first speaker..."

That was Ray's cue to wake up. He hurriedly grabbed under his seat for his package and made an attempt to straighten his cheap polyester tie. "...Ray J., who is going to give us a briefing on what could be a potentially interesting new find." There was some sporadic clapping as Ray moved through the crowd of generals, middle-managers, and contractors to the podium. In his hands was a large orange bag, similar to the one that he had carried with him to Groom Lake six months before. He accidentally bumped against a few people on the way up. Finally he reached the stand. He wasn't used to speaking in front of people and felt rather awkward in his suit. He fumbled through his coat pocket for his cue cards, but he didn't really need them. He knew what he was going to say.

"Ladies and Gentlemen, this briefing will be given at the Top Secret/Majestik-12 level. If anyone here doesn't have that caveat, you should probably leave now." No one got up, nor was anyone expected to. It was just formal procedure to ask about clearances before a briefing. "Here at Beachcomber, we are used to getting trash. Most of the pieces that we bring in are found to be meteorites, or hoaxes, or parts from airplanes. A lot of the research papers that will be presented today will talk about those things. They will talk about how we spent $25k on a metallurgical analysis of a screw, only to prove conclusively that it fell off a Cesna into grannie's back yard. Today I've got something different. In this diplomatic pouch, I have something that could be a very key find for the Beachcomber project. Potentially, this one object could justify the entire Beachcomber budget for next year." He broke the diplomatic seal on the pouch and pulled out a silver cylinder. It was about two and a half feet long, and maybe eight inches in diameter. One end was pointed like a missile. It was smooth and polished. You could tell that it had once been rather shiny, but the pointy end was blackened considerably. All down one side of the cylinder were small holes, about a few millimeters in diameter each.

Ray dropped the bag to the floor and rotated the cylinder around for the room to see.

"This here is what I consider to be one of the most intriguing items that the Beachcomber project has found in the last forty years. I personally picked this up from our station in New Delhi last month. It had been found lying in a field by some school children a few weeks before and was being stored in a local police station pending identification. The schoolchildren said that it was in a pit. I visited that pit and here's what it looked like...," Ray handed a slide to the contractor who placed it onto an overhead projector. "As you can see from the pit dimensions, as well as the blackened tip, this object obviously fell from a great height, probably from orbit. That makes it of interest to Beachcomber and to all of the Majestik-12 projects. Beachcomber originally thought that it might be an errant satellite, but it seems to be hollow and has no internal components of any kind. There is no reason to send up an empty satellite into space. Then we thought that it might be a missile casing, but we couldn't think of any reason that someone would test an empty missile. The test wouldn't be of any use to you because the missile would fly differently when filled. It was classified as an enigma and got shipped to a Majestik-12 contractor lab for testing. We've gotten some very odd results, which I think could become very important."

Ray looked around the room. Most of the generals were dozing off. They were really only here to show off how much clearance they had and to get a free weekend in Vegas. These people got their jobs based on kissing up to the right people or being well-groomed and trustworthy. It was the same here deep in the black world as it was everywhere else in the government. There was no secret cadre of superspies that kept the U.S. safe, just a bunch of schmucks who couldn't get jobs in the civilian world. None of these people had any real interest or capabilities to do the job that they had been assigned. Most didn't believe in either Beachcomber or

Majestik-12 in general. They weren't ready to accept anything outside their preconceived notions. Ray would have to make them listen. If he was right, there wasn't much time.

"The first significant thing that we found was that this material isn't typical of any known alloy we've put into space. I've had the object analyzed, and it has a very strange isotopic spectrum. It's primarily made of steel and tungsten, but the isotopic ratios are unlike those typically found on earth. There's more ^{59}Fe than one would expect. That would imply that the material used to fabricate this object didn't come from Earth." That got some people's attention. Since the Soviets had self-imploded, all of these generals were going around looking for an enemy. All they ever found were petty dictators and inept terrorists. Whoever made this object could be the real threat that they've been waiting for. "Now there are three possibilities that could explain this. First, the object could have been made out of a meteorite, second, it could be an elaborate hoax in which a reactor was used to change the isotopic spectrum, or third, it could be a genuine alien artifact."

A chorus of cries sprung up from about the room. Was it an attack? That was big news. Questions flew at the podium. Was he sure, how did he know, who could have done it, why were they shooting at India? Ray tried to calm the crowd down a little bit. "We don't know what the purpose of the cylinder is. It clearly didn't explode. There were no traces of hazardous chemicals. We've tested those kids, and none of them are sick. CDC databases haven't showed a spike of diseases anywhere in the world, so we don't believe that this is a biological attack, or at least an effective biological attack. This could just be a test run for something. Or maybe it's a message." The crowd interpreted that as 'no casualties, nothing to worry about,' and began to slump back into their boredom-induced catatonia. Once again, Majestik-12 blows the whistle on something that initially sounded big, but turned out to be nothing in the end.

"One more thing," continued Ray. "Unlike most of our other anomalies, this object is not unique. Beachcomber has been finding these all over the place." Ray moved to a curtain that covered the back of the podium and pulled it aside. There, lined up on the floor were about a dozen objects identical to the one he had just pulled from the diplomatic pouch. "Gentlemen, Beachcomber has been picking these objects up for about eight months now. They seem to be falling indiscriminately around the world. We've picked up objects from most of the continents, all with the same characteristics, same isotopic spectrum. And who knows how many more we haven't found yet, or how many the Russians have picked up? I've been in contact with experts in other parts of the Majestik-12 program, and we are of unanimous opinion. We believe that these objects can only be explained as the beginning of contact from an alien intelligence."

The crowd replied with an even louder chorus of cries and questions. Ray bit down on a bagel. This was going to be a long meeting.

Two months after the Beachcomber annual review meeting, Tyler Memorial Hospital, Tyler, TX

Tom Miller was sitting in Dr. Thomas's office at Tyler Memorial. He felt a little nervous being here. He was more used to being out in a field dressed in overalls and dust. He wasn't used to offices. The only time he ever went to an office was to get his loans approved at the bank. Being in a fancy office like this made him feel uncomfortable and underdressed, just like church. It was almost as if they did it on purpose. Made the office real fancy and all so that you would feel a little inferior. Maybe the doctors figured that they wouldn't get as much back-talk that way. Maybe they thought that if they looked all fancy you wouldn't mind paying the ridiculous amounts they charged.

Tom had no intention of giving any back-talk or arguing about bills. He just wanted to find out if he could finally take his kid home from the hospital. He'd been here his entire life. Eight months now of being probed and poked and who knows what else by a team of doctors from all over. They even brought a few in from Dallas a last month to take a look. They all wanted to gawk at the freak, he guessed.

Dr. Thomas paged through the file on his desk. He and his team had gone over all the data and still didn't really know what was going on, even after eight months of probing and poking. "Well Mr. Miller, we've done every test that we can think of, and we have no real conclusive explanation for your son's malformities." Tom hated the word 'malformities,' it was just another way of saying 'freak.' Why didn't the doctors call a spade a spade? Everything had to be cloaked in medical mumbo-jumbo doublespeak. "However we have positively diagnosed the problem. It looks like your son is suffering from a very rare disease called Handel's Syndrome. There are only a dozen or so known cases, mostly in Europe.

It was only first documented in the literature a few months ago. It is a genetic defect that we've just discovered. Most humans have 46 chromosomes, your son seems to have 48."

"What does that mean doctor?"

"Well, chromosomes are the instructions that we have in each cell. It's like a blueprint. Every species on Earth has them, animals, plants, everything. Some have more than others, some have less. Every species has a different set. Somehow your child got some extra instructions in him and that is what is causing his malformities."

"So, are you saying that he isn't human?" Tom was a bit confused.

"No Tom, he is as human as you or I. Kids with Downs Syndrome have sort of a similar problem, they have an extra chromosome. But they're still human. Kids with Handel's Syndrome are still human too, even if they don't look exactly like us."

"Can you fix it doc?"

"No. Unfortunately, there is nothing we can do to fix it. There are some experimental gene therapies that are being developed, but no one is expecting those therapies to handle something as severe as Handel's Syndrome. Genetic damage like this is something that child is going to have to live with his entire life." The doctor picked up the child's chart and opened it for Tom. "There is good news however. Other than his outward appearance and an irregular heartbeat, he seems to be healthy. He is growing and responding to stimuli. We have no reason to believe that he won't be able to live a full and productive life." The doctor smiled, trying to put a good face on the news. Optimism was very important in cases where no treatment option existed.

Tom wasn't at a stage yet where optimism really helped. He leaned forward in his chair and said hesitantly, "But he'll always be a freak, won't he?"

"Now don't say that Tom. Your son is going to have a hard road ahead of him. There are some things that we might be able to do with plastic surgery, but there is little chance that he'll ever look like you or me. You'll have to accept that, and you'll have to be strong for him. He is going to need a lot of support as he grows up. Let me give you the name of a good counselor." He took a business card out of his desk and handed it to Tom. "That's the name of a good specialist in Dallas who is an expert in child malformities. She should be able to help you and your wife. It's going to take a little extra work, but you'll make it. A lot of other new parents have had to deal with a lot worse, and they've found the strength to be there for their children." Dr. Thomas started to get up out of his padded leather chair. "But, from a review of the literature, there doesn't seem to be much point keeping him in the hospital any longer. We'll need to do checkups on him every few months of course, but you and your wife can take him home. That's probably the best place for him to be right now."

Tom stood up and brushed the seat off a little bit. He still felt a little awkward. Dr. Thomas led him to the door of his office and out into the hallway of the maternity ward. They walked down the sterile corridors to the visiting room. His wife was sitting in a cushioned chair. She was holding the baby in her arms, rocking it back and forth slowly. It was tightly wrapped in a large, blue blanket. Her long brown hair had fallen into her face a little, and she looked beautiful as the light from the window spread rays across her body. She didn't react to the men's arrival for a few seconds, like most mothers she was fully absorbed by her child's sleeping face.

"Lorraine, we can take him home. The doctor says that we can take him home today," Tom said flatly.

"Really?" said Lorraine, lifting her gaze to the doctor. She had a look of expectant joy on her face. She stood up carefully, so as not to wake the child. "We can take him now?"

"All we need to do is have you fill out the release paperwork, it should only take a few minutes," said Dr. Thomas. "I'll take you over to the duty nurse."

The three (technically four) of them began walking down the corridor to the exit of the maternity ward. Tom was amazed at Lorraine's response. "I guess it's just a girl thing," he thought to himself. How was it that she was able to love so unreservedly? She chatted with Dr. Thomas about care and feeding as they walked. The question of what had happened to the child never crossed her mind. She didn't care about that. She only cared about being with the people she loved, no matter what they looked like, no matter what problems they had. "She's quite a woman," Tom thought. He felt lucky to have her. He was going to have a hard time with this, no matter how open-minded he wanted to be, he was still a simple farmer from Texas, and he knew that. It was going to take a lot of effort on his part to be a good Dad. Perhaps more than he could give. He let out an inaudible sigh.

Tom stopped in front of the window to infant care ward. He looked at their faces, row after row of little bundles of joy wrapped in blue and pink swaddling. A few nurses moved in and out of the rows, distributing bottles, blankets, diapers. All the infants smiled back at them, their faces bright with hope for the future. All the faces were normal, all but his. His child was a freak. Why did this have to happen to him? Here were hundreds of normal babies, why didn't they have any "genetic malformities?" Why had God saddled him with this responsibility? It could have just as easily been someone else. He could have had one of these kids. He could be looking in this window at his kid right now, tapping on the glass at a beautiful boy, with hair and eyes and pink skin and all the trappings of normalcy. But no, he had a freak to deal with.

Lorraine sensed that her husband was no longer beside her. She stopped and turned to see him staring blankly in the window. She walked back to him and put her hand on his shoulder. She knew what he was thinking. She knew what he was feeling, because deep down, she felt it too. But she knew that this was the way it was supposed to be, that she had been given this child not as a burden, but as an opportunity. A way to show how much love could achieve. She knew that her son would grow up to be a great man someday, in spite of his problems. She was just sure of it. Tom turned and faced her. "Come on, let's go home," she said to him in a quiet yet hopeful voice. "Yeah," said Tom dejectedly, "Let's get home." Together they walked out of the maternity ward.

The same day, Washington Square Park, New York City, NY. Under the brush.

The first time the girl knew she was pregnant was when her water broke. She was lying under a tree at the corner of the park, away from the tourists and pigeons. A chill was in the air that morning, the grass was wet with dew. "Winter is coming," she thought as she pulled her ratty green jacket around her. It wasn't much to ward off the cold, but it was all she had. Well, that's not totally true. She also had several slugs of liquor in her, and that was warmer than any blanket. She lay in the grass under the tree, trying to will herself into more of a drunken stupor than she could expect from the amount of alcohol she could actually afford. Her legs felt wet. She looked down. At first she didn't understand what was happening. "Perhaps it was all a hallucination," she thought. She tried to ignore it. As with a lot of stuff, if you don't think about it, it just goes away. But then the cramps started. At 16, she didn't know much about the process of birth. Her life consisted of running and hiding and searching for food. Of defending herself against attackers, and giving in to them when she thought that she could get something out of it. She staggered to her feet and made it to the public restroom before the cramps overtook her.

The public restrooms in any park leave something to be desired, but in downtown Manhattan, they are exceptionally bad. The smell was something unidentifiable– an amalgam of dozens of other scents, each offensive in its own way. The floor hadn't been swept in months, if ever. The girl made it to the one stall with a working door and collapsed on the floor. The child began to come out. "No, no, no," thought the girl. "I don't need this, I don't need this." She tried to stuff the little thing back inside her in a vain attempt to solve the problem, but that obviously didn't work. The child came. It pushed itself into the world through sheer force of will.

The girl lay on the floor for quite a long time. She could feel the fluids leaking from her. She could feel the wriggling of the newborn. She could hear its faint cries and gurgles as it attempted to clear its lungs. After a time she gathered the strength to stand back up. There was a large puddle of fluid spreading across the floor of the stall, leaking into the corridor. Around here, no one would notice. The girl didn't know what to do. She looked down with complete shock. It wasn't a real child that she had just borne, it was some kind of freak thing. Its head was big, far larger than normal. The rest of its body was thin and underdeveloped in comparison. The thing looked up at her with its two large, insect-like, black eyes. A cry came from its tiny mouth– familiar sounding at first, but it grew more and more inhuman the longer you listened to it. The girl stared in disbelief, "What the hell is that?" Living on the streets she had never heard of Handel's Syndrome. To her it was just some sort of baby monster. "Perhaps I'm just hallucinating again," she thought. She hadn't had any hard drugs in almost a week, but maybe it was a flashback or something.

The girl was scared. She didn't know what to do with the little mess that was wriggling around. She scooped the thing up in her green jacket. She brushed herself off a bit, straightened her hair. She carried the child out of the restroom, and, looking carefully around to make sure that she wasn't spotted, dropped it into one of the wastebaskets at the bathroom entrance. "Well, that's over with," said the girl, as she staggered off through the park. The smell of vendor's hot dogs and roasted peanuts was starting to fill the air.

The child lay in the swaddling, kicking instinctively. There wasn't much air. But it had made it this far, it had pushed its way into life, and it wasn't going to go back to the void so quickly. On some instinctive, fundamental level, it knew that it needed to extricate itself. It pushed and pulled, testing its new limbs. It began to cry. Although muffled, the cries would eventually attract the attention of a passing police officer. The child would survive.

Five months after Lorraine Miller took her child home from the hospital, inside a BL-4 Laboratory at the U.S. Army Medical Research Institute of Infectious Diseases, Ft. Deitrich, MD

Colin Hayes worked furiously over the samples he had prepared. He was transferring liquid from one vial to another with a pipette. It was slow going, even with all the advanced equipment available. There were a lot of samples to run. He didn't like working in the BL-4 lab. BL-4 was where the most infectious and dangerous diseases were kept– maximum safety protocols. That meant respirators, full body suits, and other safety equipment that made him uncomfortable. There were no chairs in the room, but you couldn't sit down in the suit anyway. Strangely, Colin found the discomfort of the safety equipment more distressing than the prospect of catching a deadly disease. He was pretty nonchalant about working with deadly diseases. He had been employed here for almost ten years. He had done work with everything from Marburg to H5N1 influenza to moon dust. Any fear he had about catching something had gone away years ago. The excitement he had when he was just a grad student had also diminished for the most part. The novelty was gone for him. At this point, working with deadly diseases was as routine for him as tightening screws was as routine for the people who work on automobile assembly lines. It was just a job.

He wasn't even sure exactly what agent he was dealing with. He just knew that it was important and that it was supposed to be dangerous. He had been given this assignment by none other than the head of USAMRIID herself. The task was to figure out what the function of this virus was. Viruses are very specific; they attack only a particular type of cell. Knowing what cells a virus attacks is the first step in finding a vaccine. He looked around to the other side of the lab, where the metal cylinders lay. He hadn't been given much information, only that there was a virus located in these cylinders and that some important people needed to know the answers. He was used to working in an intelligence vacuum. He often worked with samples that came from "somewhere." He didn't need to know where the cylinders came from. What was unusual was the lack of any supporting information on what they suspected the cylinders to contain. He first figured this was some sort of a blind test, to see if he could identify a virus properly with no information.

Colin had already done all of the standard assays and proved that the virus wasn't similar to any of the well-known bioweapon agents. Whatever this was, it wasn't something typical enough to have a standard assay procedure made for it. The next step in the process had been to do a DNA breakdown of the virus to see if it was close to any known species. It had actually taken him a while just to isolate the virus DNA. It wasn't quite like any he had seen. It had a protein coat that was different somehow and that made it hard to detect. It was certainly a new class of virus. It had some similarities to a retrovirus but not quite. It was exciting and frustrating to work with. He was now trying to find out what sort of cell it attacked. He had been told by the person who had brought in the cylinders that it was probably a human phage, and that he should start there, but Colin was having trouble activating it.

He had some suspicions about the bug that he hadn't shared with anyone yet. He thought that it looked manipulated. He wasn't a bioweapons expert, but he could guess that from the cylinders he scraped it out of and the hush-hush secrecy of the whole operation that it was some sort of genetically manipulated virus. He had heard of these things before. There were all sorts of rumors about what the Russians had been producing during the Cold War (not to mention what was going on in other parts of this very facility). It was probably something that they had dug up in a field in Kazakhstan. Colin would never know. He had been hired as a researcher, he wasn't privy to any of the secrets they kept around here, and there were a lot of secrets.

He elucidated the final sample for the day. He was mixing viral samples with different types of human cells to see if he could find a substrate that the virus would grow on. That would give him some idea of what sort of infection it caused. He was anxious to get finished. He didn't like being in all this protective gear. Besides, his wife was now pregnant, and he needed to get home to help fix up the baby's room. The child was due in three months.

He looked up at the double reinforced glass window that separated the BL-4 from the rest of the Institute. Looking through the window back at him was a man that he only knew as Ray. A bead of sweat ran down Colin's temple. He really wanted to be done for the day and get out of that damned suit.

Late morning, The Watley family residence, Tyler, TX

Lorraine watched the wisps of steam rise from the coffee mug. The light streaming from the window made the vapor seem brighter, more three-dimensional. She wasn't even listening to Joyce's droning on and on as she fixed the muffins. She just stared as the steam played around in the light. It wasn't the sound of Joyce's voice, nor her sitting down at the kitchen table that brought Lorraine out of her self induced oblivion, it was the motion of air that Joyce made as she roughly lowered her bulk into her seat. It disrupted the steam. Lorraine shook her head and looked up.

"Why Lorraine, I don't think that you've heard a word I've been saying. This whole thing really has you torn up." Joyce was Lorraine's neighbor. Their houses sat reasonably close together, nestled between the fields of corn. Joyce's husband was also a farmer, and the two men were out on their tractors, preparing the fields for the spring planting. Joyce was a big, wild Texan of a woman. She had always lived in Tyler. She couldn't imagine living anywhere else. She couldn't survive anywhere else.

"I'm sorry Joyce," Lorraine said apologetically, "It's just kinda sad, you know. I thought that having a baby would give me what I wanted in life. It's what I've been talking about ever since I was a little kid. But it's not working out to be what I thought it would be." Lorraine didn't have many friends. She lived outside of town and had given up most of her previous world to helping her husband. She didn't resent that her life turned out that way; in fact, it was what she wanted, but sometimes it got a little lonely, especially during planting season. She was glad that Joyce was just down the road to talk to. She came over here a lot, and not just for the fresh muffins.

Joyce sipped her coffee. "That's just new mother's syndrome. All women get depressed after having a baby. It's natural. Hell, you should have seen me after I spit Harry out. I didn't want to have nothing to do with nobody. It gets better though." She stopped talking momentarily to pick a bit of blueberry from between her teeth. "I can only guess how you feel having a deformed kid like that. I don't know what I'd do if any of my kids turned out that way. I truly don't."

"It's not that. I mean, Jim isn't that much more work than a normal baby." She looked down at the child, sleeping in its tote. He still had the bottle of juice hanging out of his mouth. "I can deal with the HS. I'm worried about Tom though. Things have been so... strained since the baby."

"What do you mean sugar?" Joyce shifted her bulk around in the chair.

"Well, he puts on a good front, but I don't think that he is happy with Jim. It's like he doesn't even acknowledge him. I thought that having a child would bring us closer together, but it hasn't done that at all. I hardly even see Tom anymore, he spends so much time out in the fields."

"Well, it is planting season. He's probably just busy. You're just feeling oversensitive because there's so much extra work to do around the house."

"No, there's more to it than that. It's like he's ignoring me. It's like he doesn't want to be around the baby. He doesn't want to face up to the HS. Ever since he got out of high school Tom has been talking about some football-star fantasy that he was going to live out through his child. Now that isn't going to happen, and I don't think that he knows how to react. I mean, he is doing his job as a parent and a husband, but it seems that he's only staying around because he has a sense of duty, not because he wants to be a part of the family."

"Oh, stop talking like that. Tom's a good man. He won't turn his back on you because of this. It's just going to take him a while to get used to the idea. I mean, look at him." She pointed to Jim. "It takes a while to get used to that. The first time I came over after the birth I almost fainted dead away. I don't think that you have anything to worry about."

"I guess you're right Joyce." Lorraine halfheartedly took a bite of muffin. "I just don't know how to talk to him. You know how Tom is. I don't want to make it seem like I'm accusing him of anything."

"Just give him time, he'll come around on his own. And if he doesn't, just slap him around some. That's what I always do with Larry. You've got to make him understand who's the boss. Man, I just put up a fist and he does whatever I say." She held up a hammy, balled fist. "The little wimp. I love him."

There was a loud crash from the other room. Joyce turned her head and shouted, "What the hell was that!" She turned back to Lorraine. "Hold on a sec Lor, I got to go deal with my brats." She got up creakily and began walking down the hall. "What the hell are you kids doing in there, don't you know I got company. I'm gonna beat you kids stupid. Where the hell did you go...." Her voice faded as she left the kitchen, chasing after the children. Lorraine put down the coffee and reached into the bassinet. She touched Jim lightly on the forehead. His skin was soft. If she closed her eyes she could almost imagine that he was normal.

A radio was humming softly on the windowsill. "Crazy, crazy for being without you...." This was a hard road that the Lord had put her down. It was going to take a lot of her inner strength to make it through. She just hoped that Tom had enough inner strength as well.

Two months before Colin Hayes performed his viral assay, Saint Maria Inglasias Hospital, Bronx, NY

The orderlies were at work cleaning the infant care ward. They moved furiously, with a drive that was seldom seen in this dreary place. Child Protective Services was coming today, and if the floor wasn't clean, they would hear it from the nurses. They mopped all around the little cribs, being very careful. This was the ward for the sickest children. Incubators lined the walls. They had to be very cautious in here. All of these kids had problems. If they woke up even one, all the rest would soon join in a din of cries and screams. But the orderlies did their work gently, and all the children slept quietly, even the little freak that the cops had brought in three months ago.

Two nameless CPS officers walked down the cold, tile hallway. You could hear the clack-clack of their heels all the way down the hall. It was an old hospital, built in an almost forgotten age when arches, wood stylings, and pressed tin ceiling tiles were in fashion. You could still barely make out the classic style as it attempted to get through the layer after layer of thick white paint that covered everything. The officers, one male and one female, were on their way to meet with the staff pediatrician, Dr. Julio Espisito. They took their job seriously, and this case would be difficult. "So, what are the special procedures for this kid again?" said the male CPS worker to his female colleague.

"I'm not sure. This one has got...," she flipped through her notepad to get the answer, "...Handel's Syndrome. It says here that there are severe defects to the eyes and facial features. There is a discoloration of the skin. Hmmm, what else... There doesn't appear to be any decline in motor skills or intelligence."

"Appears to be? What do you mean, appears to be?"

"Whatever this disease is, it is pretty new. No one knows what causes it. The first known cases just started popping up about a year or two ago."

"So no one knows what the long lasting symptoms are?"

"That's right."

He sighed, "This is going to be a tough kid to place then isn't it?"

"That's what I thought. I doubt that any foster parents will take someone with such a rare condition. And even if we did find a parent, would a judge allow it? The rules are more stringent for handicapped kids. The parents would have to show that they knew how to meet the child's special needs, and that may not be possible since we don't even know what those needs are."

The two officers arrived at Dr. Espisito's door. It was made of old, cracked wood with a large glazed glass window set into it. The light was on inside. The agents opened without knocking. Dr. Espisito was sitting at his desk reading a trade magazine. He immediately recognized the agents and stood up to greet them. "Ah, you must be the people from CPS that called this morning. Agents Anderson and Davidson I presume."

The agents exchanged pleasantries with the doctor and sat down in threadbare but comfortable chairs. The doctor offered some coffee from a drip machine on a bookcase shelf, but the agents refused. "I assume that you are here about Baby Doe?" said Dr. Espisito as he sank back into his chair, steaming cup of coffee in hand.

"That's correct Doctor. We've just been assigned to the case."

"You know, he's been here for almost three months now. You've taken your sweet time getting here. I haven't heard a word from you guys since the police brought that child in."

"I'm sure that you can understand the workload we're under. Sometimes things like this slip through the cracks for a while. Rest assured that the state is very interested in the welfare of this child, and we are going to do everything to make sure that he's brought up in the best possible fashion."

"Of that I have no doubt. I'm not upset at you in particular, it's just this city government we have. There aren't enough people to do the job. I get cases all the time that require your attention, but all I hear about are waiting lists and need-based care."

"We can agree with you on that. We're doing our best."

"Well, now that you are here, let me take you to see little Mr. Doe." The doctor stood up from his chair and guided the agents to the door. They walked a short way down the tile hallway to the maternity center. Inside were row after row of babies. All in little cribs, all identified only by small paper bracelets. Most were fidgety in their little beds. Some slept. A pair of ragged looking nurses were moving back and forth, trying to feed the hungry ones. "This is the intensive care part of the maternity ward," said Dr. Espisito. "Mostly premature births and drug addictions." Dr. Espisito looked downward, "We get a lot of drug addictions."

Dr. Espisito pointed at the child nearest to him. It was quite small, and shook quietly in its crib. "This one here had a mother who thought it was ok to use cocaine while pregnant as long as you chased it down with some depressants."

"What about baby Doe?"

"Well, we tested the kid when he got here. He tested positive for cocaine as well as a few other drugs. We were expecting to have to deal with the addiction factor as well as the HS, but that hasn't been a problem."

"What do you mean?"

"Let me show you." They walked over to Baby Doe's crib. The child was sleeping. Its large black eyes were closed into almost undetectable slits. The nurses had assumed that since he didn't have hair he would be cold, so they had given him a rather funny looking cap to wear. It snuggled with a small stuffed bear, sucking its thumb. "He's asleep. That's unusual.

He doesn't sleep much." The doctor grabbed the child's chart and showed it to the two officers. "You see, we were expecting the child to have all sorts of medical problems stemming from the mother's drug use, but we haven't seen anything like that. The heartbeat, the growth rate, food intake; all normal, normal at least for a child with HS."

"Why do you think that is?"

"Well, it's my guess that whatever genetic deformity causes HS is also somehow involved in brain chemistry. Somehow HS kids are not susceptible to cocaine addiction; maybe they're missing the receptors? It could be a breakthrough for the drug addiction community. I'm writing a paper on it."

"Funny," said the female agent.

"What's that?" said the doctor.

"This kid has all these problems, he's like the unluckiest kid in New York, but somehow all that bad luck cancels itself out. And he might be able to help millions of people break their drug addictions. It's a funny world isn't it?"

The three people agreed. They continued standing over the child's crib for a long time– just watching, and imagining. The child just slept.

Excerpt from "The Reality Behind the Myth," Published in Fortean Times Magazine, about six months after CPS finally came to see Baby Doe.

"...and the phenomena of superstitious villagers turning deformity into myth has even continued to this day. In the past it was people with pygrophia being labeled 'vampires' or people with stunted growth being labeled 'leprechauns.' Today it is people with Handel's Syndrome being labeled as 'aliens.' The evidence is clear that although Handel's Syndrome was only recently 'discovered' in the Western Medical Literature, it has been with us for time immemorial. In the olden days, those with HS were labeled as 'elves' or 'pixies.' They were shunned by their families and forced to live in the forests, robbing and murdering for a living. Now, with our more 'sophisticated' society we have abandoned such notions of magic and fantasy, only to see them replaced by notions of alien encounters and flying saucers. As I've already shown, all so-called UFOs are easily explainable by a variety of naturally occurring and man-made phenomena. I now put it to the reader that the people who claim to have seen 'aliens' have instead seen nothing more than a person suffering from HS. Look at how similar the description of HS is to that of the so-called 'grays.' HS sufferers have bald heads, discolored skin. Their eyes are larger and different from 'normal' eyes. They have small noses and mouths, long fingers and spindly limbs. It's clear from the description that we are talking about exactly the same thing here people! When will this lunatic fringe of society finally accept the fact that there are no aliens, that there are no pixies or vampires? As long as society continues to tolerate these myths, to enforce definitions of 'normal' then these unfortunate people will be forced to continue to eke out meager existences on the fringes of society, firmly convinced that they are some sort of creature of the night. Who knows how many lives have been lost, how many lives continue to be lost, as uneducated moralists take matters into their own hands and administer vigilante justice to these so-called monsters."

Four months after Colin Hayes performed his first viral assay, Bethesda Naval Hospital, Bethesda, MD

The maternity ward at BNH has a set of large, double doors that swing open. Usually the only time they fly open is when a woman in labor breaks through on a gurney, screaming in pain, husband, nurses, doctors all in tow. But on this day the doors burst open to reveal a very different entourage. Ray Johnston has just broken through. He was disheveled. He looked as though he hadn't slept in days (in truth he hadn't). His hair, which was usually so well trimmed in a military cut, had grown ragged and mopish. His tie was skewed to one side, and the top button of his blue polyester dress shirt was undone. His tan raincoat clashed with his dark suit and black shoes. He pushed the big double doors to the maternity ward open with both arms. It was a more difficult task than one might think, because each arm was being held by a nurse. "Sir, sir, you can't just barge in there like that," said the nurses. Ray didn't care. He had other things on his mind.

"Get these people off me," he said to his compatriots. Three men dressed in dark black suits pulled the nurses back. The men wore dark sunglasses and had little white earphones in their ears. They were much larger than the nurses, and well schooled in a variety of personal combat techniques, so they removed the nurses from Ray's arms with very little effort. The entire entourage made a fair bit of noise bursting in like that, which attracted the attention of the head nurse. She was taking the temperature of one of the babies. She stopped her work and looked up at the mob of people that had entered her ward. "What the hell do you think you are doing?" she said. "Who the hell are these people; where's security?"

Ray just ignored her. He moved amongst the newborn cribs looking for something. He moved down the aisles with precision, sometimes lifting a blanket to see underneath. The babies began crying. Of course, once a few start, they all begin bawling. The ward became filled with the din of babies woken prematurely from their afternoon naps. The head nurse moved to stop Ray, but her arm was grabbed by one of the black-suited thugs. She glared up at him and raised her free fist to strike him. He looked down and calmly shook his head in a "don't even think about it" sort of way that was intimidating enough to erase the violent thought from her mind.

Ray finally found what he was looking for. He had stopped at one of the HS babies that the ward had. He lifted the little pink blanket and pointed. "This one," he said. Colin Hayes arrived just in time to hear the command. He had been left behind in the scuffle in the hallway. Ray was crazed with adrenaline, and Colin sometimes had a hard time just keeping up. Colin opened a small case and pulled out a rather large needle. He moved toward the child. "What the hell do you people think you are doing?" said the head nurse. "You can't just burst in here like this!" She struggled against the man in black. "Who the hell gave you the authority?"

"Sorry ma'am. National Security," said Ray. He held the small child's frail arm. Colin began pouring alcohol on a cotton swab.

"National Security? You just can't come in here crying National Security!"

"I'm afraid they can, Nurse Adams," said the voice coming through the door. It was Dr. Rourke, the head administrator of the hospital. He entered the room accompanied with two more of the men in dark suits. He held in his hand a slip of paper. "Despite their poor manners, these people have the authority to take blood samples from your patients. Please give them your full cooperation." Dr.

Rourke didn't look well. He didn't seem too pleased with what he had just said, as if he secretly knew better, but had no choice in the matter.

Colin finished taking the sample from the first HS baby. By that time Ray had already identified the other two in the ward. Colin repeated his procedure, carefully cataloging and storing each sample in his case. Nurse Adams was not pleased with the events, but there was little that she could do without Dr. Rourke's backing. "Who the hell do you think you are?" she said out of frustration. "Who do you work for?"

"Center for Disease Control ma'am," said Ray, not really paying attention to the question. He had other things on his mind.

"CDC? You guys don't look like you work for the CDC. I want to see some credentials."

Ray silently looked up at the men in the dark suits. They got the message. They grabbed the head nurse by both arms and politely escorted her out of the maternity ward.

Several hours later, the Miller farm, on the outskirts of Tyler, TX

2 am. Tom sat in the almost complete darkness of his child's room. His eyes had gotten used to the dark though. He could make out most of the things around him with just the starlight to see from. The nights around here had been getting brighter and brighter as the city moved closer. He remembered being out at night as a kid. You couldn't see your hand in front of your face. Now he could see the items in the room quite clearly. The mobile above the bed twirled slowly in the light breeze from the open window. The crib lay before him. Inside was his son, motionless, asleep.

He had been sitting here for almost an hour, immobile in the darkness. Outside the window there was the occasional sound of a cricket, or maybe a car in the distance, but that was it. On his lap he silently stroked a brand new, kid-sized baseball glove. He had gone a little overboard when he found out Lorraine was pregnant and bought a whole bunch of toys for "his boy." Off in the corner a veritable treasure chest sat, filled with baseball bats, balls of all sizes and shapes, a few toy six-shooters. Toys that little Jim wouldn't have been able to use for years, even if he had been healthy.

"Jim," thought Tom. "My son is named Jim." When Lorraine first found out that she was pregnant, they had gone through all sorts of ideas for names. She even bought a book. They had settled on James, since it was her father's name. When the child had arrived so deformed, they seemed to unconsciously delay filling out the birth records. The kid had gone officially unnamed for several months. Neither of them really wanted to talk about it. You're supposed to name your kid after someone to honor them, Tom thought to himself. What kind of honor is it to have some freak named after you? Tom quickly retracted the thought. He had talked to the doctors and counselors. He had read all the pamphlets that Lorraine had brought home. He understood that he needed to be more sensitive. He understood that he needed to be more politically correct. He understood that he needed to be strong for the sake of his family, and to be accepting and loving and everything that a good father should be. He understood all this in his head, but that understanding hadn't made it down to his heart just yet. He fingered the tiny baseball mitt he was cradling in his lap. It had seemed so perfect when he had bought it. Now it felt useless. With those long, spindly fingers and weak, fragile arms, Jim would never be able to fit into it. He would never have the son that he'd dreamt of all these years. He wanted to grow old watching his kid win the little league championships, make the football team, grow smart and strong and popular. He wanted someone who could take over the family business and would love the soil as much as he did. He wanted someone who would carry on his legacy and the family name. From what little they knew about HS, it seemed very unlikely that those things would happen now. "I'll be lucky if he's not a complete retard," he thought.

Tom wanted a smoke, but his wife wouldn't let him smoke in the house anymore and he was too lazy to go outside. He sat for a while longer in the darkness, not really thinking about anything in particular, just enjoying the quiet and watching the curtains move slowly back and forth in the breeze. Eventually he decided to get up. Not to go to bed, but to go to the kitchen. He hadn't been sleeping well since the baby came. It wasn't the crying or midnight feedings either. Most parents of newborns don't get a lot of sleep in general. But for Tom the problem was internal. Nothing he could put a finger on really. Just a sadness, just some post-partum depression that kept him up late worrying about the future, about what other people were saying about him. He hadn't had anyone over since the birth, even though a lot of the neighbors expected it. He didn't want to admit to what sort of child he had spawned. Not just yet. Of course, there were rumors all around town, but for now they were just rumors, and the people had enough class to keep them quiet. Once the story broke though, geez would lips start flapping. "What went wrong?" "Was it his fault?" "Was there something wrong with his genes?" Tom could almost hear all the voices of the neighbors in his head. Yapping and yapping about stuff that just wasn't any of their damned business anyway.

Tom sighed audibly and stood up from his chair. He could already taste the beer on his lips, hear the satisfying hiss of the can opening. As he turned to leave the room, he heard a small cry from the child. Nothing really, just a murmur as the baby shifted positions. Tom stopped in his tracks. "That sounded just like a real baby," he thought. With the lights off like this, it almost looked like a regular baby– all bundled in his little blanket, just the top of his head visible. Tom moved over to the side of the crib and rested his arms against the railing. He had never really looked at his child before. I mean, he had seen him, but he had always averted his eyes a little. Never really appreciating the child, as if in some unconscious way believing that if he didn't look too closely, all the problems would go away. Maybe if he never really acknowledged the child, the problems would never be fully real. But now Tom did look at his child. He looked at it with fascination and with wonder. There was a slight movement from beneath the covers as the baby shifted again. A small hand slid out from under the blankets. "It's so tiny," thought Tom. He put out his big, calloused finger and touched the hand. The small fingers wrapped around their father's thumb. "Well, at least he's got a good grip," Tom whispered to himself. He remained motionless for some time.

Tom thought that his whisper went unheard by anyone except himself and perhaps God, but he was wrong. In the doorway to the room stood Lorraine. Since the baby was

45

born, she had been having trouble sleeping as well, but not for the same reasons as Tom. She was worried about her family and how they would survive. She had felt Tom getting more and more distant over the past few months, and inside she felt a rejection, as if he somehow blamed her for their child's disability. She had gotten up to see where her husband had gotten off to, to ask him to come back to bed. But there in the darkness, she realized that things were going to be ok. That it might take him a little while, but that he would bond with his child, that he would protect and love his family. She just had to be a little patient, that's all. With a tear in her eye she quietly backed out of the doorway and went back to bed. There was no need to disturb Tom. She would be able to sleep now, things were going to be all right.

The next morning, Holy Trinity Orphanage, Bronx, NY

Sister Mary Helen was up with the first light of dawn. That was the best time to pray. That was the best time to feel close to God. She knelt in her quarters looking out the small window as the first rays of sunlight began to cascade over the horizon. The room was filled with a brilliant orange light as the sunbeams reflected off all the tiny motes of dust in the air. It was a beautiful sight, and Mary Helen wasn't about to miss it sleeping.

Mary Helen's motivations for getting up this early weren't entirely spiritual though. Soon the children would wake, each with a hungry little mouth to feed, a wet nose to wipe, and a broken toy to be fixed. Dawn was about the only time that she was going to get any peace and quiet. It was quite a struggle keeping up with all the little charges in the nursery, and a few minutes of solitude were most welcome, even if it meant giving up a few minutes of sleep. Of course, Sister Mary Helen never really considered it in those terms. Her mind was on God and she needed to make her daily penitence and her daily requests– nothing ever for her sake, just for the children. She asked God for the food and money needed to keep the place running, she asked for a sunny day and for no one to get hurt on the playground at lunch. She asked for parents to come and adopt the children, since they were all great kids after all. But today she was especially penitent, because she had a special request.

After she had gone over all the things that she had done wrong since last morning, she hastily asked for the strength to be a better person and a better nun. She read through her standard list of prayers quickly. Then her mind turned to the child that had come to her yesterday, the sickly little thing that CPS had brought from the hospital.

"God. I have one more request to make of you today. The little boy that was brought in yesterday. The one with HS. He needs your help God. He needs your help more than any of the other children. He's sick, and he has had such a hard life so far, being born under the most horrible of circumstances. Abandoned at birth and all. I know that you have a great plan for each of us, and I know that your wisdom to bring such a child into the world is above reproach, but I implore you to give me the strength to make his little life more comfortable, and I pray that you send me some parents who would love someone like him, in spite of all his problems. I can tell that he's a good kid at heart. Amen."

Sister Mary Helen looked up at the sky for an answer to her prayers, but nothing apparent was forthcoming. The sun had completely risen now– morning had officially begun. The children would be waking soon. Sister Mary got up on her feet with a slight groan, straightened her habit, and got ready to start another day.

Two weeks after Ray Johnston's hospital visit, in the hallway just outside of a BL-4 Laboratory at the U.S. Army Medical Research Institute of Infectious Diseases, Ft. Deitrich, MD

Ray waited impatiently in the pale green hallway. He paced back and forth on the smooth concrete floor. It was green too. If Ray had been a more aesthetically-minded person he would be wondering why everything here was painted the same pale green color. He could hear footsteps in the distance occasionally, but it was late in the day and the number of people had been gradually diminishing as the sunlight coming through the windows dimmed and turned orange. He decided to take a chance on a cigarette. He pulled a ragged pack out of his pocket. It was a little bent, but the tobacco was still good. Ray looked up at a sign painted on the wall years ago. It said, "no smoking." He decided to ignore it. He pulled a cigarette from the pack with his teeth as he fished in his coat pocket for a light. He pulled out a silver lighter. It wasn't really apparent unless you looked close, but one side of the lighter was engraved with a 'thanks for your assistance' sort of dopey message. The other side had the CIA logo on it. He struck the flint once and the flame roared to life. Just before he could ignite the tip, his eye caught a smoke detector attached to the wall near the ceiling. Ray only hesitated a minute though before taking his first puff. He had much larger problems than worrying about setting off an alarm.

Once the cigarette was safely lit, Ray stepped away from the detector, towards the window of the BL-4 lab. He looked inside. Colin Hayes was manipulating samples along with two other technicians. There were small vials filled with blood all over the workbench. Ray knew that the final analysis wouldn't be available for several more weeks, but he was a good reader of people, he had to be in his line of work. Ray looked through the glass at Colin's face. The look of resignation and disappointment told him all he needed to know. He began walking down the hallway. He needed to call General Dumphries immediately.

Adopted Son

That same afternoon, Tyler Memorial Hospital, Tyler TX

Dr. Thomas could see the Millers coming down the hallway. He was encouraged to see that Tom was holding the baby. Dr. Thomas had been a little concerned that the father was getting distant from his child due to the HS. A lot of parents of disabled children have experienced similar problems. He hoped they hadn't been lying about seeing that counselor in Dallas. Thankfully, since the last visit Tom seemed to be adjusting better. He stopped them as they walked past.

"Tom, Lorraine, how are you two doing today?"

The new parents moved to the side of the hallway to allow traffic to pass and stopped to chat. "We're fine Dr. Thomas, it's good to see you again."

"Is there a problem? How's little James today?" He reached over to the bundle Tom held in his arms and uncovered the top blanket to reveal a little head, fidgeting about.

"Well, Jim was up last night sneezing, so Tom thought we should take him in to get him checked up. The doctor in the emergency room said that he was ok this morning, no temperature or nothing. We got a prescription just in case."

"It was good that you brought him in anyway. It's best not to take chances with someone so young," said the doctor.

"Tom's been getting so overprotective lately with him, it's like walking on eggshells when they're together. He frets over every little thing," said Lorraine.

Tom continued. "It's the HS doc. You just got to be careful. I don't want to make a bad situation worse."

"That's true. With something so rare as HS, you can't tell how their body is going to react to a disease. Sometimes what just starts out as a sniffle can lead to something serious in a hurry. Whatever the genetic defect that causes HS is, it looks like it affects the immune system, HS babies may not be as resistant to simple diseases as regular babies. Have you gotten him immunized yet?"

"Yes sir, we're up to date," said Lorraine. She waved the baby's medical papers to emphasize the point.

"Well then, you three best be on your way. It's a great day outside, you don't want to miss the weather."

The new parents thanked the doctor and continued down the hallway on their way out of the hospital. They chatted between themselves at how nice the hospital staff had treated them. On their way out, they passed by the maternity ward. Lorraine, who just loved babies in general, demanded that they stop and look in the window at all the other children.

They glanced around a bit and then went on their way. Lorraine seemed pleased by the experience, while Tom found it a bit troubling. Something the doctor said was sticking in his head. "HS is a very rare disease," the doc had said. If that was so, why were there three newborns in the maternity ward that were clearly HS positive?

Three weeks after Tom Miller noticed something strange. The White House, Washington DC

Ray Johnston waited impatiently outside the White House Situation Room. Everything was smaller than he expected it to be in here. There was barely room in the hallway for a pair of chairs for people to sit in. He wasn't feeling all that comfortable in his suit. He was also sweating quite a bit. Was it too hot in there? The presentation had gone pretty well. Ray had been giving a lot of presentations recently. He was sure of his facts. But this one was to some pretty high-ranking people. It was so important a topic. He wasn't sure that he had been taken too seriously though. He wouldn't have taken himself that seriously if he hadn't gathered the evidence personally. But he was sure that in the end, they would do the right thing. That's why they had been elected after all, wasn't it?

The door to the conference room opened and General Dumphries came out. "Ray, they've finished their debating, come on back in here." Ray got up and grabbed his briefcase. He had forgotten to lock the clasps though and it tumbled open when he lifted it, spilling slides marked Top Secret/Majestik-12 all over the floor. He quickly stuffed them all back in his case and ran inside. You don't keep the President of the United States waiting.

Ray entered the Sit Room. It had been a spare bedroom back when the West Wing was built, and there was barely enough room for the large central table. You actually had to ask an NSC member to move their chair if you wanted to get to the podium. Ray squeezed his way front and center and awaited their reaction to his presentation.

"Mr. Johnston," began the President, "I want to thank you for taking the time to put together this fascinating briefing." He tapped the cover of the 400-page document that Ray had assembled over the past year. "It's quite an impressive piece of work." Ray wanted to say thank you, but he didn't want to interrupt the President. "I can't say that I understand all the technical details, but it is clear that you've found some very interesting things. Unfortunately, the NSC has chosen to take no action on this issue at this time."

Ray was shocked by the decision. Didn't they understand the implications? Didn't they understand the threat? How could they choose to take no action at this time? "Well Sir, when will be the time to take action on this issue?" he asked incredulously. "How can you choose to ignore this?"

"It's not that easy son," said the Vice-President. "You can't just go to the people with something like this. They won't believe it. They won't accept it. I mean come on, if the President released this to the press, he'd be laughed out of office."

"That's what the report was for, Sir. All the data is in there, it's incontrovertible."

"That's what you say. I must have had five meetings this morning with different lobbyists, and they all have incontrovertible proof of one thing or another, most of it contradictory. There's a lot of play here. We'll task this out to some national lab people, they'll try and confirm, but I think that it is way too premature for any of this to be released to the public. We don't even have a solution for any of this. We need a game plan."

"But you can't just wait on this. There isn't any time left. Every minute we delay is going to hurt our chances of surviving."

The President said, "You just don't understand all the political ramification of this thing, Mr. Johnston. I can understand how you feel the way you do from your perspective. But remember, your job is to find way-out threats and bring them to our attention. But there are a lot more parts to the puzzle. We've got to worry about the employment figures, foreign relations, the environment– a bunch of other things. We can't just go off half-cocked on something like this. We've got to spin it right. We've got to give the American people a 'warm fuzzy feeling' about it. Otherwise there'll be panic in the streets, and we wouldn't want that now, would we? We'll take your report under consideration, and we'll monitor the problem very closely. I'll put one of my top aides on it. You just go back and try and uncover some more info on this. Good work, son." He presented Ray with a thumbs-up.

The President was interrupted by one of his aides, "Sorry to interrupt, Sir, but you've got four more briefings to get through before lunch."

"Yes, good, send in the next briefer," the President said to his aide. Then he turned to Ray, "Great briefing Mr. Johnston. Great briefing. Keep up the good work." General Dumphries smiled and began to guide Ray out of the chamber. The President continued, "...and Mr. Johnston, remember to pick up one of my signed photos as a souvenir. Ask the secretary. Great briefing."

The last image that Ray had of the room was of a new briefer beginning to show slides about Russian Air Defense units. The President was already deeply engrossed in the new brief. He wouldn't do anything about this. He wouldn't even remember it ten minutes from now. "Ray, I thought that went great. I'm always proud of my boys when they can get some face time. This presentation will be a great addition to our yearly highlights report."

"Well, what the hell do we do now?" Ray said to the General, ignoring the empty congratulatory statement.

"You heard the commander. We go back and look for more evidence. We take it slow."

"But there isn't any time. We've got to take action now. Before it's too late. Hell, it may already be too late."

General Dumphries picked up his beeper from the tray on the secretary's desk. No electronics were allowed in the Situation Room. As he stretched to clip it back to his belt his shirt strained to remain tucked. "Calm down Ray. You've done your job. Remember, we don't make policy. We were hired to inform the policymakers of the facts. What they chose to do with those facts is up to them. All we can do is be good soldiers, that's all."

"But they're not going to do anything. They are going to take that report, classify it so deep that no one will ever be able to read it, and they'll do nothing. Then it will certainly be too late." Ray was clearly getting hot under the collar.

"Don't worry, I've already written a commendation for your work. It is documented how you were the first person to pick this up. When the story finally breaks everyone will remember that you were the one who was right. It'll all be in your personnel record."

"Damn it! Is that all you people think about? We're talking the end of the freaking world here! This isn't some bureaucratic crap. Are people so not used to dealing with serious threats that they've gone blind to them?" The General put his arm around Ray, and tried to calm him down. Ray pushed him aside and headed towards the door. "I'm not going to stand for this. I won't stand around and let the whole world end just to have a freaking gold star on my personnel file. Screw my personnel file." Ray left the office.

The General wasn't going to let Ray's behavior bother him. He was a company man. He had made his rank by maintaining a cool head and following orders. He had taken some management courses. He knew that primadonnas like Ray often get frustrated by the bureaucratic nonsense that goes on in today's government. It was best to let them blow off a little steam. Then everything will be ok. The presentation to the NSC would look great on the General's file when he came up for promotion. He couldn't see anything bad that happened today. He calmly walked down the hall, stopping only to pick up a signed picture from the secretary and a handful of candy from the jar on her desk.

Excerpt from an Editorial in the Sacramento Bee, Health Section, page H4. Three days before Ray met with the NSC.

"Is HS the Latest 'Environmental' Disease?"
by Dr. Alan Franks, health editor

The latest statistics released from the NIH this Thursday paint a stark picture of our nation's newest epidemic. The number of Handel's Syndrome children has been increasing at an alarming rate. In the last year, the number of cases has increased almost ten-fold. The figures for prior years are even more disturbing. There wasn't even a name for the disease up until about two years ago, and epidemiologists have yet to uncover a confirmed case of HS dating back more than five years. You're probably not even familiar with the symptoms; deformed features, stunted growth, enlarged eyes. What's more alarming is that NIH is still unable to identify a cause for this disease. Despite rumors on the internet, HS is genetic in nature (HS children are born with an extra chromosome), it is doubtful that some sort of germ or virus is the culprit. However, since it only appeared recently, it cannot be considered akin to Hodgkin's or Diabetes or any of the traditional genetic diseases that have been around since time immemorial. It is more likely caused by some new mutating agent. But what sort of agent could do this? With the Thalidomide scare of the 1970s, the symptoms showed only in patients whose parents had ingested the drug. But HS doesn't seem to have any sort of epidemiological consistency. Physicians worldwide have reported cases. There doesn't seem to be a focal point or any feature that links the patients. They come from rich and poor backgrounds, warm and cold climates, their parents have varied access to drugs, foods, and industrial chemicals.

One answer may be that the chemical causing the mutation has become ubiquitous, much in the same way that DDT is. DDT was banned from most industrialized countries decades ago, but detectable levels are still found in the livers of polar bears, who certainly have no recent direct exposure. It is possible that some chemical we have been taking for granted all these years has actually been building up in the food chain, and has finally reached levels where its mutagenic effects can be seen.

One good guess at the mutagen is the class of chemicals known as 'environmental estrogens.' These industrial by-products are chemically similar to estrogen, and they are rumored to have effects on the human metabolism. They are thought to be primarily responsible for the alarming decrease in human male sperm production that has been recorded over the past few decades. It is also possible that these chemicals are responsible for the mutated frogs that are being found in lakes all over the country. Due to their thin, porous skin, amphibians are usually more affected by small doses of chemicals than mammals are. Do the frogs represent the future for the human race, smothered and mutated by the weight of our industrial by-products?

The medical community should make a strong effort to find the cause of HS, and to develop an understanding of how the disease is contracted. I urge politicians to increase funding for HS research. While the number of patients with HS is still very low, the alarming increase over the past few years should make HS research a priority. Whatever the cause, it needs to be identified and controlled in a hurry, before even more children have to grow up with the disease. Let's not repeat the mistakes that have been made with other diseases. Now is the time to increase funding. We can't afford to wait until the disease reaches epidemic proportions.

Two months after Baby Doe was brought home. Holy Trinity Orphanage, Bronx, NY

"Well, thanks for stopping by, just the same. We'll call you if the situation changes," said Sister Mary Helen to the couple as they walked out the orphanage door. Her dejection was readily apparent in her voice. She stood in the doorway for a while, watching them walk down the street hand in hand. It was starting to get cold out. Winter was coming. She went back inside and closed the door.

Father Blythe was waiting for her in the hallway. "Well Sister, is there any good news?"

"No Father," said the nun. "They wanted an infant, but they weren't too interested in taking on the responsibilities of a disabled child."

The two of them walked down the drafty corridor of the orphanage. "Don't look too harshly on them Sister. It's a big responsibility. Not many people are willing to shoulder that burden. That is why we are here. Our job is to take in those that no one else wants. The children here will never be unloved because of us."

They reached the infants' room. It was empty except for one crib. It was usually pretty easy to place infants. People wanted the ability to raise a child from scratch. They wanted an empty slate to work with. Infants were usually not the problem. It was only the older children that the orphanage really had a hard time placing. But this new baby was different. He had a hard beginning. Found abandoned in a garbage can, addicted to drugs. And, to top it off, the child had a rare and disturbing disease.

They looked in the crib at the sleeping newborn. Its giant eyes were just slits. It sucked on its spindly thumb as it slept. The Father carefully patted the child on the head. "We'll find a home for him someday." Its skin was thin and slick, not unlike a frog's.

"I think that his time is running out Father. After they hit about a year or so their chances of ever leaving start to go down. If we've had this much trouble with him so far, I don't think that he'll ever be adopted."

"Well Sister, then it'll be a blessing for us, won't it?" replied the Father, trying to convey good spirits. "Everything has a purpose in this world, and if God has decided that the boy will stay with us, then there must be a reason for it."

"I suppose that you are right Father." She took the blanket and tucked the child in a little better. It was drafty in this old house. The blankets were thin, but serviceable. "I guess that we can't keep calling him 'Baby Doe.' If he's to stay with us, we should probably give him a name." They'd named children before. As the guardians they had the legal right to do so for children that had no birth record. They didn't like to take that step though, because they believed that a person's name should be a reflection of their history. With no history for these kids, it was unfair to name them. That was a job better left to their adopted parents. However, it had happened in the past that a child got too old to be called 'baby' and so they created an official name. The standard last name they used was 'Trinity' after the orphanage. The first name was usually left up to the head Priest.

Father Blythe had his hands in his pockets. He usually had his hands in his pockets, it was a nervous habit. He rummaged around for a bit and pulled out everything he had. "Well Sister, let's see if anything in here will inspire us." There wasn't much there– a pocketknife, a screw, and a crumpled ten-dollar bill. Father Blythe unfolded the bill and looked at it. "Hamilton...? Sister, how do you feel about the name Hamilton? That's a name, right?"

"That's not a good name Father. Our new boy is only worth $10? Sounds cheap. Who's on the hundred?"

"Ben Franklin I think."

"Franklin Trinity," replied the Sister. "Now that has a certain ring to it. Classy. I'll tell the rest of the Sisters that our Baby Doe is now officially Franklin Trinity."

Handel's Syndrome Research Laboratory, National Institutes of Health, Bethesda, MD

"Dr Mensen, I think that we have a problem with those samples that you gave me." Nancy Collins, stood at the doorway to the doctor's office. He looked up from his computer.

"What's that you say Nancy?" He had been doing some internet searches for information. Dr. Mensen preferred the old days, when journals still came in paper form– something that you could flip through while sitting on the can. He didn't like these new 'searchable' on-line journals. They were too focused. Sure, you got the information you were looking for, but you never learned anything else. It was too easy to click a button and flip to the next page. Everyone was becoming more and more adept at their little piece of the puzzle, but less and less informed about the rest of the world. No one had the capability to put two disparate pieces of information together anymore. None of his post-docs had the capability to think outside the box. They were so used to being able to get exactly what they needed, that they never bothered to learn how to do things a different way or to figure out a work-around for an intractable problem.

"Well, I was doing some of the DNA mapping, and there seems to be a problem with the blood samples that we have. I couldn't get any acceptable results."

An exasperated Dr. Mensen sighed inaudibly. Couldn't these post-docs do anything right these days? From what he remembered, post-docs used to be able to do simple experiments without needing you to look over their shoulder. Nowadays no one seemed to be able to do anything. What was going to happen to the NIH once he retired? It would be chaos. He stood up and moved around the desk, "Show me the problem," he said.

The two walked down the hallway to the main laboratory floor. The place was filled with beakers, vials, biohazard symbols, and other paraphernalia. They passed two of his other post-docs, who were busy abusing his precious PCR-sequencer. "Good afternoon Dr. Mensen," they said in unison. Mensen grumbled a greeting as they walked past. "OK, tell me what you did."

"Well, Dr. Mensen, I'm working on how HS is transmitted to children like you said to do. I was trying to look at mutations in the parent's genes that may have led to the mutation in the children. According to biology, the gene defects in the children should show up in the parents."

"Yes, we don't yet know the cause of HS. It could be some sort of mutation that happens because the ovaries mess up the creation of the eggs, like in Downs' Syndrome. It could also be caused by some rare recessive gene. If both parents have it, you've got an HS child."

"Well, we got a batch of child blood samples, along with blood samples from their respective mothers. As a first step, I did a Southern Blot test to ensure that the samples hadn't gotten mixed up in transit. I wanted to make sure that each sample from a mother was attached to the correct child sample."

"That's a pretty simple procedure, why couldn't you do it correctly?"

"Well, I couldn't get any of the samples to match up Dr. Mensen." The post-doc reached across the lab bench and picked up the gels that she had run some of the tests with. I couldn't get a single mother-child match. They're not the same at all." She handed the gels to the Doctor.

"Maybe there was systemic problem and all the samples got switched. Just check each child against all the mother samples until you find the right one.

"That was my first thought Dr. Mensen, but none of the samples matched up. None of these mothers match up to

63

any of the children. I think that the batches must have gotten mixed up."

"That can't be, there was only one batch. The parent samples were taken at the same time as the child samples, it was all shipped in one shipment. There should be a match somewhere."

Damn grad students can't do anything right, thought Dr. Mensen. Now he was going to have to spend all afternoon tracking down the samples and running them himself.

Four months later, at the Hayes residence, Fredrick, MD

Colin was in the process of tucking in his child for the night. He could hear his wife washing dishes in the kitchen. The light was still on, but the boy was already asleep. He had fallen asleep in the living room while the family was watching television. Colin carried him into the bedroom himself. He paused to rub his son's head. Already his hair was full and thick and red, just like Colin's. He looked like a very normal, one-year-old child. That was a bit disconcerting for Colin considering all the research he had done lately. He knew what was going on. His research had confirmed what Ray had been thinking. It wasn't good. He wondered about his child's life. How would it be? How would he deal with the coming storm? How lucky he was. He'd made it just under the gun.

Colin's wife turned off the faucet and came to see what Colin was up to. "Let him sleep," she said quietly, so as not to wake the boy. Colin left the room stealthily and joined his wife in the hallway. As he stepped from the room she reached inside and switched off the light. Colin gently closed the door. "Hopefully he'll sleep through the night," she whispered as they walked down the hallway. Their house was plain and a bit old, but it was clean and warm. It needed new rugs and a coat of paint, but Colin hadn't had time to do any fixing up during the past few months. He had been working so much overtime lately at the lab. The money was great and all, but Colin's wife really would have preferred if he was home more often to help with the running of the household.

"I'm sorry that I haven't been around so much Janice. That'll change soon. This project is almost done. Maybe then we'll go away together. We'll take a long vacation. Up in the mountains, maybe."

"...Or maybe we could have another baby?" Janice said hesitantly.

"What? Janice I don't think that's a good idea. I really don't."

"But Colin, you promised. Don't you remember, back when we were first going out? You said that you always wanted two children. You said that you didn't want to space them out too far, so they'd be able to relate to each other."

"It's out of the question right now. Maybe someday, but now is a very bad time."

"But you said that your project is almost done. You want to spend more time at home. We don't have any money troubles. What's wrong with doing it now?"

"You don't understand Janice. Things are changed... will change. It just isn't a good time. You don't know what's going on. There's a lot that you don't see. There are... problems. It's out of the question."

"Just like that? You don't even want to discuss it?" said Janice pleadingly.

"No. I don't want to discuss it. Let's just be thankful for what we have. You've got a beautiful baby boy in there, console yourself with that. I'll explain someday, but I can't today. You'll just have to trust me for now."

This was unlike Colin. He wasn't usually so stubborn. In fact, he was often pretty easy to manipulate. Janice figured that there must be something unsaid that was bothering him. Something he didn't want to talk about just yet. She would get it out of him sooner or later. She had a way with these things. She would keep subtly bringing the issue up until she found out what was wrong, neutralized the threat, and got her way. She didn't consider herself so, but she was really a very manipulative person. She dropped the subject for now. Colin just went wordlessly into the bedroom, leaving Janice to turn off the lights and close up the house for bed.

She went back into the kitchen and put away the rest of the dishes. Then she walked through the various rooms and made sure that the lights were off and the doors were locked. On her way to bed she stopped by her son's room. She opened the door quietly as to not wake him. It was dark, but the moon provided enough light to make out the outlines of the crib and furniture. She moved towards her child instinctively. She could hear him breathing lightly under his covers. She stood there watching for a while, thinking about Colin's reaction. She had always wanted many children. She didn't think it would be fair to only have one. He'd grow up so lonely. What could the problem be? Colin had always expressed a desire to have several kids. That's one of the things that first attracted her to him, he was a family man.

Was he sick? Maybe that was the problem. Maybe he had come down with cancer or something and he hadn't told her yet? That would be like him, always trying to play the hero, always trying to be the strong one in times of adversity. Janice quickly dismissed the thought from her head. No, he wasn't sick, he couldn't be. Perhaps the thought was too horrific to finish, perhaps she subconsciously believed that she understood her partner enough to notice if he was sick, but for whatever reason she dismissed the thought.

She considered other possibilities, sexual dysfunction, money problems, fear of nuclear war. Nothing made sense. She eventually decided that it was just the stress of his job that was bothering him, and that he would go back to his old self as soon as he stopped working so much overtime. Perhaps she would suggest that he find a new job. There were a lot of places a biochemist like Colin could go. Maybe move out of the DC area, somewhere with better weather. She looked down at her son. Her maternal instincts were revving up again. She had been feeling a strong desire to have another child for some time now. Almost since she gave birth to her first one. She considered the possibilities for a long time. She thought of all sorts of ways that she could approach the subject again without riling Colin too much. She considered different things that she could do to change his mind. Eventually, after almost a half hour of standing in the dark, she had formulated a plan. Everything was going to be all right. She headed off to bed.

A few days later, at the residence of Dr. Heinrich Mensen, Potomac, MD

After cleaning up from dinner, Dr. Mensen was just sitting down in a big, comfy, leather chair in his wood-paneled living room. He had just poured himself a snifter of brandy and was about to settle down with a good book for the evening. He needed to do some relaxing after a difficult day. He had always wanted to be a scientist, to probe the secrets of life itself, to help people. But more and more he found himself to be just an administrator, just a middle manager. He shouldn't have to spend half his day begging for grant money. That job should be left for someone better qualified at schmoozing. He needed to get back to the lab. He had been thinking lately that he might resign his position as department chair and go back to pure research. But thoughts like that could wait until tomorrow he decided. There was no point in ruining a perfectly good evening by thinking about work. He settled down into his chair and picked up his novel.

Riiiinnnnngggg.

The phone rang. Perfect timing. The doctor considered just not answering, but he decided that he must. It could have something to do with the grant applications that he had been submitting all week. He rose from the big, comfy, leather chair and moved across the study to the phone sitting on the wood desk.

"Hello?" inquired Dr. Mensen.

A voice that sounded suspiciously like Ray Johnston (although at the time the doctor wouldn't understand the significance of that name) was on the other end of the line. "Dr. Mensen, it is good to finally speak with you. I read your paper on the causes of HS."

"Who is this?" said Dr. Mensen. "How did you get this number?"

"Never mind who I am Doctor, and how I got this number doesn't matter. I'm a friend. I want to help you. I know that your funding has been cut back severely, and I know why. I have some information that you might find very useful."

"My funding has been cut back because the appropriations committee didn't give NIH as much money as last year." He had been told that HS was not a very common disease, and cuts had to be made somewhere. "What are you implying sir?"

"I'm implying that there are forces at work that don't want your research to succeed. They don't want to hear what you would tell them. They aren't ready to face up to this news. But I'm going to give you a valuable piece of the puzzle." The person on the other end of the line certainly had a flare for the dramatic.

"Who is this?" demanded Dr. Mensen again.

"I read your paper on HS genetics. You've noted that the children have a mutation that doesn't appear in the parent. Your report likens HS to Downs' Syndrome. You make the assumption that there is some problem during fertilization, that the DNA in the egg gets mixed up. That's why the kids have little genetic similarity to their own parents."

"I know my own research."

"Well, I want to tell you that you are off-track on this. I can't explain how I know, but I want you to do a test. Find a woman pregnant with an HS child. Do a DNA test on both the blood and the amniotic fluid."

"What's that supposed to prove?"

"That's what you are going to find out doctor. That's all I have to say. Do the test, you won't be disappointed."

The voice on the other end of the phone was replaced by a click as the phone was hung up. Dr. Mensen stood by his desk for a while, receiver still in hand. He wasn't used to getting strange calls in the middle of the night from unnamed men telling him to perform experiments. And what was the voice implying about his inability to get grant money the last few months? The phone started beeping in his hand with the 'off the hook' sound, so the doctor hung it up and went back to his chair. He wasn't too happy about the call, but perhaps he should follow it up. The experiment that was suggested was simple enough after all. He could get Nancy to do it in the morning. Of course, if this guy was a researcher, why was he using such strange tactics? If he was legitimate, there are many journals that he could publish in, why resort to spooky phone calls? Dr. Mensen shook off his thoughts. He'd worry about it in the morning. Now it was time for relaxation, brandy, and a good book.

Dominic Peloso

The Miller farm, on the outskirts of Tyler, TX

Tom sat on the floor of his living room. A few feet away from him was his son, who was sitting up on his own now. The doctors had been worried that the child may never sit up straight. His head was so much larger than the rest of his body that it might be tough for his neck muscles to support the weight. But the doctors were wrong, doctors are sometimes wrong. Tom sat across from his son. Now that the kid was a bit older, and was wearing clothes, he looked almost normal. He sat in his little blue jeans and a striped shirt that Lorraine had made for him. He had to wear special shirts because the ones from the store wouldn't fit over his head. Tom had been hoping that the kid would grow some hair, but as for now little Jim was still bald as the day he was born. Lorraine was sitting on the couch, watching TV and doing the crossword puzzle. Tom was trying an experiment. He was still hoping for a sports career from his son and, as everyone knows, you have to start them early on that path. Tom had a little pink rubber ball he had picked up last time he was in town. He rolled it slowly towards his child. As the ball passed by, Jim made no move to get it, but he did turn his head and watch it pass by. That was a good sign. The doctors had told Tom that his kid was likely to be blind, or at least have very poor eyesight, but as far as Tom could tell, he could see just fine. He played with his mobile, he turned his head when you walked into the room. No, that boy could see just fine. The doctors were wrong. The doctors were often wrong.

Anyway, the ball experiment wasn't a success, but Tom wouldn't give up so easily. He went and retrieved the ball and tried again. Same result. A third experiment resulted in the ball bouncing off Jim's shoes. The fourth time was a charm though. As the ball rolled past, Jim reached out for it.

72

He missed and fell flat on his face, but it was a good attempt. He was getting there. Tom was very happy with the effort. "Ho ho Lorraine, would you look at that! A diving catch!" Tom exclaimed. "If he keeps that level of effort up he'll make the majors no problem." Lorraine glanced up from her puzzle but mostly ignored the comments. Jim was only one year old now, and Tom had been talking about 'the majors' for the last four months. Lorraine would be happy if Jim grew up to be a good man who held down a job and could raise a family. She didn't need glory to feel like a successful parent.

Tom sat Jim back up and got the ball back. He rolled it toward him again. Jim once again grabbed for the ball. He didn't get it, but at least he didn't fall over. Progress was being made. As Tom went to get the ball again, there was a distinct giggle from Jim. He was enjoying himself. That made Tom happy. If you're going to succeed at something you've got to enjoy it. Otherwise you'll never make it. Tom kept at it.

Another twenty minutes of rolling passed by, and there were a few successes. Jim was able to stop the ball a few times, although nothing that could ever be considered a 'catch.' It was more like he fell on the ball. "Perhaps he'll be a goalie. That'd be all right I guess," said Tom. Lorraine ignored him.

"Why don't you teach him something useful, like driving a tractor, which is what you should be doing," she said with mock irritation.

"This is useful," protested Tom. "You can't get the girls without being able to play ball. You want him to get the girls don't you?" He rolled the ball again. Another catch. "Man, this kid's awesome. Awesome I tell you. If he's this good now think about how great he's going to be in a few years. It's those long fingers, he's gonna have quite a grip I bet." He retrieved the ball. "We got to do something about that bald head. Can't you knit him a cap or something? He's going to catch cold." Lorraine just sighed.

He rolled the ball a little faster this time. It went right past little Jim, who fell over trying to make the grab. Then an amazing thing happened. Jim rolled over, stood up, and galloped towards the ball. He didn't get very far, just a few feet. Then he fell over on his face. "Holy! Lorraine, did you see that! He just took his first steps! And a run too! Holy Gee he's gonna be fast, fast I tell you." He went over and picked his kid up. "This calls for a treat. Lorraine, where's the ice cream?" Tom strutted into the kitchen with Jim on his shoulders. "We are the champions, we are the champions..." he sang as he left the room. Lorraine just shook her head. It was tough having two children to deal with.

.

Eight months later at the World Health Organization Annual Conference on Birth Defects and Childhood Diseases, Geneva Switzerland

Dr. Mensen sat in the back of the auditorium. He was only half listening to the presentation on HS oncology. The man on stage had been performing research to support the theory that the genetic defects from HS were the result of the mother's eggs being deformed by uterine tumors. Mensen had counted at least three errors in his presentation so far. That was usually his limit of attention. The Doctor was quick to judge other people, and god forbid that he judged you as an idiot. He turned his attention to flipping through the notes for his presentation. The research contained therein was remarkable. He should have been chosen to chair this session. He was clearly the most qualified person here. If only they hadn't cut his funding. He had been one of the top researchers in the HS field, but now with his budget slashed by those morons at the NIH, he didn't have the clout to push through big projects quickly. Not like Foucoult. That French twit had a virtual research paper factory running in Paris. That's why he was picked to chair the HS session. Dr. Mensen considered his presentation. It was going to really drive the final nail in the coffin for Foucoult's theories. Mensen was sure that the disease was being caused by some sort of retrovirus. Foucoult stubbornly clung to the mistaken belief that the disease was genetic.

Mercifully, the man on stage finished his presentation and moved away from the podium quickly. He was replaced by Foucoult, who began his next introduction in an annoying French accent. "Our next speaker is Dr. Heinrich Mensen from the United States." Foucoult said the words 'United States' as if they tasted bad. There was a lot of rivalry in the scientific community. Dr. Mensen knew that Foucoult would have preferred if he hadn't been invited at all. He couldn't get away with that though. Even with his reduced funding level, Mensen was considered a pioneer in the field. There was no way that Foucoult could shut him out of a meeting of this caliber, even if he didn't like what Mensen was going to say.

Dr. Mensen took his time getting up to the stage. He was in no hurry, and the longer he walked, the longer the applause lasted. Not that Mensen was a vain man. He didn't need the applause. He just knew that it grated on Foucoult's nerves, and that was reward enough. He walked up to the fake wood podium and began to give his speech. He had brought notecards with him, but he didn't really use them very much. He didn't see that well up close. He knew what he was talking about, and the slides being projected were enough to keep him on-track.

The first slide came up. "This presentation is entitled, Handel's Syndrome as a Consequence of Chromosomal Damage by Retrovirus." He cleared his throat, and took a sip from the glass of ice water that had been provided for him. The next slide came up. He adjusted the silver microphone a little, resulting in some static and the annoying whine of feedback being projected through the speaker system.

"Ladies and Gentlemen of the scientific community. It is my firm belief that HS is a genetic dysfunction that is caused by prenatal exposure to an as-of-yet undiscovered retrovirus. After my presentation you will also hold this belief." He looked over the podium at the audience. Foucoult and a few of his boys sat on the side, affecting disinterest. They remained sure that it was some sort of genetic abnormality. "Next slide please."

The next slide appeared, showing some of the contrasting 'DNA Lines' that are made by Southern blotting. "Here are three DNA samples. The first shows a child afflicted with HS." He used his pointer to show where the lines were on the slide. The second set of lines are the DNA samples taken directly from the mother's uterus. As you can see, they line up completely, as would be expected. The match proves that this child is the progeny of this mother." He waved the pointer around again, emphasizing the fact that the lines from the first sample matched the lines from the second sample. "Now, here is the kicker. The third DNA sample is also from the mother, but taken from her blood serum. As you can see clearly, the DNA does not match up to either that of the child, nor her own uterus!"

Mensen waited a few seconds for the murmuring to die down. "Next slide please." More data appeared. "As you can see, there is some genetic defect in the mother that has changed her reproductive system on a fundamental level. In most cases, all of the RFLP markers have changed. Portions of her reproductive system have been completely warped by some agent. This is also true for the father. Next slide please." More data appeared.

"This slide shows, some DNA sampling that we took from the HS child's father. As you can see, the DNA sample from the father's reproductive system matches the child's. This boy is clearly the child of the man. However, again, we see that the father's blood serum genetics do not match that of his own reproductive system!" Again, there was murmuring in the audience. Foucoult and his group looked unconvinced. They whispered amongst themselves. Mensen knew what they were saying. They were accusing him of cross contaminating the samples. They were assuming that a mistake had been made.

"Of course," continued Mensen, "One case is not enough to make a diagnosis, so I did some further testing. Next slide please." More data appeared. "I had labs at Hopkins and UC Berkeley run split samples on almost a hundred HS children and their parents. I received a one hundred percent correlation rate. Every HS case that I tested for showed a significant abnormality between the parents dominant genetic code, and that of their reproductive system." He pointed to the data on the slide.

"Now, it is possible that the parents are suffering from some rare genetic mutation. It is not entirely unknown to have some cells mutated from the normal. After all, a cancer tumor has a different genetic sequence than the rest of the patient's cells. This could be a natural mutation, albeit more severe that previously known."

"I did some more research on the subject. I attempted to pollinate an HS-positive egg with normal human sperm. This was unsuccessful. It was only possible to unite the HS-positive egg with HS-positive sperm. Now, if this HS genetic mutation was as rare as we would think, it would be almost statistically impossible for two HS carriers to meet and conceive, and that fact bothered me." He waved to the technician to switch slides.

"I've been conducting some studies on patients at fertility clinics. I'll be publishing on that topic soon. But the bottom line is that we found that in approximately six percent of the cases, one partner was HS-positive. The genetic differences were preventing conception." Dr. Mensen moved to his conclusion slide.

"There is only one conclusion that can be drawn from this information. Some sort of retrovirus is targeting the reproductive systems of individuals. This virus is resulting in significant genetic damage that is asymptotic and goes unnoticed in the patient. This disease renders the patient incapable of conceiving a normal child. However, the disease does appear to be contagious. Those people in close proximity to each other, such as spouses, can pass the virus on. This results in two damaged reproductive systems that are mutually compatible, resulting in a child exhibiting the symptoms of HS."

Dr. Mensen stepped back from the podium for a moment and took another sip of water. The question period was already commencing, and Dr. Foucoult was right at the head of the line. Dr. Mensen looked around for a few seconds, pretending that he didn't see him, but he eventually recognized Foucoult.

"Dr. Mensen," began Foucoult, "How do you know that this genetic drift you speak of comes from a viral vector? It could be any one of a number of mutagens, or it could be some sort of hereditary defect."

Dr. Mensen had of course anticipated that question. He responded, "I wondered that as well, Doctor. I came to the conclusion that it is not a hereditary defect because every case we've seen so far of a parent with an HS reproductive system has birthed an HS-positive child. If this was a hereditary defect, it would have shown up in the literature a long time ago. There is no precedent for this sort of thing. If all of the genetic ancestors of an individual have HS tendencies, why have they all given birth to normal children up until now? No, this must be a new event." He took another sip of water. "As for another mutagenic agent such as radioactivity or chemical contaminant, I can't rule those out. I do believe that they are unlikely for several reasons. First, the parents were screened for toxins and came up negative. Second, they are from very different economic and geographical regions, so there is little chance that they would all come into contact with the same toxins. Unless that toxin is almost universal."

"If the genetics have changed so significantly, why doesn't the body reject this alien tissue?"

"I can't explain that. Perhaps the genetic differences don't result in changed surface receptors."

One of Dr. Foucoult's grad students raised his hand. The impudent man didn't even wait to be called on before speaking. "Dr. Mensen, this theory you have is interesting to be sure, but without any hard data it remains quite fanciful. Have you isolated any potential viruses?"

Mensen had little choice but to answer. "No. As of yet I have not isolated any viruses in the patients that could account for this genetic damage. I'm basing my viral theory solely on the epidemiology and the fact that it's the simplest explanation." The reason Dr. Mensen hadn't isolated a virus yet was that his funding had been cut. He didn't have the resources for a good virologist post-doc. He wasn't going to admit that in front of Foucoult though.

Foucoult took up the questioning. His team operated like a pack of wolves. "Well, Dr. Mensen, then you've got your work cut out for you. Why don't you go back to America and start looking for this virus of yours?" Foucoult made a gesture implying that the 'virus' wasn't a real thing. "Maybe you can come back next year and present your findings. We all anxiously await your results of course, but until we have a good candidate, I'm afraid that your theory must remain just that; a theory."

A man seated in far the back of the audience stood up and began moving forward. "I believe, Dr. Foucoult, that I can be of assistance here." He walked to the front to the podium and hopped up on stage. He was followed by several large men in dark suits. "My name is Ray Johnston."

Dr. Foucoult stood up defiantly. This was his session, he was the chair, he would decide who would speak and who wouldn't. "Sir, you have not been called. Please return to your seat." He said, trying to sound as outraged as possible at this breach of protocol.

"I don't think so Frenchie," replied Ray. Dr. Mensen instinctively stepped away, allowing Ray room to take the microphone. Dr. Foucoult took a step forward, determined to have this man removed, but he was blocked by two of the men in black suits. No one but Foucoult could see, but the men each had handguns under their coats. Foucoult was arrogant and outraged, but he wasn't stupid. He sat back down defiantly.

"Ladies and Gentlemen. My name is Ray Johnston. I work for the U.S. government. I am sure that you have never heard of me, but I have spent the last year of my life delving into the mysteries of this disease that you call HS. I have a lot of information that you need to have.

"Time is running out for an epidemic the likes of which have never been seen on this planet. I have information crucial to stemming the tide, but I've been blocked by my own government. They have been trying to stop me because they don't want to panic their citizens. Well I say that it is time to panic. Panic is the only way that this issue will get resolved. We must panic and panic effectively. I have been working behind the scenes, doing what I could, passing information to some of you clandestinely. Many of the people in this room have already spoken with me, but they haven't known who they were talking to. Hopefully the fact that the information that I gave you turned out to be true and very helpful will give credence to what I am about to say. I wasn't sure what I was going to do today, if I was going to stay quiet and allow the scientific process to function on it's own time scale or if I was going to break every oath I've ever taken and reveal myself in order to speed things up. But I can't wait a year or more while you people dither around, we don't have the time. I have prepared packets for each of you." Some of the men in dark suits began distributing large manila envelopes to the crowd.

"Hopefully the scientific community has reached a point where they are willing to listen to what I have to say. I couldn't talk openly before without seeming to be a crackpot. I am not a crackpot. I am very serious about what I do. My information comes from the very best sources. In the packet you will find information about the organization that I work for. This organization is highly classified, and their existence is denied by the U.S. government. By revealing the nature of this organization, I am effectively committing treason. But I feel that I must speak and I must speak now."

"Also in the packet you will find several detailed papers relating to the subject that Dr. Mensen has been talking about, namely a virus that is causing the HS mutation. This information comes directly from the U.S. Army Medical Research Institute of Infectious Diseases. You may remember these guys as the ones responsible for our nation's biological weapons program. They are world-class scientists. I believe that you will find their procedures and scientific processes to be impeccable and their conclusions irrefutable."

"In addition, you will find several small vials of material. Do not open these outside of a BL-4 facility. They contain live samples of the virus that causes HS. This virus is highly contagious. I've provided samples because I want you to perform your own tests. I want you to confirm the results of the USAMRIID study I've given you."

The scientists were beginning to open their packets. Some had pulled out the USAMRIID study, others were examining the vials. Some were looking at small bits of metal that were also included. Ray took the opportunity to sip some of the same water that Dr. Mensen had been drinking.

"Now, you may ask why this information has been withheld from the scientific community. The answer to that question is contained in the small metal bits that I have included, as well as the final report. What I am about to say is going to be hard to believe. I know that you will all immediately attempt to dismiss me. However, I know that you are all highly respected scientists, and that you are all familiar with the basics of scientific procedure. I'm sure that you will take my studies, and the material that I have given you, and go back to your respective labs and do the tests yourselves. Once that happens, you will be led to the same irrefutable conclusions that I have been led to."

"As hard as it may be to believe, you will begin to understand that the virus in the vials is not a naturally occurring viral species. It has been bioengineered. You will also come to the conclusion that this material is indeed a biological weapon... and that we are under attack." Hushed whispers began to come up from the crowd. They didn't know how to react to this. The entire scene was very unusual. Scientists aren't the sort of people equipped to deal with events like this. Ray was used to talking to military men, who were trained to process information rapidly and change their entire viewpoint on an issue in a few seconds. Scientists take a slower, more methodical approach.

"The final conclusion that you will make, as I have done, is that this virus is not terrestrial in origin. It has come to the planet from outer space. The metal included in your packets is a small sample from one of the casings that my organization has been digging up all over the planet. The classified report on unknown objects falling from the sky should back up my claim that these bombs have been dropping all over the world for several years now, and that they continue to drop to this day. The material of the bombs is an alloy that is not common on earth, and the isotopic distribution of the elements are unlike any terrestrial ore. The only conclusion that one can make is that some extraterrestrial intelligence is engaged in a deliberate, systemic act against the people of Earth, and that the consequence of their actions is Handel's Syndrome."

"Epidemiological research performed at USAMRIID has shown that almost 3% of the population is already infected with the virus, and that number is growing everyday. I take this action against the wishes of my government because I believe that we must face this threat and face it quickly, otherwise it will be too late for any of us. I urge you to take this information back to your laboratories, verify the results I have presented, and immediately begin work on ending this threat now, before it is too late. I'm having copies of these packets sent to many major news agencies as well as to premier biological research facilities all over the world in an attempt to ensure that my message will be received, understood, and acted on. I'm going to get into a lot of trouble with my government for providing this information to you. Please do not let my sacrifice be in vain. Thank you."

With that, Ray walked off the stage and out of the auditorium, followed by his goons. No one said anything for several seconds. Then the whispering began. The volume increased to chattering, and then to arguing. As the scientists read more and more of the information presented to them, they began to realize that this strange man was not a kook. Many rushed out of the conference in order to catch the next flight home. Everyone wanted to be the first to confirm the results. To prove to the world that this was some form of extraterrestrial life, and to begin to counter the most serious threat that the human race had ever known.

Book 2: Revelation

The Oval Office of the White House, Washington, DC

"30 seconds Mr. President," someone off to the side says.

Hank Dillon was feeling nervous. More nervous than he usually felt when talking to the American people. The stylist finished brushing his shocking white hair and pulled back out of the shot. His tie felt a little tighter than it usually did. The makeup artist finished removing the shine from his forehead and stepped back out of the shot. She returned momentarily to retrieve the makeup bib she had inadvertently left around the President's neck. Hank collated some of the papers on his desk. They didn't have anything written on them. They were mostly just a prop, something to play with as he spoke. He looked up at the cameras. The wardrobe person finished brushing the lint off his shoulders and moved out of the shot. "15 seconds," says someone. Hank can't really see, the lights are pretty bright in his eyes. The producer steps forwards and does one last spot check to measure the light level. Then he steps out of the shot. Hank didn't want to give this speech. He didn't want to have to admit the things that he was going to have to admit. The people of this country elected him to lead, to protect them. Now all he could do was sit on TV like some fat, stupid, cow and tell the people who voted for him that once again the government was caught covering up the facts. Fact about a disease that could affect every American home, and that he, the President of the United States, had no answers. The spin doctors would try to show the plus side in this, but the public always saw through the spin when the situation was really awful. His approval rating was going to take a tumble after this for sure. It was a good thing for him that the election wasn't for several years.

He glanced over to his Chief of Staff who stood off to the side. She was far enough from the lights that he could make out her face. She was moving her fingers in an upside down arch across her face. Smile. The President perked up. He was going to have to be strong. Any weakness during this speech would really reduce the people's trust in his government's ability to protect them. "It's going to be ok, it's going to be ok," he repeated to himself.

Everything began to go silent. A lone voice from behind the lights cries, "We're live in 5...4...3...2...__..."

"Good evening fellow Americans." Smile.

"Over the last few days, there have been many rumors going about concerning the disorder called Handel's Syndrome. Some of what has been said is true. A lot of what has been said is untrue. I am speaking to you tonight in an attempt to clear the air about this disorder, what it means to your family, and what it means to the American people in general. Some of you won't believe what I have to say. Others won't want to listen. You might become angry, might feel frustrated. You might wonder why more hasn't been done. But I hope that you'll hear me out. Listen calmly, and then act calmly and rationally. The situation is not as grave as some unscrupulous elements in the media have led you to believe. There is no imminent danger. There is no reason to panic. Yes, there is a hardship that we are all facing. It is an unexpected hardship, an uncertain hardship, and yes, perhaps, a challenging hardship. But I believe that the people of the United States of America are the best people that ever lived. And I promise you that we will defeat any threat to our health and our freedoms. I am going to be quite frank with you about the current situation. You deserve that much. And then I am going to call on you, the American People, to stand united with me and help to meet this threat head-on." Pause.

"Let me start by repeating what the media has already said about this issue, and telling you what we have learned.

The scientific community now seems united in saying that Handel's Syndrome is indeed caused by a virus. You catch it in the same manner as you would a cold or the flu. We've isolated the virus. It is also true that this particular virus doesn't make you sick, in the way that you become sick when you catch the flu or the mumps. This virus scrambles the DNA in a person's reproductive system. When two people who have been infected conceive a child, that child is born with the scrambled DNA, and has what we have termed Handel's Syndrome."

Hank turned to camera two and the second prompter. "It is also known that once a person has had their system scrambled by the virus, the damage is permanent. That person will almost certainly never be able to conceive a 'normal' child again. This is also a known fact. Perhaps some day medical science will come up with a way to unscramble DNA, but under present technology the damage appears to be irreversible."

"That is the extent of what is known about Handel's Syndrome at this time. There are so many rumors floating in the press these days that it is easy to become confused. So, let me tell you what is not true. First of all, there are a lot of people out there saying that the virus is artificial, that it has been engineered for this purpose. This is not true. We are in the process of researching this virus, and our scientists say that it is much too early to make any determination of that sort. As far as they can tell, this virus is simply a product of nature like any other virus. While its appearance is certainly unfortunate, it is no more a manufactured virus than Ebola, Small Pox, HIV or any of the other scourges that man has had to put up with since time immemorial."

Back to camera one. "There have also been wild rumors circulating in the press that this virus is somehow extraterrestrial in origin. This rumor started because some unprincipled members of the press speculated that the victims of Handel's Syndrome have many of the characteristic of so-called 'gray aliens' that we've all seen at the movies. Now people are even saying that the virus was first found inside of a meteorite. This is preposterous. Nothing could be further from the truth. Our scientists at the various national laboratories assure me that this virus is terrestrial in origin. It comes from good old planet Earth. There is nothing to fear about this."

"I've also heard rumors that this is some sort of biological weapon developed to destroy certain races. That certainly isn't true. The virus seems to infect people of every race, creed, and ethnicity in the same way. There are so many statements about this virus that are simply untrue. I've heard that the virus is spread through sex, and I've heard that it's airborne, and I've heard that it's spread through drinking water. I've even heard that it can somehow transform an adult who is exposed– like someone who's been bitten by a werewolf. All this speculative and malicious gossip has led to some panic in various places. People are starting to hoard food, to avoid contact with people, to skip out on work. This is not helpful. The plain truth is that we don't know how the virus is spread yet. I can't give you any advice on how not to catch it. But I can tell you that we have our best scientists working on the problem as we speak. I am authorizing the National Institutes of Health to place Handel's Syndrome on their list of highest priority diseases. I have just signed an executive order that increases the funding for HS research ten-fold. I have no doubt that other countries are also increasing their research efforts in this field, and we are prepared to work with the international scientific community on a cure."

Time for the big close-up finish. The camera zooms in until his face fills the entire screen. "This is not the time to panic. Yes, this is a potentially serious threat, but it is not beyond the capabilities of the American people to overcome it. We overcame the odds in World War II, we have overcome countless diseases, from the Plague to Small Pox to Tuberculosis. I am calling on you, the American People, to rise to this occasion and help me fight this disease. Panicking will not help, hoarding goods will not help. Trying to eradicate the virus by committing acts of violence against those infected will not help. We need to stay calm, clear, and rational. I know that if we work together; there is nothing that we can't do. There is no challenge we can't overcome. Yes, the road ahead may be bumpy, but my friends, we will get through this. Mark my words. We will not only survive, but prosper. Adversity always brings out the best in people, and I'm counting on you to do your part in helping to maintain America's honor and dignity. Thank you, good night."

The red light on the top of the cameras switch off. "Ok, we're clear," says the producer.

Hank looks around the room. "Jimmy, get me the poll numbers as soon as they come in." He gets up. He reaches up to his forehead and wipes off a bead of sweat. It's hot under these lights.

That same night. The Miller farm, outside of Tyler, TX

Lorraine sat blankly as the TV went back to its regularly scheduled programming. She didn't know what to say, what to think. The morning newspaper still lay on the floor. In bold letters the words, "Is your child from Mars?" stared up at her. Special reports had been on the television all afternoon. The President's speech was the final capstone. She stared at the TV for what must have been a good ten minutes before she became cognizant enough to realize that Tom wasn't in the room anymore. She hesitantly got up off their old, gold velvet couch and went looking for him. She found him of course, right where she expected. He was in Jim's room, in the dark, standing over the crib. She could see in the dim light that both of his hands were clenched tightly. She was worried. Jim was so small, and Tom's hands were so big. She didn't know what to say, what to do, how to act. She slowly crept up on Tom and tried to put her hand on his arm. She moved slowly and attempted to be as comforting as possible. Tom just stood oblivious to her touch. She rubbed his strong shoulder and felt the tension deep within the muscles. She didn't say a word, she didn't have a word to say.

All of a sudden, Tom turned and left the room. He walked deliberately through the house, not taking notice of Lorraine. He pushed his way through the hall. The baby stroller was partially blocking the doorway. Tom knocked it over with one swoop and kept going, right out the front door. Lorraine followed him out into the yard. She watched him move purposefully toward his truck. She panicked for a moment when she realized that Tom kept his shotgun in the truck, but only for a moment. He calmly got into the dusty, red pickup, turned on the lights, and drove off into the night.

Lorraine didn't know how to take that. This wasn't like Tom at all. She was worried about him. He never liked to talk about his feelings much, but he didn't normally just storm off like that. She didn't know what he would do. Maybe he wouldn't come back, maybe he would do something bad. Even for herself, Lorraine didn't know what the future held. What were they going to do with an alien baby? What the hell did the President mean? Why didn't he address all the facts, like those bits of metal they found? He didn't give any advice on what to do. Maybe Doctor Thomas would have some ideas. She'd call him first thing in the morning. Maybe the doctors had been given more information. Lorraine was a very practical woman who had a healthy respect for authority. She knew that whatever was going on was beyond her, and she knew that someone would have a plan. The government always has a plan for things like this. Nothing really bad is allowed to happen. All she needed to do was to stay calm and wait until someone told her what to do.

She stood out on porch in the cool Texas night, watching the taillights of Tom's pickup get smaller and smaller as he drove down the long, straight country road that connected their home with the rest of the world. She bundled the neck of her robe close up to her throat to keep out the chill. Things were changing. She could feel it even out here. Today wasn't a typical day, everything was going to be different from now on.

It was quiet out here in the country. Even the almost constant wind that blew across the fields made no sound. A phone rang. "That must be Joyce," thought Lorraine. She must have been watching the TV too.

A Senate Hearing Chamber. Five days after the President's announcement.

"Would you state your name for the record?"

"Raymond Montgomery Johnston"

"And also, for the record, could you please state your employer?"

"I work for the Defense Intelligence Agency Senator, although most public records will show that I work for the State Department."

The lights were bright and hot in the Senate chamber. The twelve senators that make up the Intelligence Committee sat on the podium, above the crowd. Ray had to look up to see them. He was sitting at a small table, giving testimony. He was worried because the hot lights were making him sweat a little bit. Sweat is an indication of deception. This was the beginning of his third day of testimony. They had already grilled him on the specifics of the virus, on Project Beachcomber, on his involvement in the 'cover up' of information that supposedly had occurred. The press reports said that today's testimony would focus on why Ray decided to take the rather drastic actions that he had taken, and the security implications. Ray had not been looking forward to answering those questions, and hadn't gotten much sleep the night before. Still, he looked good in his new, crisp suit. His lawyer suggested that he not be seen in front of a national audience in the same ratty polyester outfits that he had been wearing for the past ten years, so he treated himself. It was important that he was believable, for the sake of the world.

The Intelligence Committee meetings were usually held behind closed doors. They are the one Senate committee that isn't usually open to the public. But this time was different. A stir had been created. The government had been accused of hiding important health concerns from the American people. After the Gulf War Syndrome fiasco, those who want to be reelected shudder at the thought of being accused of secretiveness and conspiracy when it came to health issues.

Senator Blaines, the head of the Intelligence Committee continued his questioning.

"Mr. Johnston, I have to ask again, do you understand why you are here?"

"For telling the truth." Several claps came from the gallery. A lot of the people that showed up for this hearing were involved in some way with HS. A few were researchers, some were consultants trying to get a piece of an appropriation, but the majority were parents who had an HS child. The claps comforted Ray as much as they infuriated Blaines. They were an indication of the popular sentiment towards Johnston. Ray felt strange receiving accolades. He wasn't used to people supporting him. The Senator banged his gavel twice.

"Mr. Johnston, you are here because you chose to reveal sensitive, compartmented government information to a group of foreigners. Now, did you or did you not sign a secrecy agreement when you joined the DIA?" Ray leaned in to the microphone to speak, but the Senator didn't wait for an answer. "We are here today to examine the implications of this breach of security for the American people."

Senator Walker raised his hand. "The chair recognizes the junior senator from Kansas," said Blaines.

"Senator Blaines, I can't believe that you would question the motives of man like Ray Johnston. Here is a man who worked..." Senator Walker paused a seconds while he flipped through his dossier, "twenty-one years for the intelligence community without a single blemish on his record. He did what he was told to do because he believed it to be in the best interest of the people of these United States. He attempted to break this story through normal channels, but he was rebuffed. So, he did the only thing that he could do. Senator, this man here is a real American. He's the kind of person that we need more of in this country. Begging your pardon sir, but the old way of bureaucracy and rigidity are going the way of the dinosaur. It's a mode of thinking that has hurt us in the past and will hurt us again in the future if we allow it. Whatever this virus is, we need to stop it and stop it quickly. Waiting around for vital information to get cleared for release is a bad strategy. Mr. Johnston here has given us months, probably years, more warning than we would have had if you were running Project Beachcomber Senator. I believe that Ray Johnston's actions may have saved the entire human race. How dare you accuse him of breaching his secrecy agreement? Hell, we should give him a medal!"

With that, a roar erupted in the crowd. Many of the people in the back began clapping and shouting at Senator Walker's remarks. Some even stood up. Senator Blaines banged his gavel, "Order, Order," he said, but to no avail, the people had spoken. Ray concentrated on suppressing his smile. By the time that Blaines had gotten the crowd calmed down enough to continue the testimony, Ray knew that his actions would be vindicated. Although he was no longer a company man, he still had the best interests of the American people in his heart. He knew that his actions in Geneva two weeks ago would unite the world against this threat. Part of him, only a small part mind you, was beginning to believe Senator Walker's grandiose statement that he, Ray Johnston, had single-handedly saved the human race.

The night of the President's announcement. A lonely road outside of Tyler, TX

Tom Miller is driving down a long, straight country road. The old, red pickup rattles and groans as he presses the accelerator. The truck wasn't built for going fast like this. It rattled to the point where you would believe that it would fall to pieces any second now. Tom was used to it of course, and so he didn't even notice. The night was dark. There was almost a new moon, and the sky was a flat black. You could really see the stars out here in the country, more points of light than those who have grown up in the city would believe. Tom was also used to the stars though, and he noticed them less than the rattling of the old truck. The radio was playing. There weren't many stations out here, and even less if you didn't like country or oldies. "...I fell into a burning ring of fire...." Tom wasn't listening to the radio. He didn't even really know that it was on. He was concentrated on his thoughts. "...I went down, down, down, and the flames went higher..."

"An alien." That's all that was going on in Tom's mind. "An alien." There wasn't a lot more to say was there? It was all explained, and despite the President's promises and explanations, he knew what was going on. Tom wasn't a scientific man, but he was bright enough to put together logical facts. In his mind, all the pieces had fallen into place. Some aliens somewhere had decided to take over the planet, and use our women as surrogate wombs for their next generation of invaders. He was a jumble of thoughts. It was so hard to believe wasn't it? If it hadn't come directly from the President, in a national news conference, he wouldn't have bought a word of it. It was too weird, too strange. This sort of stuff didn't happen in real life. It was too much to take.

Those damn aliens, how could they do this? How could they treat his wife like that, treat him like that? He felt dirty and violated. For the last year he had wracked his brain with guilt because somehow he was deficient, somehow his bad genes had ruined his son. But it wasn't him after all was it? It had been some sort of trick, some sort of attack. Like those cuckoo birds that hid their eggs in other birds' nests, expecting them to sacrifice their legitimate children feeding this intruder. What was he supposed to do about his son? "My son," Tom thought, "it isn't my son at all, it's some parasite, some invader. I don't have a son." How dare those aliens try to trick him into raising their progeny. How dare they trick him into working his hands raw in the fields to earn money to feed the little monster. How dare they trick him into loving the little beast. Yes, he had loved little James. He didn't want to at first, but he did. He had dealt with all those feelings of failure and revulsion. He had dealt with all those feelings of inadequacy in producing a deformed baby. All this time he had been thinking that it had been his fault, that he had somehow been to blame for whatever accident had caused James' HS. But now, only after he had spent countless nights agonizing over what went wrong, and trying to find the courage to deal with the problems and be a good father because James needed him, only now does he find out that it's all a big scam. A big joke at his expense.

He drove on through the night down the straight country road. Past the farms that were filling with crops, past the sleeping longhorns and barbed wire fences. He didn't know where he was going at first, he just knew he needed to get out of there. He needed to remove himself from the situation and think things out. He didn't really know what he was going to do. He couldn't go to his friends. He knew them; they'd accuse him of being some sort of traitor to the human race for harboring that little freak for so long. He couldn't go to the authorities; what would they do? He wanted to drive it back to the hospital and drop it off, 'Return to Sender;' but that didn't seem to be a possibility. He found himself heading south, unconsciously driving towards his parents' farm. It was only when he was approaching the exit on the highway did he realize that's where he had been headed all along. "Dad will know what to say," thought Tom. Tom's father had been a farmer for so long now. He was in his sixties and he still did all the work out there. Tom's Mom had died a few years ago, and Tom had asked his father to move up to Tyler, but he refused. He was an independent man, he was a strong and stubborn, he was a wise man. If anyone knew what to do it would be Dad. As Tom drove up the driveway that led to the farmhouse, he could see the light was on in the kitchen. It was late and Dad was usually asleep by this time, but he was up. Tom instinctively knew that this was a subtle invitation. Maybe he saw the President's speech, maybe Lorraine had called him after Tom had left so abruptly, but however he knew, he knew that he would be needed that night. Tom was immediately uplifted by that kitchen light.

Tom was already starting to cheer up as he stopped the car. If anyone could make it better it would be Dad. Tom started to the front door, but changed his mind when he saw how dark the living room was. He rounded the side of the house to the old screen door that led directly to the kitchen. As he approached, he could see the silhouette of his father standing in the doorway. He climbed up the three peeling green steps as Dad opened the door and welcomed him inside.

"I had a feeling that you'd stop by tonight. I've put on some coffee." He stepped aside and Tom came in. As he did, the father put his callused hand on Tom's shoulder. It was comforting. The elder Miller was not an affectionate person by nature, and this gesture was the equivalent of a big hug to Tom.

"Did Lorraine call you? Is she looking for me?" Tom said, as he sat down on the wooden kitchen chair. He sat in the same chair that he ate dinner at as a child. It was a bit more rickety now, but it still felt natural and normal. Tom's father didn't answer right away. He turned to the counter and poured some coffee out of an old-style, chrome percolator. He had been given a drip-machine as a gift years before, but it was still in a box in the closet. Percolators made a better brew. Once the coffee was poured, Tom's father turned and walked to the table with a cup in each hand. He placed them on the table and sat down. "Lorraine did call, she's worried about you. But I knew that you were coming even before that."

"You saw the President's speech? You know about the aliens?" said Tom.

"I did. It interrupted the ball game. What choice did I have?" He chuckled. "You must be pretty torn up inside right now, I assumed that you'd come over here. I couldn't imagine you staying at home tonight. You always did run when things get tough. That's why you were a running back in high school." He lit up a cigarette.

"I didn't know what to do Dad. It's not my kid. It's some kind of alien monster. I've been tricked."

"What difference does that make?"

"What the hell are you talking about? 'What difference does that make?' 'What difference does that make?' That thing isn't a baby, it's a monster. It's not my kid, it's some kind of alien-virus kid, it's... it's... I don't know what it is." Tom put his head down on the table.

"What difference does that make?" repeated the father calmly. He sat back in his chair and took a sip of coffee, black of course.

Tom knew that when his Dad repeated the same thing over and over again, he was trying to get some point across. That was his way. He didn't just come out and say what he meant, he made you figure it out for yourself. Tom looked up from the table, his head still partially covered with his hands. "What are you trying to say Dad, I don't have time for your games. You know what difference it makes."

Tom's father got up and walked to the counter, and put his hand on a photo album. With his back still to his son, he said, "I promised your mother that I'd never show you this, but I think that the situation has gotten to the point where this'll do more help than harm." He picked up the album and brought it over to the table. Tom sat back up as his father handed him the album. "This is something your mother put together about the time that you were born. I didn't have nothing to do with it of course, being as I'm not into that sentimental stuff, but she wanted to have some record." The cover to the volume said "Welcome Tom Miller" in his mother's handwriting on lavender paper with the edge trimmed to look a bit like lace. He flipped through the pages. There were some photos of his parents bringing Tom home for the first time. There was a shot of Mom getting out of the family's old, black Plymouth carrying a sack of blankets that could only be little Tom. There was another shot of the proud parents standing in front of the door to the farmhouse. It was winter in the picture and everyone was bundled up. More pictures inside of first birthdays, Tom in the bathtub, Tom crawling on the floor, Tom's face covered in food, that sort of thing.

"Why didn't Mom ever show this to me before? I've never seen these pictures," said Tom.

"Your mother was a sentimental woman, she wanted to keep a record for herself, she needed it for her peace of mind. She couldn't show it to you of course, because she didn't want you to find out her secret. So she hid all the stuff like this. I got a whole box of pictures and crap. After you got married and moved out, she looked through that box almost every night." He took another puff on his cigarette and coughed a few times.

"What secret, what didn't she want me to know?"

"Keep looking," said Tom's father. Tom kept flipping through the album. The front half was filled with pictures, but the back half was filled with records. There were pages with Tom's immunization records, an old crayon drawing of a cow, Tom's birth certificate. "I don't see what I'm supposed to find in here..." Tom dropped off as he saw the document. It was an adoption record. There it was, in clear type, notarized by some long-retired Texas official. Tom had been adopted by the Millers.

"I'm adopted?"

"That's what it looks like, don't it?" replied the elder Miller. "Your momma never wanted you to find out. She thought that you'd go away, off on some hot-headed quest to find your birth mother. Seeing how you turned out, she was probably right."

"Jesus Dad!" Tom slammed the book down on the table angrily and stood up. "What the hell?– Ya spring this on me now?" He paced around the kitchen frantically. "I got my own problems to deal with. I came to you for help, now I got two problems to deal with."

Tom's father was unfazed by the display of emotion. He knew that Tom had a temper, he took after his old man. The elder Miller had learned how to deal with Tom a long time ago. "No, you got the same problem to deal with, you're just on the other side. See, I've given you the answer. You're just too thick-headed to get it just yet. But think about it. It'll come to you."

"I don't have time for your puzzles again." He sat back down and opened the book once more. Incredulously looking at the birth certificate, scanning for some hope, some sign that it was a fake, some kind of a joke.

Tom's father leaned forward across the table. Tom could smell the stale cigarette smoke on his breath. "You see Tom, you ain't my son. You ain't from my belly. You don't have none of my 'genes' or whatever. But that don't mean nothing does it? No, it don't, and why's that? Cause I raised you, that's why. I made you my son. Why the hell do you think you farm corn? It is because of some daddy somewhere that you've never seen? Hell no. It's because of me. That's what's important." He sat back in his chair.

Tom was silent. His father continued. "You farm corn right? Whose corn is that out there in your field?"

"That's my corn," Tom said hesitantly.

"But that corn ain't got none of your 'genes.'" When he said the word 'genes' he always slurred it and dragged the sound out, as if in contempt for science. "But who made that corn what it is? You did. Whose sweat and blood go into that corn? Yours do. Who does that corn belong to? You. And damn if you won't take a shotgun and defend that field against anyone who would come and take your corn away. So, whose that corn's Daddy?"

"But that corn ain't some alien freak."

"Where that boy comes from don't mean nothing. What if your real mommy came from Israel? That don't make you Jewish. My kin came here from Ireland. That don't make me Irish. We're Texans boy. We're Texans from birth and by God's will. That's the important part. Who the hell cares what some scientist says about the boys 'genes.' That boy is yours and by God he's a Texan too. You got a responsibility to raise him."

"Even if he's a freak?"

"Especially cause he's a freak. Who the hell do you think is going to do that job if you don't? The government?" He said the word 'government' with the same dismissive sneer as he said the word 'genes.' He moved in close once again. "Look here. I ain't gonna be around forever you know. Somebody is going to have to take over this here field. Somebody with the Miller name. I am not about to let this place go to the corporations. Sure, it ain't ideal and all, but that boy is gonna have to learn to farm, and you're the guy who's gonna have to teach him. A year from now and those liberals will all be saying that kid ain't no alien, he's an

'Alien-American.'" He chuckled. "You raise him right and he ain't gonna be no alien no more than I go around collecting shamrocks. He's gonna grow up to be a Texan, just like his old man. Hell boy, you can't skip out on your responsibilities just cause you don't like the way things turned out. I raised you better than that." The old man leaned back in his chair and took another sip of coffee. The chair creaked.

Tom sighed. He ran his hand over the plastic sheeting that held his adoption certificate. He felt better. The old man was right. It didn't matter where that kid came from. He was still sort of Tom's kid. Tom did teach him how to catch and all. And, Tom supposed, Lorraine had gotten attached to the little thing. It wouldn't be right to just walk out. That kid needed raising. He had already dealt with the whole HS thing. He already knew that he could grow attached to someone who wasn't perfect, someone who didn't look like him. This was just one more step down that road. If he kept thinking that Jim was adopted, he knew that he could make a good father. He wanted to do right by Lorraine. He wanted to make his father proud. He didn't want to let down the people that were counting on him the most.

Tom didn't even wait to finish his coffee. He had to get back to his farm. Lorraine and Jim would be worried about him.

Article in the Journal of Biochemical Virology, published three months after the President's announcement

Morphology of Handel's Syndrome Virus Methyl-Transferase 1 (HSLVM1), and HSLV Promoter Sequences
Dr. Heinrich Mensen*, Dr. Nancy Collins*, Dr. James Bluefeld[†],
Dr. Hong Lee[†], Dr. Wilma Sommers[†]
*Handel's Syndrome Research Laboratory, National Institutes of Health, Bethesda MD.
[†]Department of Virology, the Johns-Hopkins University, Baltimore MD

ABSTRACT: Based on its large genome, Handels' Syndrome Virus (HLSV) may represent a new class of DNA viruses. While most known viruses encode between 5 and 250 genes in their genome, HSLV contains significantly more open reading frames (ORFs). Based on the amount of genetic material present, it is estimated that there are up to 500 unique ORFs in the HSLV genome. It is possible however, that much of this material may turn out to be so-called 'junk' DNA that is not expressed. The first gene to be isolated from HSLV is Handel's Syndrome methyl-transferase 1 (HSLVM1). This DNAse seems to have similar morphology to other known methyl transferases in the human genome. HSLVM1 functions on a specific, highly-conserved DNA sequence in the human genome known to be associated with gene promoter binding sites. It is thought that HSLVM1 functions by irreversibly methylating promoters thereby stopping the human gene from being expressed. DNA probes have shown that the HSLV genome contains sequences almost identical to the human promoter sequences bound by HSLVM1. However, the HSLVLM1 does not attack promoter sequences in

HSLV due to the presence of a highly conserved sequence that appears directly before the HSLV promoter sequences. This sequence seems to inhibit HSLVLM1 activity against promoter sequences in the viral genome.

"Live Talk! with Bill Garcia," broadcast nine days after Ray Johnston's testimony before Congress.

"...Available wherever quality products are sold."

Three seconds of black screen.

Bill: And we're back with 'Live Talk!' I'm Bill Garcia. We're sitting here today with whistleblower and alien investigator Ray Johnston. Now Ray, you've been telling us all about this so-called 'alien plague' but what everyone wants to know is what made you come forward. Isn't keeping secrets number one priority with your people?

Ray: Well, Bill. Something needs to happen and something needs to happen soon. I had tried all of the usual channels and I was getting nowhere. What else could I do?

Bill: That must have been hard for you. You spent your entire life *not* talking to people.

Ray: That's true Bill, but let me tell you, the people working in the intelligence community today aren't the same ones that I knew when I started 30 years ago. Back then, during the Cold War, we had a purpose, a raison d'être. The men were motivated by a vital mission. Today's agents are just bureaucrats. They can't do anything right. The same goes for the military.

Bill: So it was incompetence that motivated you?

Ray: I came forward because I knew the bean counters who run the procedure for distributing declassified materials, and because I knew that beating your way through bureaucracy is like sucking molasses through a straw. I felt that the only way to get the information to the people in time was to take drastic action. I'd already wasted a whole year trying to go through the system legally.

Bill: That was quite a risk, do you think it was worth it?

Ray: Of course it was worth it. Now the scientists can get a handle on this problem. I've talked to some of the leaders in this field. They think that the disease can be stopped. But, it's going to take time. Time we may not have. Time we certainly wouldn't have had if I kept quiet on information of this importance. We had already isolated the virus for God's sake! A virus that is turning our kids into monsters, and the government wanted to keep it quiet until some pen pusher in Washington who doesn't know a virus from a jellybean could 'review the data' and put the proper spin on it. Hell yeah it was worth throwing away my career. This thing is bigger than me.

Bill: The Administration has come out strongly against you, but there has been a lot of public support for your decision. The military has withdrawn their attempt to prosecute you. You've been honorably discharged from your duties. The press is calling you quote, "The only 'Real American' in the federal government."

Ray: hmm.

Bill: So what are your thoughts on what to do with these HS kids? Should we round them up and shoot them?

Ray: I'm not a sociologist. I don't know how those kids are going to react when they grow older or how society should treat them. I don't know what the solution is. But I'll tell you this; the longer we wait, the more drastic our solution is going to have to be. We can't sit around hoping things turn out ok. The answers must come and they must come quickly, or society as we know it is going to be in serious trouble.

Bill: You know the President is still denying that the virus is extraterrestrial.

Ray: I can't control what the President says. The evidence is out there for people to judge themselves. I leave it to the scientists.

Bill: Any thoughts on the future? You can't go back to spying.

Ray: You know, I haven't really thought about it. My entire life I assumed that I'd be retiring on a government pension. I don't know what I'm going to do. I have some speaking arrangements scheduled for the next few weeks, but beyond that, who knows?

Bill: Rumor has it that there's grassroots campaign gearing up to have you run for Senator Blaine's seat in Congress. Any truth to those rumors?

Ray: I've got no desire to run for office. I see myself as more of a motivator, someone who works behind the scenes. Congress has gotten fat and weak over the years. They need some new blood. People who are willing to go out on a limb and actually do something. What we don't need are bureaucrats who sit around all day extorting money from lobbyists and filibustering each other. Government needs to work, not discuss. We need people of action to lead this nation.

Bill: Some 'Real Americans' huh?

Ray: hmm.

Bill: We've got to go to a commercial break now, we'll be back with your calls for government whistleblower Ray Johnston on 'Live Talk!'

Fade to black.

Six months after the President's announcement. Holy Trinity Orphanage, Bronx, NY

The living room is dark at this time of night. Everyone is asleep. Well, almost everyone. It is still possible to maneuver your way through the maze of threadbare furniture and soiled toys by the light coming in the window from the street lamps outside. This is exactly what Sister Mary Helen is doing. Rain is falling against the windowpanes this evening. The sound is enough to blot out the noise of distance sirens and car horns that can keep the children awake at night. However, it is not loud enough to keep out the sound of a knock against the front door. The dreaded knock. It was later in the evening than most, the knocker was lucky that Sister Mary Helen was up. She usually was fast asleep at this hour. Something had kept her awake, something had made her decide to boil some warm milk before bedtime. The knocker was lucky that she was awake, or, more to the point, the child was lucky that Sister Mary Helen was awake. That was what the knock was all about wasn't it? It was safe to assume that it wasn't someone coming round to sell encyclopedias. This was another case of an unwanted baby being abandoned on the steps of the orphanage. These cases had been growing in regularity of late. "Perhaps...," thought Sister Mary Helen as she walked to the door, "...we should consider hiring a night watchman. For practicality." Mary Helen began twisting open the bolts on the outer door. She dismissed her previous thoughts about the night watchman. She knew that everything happened for a reason, and that God wouldn't let these children down. She trusted her instincts. She knew that when the next instance occurred, God would once again revive her insomnia so that she could be there for the child.

As she feared and expected, the top step contained a large pile of blankets, gently wriggling. She knelt down to pick up the bundle. She was getting older, and her back wasn't what it used to be, so she had a bit of trouble getting back up with the babe in her arms, but she managed, she always managed. She took the child off the damp, tile floor of the entryway and brought it through the darkened living room to the bright warmth of the kitchen. She lay the child on the table and turned off the stove. Her milk had almost boiled over. Once that was accomplished she returned to the pile of blankets. She knew what she would find inside. She undid the top few folds and revealed the baby's head. Its huge, bug-like eyes were closed, but it twisted fitfully in its sleep. She looked around for the obligatory note from the mother, but there was none in this case. "Well, at least they bothered to give the child a blanket," she thought.

At that moment a creaking could be heard coming down the stairs. It quickened its pace when it reached the point where one could see that the lights were on in the kitchen. A few seconds after that, the form of Father Blythe could be seen entering the room.

"Sister, I thought I heard a knocking. It's another child isn't it?" the father said dejectedly. While he was happy to care for any child in this world, he pitied the mother, pitied the fact that anyone would willingly give up such a gift from God. He would pray that the woman would have the strength to live with her decision. The fact that the orphanage's resources would have to be stretched further to accommodate this new resident didn't cross his mind. They always managed.

"Yes Father," responded the Sister. He moved towards the child.

"HS?"

"Well, duh," she responded. He looked down upon the child, putting his hand upon the girl's oversized, bald head. The child responded by fidgeting around and freeing one arm from the swaddling. Father Blythe put his finger out, which the baby grabbed tightly before returning to sleep. Sister Mary Helen returned to the stove to finish her cooking. "I have some warm milk Father, if you'd like some."

"No thank you sister, that'll put me right to sleep. I've got to find a place for this little one before I go to bed."

"This is the seventh HS child we've gotten in the last two months. It seems to be a trend doesn't it Father?"

"People are scared of the unknown Sister. They don't understand what is happening to them. They look at these kids and they just see 'monster.' There has been so much on the news about it. It is no wonder that they choose not to deal with it."

A tiny voice came from the foot of the stairs. "Am I a monster Father Blythe?" said the voice. A face came into view. A little boy. He was wearing yellow pajamas and dragging a stuffed rabbit by one ear. His oversized, bald head was covered by a rather ridiculous-looking purple nightcap. As silly as it was, he never took it off. The Sister had made it for him.

"No, you're not a monster Franklin. But you should be asleep."

"I'm sorry Father. I heard the noise down here. I came to see." He waddled across the kitchen, the plastic feet of his pajamas scuffling across the linoleum floor. He climbed up on one of the chairs as one would mount a horse. He stood on the seat and peered into the blankets. "Another one like me," he said matter-of-factly.

"Yes Franklin, it seems as if you have a new baby sister." Franklin poked at the child with his long, bony finger, perhaps to assure himself that the little thing on the table was actually alive.

"What's her name?" said the boy.

"You can look at the baby in the morning Franklin, you should be in bed now. It's late."

"Yes Father," the child said. The priest picked Franklin up and threw him over his shoulder like a sack of potatoes. He turned to the nun. "I'll be back in a minute Sister," he said as he carried Franklin back upstairs to the bedrooms.

As the pair was walking out of sight, the bouncing form of Franklin lay half limply across Father Blythe's shoulder. The cloth rabbit looked increasingly distressed as it bobbed up and down. Franklin remained focused on the Sister as he was leaving. "Sister," he said, "Are you going to make this little girl a hat like mine?"

The Sister just smiled wistfully. She sat down in the chair that Franklin had been standing on, and took her first sip of warm milk.

20 miles north of Thule Air Force Base, Greenland.

The ice was too frozen here for the corer to go in smoothly. Dr. Collins was pounding on the top of the device with a rubber mallet, straining to get the thing to go in the required six inches into the snowdrift. Trying to grasp the hammer while wearing thick mittens was difficult, and it took her quite a while to even get it in halfway. One of the marine guards assigned to the project saw her struggles, and being the gentleman he was, came to help. While she held the corer steady with both hands he began stomping on the thing with his big, black boot. That seemed to do the trick, and soon it was in the full six inches. The fact that the two were able to act together was surprising, since the wind and snow were blowing hard enough here to make hearing each other's conversation impossible. They both had to rely on just knowing what the other wanted.

Nancy grabbed the metal tube and pulled it from the ice. It was easier to get it free than to get it in. It slid out, containing a perfect core of stratified ice. She took the sample and placed it in a plastic bag that had a little white label on it. Then the bag went into a cooler. The marine guard and the biologist then carried the cooler back to the helicopter to wait for a suitable break in the weather to take off, fly another few miles, and take more samples.

The next day, Nancy sat in her laboratory in the Air Force Base. It wasn't much of a laboratory really, it was more like a disused office. There wasn't much furniture, just an old desk and a chair that flaked tan paint when you sat on it. It was filled with boxes though, boxes that Nancy had brought with her. Most contained equipment of various types. She had tried to make her lab as mobile as possible, but it still weighed almost a half a ton. On the desk, and all over the floor, lay reagents and diagnostic equipment. Sequencers, antibody stocks, other obscure scientific items she needed to do her job. In one corner sat the cooler containing the samples. Nancy had worked for most of the morning setting things up and running diagnostic tests and control samples. She was now ready to begin. It was cold in the office, partly because it was, after all, in Greenland, but also because the ice cores needed to be kept frozen. She walked over the to cooler and pulled out the first sample. It was labeled with the GPS coordinates of where it was taken, N77 30' W065 30'. It also had the vague and pointless statements, 'Ice Core Sample,' and 'keep below freezing.'

Nancy put on her rubber gloves and took the core out of the bag. She placed it on a cutting board at the end of the table. She carefully removed the outer, plastic sleeve. This left a cylinder of pure snow. With a large, sharp pick Nancy broke the sample into one inch segments, and placed each segment in a plastic cup. The cups were sequentially labeled 0" to 5". The top segment she broke into four quarter inch segments, each getting its own cup. The cups were sealed. She repeated the process with a number of other cores. Once that was done it was time for some coffee. After all that work trying to keep them frozen, now the ice needed a chance to melt.

After her short break Nancy returned to the solitary room. She took each sample in turn and drew off 10ml of water. These samples would go through several processing steps. First, they would be sonically shocked in order to break up any virus particles that may be inside. Then the samples were run through a PCR machine. This machine looked for a specific DNA sequence, and if it found it, would exponentially increase the amount of it in the sample. This allows for the third part of the test. The samples are examined using certain immunoprobes to test for the specific DNA sequence. The entire experiment takes about five hours to do, not including control samples. The 50's vintage

Air Force clock on the wall loudly ticked off the seconds as Nancy poured and measured, transferred and examined.

It was late when she had finished her work with the samples. She looked at the results on the printed readout. She picked up the phone to call Dr. Mensen, but then thought the better of it. There was nothing new to tell him, no special insight that would change their theories. The data that came out matched the data that Nancy had collected in Tierra del Fuego, that she had collected in American Samoa, that she had collected in Macau. The test for the HS virus showed that there was no virus in the core sample at the lower depths. However the samples on the top surface were positive. That meant that whatever this virus was, it had not be around very long. It hadn't been deposited on the ice until about five years ago. Then inexplicably it shows up. It shows up worldwide. However this virus came about, it didn't seem to exist five years ago, then all of a sudden, it was airborne and it was everywhere. Nancy put away her equipment. She still had some more cores to do tomorrow. If she hurried though she might still get to the base cafeteria before it closed for the night.

11 months after Ray Johnston denied having aspirations for a Senate seat. State House, Albany, NY

Albany is never a warm place, especially not in March, but they were waiting just the same. They stood on the cold, beige steps of the State House and they waited. All sorts of people waited. Some were from the news media and were getting paid to be here, but many weren't. They came from all walks of life. Some had come all the way from Buffalo to see the ceremony. They didn't have to really. It would be all over the evening news, of course. But they came and they waited. They waited because they wanted hope. They waited because they felt the oppressive weight of history falling down upon them and they wanted to catch a glimpse of the one person in the country that they felt could be their salvation.

"Let them wait," Ray thought as he stood in the antechamber. He looked down the hundred steps that connected the doors of the Statehouse to the rest of the world. There were banners and signs scattered throughout the audience. Some were the ones that his campaign staff had printed up, Ray's smiling face on a field of blue. There were stars surrounding him like a halo. It said in solid-looking print: "Vote Ray Johnston, A Real American." But Ray was surprised to see a bunch of other signs as well, some hand-painted on old bedsheets. It was like a sporting event out there. The signs said all sorts of things. Most were encouraging. "We're with you Senator!" "Together We'll Beat the Virus." A few signs were taken from soundbites from his campaign speeches. One sign, near the back, disturbed him a little. It showed an alien head surrounded by a big red 'No' symbol. Underneath were the words, "Kill the Invaders!" Ray knew that his campaign had brought out some extremists, but he hoped that they wouldn't show up in large enough numbers to ruin his inauguration.

Ray stood and waited in the antechamber. The doors were opened, and some people started out down the steps. The governor of New York went first, followed by the Chief Justice of the State Court and a few hangers on. Senator Walker stepped out onto the stairs. He had come to show his support for Ray and his agenda. As soon as the doors were opened, a cheer rose from the crowd. They were expecting Ray himself. The cheer died down as the doors were closed again. Ray went over the speech that was prepared for him. A few makeup people finished combing his hair and brushing his face with powder. A band began to play a suitably patriotic theme. That was his cue. He looked at his makeup guy, "How does he look?" said the campaign manager. The man responded with a 'thumbs up' sign. The doors of the Statehouse were opened again. Ray cleared his throat once, and stepped onto the top stairs to cheers so loud that they drowned out the band.

He made his way to the podium, which was located about halfway down the steps. Somewhere, a button was pushed and a video screen that had been affixed to the wall of the statehouse sprang to life. Patriotic music played in the background as a montage of still photographs began to flash across the screen. Some were pictures of typical New Yorkers going about typical New York business. Others were shots of Ray on the campaign trail; kissing babies, shaking hands, boarding airplanes. The video culminated in a few shots of Ray smiling wildly on Election Day as red, white, and blue balloons fell onto his head. The last image was of Ray standing in a long line of new senators taking the oath of office at the Capitol.

Of course, Ray himself wasn't watching. He had seen the tape beforehand. He had even given it his 'approval' whatever that means. His campaign manager really made all the decisions. His approval meant nothing. It was quite an embarrassing and self-indulgent display, not the sort of thing that Ray wanted at all. In fact, spectacles like this were part of the reason that Ray decided to run for office in the first place. He wanted to replace the spectacle of politics with the work ethic of someone who was prepared to get the job done. He found himself blushing slightly and smiling quite uncontrollably at the movie as it reached its crescendo. But he got a grip on himself, coughed a few times, and began speaking just as the video faded to black.

"People of New York," he began, reading from the teleprompter, "Let me first express my sincere gratitude to you for giving me the chance to serve you as your newest Senator!" A cheer came up from the audience. Ray waited for it to die down before continuing. "You should be congratulated. Congratulated for choosing message over flash, for choosing substance over style." More cheering. "I have never claimed to be a politician. I never wanted public office. I just wanted to serve my country in the best way I could. For years that service was in the form of a low-level civil servant. I tried to make a difference instead of making money; working on getting to the root problems we face, instead of working on getting promoted. I was just like all of you out there. I was just a guy trying to get by and do his part. But the system failed me. The system failed us! Those bureaucrats in Washington faced a threat that they couldn't even comprehend, nevermind fight against. They put me in a position where I had to choose between my country and my government. And I'm sure that you'll all agree with me when I say that it is our country that is more important!" Ray took a second to sip some water. In the cold March air it was almost frozen. He wished for something hot instead.

"So I did the only thing that I could do. I knew that I had to change the government. I had to make those at the top responsible for their decisions. I couldn't do that from where I was, so I risked it all. I never intended to run for office. I don't have the silk suits, I don't have the bright white teeth, I don't have the ability to stand up in front of a crowd of working men and women and tell them lies and platitudes with a straight face. But you, the people of New York, have spoken. You have welcomed me into your arms. You have sent a message to those professional politicians that we will no longer stand for their pandering to the media and special interest groups. Today is the start of a new era! An era in which your government works for YOU! An era in which the phrase 'for the people' is not lost when the founding fathers' names are invoked. An era in which we can once again rely on government to look after our interests, and to protect us from threats domestic, international, and extra-terrestrial!"

The crowd noise became so loud that Ray couldn't be heard anymore, even with the PA system. He looked at the teleprompter, it said calmly 'wait for crowd noise to subside.' The speechwriter was good, he knew exactly when the crowd would react. He should be good, he cost enough money. Ray cleared his throat again, just like the vocal coach had taught him, rubbed the tip of his nose with his leather glove, and continued.

"Yes my friends, I say domestic, international, and ALIEN!" Another roar from the crowd, but smaller this time. "We have a problem in this country. The HS virus. It is my pledge to you that I will work as hard as I've ever worked to bring this issue to the forefront of American legislation. I promise you now, as I've promised you all down the campaign trail, that I will get funding for research into this horrible disease. We will find a cure for this plague, we will arrest its spread, and we will reverse its effects on our children. This must happen now. We must divert funding from bloated government programs in order to combat this thing. I've said all along that I believe the HS virus to be the largest, most insidious threat to humanity that we've ever had to face. But I am sure that we will rise to the challenge. You've taken the first step. You sent a message to the government that this is important. Now it's up to me. I'll take up the ball from here. I hold here in my hand, no less than fourteen bills that I am ready to submit to vote on the very first day of the new congressional session. I'm not going to wait until I get a feel for the place. I am not going to defer to some old coot because he has a few years more experience. No way! I'm going to take the message of the people of New York and ram it down those congressional throats until everything that can be done, every resource that the federal government can direct at this problem, is properly tasked and funded. We live in a great country. We have tremendous resources at our disposal. We can combat this threat, we can defeat this disease, we can triumph in the face of adversity. We CAN and we WILL! And I want to thank you for putting your trust in me, for allowing me the honor of leading the fight in your name. I know that in my heart I'll always be just a low-level civil servant trying to serve his country in the best way he can. You've given me the opportunity, now I only hope that I can live up to your expectations. Thank you again New York!" Ray raised his balled fist over his head. The crowd cheered as the speech came to a close. Some people in the front pushed against the police barriers, trying to get a little closer to the man they believed to be their savior. Some, who weren't close enough to the barriers, chose to just mimic the Senator's raised fist gesture. The people were still cheering as Ray walked back up the statehouse steps.

Off in the corner, behind the majority of the crowd, a solitary man was protesting. He held aloft a large, handmade sign. The sign had a tempura-paint rendition of an HS child's head. Underneath were the words, "These Are Our Children Too." The man went almost completely unnoticed by those who came to listen to the Senator's message. They came here to believe, to be inspired, to be assured. Assured that the future would turn out all right. They weren't looking for a debate.

A few hours after Ray Johnston's victory speech. The Hayes residence, Fredrick, MD

In most markets, the evening news that night showed at least part of Senator Johnston's speech. The election had been a very popular subject that fall, with many incumbents losing to new maverick outsiders that promised results. It was the same as most elections in that regard. The people wanted a change because they didn't like what was happening. Unfortunately, as with most elections, the only fundamental way in which challengers differed from the incumbents was name recognition. New ideas were few and far between. Of course, that didn't stop people from hoping and dreaming that the election would make their lives better. Perhaps that creation of hope is the most important function of the election season.

Janice Hayes sat on the sofa and watched the news with more enthusiasm than most of the electorate. It wasn't that she had any particular political leanings, nor was it that she had a feeling that any of the candidates were truly better than any of the others. She was excited about the election because Ray Johnston had just been elected. One might think that it was because she was excited about the new senator's politics, but that wasn't it. It was because she had a personal link to Mr. Johnston in the form of her husband. It was one thing to watch an election, but another thing altogether to actually know a senator. She almost dropped the couple's newborn from her arms when the news anchor started talking about the recent New York campaigns.

"That's him! That's him Colin," she said excitedly as the footage of the speech was played. "Isn't this exciting? You actually know him! That's him right?"

"Yeah, that's Ray," Colin said dejectedly. He was slumped in a large recliner chair, trying to ignore the television and read an article in this month's Journal of Biochemical Virology.

"I've never known a senator before."

"Janice, you don't know him now. You've never even met the guy." Colin put down the journal.

"But I will, won't I? You're going to take that job he offered you, aren't you? You have to take it, think about what that'll mean to the family."

Colin stood up and paced around the room a little. "I don't think that I want to take that job Janice. I worked with Ray for months, I don't think I want to work for him anymore. He's going to cause problems, I tell you." He left the room and wandered into the kitchen. He didn't really need anything there, he just wanted to get out of the conversation. Janice wasn't ready to let this drop. Ever since the Senator's Chief of Staff called last week, Janice had been in a tizzy. They wanted to put Colin on a very important (or at least important sounding) interagency panel to study the HS virus. The phone call had come out of the blue one day. She had heard Colin talk about a guy named 'Ray' before when he was putting in all that overtime last year, but she never in her wildest dreams expected that it was THE Ray Johnston that he had been talking about. And now, Ray Johnston wanted to put her husband on a blue ribbon panel, and he didn't want to do it? That didn't make any sense, especially with things being the way they were now.

Janice stood up and followed Colin into the kitchen, still clutching the infant to her chest. He was just standing there, facing the cupboard, an empty glass hanging limply from his hand. She walked over to him and put her hand on his shoulder. He turned to her. "You don't understand Janice. You just have stars in your eyes. Ray Johnston isn't a biologist. He doesn't understand this virus. He thinks that he can wave money and guns at the problem and make it go away. That isn't going to happen. This isn't something that we are going to be able to stop. He said that he is going to 'cure' HS kids. You can't cure HS kids, not once the virus has done its work. This thing is going to get a lot worse before it gets better. I don't want to be part of an effort that I know is going to fail. I don't want to be part of Ray Johnston's solution. He is going to get more desperate on this. Did you see some of those signs his supporters had? Who knows what those people will do when science can't meet Ray's promises? I don't think that he knows what he is getting into. I don't think that he knows what he is fast becoming the spokesman for. Can't you feel an undercurrent beneath this?"

Janice countered, "All I know is that I want what's best for our family. I want to feel secure. I don't want to live out here in some old drafty house in the sticks. I want to mingle with high society. I want what's best for all of us, what's best for Ben, and Neil."

"I want what's best for our kids too Janice, that's why I don't think we should get involved with Ray and his guys. I haven't talked to Ray in over a year. He doesn't know about Neil. I don't think that I would be on this panel if he knew about Neil." Colin pushed aside some of the blanket and exposed Neil's hand. The impossibly long fingers of the baby's hand reached out and grabbed Colin's fingers. "He says that he is for HS kids, but as this epidemic becomes more widespread, I don't know how he'll react, how the people will react. I don't know if I want to be a part of that. We've got to look out for little Neil here."

"But that's just another reason to get in there," Janice replied. "Every day I see people speaking out against HS, saying that it's dangerous to be around HS children. They say that it's contagious, and that it's somehow disloyal to have an HS kid. Well, if you were on the panel, if you got a chance to speak at the meetings, maybe you could change things. Maybe you could act as the voice of reason? Maybe you could help little Neil here." She held out the blankets for Colin. He took hold of them and began to cuddle the infant to his chest. The child's wide, black eyes stared back up at him. Colin smiled.

"You know, I didn't even want another child Janice. I knew that he would be HS-positive. I've worked around it so much I knew I had to be contaminated."

"It's a little miracle from God," Janice said knowingly. "I was taking birth control pills at the time, right? So the fact that I got pregnant anyway has to mean something doesn't it?" Actually, Janice had been 'forgetting' to take her pills for some months before Neil was conceived, but Colin didn't need to know that. "There has to be a message here. I say we listen to it. I say that you join up with Mr. Johnston and you help him. Not for the world, but for the family, for Neil, for me, for Ben. We need you more than your country needs you."

Colin relented. "I'll tell you what. I'll call back the guy from his office. I'll talk about it some more, get some more information."

"That's all I ask Colin. I love you." She squeezed up against him and put her arms around him. It felt so good, the three of them, all cuddled together like that. She closed her eyes and placed her head on his shoulders.

Two months before Ray Johnston's victory speech, Underhill Avenue, Bronx, NY

Little Franklin was struggling to keep up with the Father. Even though the priest walked slowly through the neighborhood streets, Franklin's small legs had to work overtime to maintain the pace. He was quite a sight dressed for the winter. Nothing fit properly except his hat. The dark green hand-me-down parka was at least two sizes to big for him. His pants, although cinched tightly at the waist by the Sister that morning were floppy and falling down. It was almost impossible to find the correct size for him. His legs and arms were too long and skinny, even for specialty stores. The orphanage usually had to make due with donated clothing, even if that meant that Franklin tripped over the cuffs of his pants, had his shoes occasionally fly off, and had his shirt sleeves constantly getting dipped in soup bowls. The only thing that truly fit was his purple cap, which had been hand-made just for him. Even that was getting a little tight, now that he was getting older and bigger.

Father Blythe is walking ahead, arms loaded down with a brown paper bag containing some groceries. He is wearing a black tweed coat, open in the front. His white collar and black suit are visible to people he passes, many of whom are familiar to him. They wave and say, "Good afternoon Father," as they pass. The Christmas season is coming after all, and it is a time when people begin to feel more spiritual. Father Blythe, sensing that his charge was falling behind, stopped and allowed Franklin to catch up. The two take a small break by sitting on a nearby stoop. They watch the cars pass on the street. The priest reaches into his sack and pulls out a small piece of candy, which he hands to Franklin.

"Thank you for taking me to the store with you Father," said the little boy. He had both hands on his piece of caramel, nibbling away between words like a squirrel on a nut.

"It is important for you to get out and see the world Franklin. You spend too much time alone. You have to get used to the way the world works." The boy kept chewing. "Someday you're going to leave us, you are going to need to decide what you want to be when you get older, and the only way to do that is to see what other people are doing. You can't get a good idea of the world by just watching TV you know."

"But I already know what I want to do Father," said Franklin.

"You do, do you? And what is that? A caramel tester?" He rubbed the boy's head jokingly. The child squirmed out of his grasp.

"I want to be just like you Father. I want to become a priest and run an orphanage, just like you."

"That is a noble goal Franklin, but being a priest isn't an easy life. You are young still, you should probably think about it some more. If God wants you to join the Priesthood, it'll happen, but you shouldn't spend your life trying to emulate me. There are lots of important jobs you can do."

"But I've already started. I read the Bible everyday. Sister Mary Helen has been giving me lessons. I know the Ten Commandments by heart already see..." He then proceeded to rattle off the Ten Commandments, or eight of them anyway. He became stuck on the last two. Even so, the Father was impressed by both his resolve and his capabilities. HS was still a new disease. No one knew exactly how it affected people. With their increased cranial capacity, some medical professionals suggested that the children could have increased memory and cognitive capabilities. It hadn't been proven yet, but as far as Father Blythe could tell, it was reasonable. Franklin had learned to read at only two years old. He seemed to pick up things quite quickly. The priest thought that Franklin's intelligence was a blessing. He would need something to succeed in life, considering all the disadvantages he had been saddled with at birth.

"That's very good Franklin. I think that you deserve another candy for that one." He handed the boy another piece of caramel and then stood up. "Come on, I think that Sister Mary Helen is waiting for us. She'll be quite angry if we return with no caramels left huh?" The two laughed and began walking down the block to the orphanage.

As they turned the corner of their block, Father Blythe immediately noticed something was wrong. There were a bunch of people on the front steps. Sister Mary Helen seemed to be talking to them about something. She seemed a bit distressed. The Father quickened his pace and soon pushed his way to the top of the stairs. He was about to introduce himself, but he found he didn't need to. They already knew his name.

"Father Blythe," said one man holding a microphone. "Bill Palmer, Channel 6 News. What's your reaction to the upset victory of Ray Johnston yesterday?"

"Why are you asking me that? What do I have to do with anything?" He turned towards the obviously relieved nun, "You can go inside now Sister, I'll talk to these people." She turned and went back in the door, herding a small group of curious children along with her.

"Well, you run the one of the first orphanages in the city that specializes in HS children, you must have some thoughts on his election. He based his campaign on the eradication of HS."

Father Blythe paused a moment. "First of all, I don't run an orphanage for HS children. I run an orphanage for children, period. Whether a child has HS or any other disease doesn't matter, all are welcome. Second, I have no comment on Ray Johnston or his views."

A second man stepped up. "Father Blythe, Roy Bellamy, Channel 8. There are some that say that Senator Johnston's election is going to result in a harder line towards HS. Some are even calling for a quarantine of HS children. What are your thoughts on that?"

"Regardless of what he may or may not believe, Ray Johnston is a politician, and like all politicians, he will say what the people want to hear in order to get elected. HS is a big issue right now, so of course he has made statements calling for a cure. Every other politician is doing the same thing. As for quarantine, that's ridiculous. These children are no different than you or I. They are completely harmless. HS is a genetic disease, and however you may get it, putting these children away isn't going to arrest its spread. What these kids need is to be accepted by society, as they are accepted by God. If we make them feel like freaks then all we are doing is harming our future. Like with all other diseases, people are scared, but we've got to remain rational with this. I'm sure that Senator Johnston and his fellow lawmakers will take the proper steps to combat this disease without resorting to panic. You people in the media are just going to make this situation worse by focusing on it. Go find a real news story to write about and leave these kids alone. They've got enough problems without you stirring the pot."

And with that, the Father opened the door to the foyer and prodded Franklin inside. "Good day gentlemen," he said as he followed. The reporters cried out a few final questions as the priest locked the door, but their calls were unanswered. Once inside, Franklin immediately ran to the front window and looked out at the small crowd that was still on the steps. One of the photographers saw him and snapped a picture through the window. "Get away from there Franklin," said the priest, "you're just encouraging them." The Father closed the blinds and shooed the boy away from the window.

George Austin Elementary School, Tyler, TX. Three weeks after James Miller's 6th birthday

The secretary had been warned that this day was coming, so she had been given specific orders. She was the only one with a window to the parking lot, so it only made sense that she would be the one to keep watch. She knew just what to do when she saw the old, red truck drive up and park in the visitors' parking space. She was in the principal's office before the occupants had even stepped onto the pavement. The principal, who had also been warned of this event, jumped into action. He was out the door and in front of the school faster than one would think possible, given his rather portly frame. He met the mother and child halfway down the covered sidewalk that led to the main entrance to the school. He had been given explicit instructions on what to do.

"Mrs. Miller I presume," he said to the mother as she stepped over the curb and made her way towards the school. "I'm Principal Gaffee. I was wondering when you would be arriving." That wasn't true, he had been dreading her arrival, but he had pretty much known when it would be. One of the school board members knew the records clerk at City Hall, and the birth records had been patiently scanned in anticipation of this event. Lorraine was a little confused with the special attention. She had been hesitant to do this, knowing what the prevalent feelings were in town, but she figured that it would be ok in the end. She had dismissed her jitters by deciding that this is how all mothers feel when they go to register their children for school. She had been living with HS for so long that she was half oblivious to Jim's condition. To her, everything seemed normal, and she somehow believed that everyone else felt the same way. She kept walking down the path, right up to the fat, balding man who stood in the way. Principal Gaffee was a typical teacher. He was short and fat compared to most men, and the hair had mostly left the top of his head behind, only occasionally making a return appearance as long strands that were held taut across the oily dome by judicious application of hair spray. He wore a white and blue striped dress shirt with short sleeves and a slightly off-kilter tie. The cuffs of his pants were muddy from walking in the grass behind the playground. He smiled broadly, if somewhat nervously, checked his manila envelope, and continued talking as the pair came closer.

"...and this must be little Jim," said the principal, rubbing the boy's head in a gesture of familiarity. "How are you doing today son?" He smiled again, but his smile appeared strained, as if he was being told a joke by a man pointing a gun at him. The child looked up at the strange, sweaty man with his large, dark eyes. He didn't say anything. If Lorraine could be classified as nervous, then Jim would have to be called terrified. He wasn't used to being off the farm. His parents rarely took him into town. He didn't have much contact with other people. But he had heard about school. He knew what it was supposed to be like. As much as the TV shows he watched in the afternoons made it sound like fun, he didn't want to go. He didn't want to leave his mother and his toys and his solitude behind. He didn't want to mix with a bunch of children who didn't look like him, or act like him, or played with different toys than he did. It was all pretty standard anxiety for a six year-old. Jim knew that he looked different from most kids, but he didn't attribute a value judgment to that, he didn't understand what the difference meant, or how much importance to place on it.

"Principal Gaffee, I'm here to register my boy for classes. He just turned six years old. I got a letter in the mail." She held up the piece of paper as proof of her story. "It says that I need to bring him down here to register, so here I am." Lorraine had a certain primordial respect for principals, as do most people. People really only deal with teachers and principals as children, and at that time their authority is absolute. That fear tends to stay with a person throughout adulthood, even if the actual authority dissolves away after graduation. Somewhere deep inside Lorraine's mind was a small child hoping to stay out of detention.

"Well, ye see, there might be a bit of a problem with that," said Gaffee. He rubbed the back of his greasy neck with his meaty, nicotine-stained hands and looked down at the concrete. He inhaled through his teeth. "Some folks on the Board have been thinking that you may want to keep a closer eye on little Jim here than we can really provide here at George Austin. Maybe you'd consider home schooling."

"But I got this letter," Lorraine said dejectedly. She again held up the letter from the county clerk.

"Yeah, the letter. That was a mistake from the clerk's office, someone over there hadn't done their homework. I'll take care of the clerk's office, don't you fret about that. There are just some people here in town that are a might uncomfortable having a child with your son's 'condition' here at the school with their kids." Beads of sweat formed on the fat man's forehead. He wasn't used to being so politic.

Lorraine stiffened. "What condition is that Mr. Gaffee?" she said in an indignant voice.

"You know, the whole... condition." Mr. Gaffee was obviously uncomfortable talking about this, especially in front of the child. He waved his hands up and down hoping to give visual clues as to what 'the condition' was. Lorraine caught on quickly to the situation.

"Go wait in the car Jim," she said to her child sternly. Jim Miller, happy to be free of this strange place, didn't wait for her to confirm her request. He immediately took off in a waddly run towards the truck. "Mr. Gaffee, regardless of my son's 'condition' I will have him educated. That is his right as a citizen, isn't it?"

"umm, yes ma'am, that's true, and I would agree with you. I wish all parents were as concerned with their children's education as you seem to be. I admire you for that. But you see, the thing is, ... how can I put this... we've gotten complaints."

"Complaints?"

"Yeah, you see there's a lot of people here in this town, good people, who are a bit... touchy about all the 'HS' stuff going around. You've heard what they've been saying on TV about it. People are starting to get worried. They don't want their children to be infected."

"Mr. Gaffee, there is no evidence that HS can be passed on like a cold. And even so, it don't affect people who've already been born, it can't turn anybody else's kids into... into...," Lorraine hesitated. Just what did the HS virus turn people into?

"I understand that Mrs. Miller, I really do. If it was up to me, I would have no problem with this, but it's not up to me Mrs. Miller. I have to report to the Superintendent and the school board and the PTA. As I said, people are pretty durn edgy about this whole thing. You've heard what Senator Johnston's been saying haven't you?"

"No, I don't listen to Senator Johnston," Lorraine said coldly.

"Well Mrs. Miller, the people around here do, and they're worried, and dammit, they've got a right to be. Nobody knows what's going on here, and they're scared. I just don't want there to be any... incidents."

"Is that a threat Mr. Gaffee?" She stared at him. He wiped his head with his shirt sleeve. It was hot today.

"Mrs. Miller, I understand your situation, I'm a parent myself, you know, but I hope that you'll try to see this thing from the point of view of the community. Having Jim in school is going to be disruptive. Kids aren't going want to study, they'll be staring at him. Parents won't send their kids to school, teachers won't teach him. No one wants to catch this disease Mrs. Miller and frankly I don't blame them. And besides, I'm not just doing this for the community, I'm asking you to reconsider things from Jim's perspective. I mean look at him, the spindly little thing. He ain't gonna be able to play sports with those scrawny arms. He don't have any hair. How do you think he is going to do here in school, especially with all the parents telling their kids all sorts of stories about this HS thing? If you sent him here, he'd be miserable, he'd be a pariah. A kid like that just ain't gonna fit in, and let me tell you Mrs. Miller, kids who don't fit in come out poorly."

Lorraine turned and glanced back at the truck. Little Jim was sitting in the passenger seat bouncing up and down on the cushion. He looked so innocent. She lowered her eyes and turned back around, shoulders slumped in resignation. She wasn't used to fighting for things, especially not against the perceived authority of a Principal. He did have a point about...

"I knew you'd see it my way Mrs. Miller," said the principal, smiling again. "But I don't want to just dump all this on you and leave you stranded. In this folder I've got a pile of information on home schooling, take it." He passed the file over to Lorraine. "And if you've got any questions or problems, I want you to call me personally, my card's in the folder. I might even be able to convince the Board to pay for a private tutor. We'll get through this together Mrs. Miller. You'll see, this is what's best for Jim, and best for Tyler, you'll see."

She held the folder limply in her hand as she walked back to the truck, biting her lip to keep it from quivering, trying to maintain a brave face for Jim.

The Senate Chambers of Ray Johnston (R-NY), almost three years after his inauguration.

The rumpled figure of Senator Johnston is sitting at his desk. The only light in the room is the desk lamp. He has been there since before dusk and the loss of sunlight was too slow for him to notice enough to get out of his large padded chair and turn on the room lights. A few cars can be heard crossing the street, sloshing in the rain. The only other sound is that of a lone trumpet player eerily playing the same six bars of "Happy Days are Here Again" over and over for weary Metro riders on their way home. All of Ray's staffers have left for the day. They were off celebrating the passage of another bill to increase funding for HS research. At this moment they are scurrying about the bars of Capitol Hill furtively flirting with each other and drinking enough courage to talk to the interns who were spending their summer shuffling papers for prestigious people.

Ray was reading over the text of the speech he was scheduled to give to the American Medical Association next week. It promised more governmental assistance for scientific research in general. Did it have enough references to HS? Did it have too many? Ray knew that he was elected as a single-issue candidate. If he had learned one thing in his years on the hill, it was that you couldn't stay a single-issue candidate, not if you wanted to get re-elected. He didn't want to alienate his core constituency (he chuckled gruffly at the pun), but he needed to sound more broad if he wanted to stay in the Senate and accomplish his mission. He rubbed his forehead a bit and started to make changes to the page with his pencil.

After a few minutes of scratching and erasing, he sat back in his chair. He tossed off his reading glasses and closed his eyes. It wasn't working. He was mad at himself. Mad for becoming just like the damn bureaucrats he hated. Here he was, with the biggest threat to the human race looming on the horizon, and he was writing speeches. He did nothing. He no longer was on the front lines, defending America. Now all he did was deliver speeches imploring other people to spend their money to hire people to solve the problem. What the hell had happened to him, to his dream? The Senate was too out of the loop for his tastes. He needed something to happen, some breakthrough. The research hadn't been going too well. The scientists kept asking for more money, the people clamored for more results. Nothing was happening. Ray wished that there was someone he could shoot to solve the problem. That was the way he had always been trained to handle things. Get out there and force the issue.

A phone is ringing. It wakes Ray from his self-incrimination. At first he didn't think that it was for him. As a Senator, he had people answering the phone for him going on three years now. He was used to having a secretary tell him when he needed to be on the phone. After four rings, he realized that he was alone in the office. No one was going to answer the phone except him. "Well, at least this is something that I can do," he thought as he reached for the blinking button on line 2.

"Hello?" he said cautiously into the phone. It was unusual to get a call this late. Most everyone that would call his office knew that Senators aren't in the office after about three pm. He was so unused to phone edict that he didn't even know the proper greeting that his office staff answered the phone with.

There were a few seconds of silence on the line. Suddenly, a furtive voice spoke, almost in a whisper, "Hi, um I want to speak to Senator Johnston."

"This is Senator Johnston." The Capitol Hill security staff would have had a heart attack if they had heard that. There had been briefing after briefing about not identifying yourself to potential stalkers and psychos. Of course, Ray had never bothered to attend those briefings. He had more important things to do.

"No, kidding? Is this really the Senator? Holy cow. It's an honor to meet you Mr. Senator. I've been a fan of yours for years."

"What do you want son."

"Mr. Senator, oh geez, " said the voice, "I can't believe that I'm talking to you." The boy on the other end of the line seemed a bit giddy, he giggled. Then all of a sudden, he snapped into seriousness. "Mr. Senator, I have some information for you, there's something that you need to see. I'm a Real American sir, just like you are. That's why I joined the Air Force sir. I want to serve my country just like you're doing. We all respect to you sir, that's why I've got to tell you something they're covering up over here sir. I just want to be a patriot, just like you."

The boy told Ray about the terrible secret. Ray listened intently. He wasn't sure to believe at first, but the more the boy spoke the more it became apparent that he made sense. It was all there waiting to be broken out into the open. It really made perfect sense, thought Ray, once you think about it. Of course that's what those morons who run the country would do in this case. President Michaels was no different than that oaf Dillon was. They were so worried about public perceptions and campaign contributions from industry that they would never release this sort of information. No one had the guts to do what needed to be done– no one except Ray Johnston. For the first time in a long time Ray felt that he could make a difference again. That he could actually do something positive. He reassured the Airman that he would do something about this information immediately.

As soon as the line was disconnected he called his Chief of Staff's cell phone. There was bar noise in the background. "Steve, get everyone into the office right now, we've got an emergency mission. I need plane tickets for tomorrow morning to Ohio. I need the media notified. Give Senator Walker a call at home, I need him too. Press coverage, I need press coverage. We're going to blow the lid off this thing!" He smiled, knowing that something big was going to happen. For the first time in a while, his mission was clear.

Two weeks before the mysterious phone call. Johns-Hopkins University, Baltimore, MD

"So in conclusion, HSLV uses several lines of attack against the host cell genome. First, it uses methyl-transferases to irreversibly methylate genomic promoter sequences thereby stopping expression of certain human genes. Second, it uses intronases to modify human genomic RNA before translation into cellular proteins. And third, HSLV uses integrases to write its own genes into the human genome, thereby utilizing the host's own cellular machinery to create mutant proteins. The combination of the post-translationally modified human proteins, the inserted viral proteins, and the lack of expression of key human proteins leads to the visible symptoms known as Handel's Syndrome. Any questions?"

At the request of Dr. Lee, Dr. Mensen was addressing a graduate seminar on virology. Interest in microbiology had skyrocketed since HSLV was isolated, and the number of applicants to Johns-Hopkins biochemistry program had more than tripled in the previous year. Dr. Lee had invited his colleague to speak to fulfill student demand for cutting edge HSLV information, and to give himself a bit of a break from the tedium of lecturing.

"Dr. Mensen, how many unique genes have been isolated in HSLV?"

"We originally thought that there were about five hundred genes, based on the amount of DNA present in the virus. But the more we look, the more genes we find. HSLV is very efficient and quite tightly packed. The proteins it forms are small compared to most human proteins with homologous function. The current estimate is about one thousand genes, of which we've isolated around two hundred.

Another student raised his hand. "Dr. Mensen, you say that your laboratory has isolated no less than forty methyl-transferases that attack specific human promoter sequences?"

"Yes, that's right."

"Isn't that a little hard to swallow. I mean, one or two would be believable, but how could a virus develop that many host-specific sequences all at once? I mean, it doesn't make sense. There should be a pile of similar viruses that have smaller numbers of human-specific methyl-transferases. There don't seem to be any viruses similar to HSLV, yet this one is so perfectly tuned that it doesn't make sense that it could have evolved unnoticed. Shouldn't there be similar viruses with a less perfect fit?"

"I don't understand the question."

"What I'm getting at Professor, is that, looking strictly at the morphology of course, it seems that the chance that such a virus would develop through natural, evolutionary means, is incredibly slim. What are your thoughts on Senator Johnston's claim that the virus was engineered?"

Dr. Mensen chuckled. "Senator Johnston is not a biologist. He doesn't understand what he is talking about. The people in this room all know about viral mutation rates and how quickly viruses adapt. All I can say is that 'life is wondrous.'" Dr. Mensen waved his hands over his head in a mock celebration of nature. "It certainly would seem to the layman that it is impossible for such a virus to evolve naturally, but I ask you to look at other viruses, and other life-forms in general. The more we learn about biochemistry and cell biology, the more amazed we are at how life actually works. Is it possible that HSLV was engineered? Sure, anything is possible. Is it probable that HSLV was engineered? I'd have to say no. The amount of intimate knowledge that would be required to develop a virus as complex as HSLV is astronomical. It would take decades, if not centuries of our best scientists and our most powerful computers to develop something on this scale."

"What about aliens?"

Dr. Mensen looked over to Dr. Lee, who was sitting in back, taking notes. "Dr. Lee, I thought that I was invited to give a lecture on viral morphology, not on science-fiction writing."

The morning after Ray's mysterious call, Wright-Patterson AFB, Dayton, OH

As with most military bases within the States, Wright-Pat AFB was not under any imminent threat of attack. The base guards performed a mostly ceremonial function. Right white glove to the temple for a passing officer, left white glove to the chest for a civilian. Pass, pass, pass. The perfunctory job is often performed by the low end of the totem pole, people who don't have the smarts it takes to drive tanks or fold laundry. That may have been why the airman on duty didn't know how to do anything but let the entourage pass.

And quite an entourage it was for that early in the morning. There were television cameras and vans from a dozen stations, a number of other journalists, local and state police officers, two Senators who had come along in support, a selection of scientists who advised the Senator on HS issues, and a few senate staffers that had been lucky enough to be allowed to tag along. At the center of this maelstrom was Senator Johnston himself. He moved purposefully, not like the ineffectual legislator he had become, but like the powerful intelligence officer he once had been. He rode triumphantly in the front seat of a black jeep. The airman didn't even try to stop the convoy as it drove through the gates. It was too much for him. He simply went into his little booth and called his sergeant. The sergeant called the lieutenant, the lieutenant called the captain, and so on up the chain.

The convoy made its way across the base to its target destination. It was pretty obvious to those base personnel in-the-know where Johnston was headed, given his interest in aliens and HS. By the time he reached the hangar, a crowd had gathered. Word of mouth spread quickly around here.

Some had come simply because they heard that a famous Senator was on base. Some came because they figured that there would be a ruckus of some sort. Some had come because they were bored with their menial tasks and could take this opportunity to slack off for a few moments. A few had come because they knew the truth. But, for whatever reason, there was a crowd of about a hundred people lingering around the entrance to Hangar 18 as the Senator and his media entourage came up the road. Some people even started to clap and cheer as the jeep came to a stop. Some people did not.

One of those clearly not in the mood to cheer was Colonel Hankerton, the base commander. He had gotten word from the front gate that a media frenzy was approaching. Col. Hankerton had gone through this drill many times before. Wright-Pat was used to dealing with the media for a variety of reasons. The base was often home to roll-outs of new aircraft, the hosting of summits, and other publicity-intensive projects. Occasionally people came by asking about aliens. Mostly kooks, but the base had a policy of always attempting to answer their questions as thoroughly as possible, without violating security of course. Hankerton had just been sitting down for his morning muffin when word came that Senator Johnston was approaching. The Colonel knew that there was only one place that he could be heading, only one place that could be of interest to him. The fact that the Senator had not called ahead and scheduled his visit was disturbing. It seemed that Johnston would not be satisfied with the platitudes and canned briefings that had persuaded the other members of the legislature to keep their nose out of classified Air Force programs. He had immediately straightened his jacket and drove to the hangar entrance. This party needed to be cut off, and cut off quickly.

Johnston didn't even wait until his vehicle had come to a complete stop before dismounting. It looked great for the cameras. He strode up to the waiting colonel. "Stand aside

Colonel, I'm going in!" he said in a loud voice. Over the years Ray had learned that if you sound convincing enough most people will get out of your way. Unfortunately Col. Hankerton was too experienced of an officer to be intimidated.

"Senator Johnston, it is an honor to meet you sir, I wish that you had called ahead, we could have prepared something."

Johnston moved closer to the officer. Behind him stood two other senators, and, more frighteningly, a whole host of television cameras. "The evidence is coming out Colonel, you can't stop it now. Stand aside." Shouts came from the crowd.

The officer stood at attention. "Senator Johnston, I am obliged to inform you that you are currently in violation of the National Security Act of 1945, and that pursuant to that act I have the authority to use deadly force to prevent the disclosure of classified material to uncleared personnel." Over the years, Col. Hankerton had learned that if you quote regulations in a convincing manner, most people will do as you say. The colonel motioned to a platoon of military police that stood behind him. They had their rifles aimed at Johnston and his party. They took a step closer and raised their weapons to their shoulders. "Do not make me shoot you Senator."

The gathering crowd became silent.

"Look, Colonel, we're fighting the biggest threat that humanity has ever known. Now, you know and I know what is in that hangar. We both know how long it has been there and why it has been kept a secret. This farce will continue no longer. I am entering that hangar with these folks here and we are going to open this place up. We are going to give the data to the scientific community, and we are going to find a cure for this thing. Damn your regulations. Now stand down!" He started to walk past the officer, straight towards the hangar doors. Guns didn't intimidate Ray, he'd stared down the barrel of a gun many times in his previous profession.

Hankerton took a step back and re-inserted himself into Ray's path. He quoted the lines that the base PA office had given him for just this sort of emergency. "Look Senator, I don't know what you think that you are going to find in there, but I can assure you that there are not now, nor ever have been any extraterrestrial visitors or equipment on Wright-Patterson Air Force Base. Now I again order you to leave my base!"

"Screw You," was Ray's reply. He shoved the Colonel out of the way. The officer fell over into the dust. Cameras broadcasting the event live all over the world zoomed in on Hankerton as he struggled to get up. Ray walked forward amid a din of shouts from the crowd, which was now double the size it had been when the jeep had first arrived. "Give 'em hell Senator," "We're with you!" "Johnston for President!" came from the people's voices. Only one obstacle remained. Four military police trained their rifles on the Senator as he approached. Ray walked towards them purposefully. He was prepared to call their bluff. The men looked down at their commanding officer still sitting up in the dirt. They looked at Ray and his eyes, wild with purpose. They looked at the cameramen behind him, with their lenses trained on the MPs faces. Beads of sweat came down as they went over their orders in their heads. Then, one by one, they lowered their rifles. More cheers came from the audience. The MPs stood aside. They knew that this was bigger than they were. They knew that the secret was coming out. "We're Real Americans too sir," one of them said to Ray as he passed by. He smiled as he took a bolt cutter from an airman and cut the lock off of the door. He then headed inside, followed in turn by the journalists, the scientists, and the crowd.

The hangar consisted of one large room, brightly lit once the lights had been fully turned on. It was cold inside. The chillers that were attached to the building kept the inside air temperature just below freezing. Around the outside edge of the room were workbenches and desks that held papers, tools, and odd-looking pieces of equipment. No one had been inside at this hour. The engineers that worked in this secret place didn't normally report for duty until later on in the day. Ray walked towards the center of the space without saying a word. Sitting there was a large, partially dismantled piece of equipment that could only be described as a flying saucer. It had no visible engines, but something about its shape just seemed to imply motion. Wires and piping extended limply from one side, where a section of the outer hull had been removed. Ray circumscribed the vehicle, giving it a good look over. He knew that he would never be able to understand its intricacies but he was satisfied that once the media had made its broadcast, the right people would gain access to this treasure.

After walking around the ship once, he meandered over to what looked to be a large vault of some sort. The group behind him had fanned out, trying to capture different images to sell to the papers. "Don't touch anything, don't touch anything," cried the scientists and some of the military staff. Their calls and the footsteps of a hundred or so individuals on the concrete were the only sounds in the room. The silence was not just occurring here in Dayton, but all over the world. The images were being broadcast on a variety of news stations, and people everywhere had stopped what they were doing to stare at their televisions, not wanting to miss what was arguably the most important disclosure in the history of mankind. Years later children would ask their parents, "Where were you when Senator Johnston opened the vault?" in the same way that children once asked where their parents were they were when President Kennedy was shot or when man first walked on the moon.

Ray opened the door to the vault and peered inside. No one could see over him at first. For one brief moment he was alone with his knowledge. He just stood there for several seconds, unsure of what to do. In a way, he had hoped that he was wrong about all of this. He had hoped that the only secret that Hangar 18 held was some sort of experimental aircraft design. But what was in the vault made him shiver. He had been right all along. Everything he had said was coming true. The world was indeed under a grave threat. He moved back and allowed some of the cameramen to step into the doorway. The video they shot was grainy, but clear enough. As the cameras panned across the room, they revealed several tables. On each table was a being. They were clearly deceased, and some of the bodies had been damaged. But they weren't as alien as one might think. Almost everyone who saw them recognized the features immediately. The bodies looked like human adults who were HS-positive.

Book 3: Persecution

A few hours after Senator Johnston's revelations. The Miller farm, outskirts of Tyler, TX

Tom was out in the field when they came for the boy. He hadn't been watching the news that morning. He hadn't seen the Senator's revelation. He left at dawn to begin the daily harvest. He didn't stay at home like Lorraine had that morning. He didn't see the news report from Dayton. He didn't hear about the rioting in Washington DC. He didn't hear about the looting and out of control fires that were burning across Europe. He didn't know what was occurring in Africa at that very moment (although the media hadn't even heard about that yet). He was out in the field riding his big, green machine. The corn was being pulled from the stalk and loaded into the hopper. Tom rode with his companion, little Jim. He was teaching Jim what he needed to know to one day harvest his own field. Tom was worried that the child would have a hard time reaching the pedals, but there was always the hope for a growth spurt. Jim was having fun just bonding with Dad. He watched the dust fly as the stalks fell underneath the machine row by row. He watched the crickets jump for their lives as the noisy beast bared down upon them. He was hoping to catch a glimpse of some fireflies like he had seen the night before, not knowing yet that they only glow after dark. Tom, still unaware of the maelstrom of events of that morning turned to his child and smiled. He watched as Jim poked at a bug that had landed on the dash; astutely, scientifically observing its movements. Tom rubbed the boy's head roughly, almost knocking the baseball cap off the round, slippery dome.

When he turned back to the field he noticed a puff of dust rising in the distance. It was hard to see the vehicles themselves approaching, but you always knew visitors were coming from miles away by the tell-tale clouds that their cars produced on these dusty roads. "Who do you think that could be Jimbo?" he asked the boy. "We're not expecting visitors today." The boy shrugged silently. "Maybe it's your grandpa come to visit huh?" Tom turned the vehicle from the row of corn and drove towards the main dirt road that connected his crops to the farmhouse and silos. Tractors move much slower than cars though, and he was still a fair bit into the field when the trucks met up with him.

There were three trucks in total. Tom recognized one as belonging to his neighbor, Larry Watley. The other ones he didn't recognize offhand. Each of the trucks had several people in back. They were approaching fast. The lead truck skidded to a stop on the dirt road just ahead of the tractor. The other trucks followed suit. Tom knew that something was wrong immediately. Men poured over the sides of the trucks, and they were all armed. Tom turned off the ignition to the tractor and reached around behind the seat to where he kept his shotgun. He hoped that the load hadn't gotten wet since he last used it to scare off some crows. "You stay put Jim." He said to his son in a serious tone. Then he stepped out of the seat and stood in the doorway of the tractor, several feet above the ground. At the same time, Tom's neighbor Larry got out of his truck carrying a hunting rifle.

"Hey Larry," said Tom, "Going hunting today? You should have let me know, I would have come along." He tried a smile, but it didn't come out properly on account of his nervousness.

"We've come for the boy Tom," said Larry in a deadpan voice.

"What the hell you talking about Larry?"

"I said..." he raised the barrel of he rifle and put the butt against his hip, "...we've come for the boy. Now just hand him over and they'll be no trouble. We ain't got no quarrel with you Tom." Jim wasn't sure what was happening but he knew that it wasn't good. He squirmed in his seat.

"I beg to differ there Larry. You're pointing a gun at my child, I'd say we got a problem between us."

"Didn't you see the news this morning Tom? Ain't you been listening to the radio? Senator Johnston broke the news this morning. That ain't no kid you got there Tom, that's some kind of alien invader. Johnston showed it on the TV this morning. They had a crashed spaceship hidden in Ohio. The Army's been hiding it for years, doling out pieces to companies. That thing you got there is a menace Tom." He waved the gun in Jim's direction for emphasis. "And us boys are here to make sure that thing don't go on no rampage. Now stand back."

"Rampage? Jesus Larry, are you drunk again? Jim ain't going on no rampage. Look at him, he's barely out of diapers for chrissakes. He's just a little boy Larry. Whatever the hell this 'invasion force' you're talking about is, Jim here ain't part of it. Isn't that right Jim?" He looked over expecting a nod. Jim said nothing. "So now if you don't mind..." he pumped the shotgun for emphasis, "kindly get the hell off my land." He glowered at the men in the trucks.

"You don't understand Tom. You ain't seeing things clearly. I know that you and Lorraine tried for a baby for so long. You must of thought that thing was a miracle, even if it was ugly as sin. But you have to look long term Tom. He ain't one of us, he's one of them. Someday that boy's real poppy is going to come looking for him, and when he does, guess whose side Jimmy-boy's going to be on? They're trying to get a foothold here, and we ain't going to let 'em. Ain't that right boys?" A cheer of voices arose from the mob. "So now if you'd kindly back off, we'll fix this problem and be on our way. Don't make us take you down too Tom."

The two men stared at each other from behind their respective weapons. They, like most men in this county, were quite familiar with firearms. Larry and Tom had gone hunting many times together. They were each well aware of how accurate a shot the other one was. A bead of sweat started its way down Tom's temple. Jim sat in the truck, not fully comprehending what had been said, or appreciating the seriousness of the situation. He would have been much more scared if he had. The standoff was interrupted by the sound of another car coming down the dirt path. It was a Tyler County Sheriff's Department car. It came to a halt just behind the trucks. Before the officer could get out, Lorraine jumped from the back seat and ran to the tractor. She climbed up the side and grabbed Jim, squeezing him tightly with tears in her eyes.

Officer Hamilton calmly walked up to the scene. He had his hand on his pistol but resisted drawing it. "What's going on here boys? We got some trouble?" Craig Hamilton was well known to most of the people here. Tyler was a small town, and Craig had been involved in the community since he was a youth. In fact, Larry once was Craig's scoutmaster. The officer looked at the old man with his hunting rifle. "Larry, what the hell you doing? Don't make me shoot you, your wife'll kill me."

"Stay out of this Craig, we're protecting humanity. We've got to get rid of that thing before it mutates into some monster or something."

"Larry, you're drunk again aren't you? You boys go the hell home." Tom maintained his death stare with Larry. He kept his shotgun aimed. "You all ain't got no authority here, who the hell do you think you are, the national guard?" Larry didn't speak.

Craig walked around between the two men. He grabbed the barrel of Larry's gun and pushed it downwards. "Larry, like it or not, this is a free country. And there ain't no laws against keeping aliens in your house. So you boys are out of luck. No one's going to remove that boy from this farm without the law on their side, and so far, I don't have no orders for that. I'll give you a call as soon as they come through. In the meantime, get off Tom's farm. Look at Lorraine; hell, you scared her half to death coming up here like a death squad. She didn't know what the hell was going on."

Despite the fact that Craig was one man, and was at least 20 years younger than Larry, he had a badge. Larry wasn't the type of guy to fight authority. He always gave money to the FOP. He supported the death penalty. He wasn't ready to shoot a cop. He lowered his rifle. "All right Craig. We're leaving." He said dejectedly. "But Tom, you watch your ass, ok buddy. I'm telling you as a friend, this thing is trouble. Someday we won't have the power to stop that monster." He turned back to the policeman. "You better hope that this thing gets dealt with before it gets too late." As he walked back to the truck he passed near Lorraine, who was holding Jim in her arms. As small as the child was, he was getting to big to be picked up, and his legs hung limply and awkwardly as he tried to maintain his balance. "Sorry to frighten you Lorraine," said Larry, "We was just trying to protect you after all. You folks give us a call if Jim there ever starts eating your brains." He got back in the cab of the truck. The other men followed suit. They drove off in a cloud of dust, leaving the family and the cop standing in the road. They watched as the cloud of dust shrank into the distance.

"You're lucky Lorraine called 911 Tom. You folks better be careful. Maybe it would be best if you thought about leaving. Getting somewhere safe. There's got to be more tolerant places than Tyler County, you know." Neither Tom nor Lorraine responded. "Well, call me if they ever come back. But don't worry too much about all this. That Larry is more bark than bite." He got back into his car and drove off. Tom felt a tug at his shirt. He looked down and saw his son beside him.

"I'm not a monster, am I Daddy?" Jim said innocently. Lorraine and Tom looked at each other silently.

That same morning. Underhill Avenue, Bronx, NY

"What are the first five books of the Old Testament?"

"Genesis, Exodus, Leviticus, Numbers, Deuteronomy!" replied Franklin, hurrying to maintain Father Blythe's pace.

"And who was Noah's wife?" said the old priest without skipping a beat.

"Noah's wife was named..." the child hesitated a second. "Sara!"

"Very good Franklin. You are a quick study. All those hours you've spent in your room with your nose in a book are paying off."

"I just want to be like you Father."

The two figures stopped on the street corner to wait for the traffic light to turn. "That's very admirable of you Franklin, but I'd really prefer it if you spent more time playing and being a kid. You aren't as friendly with the other children as you should be."

"I don't seem to get along with a lot of the other kids Father. I'd just prefer to be alone I guess."

"I've seen you pal around with Joshua and Gerald."

"Well, they're a lot younger than me. They need a big brother. I'm just trying to help out."

"Well Franklin, being a big brother is admirable, but you should make an effort to get to know some of the children closer to your age. The only way to grow as a person is to surround yourself with people who can teach you. As much as Joshua and Gerald need you, they are not going to provide you with any of the intellectual challenges that will help you develop." The light turned green and they crossed the street.

"The kids my own age don't seem to like me Father. I don't really fit in with them. I've tried a little, but they sort of look at me funny. Joshua and Gerald and some of the new kids, they're well... like me."

"You mean because they also have HS."

"Yes Father," the boy said apprehensively.

Father Blythe put down his brown grocery bag and knelt to the child's level. He looked directly into Franklin's huge, black eyes. "We've already had this discussion Franklin. I know that having HS makes you look different, but inside you are all the same. It is going to be tough for you to fit in, I'm not saying that it won't be. But you are going to have to make an effort. You can't just give up on humanity. People, especially kids, can be cruel, and they don't like things that seem different, things that they can't understand. But you can't let that stop you. You have to take the first step. You have to make them accept you. When you leave Holy Trinity Orphanage you are going to have to go out into the big world. And most of those people aren't going to have HS. You can't simply not deal with them. Do you understand?"

"Yes Father. I'll try."

"That's a good boy. Ok, now lets get these vegetables home so we can think about what to make for dinner."

A shadow begins to eclipse the two. Father Blythe looks up. Several men stand above him. He rises to greet them. They look angry, they look wild. "Good afternoon," the Father says, attempting to infect them with his cheeriness. He smiles awkwardly. One of the group steps forward. He is carrying a baseball bat in his left hand. He wears a dark t-shirt with the words, 'Real American' printed across the front. Some strands of wild hair peek out from his green, knit cap.

"You're that alien-lover," the man says with a sneer. Father Blythe remains silent, but stares intently at the crowd, attempting to intimidate them with his position as a religious leader. His collar is clearly visible and he presents it like a shield.

"We don't want no alien-lovers on our block," says the man. His followers move to the right and left, in an attempt to surround the pair. Father Blythe puts his hand on Franklin's shoulder and subtly pushes the boy behind him.

"Look son, I don't know why you are so angry, but we have no quarrel with you. We'll just go back the way we came. Sorry to be a bother." He smiles nervously.

The man with the bat chuckles. "That ain't good enough, 'father.' We got to teach you a lesson. You see, we don't want no damn aliens on our street." He raises his bat. Father Blythe puts himself in between the child and the man.

"Look at you, you want to beat a child? This is a child! God is watching you. He sees all that you do here today." The man isn't listening.

"You think God wants your half-breed alien scum, alien-lover? You think that we should teach that thing and feed it? What's gonna happen when his Daddy comes looking for him. He's gonna eat your face that's what. We ain't gonna let you protect that thing. None of them things that you got in that house of yours. We're taking them all out. Starting with you." The man brings the bat down. Father Blythe blocks the blow with his arm.

"Run Franklin!" he says to his young charge. Franklin, knowing danger when he sees it, takes off as fast as his spindly legs can carry him. Father Blythe gets in the way, trying to hold the men. The fall upon him like a pack of wolves. Franklin can hear the sounds of cracking bones, of club against flesh, as he runs off. Tears cloud his eyes. His hat falls off as he dashes. He stops and turns to pick it up, but thinks better of it as he sees some of the mob approaching him. He runs for his life, both hands on his head, hiding his baldness.

Six weeks after Senator Johnston's video broadcast. The Watts residence, Sierra Vista, AZ

Nancy Collins sits on plastic covered furniture in the wallpapered living room. Everything is yellow here. The walls, the couch, the rug. Even the chipped ceramic mug that Ms. Watts provided tea in is yellow. The sound of a radio tuned to an oldies channel filters in from the other room. Nancy looks out the window at the desert. There is no grass outside, just dirt. It is hot in here. There is no air conditioning, just a swamp cooler. Nancy can barely stand it, "How does Ms. Watts do it?" she asks herself. She should be listening to the conversation more closely. She should be taking notes like she is supposed to, but it is too hot. "Let the tape recorder capture the conversation, I'll transcribe it later," thinks Nancy as she politely tries not to drink the hot tea that their host has so graciously provided.

"Now Ms. Watts," Dr. Mensen says gruffly, "Let us start from the beginning. Tell us what happened to you."

"I'm so glad that you came to see me. No one ever comes to see me these days. The people in town all think that I've gone crazy, 'Crazy 'ol Ms. Watts' they say when I come to town. I'm so glad that you came. No one's ever believed me before, not even the police."

Dr. Mensen interrupts the elderly lady. "Yes, yes, we're glad to see you too. Now please get on with your story."

"Oh yes, right. My story. Well, let's see. It all started that one day in 1972, or was it 1973? I remember that it was the same year that..." Dr. Mensen flashed her a dirty look. She got the hint. "I suppose it doesn't matter after all. The important thing was that it began right down the road here. They hadn't built the mall back then, so Pebble Road was just a way to get to Tucson, if you wanted to go all the way to Tucson. There wasn't much to see on the road itself. But there I was driving my old beat up truck. I was a lot younger back then, and active, boy was I active." She turned to Nancy. "I wasn't the fat old lady you see here now, no ma'am I wasn't." She leaned in towards Nancy. "Enjoy your youth young lady, you'll miss it someday," she said in a whisper, patting Nancy's shoulder. "Well anyway, there I was out on this deserted road when all of a sudden, the engine in my car went dead. Shut off, just like a switch. Well, let me tell you, I was never much one for mechanical stuff. I had no idea what was going on. But there I was, stuck. I got out of the truck and opened the hood." She chuckled to herself, "as if I would know what to do under the hood. It was almost dusk, and I was thinking that if I didn't get this thing started soon I'd be out there all night. That road was deserted, no one came out there. This being before they built the mall and all." She again turned to Nancy, "I mentioned that this place was deserted right?"

"Yes ma'am," Nancy said unenthusiastically.

"Well, so there I am trying to fiddle with this thing when I see this light shining in the sky. I look up, and there's this giant flying triangle hovering right over me. Damned if I heard it coming. It was silent as the grave." She waved her hands over her head as if to give an indication of the size of the craft. Cigarette ashes went flying from the butt still in her hand. No wonder she had the place encased in plastic. She wiped the ashes off the cushion and kept talking. "So there I am looking up at the thing saying, 'Geesh Dorethea, that's one of them flying saucers. Ain't nobody going to believe this story.' Then, all of a sudden, Pow! I wake up on this table. I mean, I went from the road to the table in like a flash."

"And you assumed that you were inside of the spaceship." Dr. Mensen queried.

"Where else could I have gone to? It was pretty weird inside, I didn't ever see anything like that anywhere else in Sierra Vista. I mean, I'm just a country girl, and I hadn't ever been to the big city or nothing, but I can tell you, I ain't never seen nothing like that place before. The only place that come close was when I was in the hospital that one time, on account of my gall bladder."

Heading off a long story about Ms. Watts' gall bladder operation, Nancy asked, "Could you describe the room please."

"Sure, sure." The old lady took another drag on her cigarette. "I don't know much, because I couldn't move you see. That's what the weird part was. I couldn't move. So I could only see the ceiling really. The place looked like a hospital or something. It was all shiny. There were lights on the ceiling, and some metal thinga-ma-bobs on the wall. Scary. I tried to get up and leave you know, but I couldn't move.

"Why couldn't you move Ms. Watts, were you tied down?"

"No, that was the weird part, I just couldn't move, like I was paralyzed or something. I just couldn't move. But I was buck naked, I could see that much. And it was cold in there. I was on a metal table. The least those alien boys could do was give me a gown or something, but nope, they just left me there naked as a jaybird on the table."

"Then what happened?"

"Then I heard the door open, and the little boys came in."

"Little boys?"

"Aliens. Maybe like five aliens. They were dressed like doctors."

"Could you describe the aliens Ms. Watts?"

"You know, they just looked like... aliens. They were pretty much the same as that one Senator Johnston found, only not so wrinkly and rotten." Doreathea giggled to herself at what she considered to be a joke. She coughed once and then continued. "They had those big old heads, spindly little arms. I couldn't see too much, as I said, on account of me not being able to move."

161

"What did the aliens do to you?"

"They looked me up and down, all over. It was quite embarrassing you know, me being naked. They put some metal things on me. Like one of them doctor's stethoscopes or something, but more... technical." She stopped to drink some of her tea. She drained the cup to the bottom. "Do you folks want some more?" she said, straining to get up out of the chair.

Dr. Mensen was not a patient man. He was used to talking to scientists. He was used to getting the facts as quickly and succinctly as possible. Talking to people like Ms. Watts was quite frustrating for him. "No, Ms. Watts, but could we please finish this interview. It is very important." He gently guided Ms. Watts back into her chair.

"Well, ok then, just trying to be hospitable. You know I don't get many visitors these days." She turned to Nancy. "There wasn't much to say after that, they just did their business down there and then sent me home."

"What do you mean, 'did their business?'" said Nancy, trying to ensure that the information was clear.

"You know... down there." She whispered while pointing to her stomach. She seemed a bit uncomfortable talking about it. "That's why I can't have no babies. It's on account of them aliens."

"They did something to you and now you can't have children? What exactly did they do to you?" queried Dr. Mensen.

"I don't rightly know, me not being a doctor and all. But I could feel them tinkering around down there for a while. At first I thought that they were just trying to, you know, enjoy themselves, but after they let me go the doctors said I couldn't have no babies no more."

Dr. Mensen looked to Nancy for some clarification. She read from the medical report, "Due to abnormalities in the patient's reproductive system, patient is sterile..." She scanned the page for more information, "...patient seems to be lacking ovaries. This is most likely due to a birth defect, as the patient's records do not show any evidence of surgery nor is any scarring present to indicate surgery."

"See, it was the little men. That's what I told them doctors back in the '70s, but they didn't listen. You people are the first ones to listen to me. Everyone though that I was just crazy. 'Crazy old Dorethea' they used to call me. No one believed me when I said that the aliens got me. But now they do. Now I'm a bit of a local celebrity. You guys don't think I'm crazy right? You believe me right?"

"We believe every word you said Ms. Watts," replied Mensen. "We believe every word you said." He turned to Nancy. "Dr. Collins, I think that we have all we need here. Let's get back to the hotel. I want to write some things up before dinner." The two stood up to leave.

"You going to get 'em doc?"

Dr. Mensen turned around. "What do you mean Ms. Watts?"

"Are you going to get 'em? Them damn aliens I mean. You're going to get rid of them right? I don't like seeing them around, on TV and all. Walking around like they're normal people. They ain't fooling anybody you know. You're going to get rid of them right? Find some vaccine to kill them off?"

"I don't think that we're going to be killing anyone Ms. Watts. We're just trying to find a cure for HS, that's all."

"Sure, sure," Dorethea said with a wink. "A cure. That's what Senator Johnston says. We're going to get a cure. But he's alright with me. He wants to kill them all off. Put 'em in a concentration camp and kill 'em all off. And I'm going be laughing and laughing on account of what them little men did to me. Maybe he'll let me push one of them buttons." She laughed. "Bzzzz."

The two scientists politely said their goodbyes and left through the rickety screen door. Dorethea was still chuckling to herself as the door swung shut.

American Labor Federation National Meeting, Chicago IL. Four months after Father Blythe's murder.

It is almost impossible to see the crowd from the stage. The spotlights are too intense. It is difficult even to see the teleprompter, but that doesn't really matter. Ray knows what he is going to say. His steps across the wood parquet floor that makes up the stage are drowned out by the noise from the crowd. They have come here today to see him, to listen to what he has to say. Maybe that's not the way the party brass wants it to be, that may not even be the way that Ray sees it, but it is the truth. These people are fed up with the way things are, no matter how they are. Whichever administration is incumbent is the one they want out. These people live a hard life, they are looking for a ray of hope, a reason to believe that things are going to get better, a feeling that there is someone looking out for their interests, not the interests of the corporations or the foreigners or the welfare recipients or anyone else who isn't them. This is what they have come to hear, this is what Ray Johnston has come to tell them.

Ray steps up to the microphone with an air of confidence. He has received applause before starting a speech before, but this seems extra-jubilant. He puts both hands on the fake wood-grained podium and begins to speak. "Ladies and gentlemen of the A.L.F. Your government has failed you. Yes, I know that is a harsh thing to say, but I must be truthful. And so I repeat myself. Your government has failed you. They have failed to protect your interests, they have failed to protect your children. They have failed to protect your way of life. Protection is the most basic purpose of government. If President Michaels and the rest of his administration can't perform this fundamental service, then what *can* they do? Nothing! They have deliberately held the truth from you. They have deliberately kept you in the dark to serious threats to your well-being. Is this the sort of administration that you want to re-elect?" Chants of 'No!' started coming from the gallery.

"People, let me take you back to a time, almost five years ago today. I was just like you, a working guy just trying to serve his country and make a difference in the world. I compiled ream after ream of evidence of the alien threat. I presented this directly to President Dillon and his staff. I detailed to them exactly what was going on. I gave them hard evidence. What did they do about it? Nothing! I originally thought that the administration was just incompetent. That's why I ran for Senate in the first place. But now we know the truth! We were lied to. We have been lied to since 1947. 1947! When the alien ship crashed in the Nevada desert, was the information released to the American people? Was the data given to scientists and sociologists to help combat the threat? No it was not. It was purposely held from the American people so that the political insiders and their big business cronies could reap millions by tearing that ship apart piece by piece and pretending that American companies were 'developing' new technologies."

"At first, we may have been able to forgive our administrations. The Cold War was heating up, and there was a lot to be gained by keeping our collective mouth shut. There was no indication of a specific threat back then. But as more and more information came forward, successive administrations still did nothing. They were still dependent on their corporate masters for campaign money. They ignored the sightings, they ignored the hundreds of abductees. They did nothing to protect your welfare, even as they began to suspect that something sinister was going on. But then, when all the truth was given to President Dillon and the rest of the National 'Security' Staff, they continued to sit on the knowledge. They continued to hem and haw while your children were being transformed into monsters at the hands of alien invaders! I had been in the Senate for over three years before I found out about the secrets held in Hangar 18. And how did I learn about it? I was told by a lowly airman who was just trying to do his duty as an American."

"But the truth will not be held back any longer! The truth has come out! And still, Dillon's lackey, Dillon's vice president, the man who sat in that room with me five years ago and laughed in my face when I warned him about the threat, that man is now running for President! It is absurd. You can't vote for a man like that. He doesn't have your best interests in mind! He doesn't deserve your vote! If anything he deserves to be tried for treason against the American people. That's why we need a new administration in office. That's why we need Governor Bill Potter in the White House."

"What should the government have been doing for the past few years you ask? Well, let me tell you. I chair the Senate Panel on Handel's Syndrome, and my scientists have given me quite a list of things that need to be done to stop this terrible plague. We need to fund a genetic testing program that will allow parents to learn if they are HS positive before they conceive. Let's give the American people a choice! We need to increase funding to the researchers that are trying to develop a vaccine to this virus. But we need more than that. This isn't like chicken pox. Hell, this isn't even like the black plague. This virus will wipe us all out, every one if we don't move quickly. I propose that we increase educational budgets to develop more biologists to work on the problem. I propose that we develop gene banks of people, both human and alien, in order to better study the disease. I propose that we use federal dollars to create a bank of frozen human embryos that can be implanted into mothers who want guaranteed *human* children. I propose creating networks of doctors to monitor the progress of the virus as well as networks of psychologists to monitor the development of these alien children into potentially disloyal alien adults. I've made all of these recommendations to the President, but all we've gotten back is red tape and bureaucratic fumbling. "

"And what has the current administration done for those poor, unfortunate, alien children? Nothing. We need to have education plans for parents coping with having an alien baby. We need to create federally-funded orphanages to take in those thousands of infants that have been abandoned on the street. We need to protect these kids from mobs of understandably angry humans. We can't have a repeat of the violence that occurred four months ago. The longer this goes on, the more of these alien kids we'll have to deal with. We have to develop a policy on their future. As of now there are no government guidelines on what to do with these people."

"Let me tell you some of the other ways the administration has failed you. Take taxes for example..." It is difficult to hear the Senator from the wings of the stage. The loudspeakers are all facing the crowd. Governor Potter watches though. He stands behind the curtain and watches. He has come to the A.L.F. meeting for two purposes today. Primarily he is here to give a campaign speech to these unionists, but he has also come on the advice of his staff to check out Senator Johnston in action. He is impressed by the way the crowd reacts to him. He has the right look about him.

"Didn't I tell you, this guy's dynamite... dynamite!" Ron Willins repeats the last word for effect. He taps the Governor on the shoulder and repeats himself, "dynamite."

"He's got the look Ron, he's got these guys really eating out of his hand. But don't you think that he's too much of a one-issue guy?"

"That's ok, that's ok, don't worry about that. He's got what you need. He's the guy who embarrassed the hell out of President Michaels with that whole Hangar 18 scandal. He's been calling for the President to resign for months now. He's got the momentum. This guy's got Halpern's people scared stupid. He's the one you want."

"I'm still concerned about the one-issue thing."

"Yeah, sure, I'd agree with you, if it were any issue but this," replies Ron. "HS consistently polls as the number one problem that people care about. If you're going to have a one-issue guy, this is the guy. Plus, he's from New York, nominally, and you're going to need some pull in the North-East."

Governor Potter agrees. He trusts his campaign staff. Ron has been with him for years, way back to the days when he was just a state senator. "OK Ron. Call his staff, let's make him the offer."

"I'm already on it." Ron walks further backstage, pulling a cell phone out of his coat. Governor Potter turns his attention back to the stage.

"...Well, I've taken up too much of your time already," says Ray, "Let me introduce the person that you came here to see today, your next President, Bill Potter!" Amid the cheers of the crowd, the Governor steps out on stage. He greets Ray with a big handshake. He is all smiles.

One month after Governor Potter announces his running mate. Holy Trinity Orphanage, Bronx, NY

"...and God, please take care of Father Blythe." The frail boy kneels on the hard, wooden floor in front of the window. Franklin always faces the window when he prays, especially at first light. The rays of sunlight coming up remind him of the power of the divine spirit. He likes to feel the warmth on his face when his eyes are closed. It makes him feel that God himself is looking down on him, heating the boy's skin with His all-seeing gaze. A small tear begins to form at the corner of his large, alien eye as he thinks of Father Blythe. He tries to remind himself that God never lets things happen for no reason, and the incident on the streets last summer is all part of the infinite plan, and that he should accept it and learn from it. That's what the Father would want him to do. He struggles to maintain composure.

The door to his small room opens without a knock. "You're late for breakfast," says a gruff voice. It is Father Kennedy.

"I'm sorry Father," the child says meekly. "I was just saying my morning prayers." He rises to his feet and puts on the red cap that Sister Mary Helen made for him to replace the one he lost.

Father Kennedy looms large in the doorway. His arms are crossed at his chest. His black suit is neatly pressed and seems somehow more angular and sharp than the slightly rumpled outfit that Father Blythe was often seen in. "I hope that you've been asking for forgiveness for your sins," he says authoritatively.

"Yes Father," replies Franklin with his eyes lowered as a show of respect. "I was also saying a prayer for Father Blythe's soul. He was an inspiration to me."

"Give up your daydreaming boy. You'll never become like Father Blythe. He had a soul. You are just a godless thing." Franklin was stung by the accusation, but not surprised. It was something that he had been told many times before. "You want to become a priest, to become a man of God don't you? But that can't happen you see because the operative word is MAN of God. You are not a man. Pray boy, get on your knees and pray for your miserable life. Pray that God in his wisdom has the mercy to spare you for another day. That's the best you can hope for."

"Yes Father," Franklin says meekly. He pulls the brim of his cap as low as he can to avoid the piercing gaze of Father Kennedy. The priest grabs the hat from the boy's head.

"Haven't you learned any respect you little mongrel?" he says, lifting the hat out of the child's range. "I thought I told you no hats in the house. Where were you born, in a park?" The comment is meant to be hurtful. The Father grabs the boy by the chin and forces eye contact. "Is that a tear I see boy?" He drops the child and heads towards the door. "I didn't think that insects knew how to cry!" he says to no one in particular. At the door he suddenly stops and turns around, surveying the room. "When breakfast is over son I want you to march right back up here and clean this place up. We got two more of you little freaks last night, and we're going to have to put them somewhere." He tosses the hat to the floor and tromps off leaving Franklin alone.

Franklin stood in the middle of the room for quite a while. Tears rolled down his face. "The Father was a jerk, but he was right after all," Franklin thought. "I am a monster." He had seen the TV reports, he knew what he was and where he came from. Abandoned by his mother, not wanted, not even a member of the human race really. He was a monster. He required mercy, he wanted to beg forgiveness of the Lord, but how do you beg forgiveness for your own birth? He pondered the question for a while. Father Blythe would have known the answer. Father Blythe was the only human with enough compassion to care about him.

He wiped his tears with his sleeve and caught his nose on the safety pin that kept the wrist cinched tight. The pain startled him into motion. He remembered that the Father was waiting for breakfast. Franklin rubbed his face with the waist portion of his shirt until all the tears were gone. Then he started downstairs. Almost as an afterthought he went back to the room and picked up his red cap and put it back on.

The Hayes residence, Frederick, MD. Two years, three months after the birth of the Hayes' second child.

Colin doesn't have to be called in for dinner. He knows what time to come. He is alerted not by sound but by smell. The whole house is filled with an almost palpable taste emanating from the kitchen. The roast has reached the perfect level of tenderness, the butter on the potatoes has just begun to sizzle, and the carrots have become soft without losing their color. Janice opens her mouth to call her boys to dinner, but she doesn't have to. Her voice is interrupted by Colin calling upstairs to his eldest son, "Ben, dinner's ready." Janice closes her mouth and smiles, knowing that her cooking is enough to entice her husband into the kitchen by smell alone.

A few seconds later, Colin's form appears in the hallway. He is still wearing the short-sleeved dress shirt and tie that he had on at work that day. He gives his wife a hug, or at least attempts to. She is carrying a hot serving dish and swerves to avoid spilling steaming gravy all over the place. He reaches over to the high chair that has already been placed at the table. He rubs the little bald head of his youngest child, "How are you doing today Neil?" Neil, being less than three, is too young to formulate a coherent sentence. But, he is able to drop a saliva-coated, plastic toy on the floor in his excitement. Colin sits down in his usual chair and begins serving himself without waiting for anyone else to sit down.

A few minutes later, all of the food had been placed on the table, and the family had started their dinner– all except Ben. Janice looked around nervously. Colin could tell that she was disturbed about something. "Dammit Ben, get the hell down here," he cries suddenly, "I told you dinner was ready." A few seconds later, tell-tale footsteps on the stairs indicate the presence of a child. Soon, a head appeared out of the hallway darkness. Colin glares.

"I already told Mom, I'm not eating dinner," says the boy defiantly.

"You'll do what you're told. I'm not wasting food. Come in here and sit down."

The boy stands his ground. "I said, 'I'm not eating at the same table as that thing.'"

It's the same old story. This has been happening almost every night now. Colin had originally thought that perhaps this was just a phase, a stage that all older siblings go through when confronted with a younger brother. Colin and Janice had had long discussions as to whether this had more to do with Ben's need for attention as opposed to something more. Colin had had a bad day at work. He pushed his chair out and stood up. The formerly defiant young child immediately cowered in fear and ran to the table. Colin sat back down wordlessly.

"I'll sit here, but I'm still not eating with that thing at the table. It's gross," Ben says.

"That 'thing' is your little brother," Janice says in a playful manner. She had read a lot of books on child rearing and was a lot slower to anger than Colin was. "Have some respect." She served the latecomer some slices of beef. "Take the gravy."

Ben took the dish from his mother, but didn't stop talking. "That's not what Senator Johnston says. Senator Johnston says that Neil isn't my brother. None of them aliens are. They just want to suck our blood in the middle of the night."

Colin glares at Ben but allows Janice to respond. "Never you mind what 'Senator Johnston' says young man. I'm your mother and I tell you that Neil is your little brother. You treat him nice. One day your father and I will be gone and he'll be the only family you have left."

The table fell silent for a few minutes. Ben gave up his tirade for the time being, focusing instead on the delicious meal in front of him. Both Colin and Janice didn't want to bring anything up that might stir the pot further. It was a tough situation for all of them. They chewed in silence.

As the dinner progressed, the admonishment that Janice had given to Ben began to wear off and he began to muse out loud. "Hey Dad, do you think the aliens are just coming to take over the planet, or do you think that they want to eat us too?" He looked directly at his brother.

"I told you to shut up Ben."

"But Senator Johnston says..."

"I don't give a damn about what Senator Johnston says. Just shut up and eat your dinner." Colin pushed the food around on his plate in frustration. Janice sat silent. For his part, little Neil was oblivious to all the strife. He continued to play with his food.

Ben waited a few seconds and then mumbled under his breath, "Jeez, you'd think that you'd have more respect for your boss."

"I do not work for Ray Johnston. I'm just on a panel, that's all. I haven't even talked to the guy in almost a year. All we do is write reports and send them to the Senate. What he does with them is his own business."

"Dad?" Ben said innocently.

"What Ben."

"Does Senator Johnston even know that you've got an alien freak for a kid?"

Janice jumped up from the table. "That's it young man! Go to your room right this minute." She pointed at the stairs.

"That's ok," said the child defiantly, "It's starting to smell bad in here anyway." He bounced out of his chair and ran upstairs. A few seconds later you could hear a door slam in the distance.

Colin and Janice looked at each other wordlessly. Neither of them said anything, but they both knew what the other was thinking. The boy was right, Ray Johnston didn't know about Colin's second child. No one on the panel knew. Chances were pretty good that no one would care really. After all, Colin had been a valued member on the scientific panel for some time now and a lot of people had HS kids these days. But both of them could feel which way the wind was blowing. There was something palpable in the air. Something that told them that someday in the future, little Neil could prove more a liability than an asset.

As if on cue, Neil dumped his plate of mashed potatoes over onto his head. The plastic plate clattered loudly. The boy sat gleaming from behind a veil of gravy. He seemed quite proud of his achievement.

Colin smiled slightly at his child. Janice struggled to control a giggle. Then the dam burst and both parents laughed uncontrollably.

Transcript from the television show "Pundits!" First
broadcast four months after Bill Potter's election
victory.

Fade in.

Carlos: And Welcome to *Pundits!* I'm your host Carlos
          Marquez. Today on our program, we have noted
          sociologist Dr. Nicolas Boyd. He's just finished his
          latest book, 'The Enemy Within.'

He holds up the book for the camera. On the cover is a
reproduction of 'American Gothic,' but with a young HS
child positioned between the farmer and his wife.

Carlos: We've also got with us Dr. Richard Violin, author
          of the book, "Womb Raider.' I want to start with
          you Dr. Boyd. Tell us, what made you write this
          fascinating new work?

Nick: Well Carlos, I've been working with HS kids for
          almost eight years now. My research has specialized
          in family interactions. The subject of all of my
          books has been how changes within society as a
          whole are dealt with on the family level.

Carlos: Yes, I interviewed you several years ago when your
          book, 'How the Internet Will Change Our Kids'
          was released. Fascinating.

Nick: Exactly. In that book I tried to show that as the
          ability for a child to obtain information increased,
          that child's dependence on their parents decreases,
          which will inevitably lead to a breakdown of the

traditional family structure. But now, the more I work with families afflicted with HS, the more confident I am that this disease is turning into a societal nightmare.

Carlos: Dr. Boyd, you have a fantastic hypothesis that you spell out in this book. It's something that really terrified me, and I think that our viewers will really be interested. Summarize, if you can, what you think HS actually is.

Nick: Well Carlos, this is fundamental to my theory, and it is something that needs to come out in the open. That's why I wrote this book. I want there to be discussion on this topic. You see, when now Vice President Johnston opened that vault at Wright-Pat, he really created more questions than he did answers. Like most people, I started thinking about what the aliens wanted. And what HS might have to do with their presence on our planet. Some people are saying that the HS virus is just something native to the alien's home planet and has been affecting their people for years. Others have said that the virus may be a botched attempt at a bio-weapon. But I don't buy those answers. I've come to a terrifying conclusion.

Carlos: And that is?

Nick: Let me pose a question. How do you invade a planet? Sure, we've all seen 'War of the Worlds,' but could you actually do that? Not likely. We've got about six billion people on this planet, think of the logistical nightmare in bringing enough troops and equipment to win the war. You'd need a billion soldiers. That isn't practical. You could use nuclear bombs of course, but then all you win is a shattered husk. Perhaps a biological weapon would kill off the native population, but you could never be sure that a mutated strain wouldn't kill your people too. So, what do you do? You invent the HS virus.

Carlos (*coyly*): I'm not sure I follow...

Nick: It is my contention that the aliens have created a virus that changes humans in such a way that their children are genetically the same as the alien race. Now, what would happen as more and more alien children start appearing? Well, my research has shown that in the majority of families with HS children, the parents' instinctual bonds towards their children are weakened. Not in every case, of course, but because the kids are not genetic descendents of the parents, there is a disruption. You see it now every day. More and more HS kids are winding up abandoned on the streets. In some less civilized countries infanticide of HS kids is more common than raising them.

Carlos: What does it all mean?

Nick: As the family structure begins to break down, these 'alien' kids will begin to feel, well... 'alien.' They know they're different, society will treat them different. Their parents will resent them, society will resent them. They will begin to form their own society, throwing off the conventions of their elders, with whom they share no particular bond. As time progresses more and more 'alien' children will be born, eventually becoming the majority. Then the extraterrestrial 'parents' return. Who will this majority of 'earth aliens' side with? The invaders of course. So neat and tidy they've invaded our planet without a shot. Not a man lost on their side and they annex a fully industrialized planet already prestocked with loyal citizens. It's really a brilliantly efficient idea when you think about it.

Carlos: Let's turn to you Dr. Violin. What to do about it?

Richard: That's a good question. My book advocates creating orphanages to house and watch these children. If they are kept from normal society and given a proper indoctrination, perhaps they won't pose as much of a problem. At least it will keep them away from uninfected people. You may have noticed that militia groups calling themselves 'Patriot Brigades' have begun to sprout up, swearing to ensure loyalty. A well-armed militia is the key to a strong, united America. The founding fathers knew it. We should follow their example.

Nick: Oh God no. This is playing right into their hands. Loyalty oaths and concentration camps! If you put these children in concentration camps of course they are going to rebel. They are going to feel less and less human. The more resentment that is shown towards them, the quicker they will give up on their forefathers. They must be embraced, made to feel that they are natural members of our civilization. That's the only hope we have left.

Richard: Until a cure for the virus is found of course.

Nick: More like *if* a cure is found. The so-called 'Senate Panel for HS Research' is spending all of their money on scientific research. No one is prepared to address the social problems of this thing. And they are just getting worse and worse. The number of HS cases in this country is rising rapidly. In a few years it may become too late to reverse the effects. One day we are going to have to answer for how we treat these children of ours. And not a dime is being spent on that issue today.

Richard: Unlike you Dr. Boyd, I have faith in our medical community. I am sure that a cure for this virus will be found. Once that happens the human population will be vaccinated against this threat. At the current rate of infection, my models predict an alien population of two to three percent maximum by the time the cure is found. While significant, that does not represent a level high enough to present a serious disruption to American society. We should take the example of those African countries that are quarantining all aliens from birth. Those countries have a much lower infection rate than here in the U.S. where we allow those people to walk among us like normal human beings.

Nick: They're committing genocide over there! Thousands are being murdered every day!

Carlos: Well, I hate to cut off this fascinating discussion, but we've just got to go to commercial. We'll be back with more of Dr. Nicholas Boyd and Dr. Richard Violin on *Pundits!*

Fade to black.

Farmland outside of Monmouth, NJ. Eight months
after Bill Potter took the oath of office.

"I'm not sure about this speech Ron. I wish that you
would have given me a copy before now."

"Don't worry about the speech. It'll go over great. Just
trust me."

"It seems a bit... well, a bit extreme is all." Ray flips past
some of the pages. "The people elected Bill and I because
they thought we would deal with this HS problem. The first
part is great, but it starts to get pretty far out near the end.
Some of the stuff in this speech is just going to cause panic."

"Look, who's the speech writer here, you or me?"

"You're not a speech writer, you're the Chief of Staff
Ron."

"I know, and how did I get that position? I was the one
who ran Bill's campaign. I approved all of his campaign
speeches. I'm telling you, don't worry about this. No one is
going to take everything you say seriously anyway. They
expect you to be alarmist. They expect you to be way over
the edge." He poked a finger at the speech. "Very little of
this is going to actually happen. There are enough people
opposed in Congress to keep all this wrapped up in
committee. All you're going to do is rouse people up a little.
The more excited they start to get, the more they'll
appreciate you. Trust me." Ron Willins smiled with his
perfectly white teeth. A cheer can be heard from outside of
the limo. "Listen to them out there Ray. They're chanting
for you. You're on, it's too late to fix the speech."

Ray opens the door and begins to step outside. "I'm going
to give this speech Ron, but we're going to talk about this
more when I get back. I want to approve these speeches at
least a day beforehand from now on. I'm the freaking Vice-

President, I should have some say in what I'm telling people."

Two Secret Service agents in dark suits wait patiently as Ray steps out of the limo. A path is cleared for him. About three hundred people have shown up here today, along with some news media. Standing at the front of the crowd is the Governor of New Jersey and a Catholic priest. Behind them are some hangers on and staffers. To the left is a small gallery of children, all HS positive. They stand meekly, wary of the attention. Some in the crowd carry signs that denounce the children as aliens, or invaders, or worse. Police have combed the crowd and taken away some of the more offensive signs, this will be televised of course, but perhaps in order not to antagonize the crowd, perhaps because the police have some of the same feelings, or perhaps on the advice of the Chief of Staff, some of the signs and banners remain.

The Vice President steps up to the Governor and shakes his hand. He places the speech on a thin podium. There isn't much wind today, so it'll be ok to read from notes. A staffer steps up and hands Ray a chrome plated shovel. Ray holds up the shovel and leans in to the microphone. The crowd grows silent in anticipation.

"Citizens of New Jersey," he begins. "Today is a great day. I have come here with Governor Peterson to break ground on the first of what I hope will be many new facilities that will be built as part of our new initiative against HS. As you certainly must know, the Senate panel on HS has handed us three recommendations, a three-pronged approach to fighting this terrible and debilitating disease. The first and most important prong is to develop a vaccine, a cure for this plague that has been thrust upon us. The second prong is prevention. Millions of federal dollars are now being distributed to the states to start testing campaigns. People who have been infected with the virus will soon know, and will be able to decide for themselves whether or not to bring another HS child into this world. This identification program alone is predicted to lower the number of HS positive births in the U.S. by a factor of two to three." A cheer comes for the crowd. Ray takes the opportunity to clear his throat.

"But I'm not here today to talk about those two programs. I'm here to talk about the third prong of our war against HS, and that is convalescence. As the number of HS cases has grown, so has the hardship on America's families. Raising a child in the best of times is a difficult and time consuming effort, but when the added pressure of raising an infant with this terrible disease... well, it's just more than some people can bear. The incidence of abandoned children in our country is reaching epidemic proportions. Not less than 25,000 HS positive infants have been abandoned this year alone. And the number is growing. It is understandable that certain people would not want to raise such a child. There is fear of an alien invasion and what these children might become. There is a decreased maternal bond since the child is not the true progeny of the parent. There is fear of possible reprisals by the community. And there is fear of violence from that community. I can't tell you how many reports of violence against HS children and their families have reached my ears. And that is sad. Sad that we as a people can't conduct ourselves with more decorum. Let it be said that the government will not under any circumstances condone vigilantism of this nature."

"But of course, we can't be everywhere, the police can't be everywhere, family counselors can't be everywhere. And that is why I have sent forth legislation which has resulted in the construction of this new orphanage. Here, out in the countryside, away from the general populace. Here, at these houses of love, HS children will feel accepted. They will get to play with other children suffering from the same disease. They won't have to feel like outcasts, strangers, freaks. They will get the acceptance and the education that they need to survive. They'll also be safe. Safe from vigilantes, safe from criminals who would exploit them. Safe from parents who don't have the strength to provide the increased amounts of love that they need and deserve."

"And although we call this an 'orphanage,' it is more than that. Call it a 'sanitarium.' It is my vision that this place will not just be used to house those children that have been abandoned by their parents, but will also be a place of healing. Psychologists will be on hand to ensure that every child grows up loving America. Research scientists will be on hand to care for the unique health issues that HS brings with it. They will examine these children in hopes of reversing the disease and its spread. The children that will grow up here will provide an invaluable service to humanity, even if they aren't human themselves. They will be treated with the utmost care, and with full oversight by both the American Medical Research Ethics Board and the Senate Panel on HS."

"It is my belief that this building, and those like it, will become a beacon of hope. I believe that in the future, parents will not abandon their children on the streets. They will take them to this place lovingly. They will know that the United States does care about these children, that this government will not turn a deaf ear to your problems. It is my vision that parents will one day see that placing their child in a facility such as this will be superior, yes superior, to raising the child in their home."

"I'm excited about the future. I hope you are too. Now, let's get this show on the road!" A cheer comes from the crowd. Ray reaches down with his shovel and digs the ceremonial first shovelful of dirt.

In the background, the children stand shoulder to shoulder. They watch and listen as the Vice President speaks about their new home. One small child stirs. He looks about, fidgity. There are an awful lot of policemen behind him. Some in the crowd are holding signs. Enoch can't read very well just yet, but he does get the message. A lot of the people in the crowd seem mad at him. He wonders what he has done. He's always tried to do what the Father has taught him. He tugs at the sleeve of the boy next to him. Franklin is like a big brother to him. He is much older and smarter. "Franklin, Franklin. What's happening? Why is everyone mad at me? What are they saying?"

Franklin continues to glare straight ahead. He is older than his small roommate. He was there when the mob attacked Father Blythe. He knows exactly what the Vice President is talking about. He balls his fists in frustration but remains silent.

Four months after the Dallas Orphanage for HS Research opens its doors. The Watley family residence, Tyler, TX

Lorraine watched the wisps of steam rise from the coffee mug. "Well, maybe you should just think about it, that's all I'm saying that's all. It's an... option you know?" said Joyce in her deep booming voice.

"I don't know Joyce, I don't think so."

"Hey, I know how you feel, heaven help the person who suggests that I give up any of *my* kids. I love those darlings to death, even though they're such a pain in the..." Something made of glass crashed in the living room. Joyce didn't even get up. "Of course on the other hand, maybe you're the lucky one." She turned her head to the kitchen door. "Don't make me come in there!" she shouted.

A disembodied, "Sorry Mom," came from the living room, followed by a second child's voice, "It's Tim's fault. I didn't do it." "That's a lie." Then another crash. Finally, the sound of one boy chasing the other out into the yard followed closely by a slamming door.

"Sometimes I wish I'd only had one kid Lorraine. With one you always know who broke it." She tried to smile. Lorraine was still stuck on the previous subject.

"I mean, it would make things a lot easier, but I don't know if I could give him up like that. It don't seem right, you know? Plus, he's almost 12 years old now. I don't think he'd adjust well. Those camps are for little kids. Jim's too much part of our family."

Joyce snapped back to the conversation. "It ain't like you're going to be giving him up for good. It's sort of like boarding school. He'll just be going to Dallas that's all. You could visit him every weekend if you want."

"It just don't seem right Joyce. Sure Jim's got his problems, but he's our kid you know? God gave him to us to bring up. I don't want to forget my duties. I don't want to give him to the government to raise."

"There you go again with that 'my kid' thing. Jim's a good boy, but he ain't your kid. He's some alien thing," Joyce said nonchalantly, as if she was speaking about a pet.

"Hush Joyce. You weren't there. I was there. I carried that boy in my belly for 9 months. He's as much my kid as Tim and Larry Jr. are your kids. I care about that child more than you could ever know. I don't care what he looks like, he's mine. I can't even believe that I'm talking about giving him up."

Joyce took a drag on her cigarette. "If that's the way you feel Lorraine, you've got to give him up. I mean it's the safest place for him. Hell, you saw what happened that day when Larry got drunk. And he's stupider and more weak-willed than most. Ray Johnston says that it's going to be hard for people like us to protect these kids." She leaned in a little and whispered. "Larry's in this 'Patriot Brigade' now Lorraine, and I, well I hear things. These people are serious. One day they're going to do something, and you and Tom ain't going to be able to stop them."

"But I've heard horrible things about what goes on in those places. Don't they do experiments and stuff in those places?"

"I wouldn't worry about none of that. I mean, we are trying to cure this disease. All they do is take some blood samples maybe. Those kids are ok. Plus, they get to hang out with their own kind. When was the last time Jim even met another HS kid?"

"I don't think he's ever met another HS kid."

"See, that's it. He's going to grow up warped if he doesn't get any friends. None of the normal kids want anything to do with him. He doesn't go to school. He just spends all day cooped up in your house reading books and playing on that computer. That ain't no way for a boy to live."

"Joyce, I know that you mean well, but it ain't going to happen. There's no way. I know it's trying for us, but we'll pull through. We live way outside of town, I don't think anyone's going to bother us. And I know that Jim's lonely, but I don't think that putting him in one of those prisons is going to make things better. Plus, there's no way that Tom's going to give him up."

"You may not have a choice one day Lorraine. As I've said, Larry's one of them Patriots. I think he does it just to get free beer, but some of them guys are real serious. They say that someday the government is going to come and round up all the HS kids. You're not going to have a choice."

"I don't think that it will come to that Joyce."

"I hope not Lorraine, I hope not." From outside, the sound of a truck pulling up could be heard.

"I better go Joyce, I know how Larry feels about me."

"Hush, don't you worry none about old Larry. If he says anything I'll slap him in the mouth." She got up and peered through the curtain at the front yard. Larry was getting out of his truck. He had been drinking again, which wasn't that surprising. Three other men got out with him, some of his new friends. They were also drunk. "Actually, you know Lorraine," said Joyce trying to keep her composure, "Maybe you'd better go after all. Your car's out back right? Go out the kitchen door." She smiled nervously.

The Senate Subcommittee on Handel's Syndrome Research, Washington, DC. Three weeks after Ray Johnston's groundbreaking ceremony.

"The chair will hear from General Hudson." Chairman Walker banged his gavel twice for effect.

The General stood up. Lieutenant General Hudson was career military from birth. He had been hardened in combat and was raised during the paranoia of the Cold War. His face was grizzled and cracked from his time overseas. "Senator Walker, Members of the Committee, thank you for letting me speak today," he said in a gravelly voice. I have been tasked by the Vice President to provide technical support to this panel. Not in scientific terms of course, as I could never hope to match the luminaries that sit on your board in terms of biological education. But Vice President Johnston came to me and asked me to look at other areas of the HS problem. He wanted me to present my findings to you, and for you to expand your role from just a scientific organization, to one that examines all of the consequences of the HS virus. Up until now, we've treated this solely as a disease, a serious disease to be sure, but just a disease. It is now time that we face facts gentlemen. HS is more than a disease. It is a plan, hatched by aliens, for some nefarious purpose we can only guess at. It is a threat, a threat to the American way of life, to the ability of the human species to propagate itself, and a threat to the very authority of the United States government."

"We have spent years now looking for a cure, and for a way to stem the spread of the disease. We've gotten nothing from that effort. HS infection rates are still climbing. Even by the estimations of your own epidemiologists, it may be too late to save the majority of the population. We need to look at new solutions. We need to look at stronger, harsher measures to ensure the survival of our society. This has gone beyond just a disease gentlemen, this is a national security issue now. That's why I've been picked to join this panel. I won't interfere with any of the scientific research that you've been recommending. Hell, I'd love to see you find a cure and find it today. But I will be here to examine your decisions from the national security viewpoint. I'll make recommendations on that basis. Some of you won't like what I have to say, but I don't care. I've faced tougher foes than you. That's why I was picked for this job. Hopefully we will be able to work together smoothly and effectively. We all have the same goal here gentlemen, to stem the tide of this virus and to ensure that the human way of life continues on this planet for some time."

The General sat down stiffly. Senator Walker resumed control of the floor. "Let me be the first to welcome you to this august body General. I'm sure that your input will be greatly appreciated and that we will all be able to work together smoothly. I understand you have a report to present."

The General leaned into his microphone. "Yes Senator, I do. I took the liberty of tasking my staff at the National Security Council to look at possibilities for how we could deal with this threat. I'll pass those out now." An army Major walked around to each panel member and handed them a small, bound report. It was titled, 'Handel's Syndrome: The Emerging Military Threat.' Colin paged through the document incredulously. He could tell that Senator Walker was eating this stuff up. The man had been campaigning for these ideas ever since the committee was formed. Now that Johnston was the VP, it looked like political influence was going to outweigh scientific research. He wanted to speak up, to say something about this new turn of policy, but he felt intimidated. He was just a glorified lab technician really. He didn't have the clout that a lot of the other people in the room had. His eyes darted about the room looking for allies.

Heinrich Mensen also read the document with disgust. But unlike Colin Hayes, he did have the clout to speak up. He was considered the foremost authority on HS, and his words had weight. "How dare you come in here and propose these things," he said, tossing the report onto the floor. "This is supposed to be a scientific forum, not a military camp!"

General Hudson remained stoic. "Dr. Mensen, I certainly understand your frustration on this issue. I wouldn't take too kindly if you people barged into my command and started changing the way that I did business. However, all of your scientific conferences and grants have led nowhere. I don't give a damn whether you're any closer to decoding the HS virus genome or not. That isn't my responsibility. My responsibility is to deal with the consequences if you guys can't find a cure for this in time. And you've given me no indications Doctor that you will be able to find a cure in time."

Dr. Mensen was agitated. "But these measures are draconian. Do you realize what you are suggesting here General? Loyalty oaths, mandatory testing for infection, official recognition and sanction for these Patriot Brigades. What is next sir, concentration camps?"

"Yes, doctor. Concentration camps. If need be."

"Is this the United States or have we returned to Nazi Germany?" Dr. Mensen stood up. "I will not be party to this any further. If you people want to listen to this man, then you can join him in hell. Someday you will all have to answer for your actions. Good day!" And with that, the Doctor stormed out of the room.

"He'll be back." A voice whispered to Colin. He looked to his right. He was sitting next to the representative from the Center for Disease Control. "He'll be back," repeated the man. "Mensen's a hothead. He does this all the time. He won't stay away long." The man poured himself some ice water from a pitcher. Colin turned back to the proceedings.

The General continued to address the committee. "A war is coming gentlemen. It will either be a war against an alien invasion, or a war against our own children. Preparations must begin now for that war. Preparations are the key. I want this committee to recommend that Congress authorize a full-scale military buildup. I want you to recommend that Congress institute a mandatory identification and loyalty program. When the balloon goes up I don't want to be caught with my pants down. Is that understood gentlemen?"

Colin gulped and nervously fingered his wedding band. He didn't like where this was headed.

Tyler County High School, Tyler, TX. Nine years after Lorraine Miller first attempted to register her child for school.

It had become a yearly ritual here in the plains of Texas. The date was known well in advance of course, and so there was plenty of time for people to come out. It started that morning, like it had started once a year for the past ten years, with the arrival of a red truck in the parking lot of the school. It hadn't always been the same red truck of course. Tom's old beater was long dead, replaced by a model a few years younger yet just as dusty. There was never any trouble in the parking lot, no one seemed to mind the boy's presence there. It was only during the walk down the long cement sidewalk to the front door of the school that the trouble started. It had been getting worse each year. The Millers didn't hold out too much hope for today, but there was glimmer that the high school staff would be somehow different than the ones at the elementary and middle schools had been. Tom stepped out of his vehicle onto the hot asphalt parking lot. Jim looked at his father with trepidation. He didn't see much point to this yearly display and was scared and embarrassed. No 14 year-old boy wants to be the center of controversy, and Jim was no different. He would much rather have stayed at home with his books and his television and his computer. He knew how people felt about him. He watched his father standing in the open door of the truck, and knew that it would be pointless to make a fuss. Once Dad decided on a course of action, he didn't waver. It was much better when Mom had been the one to take him to school.

The pair walked through the parking lot to the long, cement walkway slowly but determinedly. The grass to the sides of the walk was filled with some of the locals. They were held back from the walkway by a thin plastic police tape. About ten members of the local Patriot Brigade stood guard wearing their traditional brown berets. At least a dozen police officers were also in attendance. The crowd chanted the most derogatory slogans. Some held hand-made signs. Every year that this ritual had occurred there were more protestors. This year there must have been almost two hundred men, women, and children in attendance. Many were people that Tom had grown up with, for in many ways, Tyler was still a small town. They didn't talk to him now, he was mostly an outcast, but he remembered all of their names. He remembered what they were like. He remembered the family picnics, he remembered the school outings, he remembered the football games. But now these people had been whipped up into snarling beasts by fear of a virus.

But Tom wasn't totally devoid of support. As he walked across the parking lot, at least a dozen other parents joined with him, each one pulling along an HS child in tow. They fell into place like marchers in a parade, all behind Tom. Although he tried to keep his eyes focused straight ahead, and tried to keep his face expressionless, Tom was excited to see how many people had chosen to join him this year. After Lorraine was snubbed nine years ago, the Miller family had, in one form or another, tried to register their child for school every season. Each time they were turned back. The first few years it had just been Lorraine versus the school principal. Then the parents of other children started to attend, backing up the school and intimidating Lorraine. In the fourth year, she had been hit on the head with a rock by one protestor. After that Tom took up the mantle. Six years into the ritual, they were joined by Jordan McReynolds and his father. Jordan was three years younger than Jim, but was also HS positive. The two fathers had tried to enter the school, but were rejected again. Every year since the families had squared off in this parking lot. One side demanding that HS be kept away from their children, the other side demanding that the county educate their children as was its duty. Every year the crowds on both sides got larger.

"What are you doing here Marty? Your kid isn't old enough to go to high school yet. Shouldn't you and Jordan be over at George Austin Elementary?" said Tom flatly.

"We're following your lead Tom," replied the father. "You were the first of us Tom, we're here to support you. I talked to the other fathers about this, and we all agree, that coming together is better than going to a bunch of different places. Hell, some of these people don't even live in the district."

Tom turned and his lips curled into a slight smile. "I appreciate that Marty," he said. He decided that if he was going to be a leader, then he should look like one. He arched his back and walked tall past the screaming crowd.

A few feet behind Tom, Jim walked with his eyes looking down. He didn't really want to be here. He preferred to be at home, where things made more sense, where he didn't have to feel embarrassed about just being alive, where he didn't feel so... different. He clutched his books tightly against his chest and hoped that he would be able to just make it through the ordeal. He had done this enough times to know what would happen. Dad and the school officials would get into an argument, and then the police would break things up and tell them to go home. Jim tried to walk with his eyes closed to see if that helped, but he could still hear the shouts of the crowd.

"Go home mutant!" "God hates aliens!" "We'll never surrender!" reached his ears along with some more hurtful phrases. There was a tap at his right shoulder. He looked around to see Jordan walking just behind him. The small child leaned in and said, "Jim, what do you think would be worse, if they don't let us go to school here, or if they actually do let us in?" He smiled nervously at his joke. It didn't make Jim feel any better.

Standing at the front of the school was the principal of Tyler High as well as the head of the Tyler County School Board, Helen Montoya. Both had their arms crossed in a symbol of defiance. Behind the two were a few more police officers. Tom walked straight up to the pair. "I'm here to register my son for school," he said.

"Tom, you know that I can't allow that," replied Helen.

"I have legal documents here with me Helen," said Tom formally, "They guarantee the right of every child in this country access to an education." He waved the document at Ms. Montoya.

"I have legal documentation too Tom. Would you like me to read it to you? It is from the County Health Board. It says...," she put on her reading glasses, "...no child with a communicable disease will be allowed to attend classes if it is believed that the child poses a risk to other students." She took the glasses off her head. They dangled from a cord at her neck. "We've already gone over this a hundred times at the school board meetings. You cannot register a HS-positive child in this school."

"But there is no proof that HS is contagious. Hell Jim doesn't even test positive for the anti-bodies."

"You try telling them that." She waved her hand at the crowd. "Tom, it would simply be too dangerous for your child to attend classes here. Not just for the sake of the other children, but for his sake too. Now, I've already made the offer to send a teacher out to home school your child, and the other children too."

"That's not acceptable."

"Well I'm afraid that's the best offer you are going to get. My hands are tied by school board policy. We are not going to register your child."

One of the Patriot Brigade militia members stepped up. "So take your damn freak kid and get the hell out of here." That was enough. Tom lunged and took a big swing at the man. The other militia members rushed forward to defend their compatriot, the other parents rushed forward to defend Tom. The police rushed forward with pepper spray. One of them tossed a tear gas canister to disperse the crowds. All of the HS children ran back to the parking lot and gathered behind Tom's truck along with a few parents who stayed out of the fight.

Jim watched the melee from the relative safety of the parking lot. Jordan was just behind him. "Well, I guess Dad's spending the night in jail again," said Jordan, "Do you want to play at my house this afternoon?"

"It's the same every year," Jim said to no one in particular.

That same day, The Hayes residence, Frederick, MD

Janice was visibly upset when Colin came home from the committee meeting. She was sitting in the living room, in the large, comfy recliner. She never sat there, she was much more of a couch person. But the recliner did have the advantage of facing the front door. It was the place to sit if you were desperately waiting for someone to come home. When Colin opened the front door he could see here there. Her presence meant that something was wrong.

Colin dropped his briefcase by the plastic mat used to hold wet shoes and came to his wife. "What is it honey?" he said.

"I was cleaning Ben's room today," she was twisting something over in her hands, "and I found this under the mattress." She thrust the object at Colin as if she were stabbing him with it. He took the brown cloth from his wife's hands and unfurled it. It was a brown beret with the words, 'Patriot Youth Corps' embroidered across the front in yellow thread. Colin stared at the object for a few seconds to grasp its meaning, then threw it on the floor.

"Where is he?" he said angrily.

"I sent him to his room."

Colin rolled up his sleeves and started up the stairs. "I'm going to have a talk with that boy." She trailed behind him, hoping that he situation wouldn't get worse. She had faith that Colin could make anything better. But lately he had become angrier and angrier, about everything. Ben had become more and more hateful, despite all of the care and attention she gave him. Neil was a handful in of himself. The child was weak and sickly, even for someone who had HS. All Janice ever wanted was the American Dream. The house with well-behaved kids and an attentive, loving husband. Now everything was falling apart. Everything was changing, warping somehow out of control.

Colin smashed his fist against the door to Ben's room. "Get out here right now Mister!" he shouted. There was no reply. "Don't make me come in there!" He bashed the door again. Still there was no reply. Janice grabbed her husband's arm as he brought it forward for a third assault on the door. Tears were in her eyes. Colin came out of his rage and jostled the doorknob. It wasn't locked. He swung the door open, ready to let out all of the frustrations he had felt that day on his disobedient child. But there was no one in the room. The window was open, and both parents knew that the tree nearby was close enough for a nimble person to climb to the ground without too much effort. There was a hastily scrawled note on the bed. It said, 'Gone to Fred's house for dinner. His Dad's a REAL AMERICAN. I'll be back when you guys calm down a little. -Ben'

Colin ripped the note in half. If he couldn't vent his rage on a person, he would vent it on an inanimate object. Then he punched the wall and broke a fist-sized hole in the plaster. He sat down on the bed, with his head in his hands. A faint sobbing sound could be heard.

"It'll be all right dear," Janice said through her tears. She tried to smile. "Maybe we'll move him to a new school. Somewhere that won't have the bad influences." She sat down beside him and put her arm around his shoulders.

"It's not about Ben. It's about the whole damn system. Ben's just a symptom."

"It's work isn't it?"

"That damn Hudson is pushing through all of his agenda. Most of the panel is with him. We're not even TALKING science anymore. No one is interested in curing this thing. They're just interested in building up an army for some attack. Do you have any idea what they're doing to those kids they've got locked up in those 'orphanages?' I do, I've read the reports. Guinea pigs, that's all. I'm not going to let them treat Neil like that. I'm not going to. But then, I come home to find their propaganda infecting my family. Damn them, damn them all to hell!" He reached across the bed and swatted at Ben's baseball bat shaped light. It crashed to the floor.

The next sound that could be heard was the patter of footsteps in the hallway. A single, insect-like eye peered around the doorframe into the room. It darted back quickly, not wanting to be seen. "Come here baby," said Lorraine. Neil ran into the room and into his mother's arms. The two parents cuddled their child for some time without saying a word.

Eight months after the Monmouth Orphanage for the Treatment of Handel's Syndrome opened its doors.

"I'm glad you came Sister." Franklin is sitting at a table in the waiting room across from a nun. He is dressed in a plain, gray jumper, just like all of the other children at the facility.

"It's your birthday Franklin, I couldn't stay away."

"Are you sure that your visit is ok with Father Kennedy?"

The nun waved her hand in the air as if to swat away the question. "What I do with my free time is none of Father Kennedy's business," she said. "Besides, he never notices me anyway. He's usually too busy with all the paperwork at the orphanage to care whether I'm around or not."

"So, how are things back at Holy Trinity?" Franklin said with a nostalgic smile.

"It's so much quieter since you and Enoch and the other boys all left. Now that all of the HS children are sent here, our house is almost empty. There are rumors that we'll be closed altogether. More and more couples are coming every day to take the children that we do have. I guess that people have decided that an adopted child without HS is better than risking giving birth to a... a..."

"An alien?"

"Franklin! You know that's now what I meant." She shook her head in mock disbelief. "Sometimes you are too confrontational for your own good. Most people don't think the way you think they do. Most people don't hate you."

Franklin looked around the stark waiting room, and then down at himself. "That's not what it looks like from here."

"You've got to have faith Franklin. You've got to believe in the idea that you will be delivered from misery one day. You've got to believe that things are going to get better. You've got to believe that everyone in their heart is a good person, and that even though most of them are scared and stupid, deep down they want what's right and they'll eventually figure it out. You've got to be patient Franklin, you've got to be patient and you've got to set a good example. Isn't that what Father Blythe taught you?"

"Father Blythe is dead Sister," Franklin said flatly. "They killed him for what he believed."

Sister Mary Helen frowned. "Don't let his death be in vain Franklin. Father Blythe was a martyr, and he'll be recognized for it one day. But you've got to educate people. You've got to show them what's right. You can't just give up on humanity because there are a few morons out there that are scared silly over some disease that they don't know how to cure." She reached across the table and took both of his hands in hers. "You watch Franklin. Things will get better. They've got scientists working all over the world on this thing. They'll find a cure. And the minute they do people all around the world will relax. They won't consider you a threat anymore. Things always look darkest before the dawn."

"I guess you're right Sister," replied Franklin. "Without you and Father Blythe for guidance, I sometimes find myself lost. It's hard to keep up hope in this place."

The nun looked down at the four hands touching across the table. Franklin's elbow was horribly bruised. "Franklin, what did you do to your arm?" she exclaimed.

Franklin grabbed at his damaged appendage as if the injury had just happened. "Nothing Sister. It's nothing. They just take blood samples for their research that's all. Sometimes they miss the vein I guess. It'll heal." He turned his face into the approximation of a smile. He didn't want the Sister to worry about him.

"But look at you. She grabbed his arm and held it into the light. There must have been a dozen visible needle marks. "Do they do this to all the children here?"

"As far as I know. I don't talk to all of them of course, but as far as I know." He chuckled. "But it's ok Sister. It's for the research after all."

Two months after James Miller should have started the 12th grade. The Miller farm, outskirts of Tyler, TX

Even for a child who has school activities to distract them, the wait can be excruciating. For Jim, who had far more time on his hands than the average teenager, the wait is almost unimaginable. Every afternoon, just after 1 pm, he treks down the half-mile or so of dusty road to where the pavement starts, to where the mailbox is. Sometimes he is early, arriving before the postman can deliver his daily load of flyers and bills. On those days, such as today, he sits and waits by the empty mailbox. It isn't that hot this time of year, and there is plenty of time after all. Studying can wait until the mail arrives. He wouldn't be able to concentrate on his studies knowing that the answer could be waiting for him in a little tin box. So he sits and waits, watching the long, straight road for signs of the van that carries the mail.

On this day, the postman drove up only a few minutes after Jim arrived. He didn't like Jim. All of these alien kids really "freaked him out," he used to say. But he was a professional and he took the job of delivering the mail very seriously. So he was cordial to the youngster if not friendly. He pulled up in the big white truck and passed the Miller's load directly to the waiting teen's spindly hands. He even managed to choke out a "Have a nice day" before he drove off.

Jim flipped through the pile of mail rapidly, looking for the letter that he hoped would arrive. At first he didn't see it. But on closer inspection, in between the cable bill and a farm equipment catalog, was the small, white envelope he had been waiting for. On its face was the logo for Georgetown University. Jim didn't even wait to get back to the house. He dropped the rest of the mail in a heap on the ground and tore the envelope open with his teeth. Inside was a single sheet of paper. That's wasn't a good sign. After fumbling with it for a few seconds, he unfolded it. It read:

Dear Mr. Miller,

Although your academic qualifications are indeed excellent, we regret that we cannot accept you at this time. Please understand that Georgetown University receives far more applications than there are slots available, and many candidates with impressive credentials must be turned down. We wish you luck in your academic career and appreciate you considering Georgetown University.

Sincerely,

Anna Chong,
Admissions Director

Tom was headed back to the house for lunch when he spotted his son standing by the road, kicking the mailbox post furiously. His heart saddened a little because he understood what that behavior symbolized. He veered off course and came down the driveway to meet his son. "You snap that thing I'm gonna make you dig a new post hole," he said lightheartedly. It was a joke really. The mailbox post was a four by four. There was no way that Jim's anemic little legs could have even chipped the paint.

"It's not fair Dad. It's totally not fair." He held up the letter from the admissions board.

"Which one is that?" the father said.

"Georgetown. That makes five for five."

"You know boy, I have to admit, I'm a bit relieved about that one. Do you have any idea how much those fancy private schools cost?" He chuckled, hoping to lighten the mood a little. It didn't work, Jim went back to pummeling the mailbox post. "Ok, ok, bad joke," Tom said, grabbing the child's shoulders to calm him down. "You can't get too discouraged by this Jim, those schools you've picked are all hard to get into. There's a lot of boys out there that're a lot more qualified."

"That's crap Dad total crap!" shouted the child. "I'm qualified as hell! I got a 1580 on my SATs, I passed all the AP tests. I did everything. And I did it without the help of those morons at Tyler High. But none of that matters. All they care about is this damn HS." He held out his scrawny arm. He raised his fist as if he was about to swing at his own elbow. He wanted to knock himself out of his own skin, to beat his own genetic structure until he was normal. But he couldn't hurt his genes, he couldn't hurt the aliens that did this to him, he couldn't hurt the scared, inbred bigots that wouldn't give him a chance. He could only hurt himself, and he was smart enough to see that there was no logic in that. He lowered his fist and burst out crying. He smothered himself into his father's chest. "It's not fair, it just ain't fair," he could be heard to whisper between the sobs.

Tom rubbed his hand over his son's bald, rubbery skull. "Crying about it ain't gonna do one damn bit of good. We'll find another way. It'll get worked out."

"What other way? I can't go to State. They've passed a resolution keeping kids like me out. All I had left was the private schools. I figured that the ones up north wouldn't be so closed-minded, but I was wrong."

"Listen son," Tom said. He grabbed Jim by the shoulders and looked him in the eye. He had to bend over a bit to do it, but this was important. "If I learned one thing from a life of farming, it's this. There ain't no one gonna give you nothing. You've got to take what you want. Sitting here crying about it ain't gonna do no good for nobody. If you want to change things then you're gonna have to get in their face and make them change things. You've got to fight your own battles now. Your mother taught you well, you're smart and strong. You've got to come up with a plan. You've got to figure out what you want, and then you've got to get it. If there are people in your way you've got to move them. Don't take nothing sitting down. That's what I've learned."

"You don't like the way things are, then change them. You got a problem getting into school, then do something about it. You got a congressman, write him a letter. Call some TV stations and see if they'll do a story. There's probably half a dozen kids in Tyler County with your exact same problem. Find out what they're doing about it. It's time to grow up Jim. Grow up and stand up for yourself."

Jim was strangely refreshed by his father's words. He had never thought of himself as someone who acts, only as someone who is acted upon. But Dad was right. There were things that he could do. He didn't have to take this lying down. He had stayed out of school and away from town most of his life because he felt small and vulnerable. It was so comforting to be small and vulnerable and helpless. But that wasn't going to get him anywhere. Tom had read the stories about how other oppressed people struggled to be free. He had always hoped that someday someone would take that struggle up for him. Now he realized that the only one who was going to fight for Jim Miller was Jim Miller himself. A newfound sense of purpose came over him. He dried his tears with his sleeve. "I guess you're right Dad. I can stand up for myself. I'm not going to let them get away with this."

"Good. Now clean yourself up a bit." They started walking up the hill to the farmhouse. "If your Mom sees you like that she's gonna think I've been beating you." The two Millers chuckled as they made their way towards lunch.

Arecibo Radio Observatory, Puerto Rico. August 6th, 25 years to the day that alien missiles first entered Earth's atmosphere.

Lights are blinking. That's all they do here, blink. Day in and day out the large bank of supercomputers sits and processes; waits, listens, and processes. The only outward sign of all this computation was a series of green, blinking lights. Jeff Hanson sits in front of the lights and waits. It is hot today, and even though there is air conditioning to keep the computers from overheating, the heat outside is still subliminally present. Jeff is sweating through his old, blue T-shirt. He has long since regretted his choice of internships. At first he thought that this would be a cool assignment; foreign travel, the chance to find aliens, to play with the most powerful telescope on the planet. But instead it has proved a disappointment. With all of the internal processing, all that happened was that some lights blinked on and off. Soon the summer would be over and he could head back to the States, back to easy access to fast food and the self-indulgent lifestyle of the graduate student. He sighed deeply and looked at his watch. It would be almost three more hours before Dr. Steinman would show up to relieve him. Jeff sat and waited. He fingered the remains of his lunch, looking for any more edible scraps that he might have missed.

At exactly 11:24 am local time, one of the computer banks began to whir and twitch. The blinking green light started to move quickly and in a regular pattern. Jeff had been working at the telescope long enough to know that an unusual data packet was being received. Usually it was just a spurious signal from a satellite or random static, but he had little else to do so he turned on the monitor. It took several seconds to warm up, at first you could hear the static, then slowly the screen grew bright and the channel listing appeared. Jeff scanned down the row of numbers until he found the frequency that was picking something up. It was an unusually bright signal, which meant that it was almost undoubtedly a satellite, random static wasn't that powerful. He tuned the display to the frequency and examined the waveform on the oscilloscope. It was a very clear signal. He rolled his chair over to another bank of computers and began typing away on the satellite finder. He ran the coordinates of all the known satellites against the position of the telescope. Nothing matched up. Was it a spy satellite? That wouldn't make sense, since usually stealth satellites didn't broadcast their location. He swerved the chair back around to the processing bank. The oscilloscope was still vibrating away. Jeff stared at the signal for almost a minute, not knowing what to do. Finally he grabbed his headphones off the table and unplugged them from the cassette deck. With some apprehension he put them over his ears and held the plug up to the oscilloscope's output port. Although most parts of his mind were telling him that this was probably nothing, some small area cautioned him to take the time to remember this moment exactly. He plugged in the headphones and listened, wide-eyed and slack-jawed.

He listened to the signal over and over again for several minutes. He checked the storage banks to make sure that the channel was being saved to disk. Then he picked up the outmoded black phone that served as Arecibo's link to the rest of the world. "Dr. Steinman?" Jeff said when someone answered. "I think that you'd better come out here right now."

That evening, in the Oval Office of the White House, Washington, DC

"...We interrupt this regularly scheduled broadcast to bring you a message from the President of the United States...."

The screen goes blank for a second. It then opens on a wide angle shot of the Oval Office. Sitting at the desk is President Potter. He has a concerned yet reassuring look on his face. Like all politicians he has the rare ability to both import the gravity of a situation while at the same time reducing the viewer's anxiety. Bill Potter's been practicing that look in the mirror for years.

The camera closes in on the President. He speaks, "Good evening ladies and gentlemen. I have historic news to bring you today. No doubt you've already heard rumors on many newscasts, but I want to give you a straightforward telling of the facts as we now know them."

"Approximately eight hours ago, researchers at the radio telescope in Arecibo, Puerto Rico recorded a signal. In the last several hours, other radio telescopes have been focused on the location and it has been confirmed. The signal is strong and it continues to repeat over and over again. We have ruled out all terrestrial sources of interference, and we must make the preliminary conclusion that the signal is alien in origin."

"It appears that the signal is coming from somewhere in the Pleiades Cluster. The repeating message is being broadcast in English, and in a frequency commonly used by Earth radio stations, which strongly suggests that the signal was meant for us and us alone to hear. It is only one sentence long. The message says, and I quote, 'Prepare children, your Father is coming.' That is all it says. There have been many rumors spread about, and many people have been going off half-cocked. I can assure you that these are the only words in the message. Currently, scientists are attempting to pinpoint the exact location of origin of the signal, and to determine if further information has been coded into the carrier wave. More details will be forthcoming in several days time."

"The fact that this signal is being received at this time should not come as much of a surprise to anyone. Vice-President Johnston revealed to the world that an apparently alien craft did crash in New Mexico in 1947. The alien HS virus is another indication that alien life was out there somewhere. However, this is a significant day in several respects. For the first time we can confirm that there actually is currently an intelligent presence in outer space that is actively trying to contact us. Second, we finally have a location to focus on. The aliens are from the Pleiades. And third, we know that they are coming. When they arrive, either peacefully or with malice, our world will change. Our lifestyles will change. This is a scary thing to think about, but it is a fact and it must be dealt with in a logical and rational manner."

"Already, an emergency session of the United Nations is meeting to discuss consequences of this momentous event. The United States will lend full support to any Security Council resolutions on this matter. Second, I am issuing an executive order to double the current level of funding for both military and scientific research. We've had the crashed alien craft for a long time now. We will continue to decode its secrets and use the technology we recover to defend ourselves if necessary." His face became ghoulishly serious all of a sudden. "We look forward to peaceful relations with our alien visitors, but let there be no debate; I speak for all Americans when I say that we will fight an invasion to the last man."

"Finally, I must plead with you to remain calm at this time. I have received reports from all over the country of panicked people being involved in acts of violence towards sufferers of HS. This is unacceptable. We have a system of laws in this country that is designed to protect all of our citizens, including ones who may carry alien DNA. I urge you to allow the military and the police to handle this problem. Random mob violence will not make the situation better. I empathize with you. I understand your frustration and your feeling of helplessness. I understand how you, you Real Americans, want to do something, anything, to protect this great country of ours. But anarchy in the streets will not help anyone. I urge all of you to return to your homes. I have advised the governors to call out their National Guard units to maintain the peace. Looting, rioting, and other antisocial acts will not be tolerated." His face once again became pleasant. "Please return to your homes and know that tomorrow the sun will still rise, people will still go to work, and the American way of life will still be in place. Thank you for your cooperation. Good night."

The President looks down at some papers as the camera pans back. Then there is another second of blank screen, which is soon replaced by a news anchorman. "That was the President of the United States with a historic message. Once again, let me report that an extraterrestrial radio signal has been confirmed..."

At the same time, at the Monmouth Orphanage for the Treatment of Handel's Syndrome, 4ᵗʰ floor dormitory.

By the time he was in his early teens, Franklin Trinity had become an astute student of politics. He always took an intense interest in what the President and other national leaders had to say about HS. He would have been fascinated in the President's speech that night if he had been able to listen. He was busy with other things. The President's speech didn't present any surprises to the American people, they already knew all about the events in Puerto Rico that morning. It had been on the news all day long. Pundits had been on TV all afternoon discussing and rediscussing the message. What did it mean? Why did they send it? When were they coming? The overall consensus was that the message was meant as a wake up call to the HS youngsters telling them that their true parents were coming. That they should take up arms and rebel against the human authorities and prepare the planet for invasion. That's what the talking heads on the news channels felt anyway.

Regardless of any potential actions on the part of any of the HS children, a distinct and vocal minority of the human people took this as a threat, a big threat. As evening progressed there were news reports about incidents all over the world. It was all still shaky at this time, but word was coming from a number of regions about assaults, executions, murders, and kidnappings of anyone even suspected of carrying the HS virus. Franklin Trinity was not unobservant. He predicted what would happen someday. He assessed his situation and decided that with a few more hours of hype, things could get very ugly at the Monmouth Orphanage. The staff, who never seemed to like the children anyway, was acting more openly hostile. As the light of day was fading, a crowd began to gather at the front gate of the complex. They held signs and banners calling for the death of the children inside. They called for an example to be made of these children, a message of defiance to send to those anonymous broadcasters in the Pleiades. Franklin's room on the fourth floor of the dormitory had a small window that looked out over the main courtyard and front gate. He sat and watched the crowd gather, and planned for the worst.

Several of his friends had come in to see him. Enoch, Marvin, some of the smaller children. As one of the oldest 'wards' of the state, Franklin was looked up to as a big brother of sorts. It also helped that he had spent his formative years with Father Blythe, who encouraged him to be confident and to be proud of who he was. Most of the children here had been dropped off soon after birth, or had been found abandoned at police stations, hospitals, or trash cans. They had been harassed, hounded, and teased their entire lives. Like it or not, Franklin had become a role model, the only one who possessed any strength to deal with a crisis.

"What are we going to do Franklin?" Enoch had asked him. Marvin Wiggins, who was new to the facility and still too young to understand the politics of hate, had been tugging on Franklin's sleeve for over an hour repeating, "I'm scared, hug me." Franklin sat and watched the crowd gather, ignoring his young compatriots. It was only when some of the older boys entered that Franklin woke from his reverie to realize that people were depending on him.

"Ok," he said turning from the window and reaching under his thin mattress. "I have a plan. Like practically everybody here, I've dreamt of escape. Of going someplace where I don't have to give daily blood samples and I can go to bed when I want. Someplace where I'm not treated like a prisoner. I'm sure you've all felt the same way." There was a murmur of agreement from the fifteen or so children who had crowded into his room. "Maybe its because I've been here longer than most of you, but I've been fed up enough to actually figure out an escape." He pulled a sheaf of paper from under his bed. "I've got drawings here of what we can do. Some lists of equipment we'll need and where we can find it, that sort of thing. It was mostly just a fantasy really. I'm almost 18, they've been saying that I can leave the orphanage then, so I've been trying not to make trouble. But it seems like we may have to put our plan in action." He handed some papers around to the people he trusted.

"Here are some lists of things that we'll need. I want you guys to go and scrounge around and get them. We'll meet back here in two hours. If all hell breaks loose, we'll put our plan into action and get out of here." The children, missions having been assigned, headed towards the door. "One other thing. This plan can't save everybody. If too many people get involved we're all going to get caught. I know that it's harsh, but we have to keep this thing quiet. The more people that know about it, the less likely any of us are going to get out of here alive." He looked around the room for agreement. "Ok, now go, we might not have much time."

Franklin spent the next few hours moving silently through the dormitories, contacting the children that he knew could be trusted and could be of value. Then he returned to his room to watch the gathering crowd at the gate.

Now, just as the President's speech was about to be broadcast, the crowd was reaching a critical mass. Some police and security guards were on hand, but they were doing little to quell the growing call for violence. Franklin and his brood were waiting patiently, watching the crowd. On the inside of the gate, a large contingent of HS kids stood in the main courtyard, watching the protesters. There is a morbid fascination involved in watching people scream for your death. The children mistakenly believed that the gate and the orphanage personnel would protect them from any real harm. Franklin watched them with a tear in his eye, wanting to tell them to get the hell out of there, that something horrible was about to happen, but he couldn't. He needed them to act as a distraction so he could get a small number of children to safety. If he raised the general alarm now, no one would be able to escape.

"Franklin, we're all ready. Let's go."

"No, not yet. We can't leave just yet. We have to stand by."

"I'm scared Franklin," said Marvin.

"I know child, I know. It'll all be over soon." He rubbed the small child's head.

Exactly forty-two seconds into the President's address, one of the protesters at the gate leveled a rifle through the bars and fired a shot. It hit one of the children square in the chest. He crumpled. Franklin couldn't tell who it was, and he was glad for not knowing. The sound of gunfire fanned the flames. Soon multiple shots were ringing out in the night. People rushed the gate. It would have been quite absurd to see the sight up close. These were normal, everyday Americans. Mothers, fresh from their kids soccer practice, men still dressed in suits from their day's labor, even children in bright clothing pressed up against the entrance to the facility, all screaming in a whorl of panicked violence. It wasn't the type of crowd that you normally connect with this sort of behavior.

"My god Franklin, let's get the hell out of here now!" screamed one child.

"Not yet, patience," replied the leader. "Right now this is the safest place to be. Patience."

Slowly the gate began to open. Someone on the inside had pushed the button to open the facility. People began to pry themselves through the opening. The children were running, scattering over the courtyard. The orphanage personnel did nothing to stop them. Some ran, some stood in silence, but no one made an attempt to save even a single child. The rioters entered the complex with bats, tire irons, whatever they could find. Soon the courtyard became a charnel house as decent, hardworking Americans murdered children in a frenzy of fear and bloodlust. An alarm began to sound.

"Now!" shouted Franklin. The group crossed the hall to Marvin's room. Marvin's window didn't face the courtyard, it faced the back of the facility. The dormitory was on the edge of the complex, and the only thing stopping the children's escape was four vertical stories and alarmed windows. Franklin entered the room and in one fluid motion threw Marvin's chair against the window. It shattered in a spray of glass. An alarm sounded, but it was drowned out by all of the other alarms and noise from below. Enoch smashed the rest of the glass out of the way with a stick. Two children began lowering a rope of tied bedspreads to the ground. Children were running everywhere. Only those who followed Franklin kept their heads about them. The facility had kept a tight rein on their charges, and most of the children didn't know what to do without the authority of their human masters to lead them. The rope reached the surface.

"Ok, Enoch, you go first, make sure that there isn't anyone around on that side of the facility, then give the signal and we'll all come down." The spry child complied and hurriedly lowered himself to the ground. He looked around in the darkness. The action was taking place on the other side of the compound. Anyone who might have been lurking about on this side had moved to the front entrance when the violence began to rage. He signaled above.

"Ok people, now we can't panic. We have to remain calm. You all know what to do. We are going down the rope one at a time, then we'll hide in the swamp. Our eyes are bigger than human eyes, we can see better in the dark. They won't be able to find us out there. Move through the swamp in small groups. We'll reconnect tomorrow morning under the on-ramp to Route 512. Now go!" The children queued up and began filing down the rope. "One at a time, one at a time," Franklin said. "Don't break the rope."

There was little that he could do at this point. He ran back to his room and watched the mayhem that was occurring below. The courtyard was mostly clear. Dead and injured children lay in groups. Rioters moved through the compound freely. Franklin could see them as they filed into some of the other dormitories. There were several fires raging. Protesters were lighting Molotov Cocktails and hurling them into shattered windows. There was the sound of sporadic gunfire and crying. "They're only children," thought Franklin. He smashed his fist against the windowsill in frustration. "They're only children."

When it became too much for him to bear he returned to Marvin's room. Most of his followers had descended. Several screams and shouts came from down the hall. The echo of a weapon discharging sounded in the stairwell. It could only have come from the floor below. "Quickly quickly," he said. The other children looked scared but they continued their decent. "Don't wait for the rest of us, just start running." Franklin barred the door to the room with some furniture. "Go, go!"

Soon the only two in the room were Marvin and Franklin. "It's your turn Marvin, go, go!" shouted the elder boy.

"I can't. I'm scared I might fall."

"You have to go, go now!" He pushed the youth towards the window.

"No, you go first, I'll follow. That way you can catch me." It didn't make a lot of sense, but there wasn't much time left. Someone in the hall rammed against the door. The furniture wouldn't hold for more than a few seconds.

"Fine, let's go." Franklin pulled his cap tightly around his ears, scrambled over the windowsill and began his decent. He went down about one floor and then looked up. Marvin was fumbling through the window. "Come up, hurry up!" Franklin shouted. There was a shot from the hallway. It snapped the doorframe into pieces. As Marvin began his decent the door cracked open and a human face appeared, mouth frothing.

Marvin made his way down quickly. Franklin watching his own decent didn't notice the face at the window until Marvin screamed. He looked up. At the window was a man. He looked down at the pair of escapees. "Marvin, watch out!" Franklin shouted. The man at the window grabbed the makeshift rope and untied the end from the radiator. The two children fell to the ground.

Franklin was about a story and half in the air at the time. He landed hard on his arm, which snapped like a twig. For Marvin, who was almost three stories up, the outcome was far worse. He wasn't moving when Franklin got to him. Franklin held the child's head. There was blood, too much blood. He wasn't breathing. "Come on Marvin, wake up, wake up," said the boy. His eyes were blurry with tears. A ricochet sounded close by. He wiped the tears from his eyes enough to focus on the window above. Two faces now looked down. One held a rifle. A second shot was fired. It missed, but not by much. Franklin looked up in disbelief. "We're only children!" he shouted to his attackers. He ran into the woods. More shots rang out. As he hit the treeline he could hear the alarms and sirens vividly. Most of the screams had died down. With the fires raging there was some light in the darkness of the bog.

He ran through the swamp, tears in his eyes for all the dead and dying. He tripped over a tree branch and fell headfirst into a foot of muddy water. He must have blacked out from the pain in his arm because the next thing he knew he was lying on his back. The stars came into focus above him bordered by trees. Something happened to him that night lying there in the mud. Franklin would later claim that he had a religious experience of some kind– that a voice rang down from the heavens and told him what to do. He was in tremendous pain and emotional distress, so perhaps it could be chalked up to hallucination. But maybe those conditions just make one more receptive to divine messages. It didn't matter if the revelation was real or imagined actually. It is only the effect that counts. Franklin came to the realization out there that the God he had worshipped was not his god, that the people who claimed to be his protectors were not his protectors. He realized what they had been telling him all along; that he was not human, that he was indeed an alien. If the people of Earth acted like his enemy then they were his enemy. Father Blythe had told him over and over that he could be accepted if he tried hard enough, if he made them accept him. Franklin no longer wanted that. He no longer wanted acceptance. He no longer wanted to live peacefully with the humans. He wanted revenge. He wanted to destroy as his life had been destroyed. The message from space was a call to arms. His true lineage was of the stars, his true faith lay above in the heavens, not here down on Earth. He was through playing human. He stood up, eyes still focused on the heavens. He threw his cap to the ground and felt the starlight on his naked head. He knew what he had to do. He knew that the only way he and his compatriots could truly be free would be to rid this place of the human plague that now infested it. By the time his parents came to reclaim him he would be in a position to present the Earth to them as a welcoming gift.

Meanwhile. The Watley family residence, Tyler, TX

The sound of truck tires was audible before President Potter had finished his announcement. Joyce Watley was sitting on the family couch, her bulk taking up slightly more than one cushion. Like most Americans, she had spent the day listening to news reports of the signal and the effects that it was having in other parts of the world. In the Middle East, several Mullahs had issued fatwas absolving anyone who killed an HS person from guilt. Areas of Africa had erupted into flames. Riots and looting were occurring at this hour in many large cities in Asia. Stock markets all over the world tumbled on the report, and there were runs on dried food, weapons, gasoline, and other items people think they need in an emergency. No one knew for sure what the message meant exactly, but they did know one thing, that 'they' (whoever 'they' were) were coming. Until now it had all seemed a dream; the alien ship in Ohio, the alien children popping up all over the place, prophecies of doom by extremist talk show hosts. It all didn't seem real somehow. No one really felt threatened. It came so slowly that people got used to it a bite at a time. Possibly most people thought up until now that it had all been just a hoax, something to keep the masses in line now that the Cold War was over. Very few people actually thought that honest-to-god 'aliens' would be coming here, not in the flesh. Suddenly, overnight, the whole world had experienced a huge shock to the system, and the results were being played out all over.

Joyce's attention was split between the President's speech and a box of cookies she was working her way through. Like most news stories, this one was starting to lose its steam. There is always a clamoring for analysis when something momentous happens, and the media tries in vain to fill that need. But there really wasn't much more to report regarding the message from the stars. Everything was just a rehash of the six o'clock news. "Do you think they're really coming Larry? Maybe they're just messing with our heads." Joyce said between bites. There was no response. "I said, 'do you think...'" Joyce looked around the room, but her husband was nowhere to be seen. His comfortable tweed recliner was empty. She rolled around like a seal and craned her neck, but he wasn't in the kitchen either. Then she heard the sound of truck tires. Her face went rigid.

Larry came down the stairs two at a time. He was wearing his hunting cap and carried his shotgun in his hand. "What the hell you gonna do Larry?" she said in a partially panicked voice.

"Stay here woman, this ain't none of your business," he replied, opening the front door. Joyce jumped from the couch, although maybe jumped isn't the proper term for how she rolled her bulk over into a standing position. She followed him out the door. Standing in the front yard were three trucks. All of them had been hand-painted with the 'Tyler County Patriot's Brigade' logo. About ten brigade members stood around wearing their traditional berets. They looked a comical sight really. To be honest they were in reality just Larry's fishing buddies. They were all old, fat, out of shape farmers. There wasn't one young, chiseled physique that you would connect with such a martial word as 'Brigade.' But they all had their deer hunting rifles with them. Joyce ran out into the driveway in her housecoat and slippers. Her hair was up in rollers and she still had cookie crumbs on her chest. It was very unusual for her to be seen by anyone in this state of dress. She usually even put on makeup when she went to the mailbox.

"Where the hell you going Larry?" she repeated.

"We're just doing our job as Real Americans. You just go to bed now," he replied. A small cheer of support came from several of the other members of the Brigade.

She grabbed his jacket. "You ain't going over to the Miller house are you? You leave them alone. They're good people."

"It's a war Joyce. We didn't start it, but for damn sure we're gonna end it. I got kids to protect. I ain't letting no alien monster get 'em." He turned to get into the back of one truck. Joyce grabbed him and spun him around.

"You get your butt back in that house. The rest of you go home to your families. Find something better to do with your time."

Larry, who weighed at least fifty pounds less than his wife struggled free. "Not tonight woman. Tonight we're taking care of our business. It's a man's job. You wouldn't understand." Joyce once again grabbed her husband and threw him against the fender.

"Gimme the gun Larry." She grabbed for the barrel. The two struggled for possession of the weapon.

"Get off me woman!" shouted Larry. Husband and wife pushed each other back and forth, rolling and pulling for the shotgun. Somehow the trigger was pulled. The shotgun had been loaded with a slug round more suited to taking down an elephant than a spindly teenager. It hit Joyce straight in the belly. The force of the blow actually lifted her off her feet and propelled her back almost a yard. Larry stared in horror at his wife, who lay spread eagle on the driveway. He looked down in horror at the smoking gun in his hands. He dropped it as if it was radioactive and rushed to his wife's side. He picked up her head and cradled it. She looked up at him with glazed over eyes and said, "Larry, you are one stupid son of a..." Her head turned to the side slightly and blood began to drip from her nose.

Larry held the dead woman's head in his hands for a long time, weeping silently. The other members of the Patriot Brigade looked around at each other, not sure what to do. Larry looked up at his house. Staring out from the large bay window were his two children.

Six months later, The Miller farm, outskirts of Tyler, TX

The sound of a door slamming fills the air inside the house. Lorraine Miller looks out the window of her home to find out why the door wasn't closed gently. What she sees is rather humorous. A small person is struggling down the hill to the mailbox. In his arms are no less than three white mail trays filled with envelopes. Her son waddles his way down the drive, barely able to keep from falling over. Lorraine sighs and puts down the dishtowel she was drying her hands with. She goes into the laundry room and picks up a cart that was designed to carry luggage. She rolls it out the front door and has soon caught up with her son, who was on the verge of spilling his heavy load.

"Glory! I just can't understand how someone who is supposed to be so smart can be so dumb," she said out loud as she got within hearing distance. "Or maybe you're just stubborn. Your father's the same way. Now here, use this cart before you fall over and hurt yourself."

"Thanks Mom," said Jim, handing over his load. "I was in a hurry, I don't want to miss the mailman. I've been licking stamps all morning." He stuck out his tongue as if to show how worn out it had become.

The two started walking toward the mailbox together. She looked through the contents of the mail tray. It was filled with identical magenta colored sheets of paper, folded in thirds and stapled. "Is this another issue of that newsletter of yours?"

"Issue Four of 'Genetic Equality: The Official Newsletter of the Johnannes Handel Anti-Defamation Society.'" Jim beamed with pride. "Dad, Jordan and I just finished it last night. I've got to get it out today, we're on a deadline."

The two rolled to a stop by the mailbox. It was almost 1:30 pm now, the mailman was already past due. Jim checked the box just to make sure that he wasn't late, but it was empty, the mail hadn't been delivered yet. "The 'Johannes Handel Anti-Defamation Society' huh? Well, I'm glad that you've been keeping busy these last few months. You were pretty down after the college rejections you know. Not me though, I'm glad that you're staying around the farm for a little while longer. Things would seem so lonely if you went away. Just me and your father. Even Joyce is gone now..." Lorraine cast her eyes downward and let the rest of her sentence trail off.

"It's gone past that Mom. I know that when we started I just thought that the newsletter would be a way to keep busy, but I've found out so much and corresponded with so many different people. There are serious issues that no one in the mainstream press is really giving much attention to. Did you know that Johnston has a bill before Congress right now that would *require* testing of all humans? And those that tested positive for HS would have their names publicly released? Right now it's totally legal to fire someone just for having an Alien-American child." Jim started counting on his fingers. "And what about the violence of August 6th? Thousands of Alien-Americans were killed, property was destroyed, and there hasn't been a single prosecution."

"Alien-American? That's what you're calling yourself now?" Lorraine chuckled.

"That was Dad's idea. It makes it sound less like a disease or a disability." He continued without letting up, "Third, there are stories coming out of other countries that make what happened here six months ago look like nothing. They're now estimating that the world population is actually decreasing with all the infant killings that are going on! Fourth, every day gangs of ignorant thugs beat up and murder Alien-Americans and the cops don't do anything to stop these people. Fifth, the military buildup for this vague threat is resulting in decreased social services and..."

"Ok, ok, calm down. You're preaching to the choir here," said Lorraine. She patted her child on the head. "I've got to listen to your father rant on and on all day about this. I don't need it from you too."

"Sorry, Mom, it's just that I get so excited. I mean, I'm doing ok here, but there are a lot of people that are in way worse shape. Have you heard about the things that go on in those orphanages? I mean it's..." Jim caught himself before he started another tirade.

"So what's the big deadline?"

"Huh?"

"You said that you had a deadline to meet."

"Oh, yeah, we're planning a march."

"A march, where?"

"Washington, D.C."

"Does your father know about this?

"He's the one who's driving."

"How are you planning a march?"

"I know, I thought that it was a crazy idea at first too. I mean, I don't know how to plan a rally, but I said to Dad that we needed a rally, and he told me to figure out how to do it. I started by calling other minority groups and asking them questions. Some were pretty friendly. Then I called the City Hall in D.C. and asked them how to get a permit. I've still got to paint up some banners and all, but we've got a permit for two months from now. So, I've got to warn my subscribers to come if they can make it. I'm hoping to get a hundred people. We're gonna march from the White House to the Capitol. Maybe we'll even have some speeches, if I can figure out where to get a microphone."

"Where did you get the money for all this. It ain't like you got a job or nothing."

"Donations, donations, donations. I've got checks from a bunch of people. I never asked for any, but people send me

225

money anyway. Plus, there's this guy, he's the CEO of an oil company. His daughter is an Alien-American. He's said that he'd put up a hundred thousand dollars if I needed it."

"A hundred thousand dollars? I don't know about this James. That's a lot of money. These people are expecting something serious. You're just a teenager. Maybe you should let someone else handle this."

"There isn't anyone else Mom. When I started this thing I didn't realize it, but no one else had stepped forward. I'm one of the oldest Alien-Americans around, so a lot of the younger kids look up to me. Sure, there were some groups that have been dealing with HS as a disease, but they're all small and local and misguided. No one before me has come forward and talked about the human rights issues associated with this thing. Now everyone's looking to me for guidance. I've become a leader." He puffed up his chest proudly, "I've got a mandate from the people."

Lorraine looked down at the pile of newsletters. "What do you have there, a thousand letters? That's not exactly a 'mandate from the people.'"

"Oh these, these are just for those people that don't have email. I've got about fifty times this number of people who I sent newsletters to electronically."

Just then, the mail truck appeared in the distance. It drove closer and closer trailing a cloud of dust. When it arrived, Jim helped the mailman pick up the newsletters and put them in his truck. The driver then reached around back and pulled out two large sacks of mail each as big as the boy himself, which he dropped at the young leader's feet. "Good thing we brought the cart, huh Mom?" Jim said.

Two weeks before the J.H.A.D.S. Rally. An alley in downtown Fredrick, MD

"I'm telling you man, if you want in, you're gonna have to jump a baldie. That's like the rule." The teenagers, just boys really, sat in the alleyway hidden from the view of the street by strategically placed garbage cans. They all wore the brown berets that they were so proud of. Two of the boys had black leather jackets with a strange symbol hand painted on the back. It was a gray, upside-down teardrop with a large red 'X' overlaid on it. You could tell that the decoration was fashioned in a hurry since small rivulets of paint had dried into permanent drips. One of the boys had the letters 'BK' carved into his arm, although they weren't visible with his jacket sleeves rolled down.

"I don't know you guys, this is pretty hardcore," said Ben Hayes. He was at least two years younger than the other members of the 'Baldie-Killahs.'

"Don't wuss out on us man."

"Look Hayes, you're either with us or against us. We all know that you got a baldie in your family, so you're on the edge already. You're just lucky that your Dad works with Mr. Johnston. Now you gonna prove your loyalty to the BKs or not?"

"Uh, ok, what do I gotta do?" said Colin's child hesitantly.

"Come over here." The boys moved to the front of the alley and peered around the edge of the building. "Now, you just have to wait until a baldie comes along, and then you jump him." He pulled something out of his pocket. "Hit him in the face a few times with this. That'll show 'em." He handed a homemade set of brass knuckles to Ben who took them and tried them on. The gang leader turned to his lookout. "Greg, you see anything."

"Yeah, a baldie just walked into that store. He'll be coming out soon. Then pow! He won't know what hit him." The boys chuckled to themselves. A bead of sweat dripped out from underneath Ben's beret. He looked down at his armored hand.

"Dude, you're such a wimp man. Come on, be a man. Look it's almost dark out, no one'll see you. Just hit the kid and run. Don't you hate baldies?"

"Yes."

"Don't you want to see them all dead?"

"Yes."

"Don't you want to be a real American like the Vice President?"

"Yes!" Ben was starting to get revved up.

"Don't you want to punch their little fat heads in?"

"Yes!"

The door to the shop opened and the boy came out, skipping.

"Now go man!"

"Wait," said the leader. "Get him with this." He handed Ben a switchblade. Ben hesitated a second. "Go now man, you'll miss your chance!"

Ben took the blade and ran from the alley. His long stride covered a full sidewalk segment per step. Everything flashed through his mind at once. He thought about how Dad always loved Neil best. He thought about how those freaks in school always got better grades then he did. He thought of all the irrational fears he held about being eaten alive by alien oppressors. He screamed in a frothing fury of rage and terror. He bore down on the slim child and before the alien even knew what was happening to him the knife pierced his chest. "Die Baldie!" he screamed as he delivered the deathblow. The alien frame is very fragile compared to that of a human, and the blade dove deep. Ben tried to run but the knife stuck and jerked his arm backwards. He spun around as the blade snapped off. Ben tried to regain his bearings and keep running but he didn't see the adult figure who was exiting the store in pursuit of his errant son. The two slammed into each other. Ben fell backwards and hit his head on the ground.

"Neil!" said the father rushing to the side of his youngest child who lay unconscious and bleeding on the sidewalk. The man wasn't sure what was happening exactly, he just knew that his child had been hurt. Luckily several passers-by saw the incident and grabbed Ben before he could recover from his fall. The rest of the BKs ran past at top speed, eager to get away from the scene before the police arrived. Colin picked up the head of his child and cradled it in his arms. "Neil, talk to me, talk to me, stay with me!" he cried, but to no avail. Neil would never regain consciousness.

Colin was too distraught to feel hatred for the murderer, he didn't quite even grasp what had happened on that small town street corner. This wasn't the big city. These things weren't supposed to happen here. He had decided to raise a family here because these things didn't happen in a place like this. He rocked back and forth with his dead child in his arms, oblivious to the sirens of the police and ambulance that arrived on the scene a few minutes later.

As the paramedics separated the father and son, the police took the young thug into custody. Colin stood in disbelief as they attempted to breath life back into the boy. A policeman took Colin by the hand and guided him over to the police car. "We are going to need your witness testimony to prosecute, Mr. Hayes," said the officer. "The kid who did this is waiting in car. We're going to need an ID. He opened the door. "Is this the person who stabbed your boy and ran into you just now?" he said shining a flashlight in the face of the assailant.

Through blurred, puffy eyes, Colin stared in disbelief and horror as he recognized the face of his eldest child. Ben looked back, wide eyed and slack jawed. His mind whirled a mile a minute trying to come up with something to say, but words failed him.

Two weeks later, Pennsylvania Avenue, Washington, DC

The noise of the crowd is deafening. Jim's hands are shaking with nervousness. Just an hour before, he had been a nobody, an anonymous person in the sea of a big city. He looked around for his father for support, but he wasn't here. He looked for Jordan's Dad, or anyone remotely familiar, but he couldn't see a single recognizable face in the crowd. He was alone with his microphone. He cleared his throat and began to speak.

That morning, things had gone pretty much as he had expected them to. His father, himself, and the McReynolds had gotten in the night before after a really long drive from Texas. They were excited about the march. The bed of Mr. McReynolds' truck was filled with flyers, posters, signs, and a banner that they had put together with some tempera paint and a bedsheet. All of the information Jim had sent out scheduled the march for 10am, so they arrived at the rallying point at 9am. What they saw there amazed them. Based on the few replies they had received, and their wild guesses about who would actually have the courage and motivation to come, they expected a hundred or so rallyers. An hour before the march was to start there were already over three hundred people waiting around. Many carried signs and banners of much higher quality than they ones that Jordan and Jim had painted up in his bedroom the week before. Everyone was milling about looking for something to do. Jim took out the microphone and portable amp that he borrowed from his preacher and addressed the crowd. When he announced who he was, a cheer spontaneously erupted. In the next ten minutes he was almost smothered by well-wishers and supporters. Soon after, he was greeted by none other than the Reverend Jeremiah Bentley, who was a prominent leader in the African-American civil rights movement. The Reverend introduced himself to a shocked Jim Miller. The Reverend was one of the people Jim had read extensively trying to come up to speed about the history, techniques, and effectiveness of previous civil rights struggles.

"Reverend Bentley. It's an honor to meet you sir. I never would have expected to see someone of your stature here," he said to the towering figure.

"Don't be so surprised boy. This is the front line of the newest battle for equality. My organization has been keeping track of your efforts since you contacted us. I'm here to lend our support. Our fundamental goals are similar."

"I didn't expect this many people. I'm not sure what to do," replied Jim.

"It is your time to step up son. Today is your day to alert the world to your struggle, to break the conspiracy of silence. Take command and become a leader. These people are looking up to you, don't disappoint them." He turned his head towards a group of people standing on the opposite side of the street shouting slurs, "That's what those people want. You can't fail today."

Over the next half hour, the crowd grew exponentially in strength; the marchers, the counter-protestors, and the police. Just before 10 o'clock Jim's group had grown to several thousand. They were clogging streets for several blocks. The police were standing around, trying to keep the counter-protesters at bay. There were a lot of them; many were people who were just on their way to work and saw Jim's group queuing up.

A police sergeant came up to Jim. "Is this your rally?" he said in a harsh voice.

"Yes officer," replied Jim meekly.

"Well, it's off. It ain't happening you hear. There's too many people and there aren't enough police. Tell the crowd to disperse."

"But I've got a permit." Jim held out the slip of paper he had received from the D.C. Clerks Office.

The Officer took the paper and ripped it into shreds. "No you don't. Now tell this crowd to disperse or I call in the riot police."

Jim didn't know what to do. His father was on the other side of the crowd issuing instructions to the marchers. Jim looked to the Reverend for support, and the man stood quietly, with a look of seriousness. His body language said enough. It screamed, "Take charge boy! Don't let them stop you." Jim was about to say something when another figure in a business suit arrived on the scene.

"Officer, my name is Greg Stubman. Congressman Greg Stubman. You're going to let these people march." The policeman backed off and started talking into his radio. He was trying to get confirmation from headquarters on what to do.

"Glad to meet you Mr. Miller," said the Congressman, leaning over to shake Jim's hand. "I've been reading your newsletter. My daughter is HS-positive, and I can't stay silent any longer. I'll march with you today."

Jim smiled. The Reverend leaned in. "Jim, now's the time to go, the police won't wait long, but they can't stop the march once it's started." Jim took the advice. He turned on his microphone to the maximum volume and shouted out orders to begin. All of a sudden, signs and banners arose from the crowd and people began moving down Pennsylvania Avenue in an amorphous mob. At the front of the line were Jim, the Congressman, and the Reverend. Jim looked around, but he couldn't see any of the people he came with. The crowd was so thick that it wasn't going to be possible to find them for a while. The three leaders pressed forward, each carrying a part of the large, hand-painted banner that called for equal rights for ALL Americans.

As the march moved forward, more and more counter-protestors began lining the streets. They finally had a target for their hatred. Up until that day, there was no focus for their anger, it was diffused throughout the world in the wombs of millions of disparate people. But now there was a group, a central point, something that they could use to coalesce their hatred around– something to shout at, to throw bottles at, and to curse about.

The group made their way down Pennsylvania Avenue to the steps of the Capitol. Every step was fearful for Jim, who wasn't used to having things thrown at him. But he marched on, partly out of fear of disappointing the figures on his right and left, but also partly because he wanted to help the thousands of people behind him. He wanted to give them a focus too. He wanted to provide them with something to dream in, something to believe in, something to call on in times of need. He felt alone and scared, and he didn't want others to feel the same way. The only thing that they could do was march, to show themselves on the TV cameras, and put up a brave face so that all of his Alien-American peers could find the strength to do likewise.

As they neared the Capitol steps, Jim became more anxious. He had never spoken in front of a crowd before, but he knew that these people came to hear someone speak. As he mounted the steps he unfolded his speech and prepared to address the marchers. He looked out over the crowd. It was much larger than it looked when they started marching. There were also television cameras and news reporters crawling all over the place. Jim swallowed as he realized that what he was about to say might be broadcast all over the U.S. He cleared his throat, turned up his mike and took one last glance at his two illustrious compatriots.

Then he turned and began to address the crowd.

At almost the exact same moment as Jim Miller started his march. The Senate Subcommittee on Handel's Syndrome Research, Washington, DC

It's always funny how news tends to come in spurts. For weeks, the anchorman only talks about filler and fluff, and then one day, several major events happen all at once.

The doors to the subcommittee chamber burst open as if a hurricane had blown through. That hurricane was named Ray Johnston, and he was on a mission. As the discoverer of the alien threat, he had led the vanguard towards building a defense against invasion and against the viral bio-weapon that was turning the population into the enemy, one child at a time. He created this subcommittee, he nurtured it. He hand-picked all of the members. It was the personification of his political career, and the focal point that Americans used to rally around his banner. It was the perfect place to make the announcement.

The normally staid conference room was thrown into chaos at the Vice President's arrival. He never came to these meetings, and was unexpected by all but a few in his inner circle. He arrived in large fashion, followed by reporters and hangers-on. Without saying a word, he marched straight up to the podium. This guerrilla style of speechmaking was a trademark of his. It harkened back to his pre-politics days as an intelligence agent.

General Hudson, who had recently taken over as committee chair, stepped aside knowingly and Ray stepped up to the microphone. Many of the uninformed committee felt that this intrusion was somewhat inappropriate, but it was always exciting to meet someone famous. Dr. Mensen held a silent protest by ignoring the Vice President and instead concentrating on editing a draft of his latest scientific paper. No one noticed.

One man who did know about the Vice President's upcoming visit was Colin Hayes. He received a phone call two nights ago, directly from Ray. "Colin old buddy. As you know election season is coming up and it's time to announce my candidacy. Potter's had his eight years, now it's my turn. I'm going to do it at the next committee meeting. It seems appropriate. That's where it all started after all. I want you to be there. I want you to stand next to me. I wouldn't be where I am today without you. You're part of the 'Johnston mythos' now. It's only fair that you get some face time in front of a national TV audience." It was a good thing for Colin that Ray couldn't see his face. His eyes were puffy and he looked as if he hadn't slept in a long time (which he hadn't). Ray didn't know about the incident the week before between Ben and Neil, how could he? Colin didn't say anything. He had always kept Neil's condition an open secret so as not to interfere with his career. Now he wished that he had spoken out, wished that he had stood up and railed against General Hudson's proposals. He wished that he had figured out a way to stop the tide of rhetoric that had led to fratricide. Now it was too late. He felt impotent. He choked out an 'ok' and hung up on the Vice President.

Secret Service agents took Colin from his seat at the committee table and brought him over to the podium. An anonymous campaign manager pulled him back and to the left a bit, even going so far as to bend down and show Colin exactly where to plant his feet. More people of various positions came up on stage and were guided to their prescribed locations. Within ten minutes all was ready. Ray motioned to the cameras to start rolling, and started to speak.

"Ladies and Gentlemen, we are at war. It's a subtle war. It's a war that hasn't been declared. It's a war in which our enemy has yet to fully reveal himself. But never forget that it *is* a war. And this war is the biggest war we as Americans, we as *humans*, will ever have to fight. It is a war for the very survival of our species. Yes, we are at war. A war fought not with guns but with science, a battle not fought on the field but in our wombs. And we are losing this war. Day by day our numbers shrink while their numbers grow. We are literally being eaten alive from within. Since the election of President Potter we have done much to stem the tide of HS infection. We have done much to develop a military force capable of resisting what is likely to be a technologically advanced foe. But it is not enough. We are on the correct course, but we haven't done enough. President Potter has led the fight, but his eight years in the White House are almost up. Someone else needs to take up the banner against the enemy. This is why I am formally announcing my candidacy for the President of the United States of America. Who better then me to fill President Potter's shoes? Who better than me to hold the line against the special interests that would have us believe that the alien threat is fictitious, that the alien children living in our very homes are just malformed humans? The special interests that would have you believe that any contact with an alien race will bring economic opportunities instead of annihilation." Some of the public watching the event from the gallery shouted cheers. Dr. Mensen lifted an eyebrow and noted that the gallery was usually empty during sessions, so he concluded that the politicians had brought their own cheering section with them. He returned to his editing.

"What will I do as President? How will I stop this horrible flood that threatens to engulf our genetic legacy? I think that my credentials are clear. I was the one who beat my way through the system to expose the threat in the first place. I was the one who formed this very panel that I now stand before. I am the one who enacted the legislation that has increased research dollars for the search for a vaccine. I was the one who forced the Senate to triple the defense R&D budget. I was the one who enacted the legislation to send foreign aid across the globe for HS prevention programs, for as we know, this is a global problem."

"But what will I do as President? On the first day of my administration I promise to enact an executive order requiring mandatory testing of all pregnant women in the United States, and to provide abortion services free of charge. I will create an agency tasked to deal with these so-called Alien-Americans. So far, they have not presented much of a threat, but that is only because the eldest of these invaders is barely out of his teens. This agency will be tasked to identify and track all aliens living in the United States to ensure that they are not involved in anti-government activities. I will enact legislation preventing these new, adult aliens from owning firearms, holding large stakes in key industries, or congregating in large groups."

"I plan to purge all federal government agencies of people who test HS-positive or who have alien children. These people simply cannot be trusted in times of crisis. I propose to further increase military budgets as much as we can afford. Only a strong, armed populace will be able to resist this menace. I propose to lower taxes in order to stimulate economic growth. I propose to set up a program whereby pure U.S. citizens can donate frozen, fertilized eggs to HS-positive Americans who want to give birth to normal children."

"This is what I promise you America. Now, who's with me?" A larger cheer rose from the crowd. Some of the panel members also shouted an enthusiastic "Yes!"

Colin listened to the speech in shock. He had a good idea of what Ray was going to say. He had watched over the years as Ray had gone from government spook, to paranoid conspiracist, to political conniver, and then finally to someone who believed his own hype. Colin knew that Ray had gone over the edge. He had gone too far and there was no way he could be trusted to run the government. The U.S.

would turn into a giant police state. Colin fingered the gun in his pocket.

He couldn't let it happen. He couldn't let Ray do the things that he had talked about. He couldn't let other families experience the same feelings that he had felt when he buried his youngest child. He couldn't let Ray Johnston rise to the most powerful position in the world.

Colin thought about Neil. He thought about Ben, and how he was seduced by this sort of rhetoric. He looked at Ray's back and for a minute he thought that he could see the same gray teardrop logo that the BKs wore. He blinked a few times to regain focus. His head swooned with grief and anger– anger at people like this who whooped up frenzy to further their own political goals. Ben wasn't responsible for his actions. He had been seduced. Seduced by the so called 'Patriot Brigades' seduced by the 'Real American Movement' seduced by fast talkers like Johnston who made it easy to blame all of life's problems on a poorly defined threat that had a face; Neil's face, little Neil's gentle face.

Tears streamed from his eyes as he listened to the speech. Perhaps the Secret Service agents who saw him thought that the Vice President's words were moving, perhaps they weren't paying much attention. Whatever the reason, no one noticed him in the back of the crowd. No one saw him reach into his pocket. No one saw him pull the gun. It was only when he shouted "No!" and lurched forward did any of the bodyguards make their move. But it was too late, they had been kept off stage, away from the cameras after all. No one could stop Colin as he pushed himself over General Hudson's shoulder and shot Ray Johnston twice in the back.

In front of the cameras, Ray slumped to the ground. He didn't know exactly what had happened to him. But he died believing in what he had always believed, that he was protecting the United States. Either in his public life, or in the deep, black world he traveled in before, rightly or wrongly, he had always believed that he was doing what was best for America. He was a company man to the end.

On the steps of the U.S. Capitol Building

Jim looked out over the crowd. It consisted mostly of families, one or both parents plus their child. The children were almost all HS-positive. Some people had come alone. There was a delegation of the Reverend's people, who mostly stood to the back of the crowd and looked slightly menacing in order to discourage the jeering onlookers from doing anything more than jeering. News camera trucks clogged the street and had even driven onto the grass of the National Mall. Their satellite hookups towered overhead.

"Good morning. I guess....whhheeeeeeeeeeeeeeeeeeeee," the microphone feedback drowned out the end of the sentence. Jim adjusted the volume and tried again. "Good morning, I guess you got my invitation," he joked. "I have to admit, I didn't expect to see so many of you here today. I want to start by apologizing to the police for not warning them about how big of a ruckus I was about to cause. I don't know how long they're going to let us stay here..." he looked around, "I can't imagine that they're going to tolerate this for very long, so let me get started with what I came to say." He started reading from his prepared notes. Most of the crowd couldn't hear a thing. The small PA system he had wasn't nearly loud enough to project to the back of the crowd, but they didn't care.

"Ladies, gentlemen, children. We are gathered here today, in front of these hallowed halls of liberty in order to demand our freedom. It seems strange to say that, 'demand our freedom.' After all, isn't this the United States? Aren't we guaranteed our freedoms by the Constitution? Isn't the motto of this country 'Liberty and Justice for All?' But we don't have that, do we? We don't, just because of the color of our skin and the size of our eyes. We are beaten, discriminated against, forced out of public schools. The police refuse to protect us, the courts refuse to hear us, businesses refuse to hire us. I have examples by the hundred, but I don't need to share them with you. For you, like me, have witnessed these acts in your own lives. The Tyler County School Board successfully voted to keep me out of school for my entire life. How many of you have had similar experiences?" He lifted a fist towards the sky. Many members of the crowd raised their hands in acknowledgement. "I have had the windows of my home broken, I have had my property vandalized. How many of you know firsthand what I'm talking about?" He raised his hand higher, with a similar reaction from the audience. "I personally know people who were killed on the night of August 6th. Who else here has had friends, loved ones killed?" The crowd began to shout. "We are too young for this. I'm still in my teens. I shouldn't know the face of death. This is wrong. The night of August 6th is a day that will live in infamy. It will be the rallying cry for our movement. No more will we stand idly by and let the fearful and ignorant continue to run roughshod over our God-given, constitutionally guaranteed rights. Who's with me?" Those in the crowd that could hear the boy shouted in agreement. The rest shouted in order to fit in.

"What makes me a U.S. citizen? What makes me human? Is it my genes? I can't help what my genes look like. I can't justify the actions of some alien race. But I today claim my humanity! If you cut me do I not bleed? My name is James Miller and I was born in Tyler, Texas. I am a Texan first, an American second, and an alien third. The HS virus has erased our ethnicity, but not our essential humanness. I was raised by Thomas and Lorraine Miller. They instilled in me a sense of pride, a sense of belonging. They made me more human than all of those so-called 'Patriot Brigades,' they made me more of an American than those so-called 'Real Americans.' Because unlike my oppressors, I believe in the Constitution, I believe in non-violence. I believe in God. A god that loves all people, regardless of race, regardless of ethnicity, regardless of the circumstances of their birth. I say to you that despite all the discrimination, I am proud to be an American! Yes, I say that I am proud to be an American, and I will continue this fight that we have started here today. I will continue this fight to end discrimination, end violence. I will make them see that we, the Alien-American community, are just as integral, just as valuable, as any other migrant race that has come to these shores looking for opportunity and freedom from fear. I will show them that intolerance of any sort has never proved of benefit to mankind. Only by working together will we achieve these goals. Who's with me? Who will help me show them the way?" A roar came from the crowd. People were pushing forward in order to get within hearing range.

"We will follow the model of all the great civil rights leaders, Ghandi, King, Chavez. We will fight back with love, we will fight back with civil disobedience, but never with violence. We will fight back by being model citizens and forcing them to acknowledge our value to their society. And I say we start with this." He pulled a card from his pocket. "This is a HS registration card. The federal government now requires that all parents of HS children be registered and tracked. This is unacceptable in a free society and I will not stand for it any longer." He lit a match and set the card ablaze. "That's what I think of their registration. Join me!" Small fires began to flare from the crowd, first one, than another. Tom Miller and the McReynolds moved through the crowd handing out matchbooks. Soon the place was ablaze. Jim looked back at the Reverend and smiled. The civil rights leader nodded back. The Congressman put his hand on Jim's shoulder and held his own flaming registration card up for people to see. Jim was less nervous now. It felt good to speak to the crowd. It felt good to say the things that he knew needed to be said. He turned back to the audience and began shouting, "The HS Registration Act will not stand! It will not stand!" The crowd began chanting in unison, "It will not stand! It will not stand!"

Near the back of the crowd, a ruckus was beginning. Jim couldn't hear what was happening of course, but a woman with a radio was shouting, "An alien's just shot Ray Johnston!" she didn't have the story quite right of course, but it didn't matter. As the word spread through the counter-protesters, things became violent. Ray had been their hero, their guiding light throughout all the turmoil of the past few years. Hearing that he had been assassinated was enough to send them into a frenzy. People began rushing the hastily erected police barricades and throwing themselves into the crowd. Police officers, many of whom were sympathetic to the anti-alien faction, made a half-hearted effort to keep the two sides apart, then backed off as the conflict intensified. The crowd began to flee in various directions, knocking over TV cameras and people in an effort to get out of the way of the riot. The sound of a window breaking is heard. Tom ran up on stage. "Come on, let's get out of here!" He bundled his son up in a jacket and they ran off down the street together.

The police, seeing a full-scale riot breaking loose tossed a few tear gas grenades into the crowd, which aided in the dispersal. More police cars arrived and the officers who emerged began beating whoever they saw first, most often a young Alien-American half overcome with tear gas. The anarchy would last for almost an hour before the scene was cleared out and brought back under control.

***

In the aftermath of the incident, several hooded figures walked quietly across the now-empty grounds. They milled about, looking at the blood-stained sidewalks, and kicking their way through the debris of the day's activities. They had been present for the speech, although no one had noted their presence. "Well Franklin, what do you think?" said Enoch.

"It'll never work." He pulled back his hood and exposed his head to the midday sun. "They'll never accept us. No matter what this Miller said. He's delusional if he thinks that people will consider him a Texan, and he's certifiable if he thinks that a non-violent protest is going to convince these monkeys that he's really one of them."

"He hasn't embraced his true heritage. Should we contact him, try to convince him?" said Calvin.

"No," replied Franklin. "He'll understand who he is soon enough. For now let him remain the focal point. His efforts, although ultimately meaningless, will divert attention from us. Let the monkeys worry about him for now. Meanwhile the Spearhead will continue to grow, to travel freely and undetected. Soon we'll be ready to make our move, and to pave the way for the day that our true fathers return for us. Once we claim the heritage they've given us, all of our fellow Pliedians will rally to our banner, and stop pretending that they're just monkeys. We are ever so much more."

Book 4: Union

Six years later.

"...and in business news, shares of clothing retailer 'Pants Shack' jumped three points in trading today after CEO Jack Blansford announced that his company will be developing and marketing a line of clothing specifically designed for the HS teenager. The clothing line will include shirts and pants that are resized to better fit the typical body type of an HS-positive person. Since rumors of this new line surfaced last week, some market analysts have wonder if the line's inclusion will trigger boycotts or even vandalism by people opposed to the integration and acceptance of HS into mainstream society. However, Jack Blansford dispelled those fears at a press conference today in the company headquarters in New York City..."

The video switches from the anchor desk to footage of a press conference. The CEO of 'Pants Shack' is speaking. "No, we're not worried about any boycotts. There is a reason that the Patriot Brigades have been losing members right and left these last few years. It's because every time one of them has an Alien-American kid, they leave the group. Our demographic research shows that there will be an estimated twenty million Alien-American teens living in the U.S. within ten years. Somebody is going to have to sell them clothing. Pants Shack is leading the way in this market, and will continue to lead the way. In the teen clothing business you either adapt or die. Pants Shack has chosen to adapt."

The video switches back to the anchor desk. "The new line of clothing will be called 'Alienz,' spelled with a 'Z' and is expected to be in most Pants Shack locations by mid November. For the foreseeable future, Pants Shack will continue to sell their profitable line of human-sized clothing as well."

Three years earlier, on "Live Talk! with Bill Garcia"

"Good evening, and welcome to 'Live Talk!' I'm your host Bill Garcia. Today on our program we'll be discussing the Alien-American movement, and their position that Handel's Syndrome is not a disease and shouldn't be treated as such. I've got two illustrious guests here with me tonight. In the studio with me is the young founder and president of the Johannes Handel Anti-Defamation Society, and an Alien-American himself, James Miller. And via satellite from Washington DC, we have the Chairman of the Senate Subcommittee on Handel's Syndrome Research, General Randolph Hudson. Greetings gentlemen, and welcome to 'Live Talk!'"

The two men nod politely to the camera. General Hudson is wearing his standard dress uniform. Jim is wearing a tailor-made suit he recently received as gift by a tailor whose daughter was HS-positive. The tie is a bit long, but it will do. He's not used to wearing formal clothes, or ones designed for his body, and he is a bit fidgety. But, knowing that he is on camera, Jim tries to put his best face forward.

Bill: Now let's start with you James. Your movement, JHADS, is claiming that Handel's Syndrome shouldn't be looked at as a disease, but rather a... lifestyle? Is that right?

James: Partially. Not a lifestyle so much as a separate ethnic classification, that's why we prefer the term 'Alien-American.' We believe that having alien DNA does not diminish our inherent... humanness, and we seek equal protection under the law in a manner similar to other ethnic minorities.

Bill: And General Hudson, you see it a different way.

Hudson: I believe, and I assure you that I speak with the full backing of the Senate Subcommittee when I say this, is that we are going down a dangerous path by allowing this sort of discussion. HS is not just some other ethnicity like being Irish or Japanese. The HS virus is the first shot in an interplanetary war between the human race and alien invaders from the Pleiades. We cannot allow ourselves the luxury of capitulating to these aliens just because they happen to speak our language and root for the same football teams. I feel sorry for these poor boys and girls, I really do, but if we start accepting them as full-fledged members of our society we will lose the ability to objectively develop ways to wipe out the HS virus and to create a military capable of defeating an undoubtedly superior alien threat.

Jim: I resent being labeled a threat.

Hudson: Then what about that terrorist act last month? The alien threat is beginn...

Jim: ...My organization had nothing to do with that!

Both Jim and General Hudson began shouting over each other so that neither was audible. Bill Garcia, a professional journalist, calmed the situation down.

Bill: But General Hudson brings up a good point Jim, what about the bombing of the Patriot Brigade Headquarters last month? People are looking at that as reason to support his claim that Alien-Americans are a threat.

Jim: First of all Bill, there is no evidence to suggest who destroyed that building or why. It's possible that they blew it up themselves just to increase paranoia.

Hudson: That's absurd.

Jim: And even if it is true that alien sympathizer extremist groups are beginning to form, that's just a response to the lack of inclusiveness in our society. Men like General Hudson just serve to create the very atmosphere that these groups feed off of. If we make the reforms I've suggested then these Alien-Americans will feel that they're part of human society and will feel no reason to rebel against it. Government positions that Alien-Americans are not allowed to serve in the armed forces or federal government just reinforce the stereotype that we are outsiders, which encourages separatist behavior. That may be what these 'Pleiadians' want. You're playing right into their hands General.

Bill: Now General, are we making more of a threat here then really exists. I mean, look at Jim here, he's a scrawny guy, I bet you could whip him in a fight. What's is there to be so scared about?

Hudson: Numbers Bill, numbers. Right now the number of HS victims is approximated at about a million and a half people in the US. But this number is growing. Every year more and more humans are infected with the HS virus, and the percentage of HS-positive births increases. HS births account for almost twenty-two percent of new pregnancies these days. If we don't develop a vaccine soon, we will be overwhelmed by these invaders. Other countries have been hit even harder. In India for example, almost forty percent of new births are HS-positive. As Vice President Johnston always said, we've got to nip this in the bud. The longer we wait, the more of them there will be and the harder it will be for humans to maintain control of governments and economies.

Bill (facing the audience): Ok, we've got to take a break, and then we'll be back with questions from callers. Jim, any comments before we go to break?

Jim: We need to make this message of inclusiveness global. This is a worldwide issue, and the U.S. government is just burying its head in the sand. I've got statistics here that are unbelievable. Did you know that only one out of ten Alien-Arabs reaches the age of five? In China the rate of infanticide is so high that the country's population is shrinking at almost two percent a year? In some African countries there are concentration camps that hold literally hundreds of thousands of Alien-Africans against their will in squalid, subhuman conditions. These are the Earth's children. The human race is exterminating itself.

Hudson: We are aware of the situation in other countries, but America can't be the world's policeman. We are working with these governments to develop strategies to combat population loss and to develop strategies to keep their economies intact. This is also why we are spending almost four billion dollars per year on scientific programs to develop a vaccine to the HS virus. Once the vaccine is perfected the global situation will normalize.

Jim: But General Hudson, what if they don't develop a vaccine in time?

Three weeks prior to Jim Miller's television debate. Charlottesville, VA

He is driving and he is crying. He is driving through the morning rain. It is a crummy morning, not a good morning at all. The sky is dark and rain is coming down. Not a drenching rain that comes down in sheets and washes away dirt and grime and makes the world clean. It's a weak, drizzly rain that is so pointless that it makes you wonder why it has bothered to rain in the first place. It is cold too. This fall has been exceptionally cold and wet and dreary. It adds to his depression and anger. It makes him not so upset really, in the end. It's all for a good cause after all. He is driving and he is thinking, thinking back to how warm it used to be, and comfortable it was in the enclave. Far away from the monkeys and the rats that were his tormentors in the orphanage. Far away from the life on the streets of Atlanta, scrounging an existence from theft and stealth. He thinks back to the enclave, thinks back to the leader, thinks back to his savior. He thinks back to the time he first heard of the Farm.

"Yo Joe, I'm telling you it's the truth," said the grubby kid that he lived with in a cardboard box on the outside edge of Five Corners.

"That can't be Emma. It's just a myth like Santa Claus. It's a good story for kids to believe, but I'm too old for that crap now." He wiggled under his torn, pink blanket as the two teens looked up at the Georgia stars.

"Jeez, you don't believe anything Joe, you're cold man."

"It's always paid off that way. You start believing in things then you start expecting them to get better, and then you get soft. That's when those monkey bastards come and get you. You're too much of a dreamer." He rolled over as a sign the conversation was about to end. Emma put her long fingers on the boy's shoulder and kept talking.

"Look, you didn't believe that's we'd ever escape from the orphanage, but we did. You didn't think that we could make it on our own, but we're still alive man. I'm telling you, this Farm place, it's our salvation."

"You believe what you like Emma, but you're dreaming. How the hell would one of us get a farm? It don't make sense. I'll tell you what, get back to me when you find out where this place is."

"That's just it Joe. I know where this place is. Or at least I will. I met this guy see, he's *from* the Farm. That's what he says anyway. He's got a meeting planned for tomorrow out in Grant Park. He's gonna give us maps man. It's starting!"

He remembered how joyous he felt when he learned that the Farm was real, that someone had somehow gotten hold of a real farm in the backwoods of Western Virginia. It was just for aliens. It was run by an alien. He remembered how he felt as he made his way across the byways of Southeastern America, meeting more people who were ready to follow the banner, ready to give up on monkey civilization and achieve their true destiny.

The windshield wipers scrape across the window of the van noisily. There wasn't enough rain for them to be properly lubricated, but enough so that vision was blurred without their use. He wipes the inside with a tissue to get rid of the fog, it just makes things streaky. He comes to the top of the appointed hill and stops the van. He checks his map again to be sure. He smiles nervously.

He thinks back again to the first time he met the leader, the savior, Franklin. He was so tall and majestic looking compared to the other aliens. He wore a white robe. He was so friendly and comforting. The first thing that Franklin did when he arrived was hug him and tell him, "Welcome home." No one had ever hugged him before. He cried back then as he is crying now. He thinks back to the time he spent on the Farm. How he learned his true destiny and he learned about his true parents. "They are coming for us. They haven't abandoned us," Franklin said. "We have to make the Earth ready for them. We are the spearhead. We'll present them with this world as a welcome gift." He thought about all of the great plans that Franklin had. He had an answer for everything. It all made sense. He felt his purpose. He was a true believer. He remembered the time when his destiny was revealed to him by Franklin himself.

"Now you understand Joe what I'm asking of you. It pains me to ask this of you, but remember, this whole thing here, it's bigger than all of us. And we all have a part to play in the great game. You understand that, don't you Joe? This is the first assault. The first step in a glorious war, a holy war against the monkeys that infest this planet. Will you accept this mission Joe?"

"Yes, Yes, a thousand times Yes!" he replied enthusiastically. He believed in the cause then as he believes in the cause now. He realized now he has always believed in the cause, even before he had ever been to the Farm. He understood his role in the great machine. He smiled from ear to ear as he stepped on the gas and crested the hill.

Below him was the main compound that was the heart of the enemy. He revved the engine and he came down the hillside. There was a gate, he knew that and he pushed the motor to go faster and faster, he had to break through, or else his sacrifice would be in vain. He must have been doing over a hundred when he passed the brown sign that said, 'Patriot Brigade, Headquarters Division.' He flinched a little as the van crashed through the wire fence that blocked the entrance. Calvin's words echoed in his ears, "You can't slow down Joe, they'll push the button to lift the car barriers, you've got to get past those before they can go up. He reached back and made sure that the detonator was armed, then he grabbed the wheel with both hands and headed directly toward the front door of the building. At the last second he looked up at the sky. "It's too bad it's cloudy," he thought, "I would have liked to see home one last time."

Six months after the Spearhead's first suicide bombing. Center for Handel's Syndrome Research, National Institutes of Health, Bethesda, MD

Lines of data are being tracked, pages are being turned, numbers are being counted. The lab is buzzing with activity on many fronts. Virologists study surface glycoproteins, geneticists study DNA binders, medical doctors study transport vectors. The lab is getting too big, too hard to manage, information is getting lost as more and more people are brought on board and different hands stop talking to one another. The Center for HS Research now takes up almost three-fourths of NIH's budget and it is being run more like a corporation than a research laboratory. Every section, every department believes that they are the key to solving the disease, that they are the most important segment of the program. They all demand more and more money, and since the project was given the rare status as a 'National Priority' the money flows freely. The President has said that the U.S. should work to cure HS in the same manner as we worked to get to the moon. It's full throttle.

In one small section of the Center are the epidemiologists. Their job is to track the propagation of the disease. They look at census data all day, examining which populations are the most vulnerable, and develop trends in the spread of the disease. All this is fed into the giant political machine to be used for budgets and planning, but the epidemiologists themselves don't receive much respect around the halls of the NIH. They aren't biologists after all, they aren't doctors after all. Very few of them have PhDs. But despite their status as second-class scientists, a breakthrough is about to occur.

It starts one day, as all days start, with the crunching of numbers and the development of models. Hal Sportman sits at his computer like he does every morning, entering numbers. He sits with his face up close to the screen on account of his bad eyes. He is running a program that uses historical data to develop trends. All of the information has been entered. Every case (statistically speaking) of HS has been added to the database. He hits the enter button to start the simulation. After a few seconds of whirring a map of the world appears on the screen, with everything in green. Green represents the human population. The date begins to move forward and red spots appear on the map. The red spots represent alien populations. As the date ticks forward and the computer processes the data in its database more and more of the world turns red. It reaches today's date, and almost one tenth of the globe is covered in the red stain. Then the simulation starts and the computer begins to divine the future based on what it knows of the past. The red blotches spread and slowly cover the world. The simulation shows that within seventy-five years, the human race will effectively be extinct.

Hal squints at the screen to check his model. There seems to be an error. There is still one small spot of green on the globe. Way out in the Pacific Ocean. He checks the map, it is the small island of Niue that remains green. There must be an error in the simulation, or a lucky accident of the Monte Carlo code. He runs it a second time, again Niue remains free of the red plague that engulfs the rest of the planet. He reaches across his desk and pulls out a very lengthy computer printout and begins scrolling through the data by hand to find the error. The process takes him hours. Hours of sitting and making little marks with his red pencil against the giant accordion of paper. But the work pays off, he finds something. His model isn't defective.

That afternoon, his numbers checked and rechecked, he enters the office of Dr. Nancy Collins to give her the news.

"Dr. Collins, I've found something important," he says, bursting in through the closed door. She is meeting with some vendors who want to supply new reagents. They are not pleased with the interruption. "I've found an immune population." He drops the large printout on her desk.

"What are you talking about? Who are you?" she says. She remembers a day not long ago when she knew all of the people on the HS project. Now it is rare that she recognizes the people who greet her as she walks the halls.

Hal spoke very hastily, a characteristic that most people found annoying. "Hal Sportman, I'm an epidemiologist. I was doing some simulations to show how the number of cases of HS will increase over time, but the model is based on the number of current cases, you see, the number of current cases, that's where the simulation failed, because there has never been a case of HS on Niue, so a multiple of zero is still zero, there has never been a case on Niue do you see?" he said in one breath.

"Huh?"

"Ok, ok," he said trying to catch his breath and contain his excitement. He slowed down and tried to speak more clearly. "I've got a statistical model that references our database of all known cases of HS. I've just noticed that there has never been a case on Niue Island. That implies that the native population has some sort of resistance or something because it doesn't make sense otherwise."

"Niue, I don't even know where that is. There can't be many people there, maybe they're just lucky."

"No, no, they can't be that lucky. Global HS infection rates are near ten percent. With their population they should have at least two hundred cases, but they have zero. And it's not just missing data, they've been reporting zeros. I've done some research, and they are a pretty isolated population, maybe they've got some sort of genetic resistance or something."

Nancy looked at his map and stared at the small green dot. It would make sense that some population was immune. One of the great frustrations with the HS research was that no immune population had yet been found, the virus was too universal. If an immune population could be found and studied, a vaccine could be developed based on the immunity factor. "We've got to get this information to Dr. Mensen right away," she said. "You call the CDC and confirm these numbers, I'll take this up the chain ASAP." She turned to the vendors, "I'm sorry gentleman, I've got to go." The vendors frown in disappointment.

Two weeks after Hal Sportman's discovery. On a deserted street in Muscat, Oman

Wind is blowing. It is a hot wind that comes south from the Rub al Kaliq. It is a dry wind. Autumn has arrived in this desolate place, and what few leaves there are have scattered themselves through the streets. A figure is walking down a deserted road. The figure is wearing the black burqa veil required of all women in this Muslim nation. The street is empty as the figure moves silently past whorls of leaves and paper. It floats rather than moves, its legs are covered in thick wrapping, leaving the impression of sliding rather than walking. The figure stops only once in its travels. It pauses to look at a wall covered in graffiti. It is Arabic, of course, but when translated the words ominously cry out, "They Are Coming!" The figure continues down the deserted avenue. There are very few people left in Oman these days. Birth rates have dwindled to almost zero and the majority of infants bearing the so-called "Face of the Devil" are left to die in the trash. There is no one left to perform basic services, and so a good percentage of the remaining population has left to find greener pastures in other parts of the Middle-East.

There are a few who stayed of course. Those too infirm or scared to leave, the religious police, opportunists and speculators. Parts of the city aren't as deserted as this. A few places still have some modicum of a normal life. Women still peruse the shops of the souk, men still gather in the coffee houses to chew qat and boast of their accomplishments. Few travel here though. This is the Rub al Jardon, where the demi-men live in hiding and scrabble an existence from what they can steal.

With a quick glance to ensure privacy, the figure moves into an alley of bleached stone. A rotted wooden door stands at the entrance to a small basement. Further down the alley a pile of garbage stirs. Through the veil the figure can see the masked man who waits and guards. After a nod, the figure enters the door stealthily and proceeds down a dusty, unlit corridor to a large room. The figure removes his veil and allows his bright head to shine in the dim lighting. This is one of the few places where he can be himself. The crowd sits on ornate yet ratty rugs strewn across the dirt floor. They take up every available inch of space. Their bare feet rubbing up against the qat leaves that have been scattered about for their pleasure. No one is chewing though. They are all listening. Listening to one man; the stranger, the leader, the one who walks taller than most. The one known as Trinity. He wears a dark blue robe emblazoned with three white stars. He is speaking.

"Brothers do not be taken in by the lies that these monkeys have told you all your lives. They call you rats, they call you devils. Yet you listen to them. You hide in the shadows, hide under veils, you let them beat and murder you. You must not do this. You must reclaim your heritage. You must reclaim your birthright. You must reclaim your destiny. Brothers, I was once like you. I was afraid, I was told that I was inferior, that I was a freak, that I was a mistake, that I was a pathetic wretch who had no choice but to beg God, the monkey god, for mercy. I hid my head in shame. But no longer my brothers! I have seen the light, and it burns ever so brightly. I saw the light in a glow of fire. I have walked through fire. I have seen my compatriots, by brothers, killed by the hundreds just because they had the audacity to be alive. I ran from the monkeys, I hid from the monkeys. I spent a long time just like you, here in the lightless places, cold and alone in the dirt." He reached down and picked up a handful of dirt, letting it slowly slip through his fingers.

"But I had a revelation my brothers. For so long I tried to be like them, to be a pale imitation of them, accepting of my lot as a second-class citizen. But I say I had a revelation! Yes, I saw my god. And my god isn't the monkey god, he doesn't call himself Allah or Yahweh. No, my god is real, and he comes from the stars, the Pleiades to be certain. Yes, and he speaks. We all heard his words four years ago. He said, "We Are Coming!" Yes my brothers, our father is returning to reclaim us. No longer will we live like this. We are part of a great galactic civilization that exists on a thousand worlds. Worlds of peace and beauty and unity. Worlds where we can live unashamed of who we are and what we represent. This is why the monkeys hate us. We threaten them, we are more powerful than they are. I know this sounds absurd to people like you who've lived in filth all your lives, but I tell you it's true. We will overcome and we will prevail!" A muted shout comes over the audience. The crowd has never heard anyone like this before. He represents strength, and self-pride, and purpose. He represents what they all lack– a sense of value.

"My revelation in the swamp guided me and I have since traveled the world to spread the message. I left the United States where we are nothing more than research subjects in prison hospitals. I traveled through Europe where the first of us was so brutally murdered. I traveled through Asia where we, who should be kings, beg in the streets like dogs. I traveled through the concentration camps of Africa, where thousands die of disease and starvation. Now I have come here, to a place where very few of my kind are even allowed to live. You are all lucky in a way to have survived this long. It is unfortunate that people so young as you have seen so much death."

"But that changes and that changes today. We are the Spearhead. We are here to provide the beach. Our fathers are coming to reclaim us, and we shall give them the Earth as a present. We shall beat these monkeys. We shall overcome our adversity. We shall wipe our oppressors off the face of this globe and erase all knowledge of their petty and simple civilization."

"You must stop worshiping these monkey gods and stop pretending to be monkeys. This only demeans you. You must stand up for your rights. From now on we take back what is ours. My associates will provide you with weapons and training, the means to defend yourselves. When the monkeys kill one of you, you kill two of them. When they murder a child, you execute the parents. We shall overcome. Their numbers are dwindling while we increase in strength every day. We shall prevail. Now is the time to fight. The jihad against the monkeys and their oppression begins today. We will win because right is on our side, our fathers are on our side, and because God himself is on our side!"

The crowd was unsure how to react. They liked what Trinity had to say, but they didn't trust their abilities. This wasn't a surprise to the Spearhead of course. As much as every person in the room hated the monkeys that had abandoned and hated them, and even though everyone knew someone who had been killed because of his species, they still maintained the mentality of the slave. Franklin had to prove to them they were not slaves but masters, that they had the power to change their destiny. Only then would they follow his banner with the fervor he needed of them.

"Now brothers, let me show you how powerful we really are." He pointed to a back room. Two of his bodyguards, rifles slung over their shoulders, disappeared into the darkness, appearing seconds later with a scared and disheveled looking human. He had been badly beaten. One eye was swelled shut and his shirt was stained rusty-brown with blood. The two bodyguards pushed the man to his knees before Franklin. He was hard to recognize since his head and beard had been shaved. His hands were tied behind his back. The crowd watched with eyes wide open. "This is Tarek ibn-Sanaa." He is the local leader of the religious police. "He is the one who has given orders to cut you down on sight. He is the leader of the monkeys in this area. He is our hated enemy. Let him be the first sacrifice to our new era!" He pulled a long, curved dagger from his vestments. A bodyguard grabbed the man's jaw and pulled his head back. "The Spearhead now makes the first gift of blood to our fathers." He slashed the man's throat from ear to ear. The lifeless corpse collapsed to the dusty floor. "Now who will fight in my jihad?"

Slowly, one by one, and hesitantly at first, the converts stepped forward and crowded around the body. The first few began to poke at it, still scared that somehow it might be dangerous. It did not stir. Franklin looked at his two guards with apprehension. The reaction of the crowd would determine whether he had won them over to his cause.

A young man of about twelve was the first. He leaned over the corpse and spit. Soon the rest were doing the same. A cheer of joy came over the group as they began to kick the body and beat it with their shoes.

Niue, South Pacific. Eight months after Hal Sportman's discovery.

A stiff breeze is blowing. A stiff breeze always blows here. It's the trade winds. A constant, non-ending flow of air that covers the island from North-West to South-East. It makes it hard to work on the beach, papers fly everywhere. There is even a dearth of rocks to keep things weighted down. Nancy sits on the front porch of what could only sympathetically be called a shack. It is a wooden hut really, but it serves her purposes, at least for now. She sits behind a table sipping from her water bottle. Below her on the sand is a makeshift clinic. About a dozen native fishermen stand in line waiting for their turn to give blood. Two local nurses, impeccably yet most incongruently dressed, are taking samples in little vials and marking them. Nancy is supervising. It isn't as hot as she expected it to be here, and the wind could be pleasant if it stopped once in a while. There is a hand at her shoulder. She turns her head to see her research associate standing behind her. "Hey Frank."

The man plops himself down in the seat next to her and passes her a bag covered with the appropriate corporate logos. "Burger and onion rings, just like you asked."

"I can't believe that you have to drive almost an hour to get food around here." The two open their paper bags and begin squirting the contents of small ketchup packages. "I didn't even think that this island was that big."

"It's not," Frank says with half-mocked cynicism. "But you're lucky if you can get up to 30 miles an hour on these roads, and that's with the 4-wheeler."

"I can't believe that I've been here for four months. I want to get back to civilization."

"That's only because you spend all of your time out here on the east side. You should hang out more at Alofi. It's getting really exciting. They've almost finished the main complex." Just then a large cargo plane flies overhead. They used to be so unusual out here. This place only had one flight a week, and that's if it even bothered to show up. Now cargo is being shipped in ten times a day. The U.S. Army Corps of Engineers had to expand the runway twice already.

"I still can't believe that we're out here. Couldn't we have found an immune population in LA or Paris? How come every time Mensen needs something from a god-forsaken place, I'm the one who's got to go?"

"Oh stop complaining. He'll be here soon enough. The facility is supposed to be operational in two months. Then they're all coming. And we'll be here for a while too."

"You don't think that we're going to find anything?"

Frank coughed and took a sip of his warm soda. Food was so far away from their location that they had long gotten used to eating cold meals with warm drinks. "Come on, you know how science works. You can't just throw money at the problem. Things take time. Even if we isolated the gene factor tomorrow we're still looking at five years of work to develop a vaccine."

Nancy crumpled up her wrappers and looked for a trashcan. She always felt bad throwing away things out here. There wasn't really any trash collection. "Yeah, but maybe...," she said getting up and returning to the hut, "...once we've got something concrete, we'll do the rest of the work back in the U.S."

"Ha ha, after the UN spent a billion dollars building the 'world's most impressive biotechnology research facility' all the way out here? It ain't going to happen honey. We're here for the long haul. All of us." He moved his fingers in a 'quote' motion when he talked about the facility. It was a giant project that dwarfed the NIH. The idea was that all HS research would be moved to the island. It was voted in the UN to make the HS-vaccine project a World Priority, and all nations were required to do their part. Of course, some industrialized countries offered to build the facility on their soil, but smaller nations were worried that the research would be politicized or withheld by their richer neighbors. After much debate in the Security Council, it was decided to build the facility here, out in the Pacific. It was remote, but it wouldn't be too hard to ship the technology in. With the large population of resistant individuals to use as test subjects, the island provided researchers with opportunities not available elsewhere. Of course being a small, independent country didn't hurt either. For their part, the islanders were grateful for the attention. It meant money and opportunities that hadn't existed before. Within months they would have reliable power, they would have paved roads, they would have malls and stores that would cater to the seven thousand scientists that were recruited to move to this desolate place. All of the top biologists in the world were coming. This program was fast becoming more high profile than the U.S. space program had been in the 1960s. Older, established scientists were drawn by grant money that flowed like water, and the opportunity to rapidly make a name for oneself pulled in the younger researchers eager for their Nobel Prize.

As Nancy stepped back out of the hut she saw two native men walking up to the porch. In their hands they carried necklaces with ornate wooden pendants attached. They presented the necklaces to the two researchers, going so far as to actually place the strands over their head. "These are for you, they are good luck charms. You are going to save the world," one said. They smiled ear to ear revealing mouths of half-rotten teeth.

"ummm. Thanks," Nancy said with a quizzical half-smile on her face. She turned to Frank. He just shrugged and tried to suppress a giggle.

Three days after the UN HS-Vaccine Research Center formally began operations. Area 51, NV

There are layers to all organization. There are levels within levels. There are meanings within meanings and purposes within purposes. Very few people are allowed access to the most inner circles. There are dozens of programs that only a handful of people have access to, and access to one doesn't mean you are allowed to even find out that others exist. This place is the headquarters of one of those programs.

A helicopter is landing. A man dressed in army fatigues guides it down to the pad. It is black, no markings at all, not the U.S. Army white star, not the organization's name, not even the required FAA call number. This helicopter doesn't exist. Its purpose is to bring people who will deny having been to a place that doesn't exist. Not even America's rivals know about this facility. It was built in the side of a mesa decades ago when those who plotted here had different enemies. Before the helicopter blades even come to a complete stop, General Hudson, looking strangely out of fashion in non-descript civilian clothes and mirrored sunglasses steps out. A jeep is waiting, motor already running. It is almost an hour drive to the facility. The landing pad is placed far enough away from the mesa to not arouse the suspicions of anyone who might see helicopters landing in this remote corner of Nevada. He gets into the jeep followed by two other non-descript men. The vehicle drives off in the direction of what everyone assumes to be an old test-shot hole dug by the military before underground nuclear testing became politically taboo. The helicopter pilot sits in his seat and swigs some water before taking off again. He watches the dust trail as the jeep moves over the unpaved surface of the salt flat. He wonders where these people go.

He doesn't know. He doesn't have the clearance to know. Not even Johnston had the clearance to know. He never suspected what was out here in the desert. Even when he was Vice President he was kept in the dark. Of course, this place was never a part of Bluefly, Majestik-12 or Beachcomber. It was designed with the Soviets in mind. The research of Project 'Zephyr-Alpha' is a very well-kept secret.

Dominic Peloso

White House Rose Garden. Seven years to the day after Jim's speech on the Capitol steps.

"...and I am proud to stand here today, surrounded by the next generation of Americans. The people who will lead the way into the future. The protectors of our legacy. No matter what the future brings, I know that our values, the core of what makes us American, will live on. And as a father myself, that's all I can ask for." The President gives a wave to the crowd of reporters.

"This way Mr. President." A press aide takes him by the shoulder and guides him over to the ornate wood table that has been brought out onto the dais. He sits in a cushy chair and examines the bill one last time. To his right are twelve gold-plated pens, one for each letter in his name. As photographers snap pictures he picks up the first pen and makes an 'A then a second 'a' with the second pen, and so on until his entire name, Aaron H. Talbot, is spelled out. He hates the way they make him sign these things. It looks like a child wrote it. It's for posterity and he can't sign his name properly because he has to create as many commemorative pens as he can to give out to supporters. "They're probably mad that they didn't elect someone with a longer name," he thinks as he crosses the last 't.' Once his arduous task is complete, he stands and shakes hands with the little man beside him. Alien skin is rather moist and slippery feeling, like a dolphin, and he has never really liked to touch them. The alien's fingers are too long for a proper handshake, they curl around his wrist and make him feel like he's shaking hands with a bony squid. But he would learn to live with it. It was just one of those things that a person has to get used to.

After the obligatory picture taking, the alien drops the President's hand and moves the podium. Unlike the first

268

time he spoke in Washington seven years ago, he is wearing an expensive and stylish suit created just for him by a known fashion designer. With no hair to speak of, his prep time for the cameras was kept to a minimum, but he still had grayish powder dabbed all over his face to look more presentable on television. He didn't argue too much, the makeup artists knew what they were doing. They had even brought in a special Alien-American makeup artist who normally worked in Hollywood painting up the handful of alien stars who were on TV sitcoms.

He looked out over the crowd and smiled broadly. The audience was mixed, with several Alien-American journalists crowded in among the throng of people that had come here to see the signing ceremony. "The amount of attention being paid here today is what I'm the most thankful for," he began. "It shows that my work these past seven years has not been unnoticed. Today is the culmination of my dream. It is a dream that many others have had. A dream that all people who come to America have– to be free. Just like the struggles of the Africans to sit at the front of the bus, the struggles of the feminists to guarantee women the vote, and the struggles of the homosexuals to be free to express their love without fear of reprisal, I too have dreamed of freedom. Seven years ago when I started JHADS I couldn't walk the streets among you. I couldn't go to restaurants and be served a meal. Even if I hadn't been so young, I wouldn't have been allowed to vote. But things have changed. I have followed the path of my predecessors like the Reverend Bentley, and I fought for what I believe in– Equality. Here today, with President Talbot's help, I think that we have achieved it. The bill being signed into law today prevents discrimination on the basis of genetic factors. It will allow people like myself to be employed by the federal government, to be allowed to fight in the military, to be allowed to rent an apartment or apply for a job without fear of discrimination. And once and for all it closes the remaining Johnston Orphanages that kept us as virtual prisoners in the name of scientific research."

"I would like to thank my Alien-American brothers for all the work they've done to bring this about. I can understand how humans might fear us, how they might not trust us. I credit each and every one of you for standing up and showing that you are just as red-blooded, just as normal, just as... American as everyone else in this country. That is what has turned the tide in our favor and made those who feared the unknown learn to cherish this new resource. And while we still maintain hope that a cure to this virus will be found, we, the Alien-American community, stand ready to take up the guard from our fathers and keep the values of America strong!" The crowd cheered.

"But this is not the end of our struggle. There are still those groups in America that hate us for the color of our skin and the length of our fingers. Even worse is the treatment we receive in other parts of the world. The infanticide and murder of innocent alien children is leading to a noticeable decline in world population. In many places we do not have the right to vote or even to be seen outside! In other places we are routinely rounded up and placed in what can only be called concentration camps. This must end! The U.S. must put pressure on the UN to force an end of these human rights abuses. None of us will be free until we are all free! So let's celebrate this victory today and redouble or efforts towards building a better tomorrow. A tomorrow where all people, human and alien, can live together in peace and harmony. Thank you."

Jim stepped off the stage to allow the next speaker to talk. He walked backstage to a rousing congratulations by some of the staffers who had worked on the bill. Someone handed him an ornate wooden box tied with a ribbon. Inside was an expensive looking gold-plated pen.

UN HS-Vaccine Research Center, Republic of Niue. Three months after James Miller's Rose Garden Speech.

"Is Stacy going to be all right?" The young alien was quite concerned. He wasn't used to this much attention. For him, attention usually meant criticism. If someone was watching him closely he must have done something wrong.

"Everything is going to be just fine Mr. Lawson, they're just prepping her. There's nothing you can do right now. Let's take a walk in the courtyard, it'll steady your nerves," replied Nancy.

The two walked out of the main hospital complex into the inner courtyard. The Project facility had been built much more ornately than it really needed to be, partially because they had to keep the researchers, who tended to be much more testy than regular people, happy out here in the middle of the Pacific; and partially because with such a high profile, the designers wanted to primp and preen as much as possible. With time being more of an issue than money, the Project administrators often had plenty of cash left for aesthetics.

"I didn't mean for this to happen you know. I really didn't," he was still a bit embarrassed by the incident.

"I know Mr. Lawson, it's ok, we're not here to judge you. Actually," she leaned in, "...as far as we're concerned here on the island, we're very glad this happened. We've been waiting for an opportunity like this for a long time."

The two sat on a bench under a palm tree. Various men and women in white lab coats scurried back and forth along the stone paths. Some carried samples, others carried packets of papers, some just wandered aimlessly, lost in thought. A brightly plumed bird flew overhead. "Who would have thought," said the boy, "that I'd ever be in a place like this. I mean I've never been outside London before you know. And now here I am on a tropical island halfway around the world."

"Yes, this place does grow on you after a while." In the courtyard, the stiff breeze was blocked and the warm, sunny air just made you feel happy.

"And I mean, you know, it's all for a shag. I thought that my parents were going to hit the roof you know? I mean, I'm only 16. Stacy's a year younger. Oh god, I was so embarrassed when I found out that we'd be the first, I mean, who wants that kind of publicity you know?" He spoke rapidly and nervously. He was wringing his hand together over and over. Nancy's cell phone rang.

"Hello?" Benji Lawson couldn't hear the voice on the other end of the line, but he knew what the call meant. It was beginning.

Meanwhile, in the gallery above the main operating room, Dr. Mensen and many of the department heads sat speculating about the upcoming event. Sonograms had given an indication, but you can't really tell a lot, and of course x-rays were out of the question. On the operating table lay a young alien woman. It was still hard to judge their ages, since none were over thirty, but something about her looked quite young. The large distended stomach was quite out of place. She was conscious and in some pain. They had given her the standard painkillers of course, but most drugs developed for humans had reduced effects on the alien metabolism. A section of the research staff here was busily developing new drugs targeted to alien populations, but that work was years from completion. Three of the best obstetricians in the world had been flown in for this procedure. No one knew what was going to happen here. As far as anyone could tell, this sort of birth had never occurred before. Complications would be inevitable.

"Remember Paul, we have $20 riding on this," said Dr. Mensen.

"And you're going to lose you old kook. I'm telling you, as Chief Virologist, I can almost guarantee that the HS virus doesn't do its entire job in one stage. There's no way a virus could have that much effect on genomic DNA. The child of an alien-alien mix is going to be some sort of different alien."

"But there was no difference when the first human-alien mix occurred last year," replied Dr. Malcolm, who ran the Microbiology department.

Dr. Mensen cut him off, "Shut up Hans, I'll fight my own battles." "As for you Paul, you seem to keep forgetting the fact that the aliens pulled from the Roswell wreck have the same genetic markers as the first generation HS kids. There's no reason to assume that the second generation kids won't have the same genes."

Dr. Helena Raskolnikova broke in, "I'm just surprised that these HS kids aren't all sterile. Hybrids are almost always sterile. In my department we have no idea how these kids even conceived." Helena was a former VECTOR scientist who now ran the reproductive technologies laboratory.

The girl on the table screamed in labor-induced pain. The obstetricians were trying their best, but were working in very unfamiliar territory.

Dr. Mensen responded. "Well, I for one am glad that they aren't sterile Helena. It means that life will go on. That our legacy will continue. Maybe in a different form, but the sentient population of this planet won't die out in the next fifty years."

"I wish I shared your enthusiasm Heinrich," said Dr. Paul Willard. "I don't think that our legacy is going anywhere. What's going to happen when these aliens show up like they promised? Those kids are going to have to fight to protect our memory, and why should they care about us? They're not like us at all."

"I'm not so sure about that Paul."

Dr. Malcolm got everyone's attention. "Well, either way folks, the future is coming right now!" he pointed to the scene below. The doctor had just cut the umbilical cord and held the sticky child up by its legs. A soft pat on the behind and a cry echoed through the operating room.

Russia, in a place that doesn't officially exist, near the border with Kazakhstan.

Snow is falling. This place used to be bustling with activity. It used to be bristling with guards, but no more. Now it is decaying, decrepit, and lonely. The fences, once ominous and foreboding, have mostly fallen down. The hundreds of guards that tended the gates have been reduced to a mere dozen people. One tramps through the knee-deep snow around the backside of the facility. The Russian government still denies their alien citizens the opportunity to serve in the armed forces. "It's too much of a risk," said a member of the Duma recently, "We don't know where their loyalties lie." So, the military dwindled as the percentage of alien births increased. There are very few eighteen year-old humans left to recruit, and even with stringent drafts, not a single unit has been able to maintain full strength for some time. With growing international cooperation in the face of a possible extraterrestrial threat, much of the mission that the troops had during the Soviet days has disappeared. Money has gone elsewhere, units have been stationed elsewhere. And here, out in southern Siberia, the depot lies almost forgotten– a relic of a war that never happened.

It isn't totally forgotten. The men that work here certainly remember. The villagers in the town several miles away sit by their fires and curse the Muscovites for taking away their source of jobs. A lone figure approaches the front gate by foot, clad head to toe in a thick fur coat. It is cold out here, and winter is coming. The figure approaches the front gate where a bored soldier waits inside the guard shack. Guarding this gate is all that he has ever known. He's been doing the job for almost fifteen years now. The way the system works out here, no one gets promoted, no one gets new assignments. Some months he doesn't even get paid. Of course he makes ends meet with some odd jobs in town. Scraping and saving for the day when he can move his family out of this god-forsaken wasteland and to someplace more vibrant, someplace where life still exists. He smiles sleepily as the figure passes through the gate unmolested. Today is his last day on the job.

The figure, not even five feet in height, is carrying two bags with him. As he ducks under the gate he quietly lays the larger, fuller bag on the stoop of the guardhouse. He then proceeds inside. The buildings here are all made of metal sheeting. It's just a storage facility after all. No one really lives here. The figure passes two guards huddling around a fire burning in an old oil drum. They should be patrolling thc grounds as well, but it is cold, and they have patrolled the grounds here for many years without seeing anything more suspicious than some errant deer and curious village children hoping to catch a glimpse of a tank. They don't even look up as the lone figure slides past them. They don't really care. All morning they have been discussing where they will go tomorrow. One intends to get to America, although he doesn't know how. The other is heading towards the oil fields of the Caspian, where there is work and opportunity. Today is their last day at the base.

The figure knows exactly were to go. He has been given a map. The signs are all in Russian, but he can tell the building he needs to visit just by looking at it. There is a second guard shack, and a double-fenced perimeter surrounding it. There are security devices all along the fence that in days long ago used to detect intruders by the vibrations of their footsteps, but they no longer work. There are security cameras that perpetually scan the front gate, but the tapes broke long ago, and no fresh ones have been sent from the supply depot, even though multiple requests have been made. The three guards that should be protecting this final barrier are inside playing cards. They don't even see the slim man walk past. They are busy gambling away their fortunes, making bets that are far larger than their monthly salaries. They laugh heartily when they lose, knowing that there is plenty more.

Not ten minutes after entering the main storage facility, the figure returns to view. This time, the empty bag is full. Something heavy is inside, and the small man has a hard time carrying it. None of the guards help though. That would be wrong somehow. Plus it would involve doing work, which they all despise. Somehow the little man manages and is soon passing the front gate and headed back towards the town where his compatriots await him. He notices that the bag he left on the stoop is now gone. It is inside with the first guard, who is busy rubbing the contents all over his face. He has never in his life seen this much money before. He wonders to himself if he must share it with his co-workers, or if he can skim some from the top before they arrive to collect their cuts. He laughs out loud.

A few hours after the Alien-American Rights Act was signed. The White House, Washington, DC

Jim was sitting by the secretary's desk just outside of the Oval Office. He was actually sitting in the same chair that Ray Johnston once sat in many years ago, although he had no way of knowing that. The alien had been sitting there for some time. He had examined his commemorative pen as much as one possibly could, he had sampled two candies from the jar on the secretary's desk, and he had paged through the pile of last month's magazines. Several men in business suits walked rapidly through the antechamber, and occasionally someone would stick a head out of the door and ask the secretary for something or other. Every time Jim heard the latch turn, a level of excitement pushed itself up into his throat. He had been told by the Press Secretary to come to a private meeting with the President after the signing, but he had found himself rather unceremoniously dumped in the waiting room.

Jim risked a short call to his office. He wasn't sure that he should be making long-distance calls without permission, but he figured that no one would really care and he didn't want to seem like a rube for asking the secretary. He phoned the main office of the JHADS in Dallas and spoke to Jordan who was holding down the fort while Jim was in DC. Jim really didn't have any specific reason for calling, but being on the phone made him feel less awkward and out of place than just sitting there.

Almost forty-five minutes after being asked to wait, the door finally opened and a whole gaggle of people rushed noisily out into the hallway. The Press Secretary waved him in, and Jim followed. Inside sat President Talbot, who was on the phone. The Secretary guided Jim to a chair opposite the President's ornate wooden desk and then closed the door. The President hung up the phone, stood up, and then extended his hand to the young alien.

"Jim Miller, glad to finally meet you, I apologize for keeping you so long." Despite the nice words that President Talbot had said about Jim a few hours ago, and the handshake they had performed for the cameras, the two had never met before. Jim had been guided to the ceremony by staffers, and only got to see the President for the first time when he stepped onto the dais and shook Jim's hand like they were old friends.

"That's ok Mr. President. I know that you've got a lot of important stuff to deal with, Alien-American rights is only one small issue."

The President sat back down in his chair. "Yes, one small issue. You're right, you're absolutely right. I told you Phil, this guy's on the ball." The Press Secretary nodded in acknowledgement. "That's why I wanted to talk to you see. This is an issue, it's a big issue, it's an important issue, but you're absolutely right, I can only spend a small part of my time dealing with it. That's why I told Phil here to send you on over after the ceremony. Isn't that right Phil?" The Press Secretary, who was standing uncomfortably close behind Jim once again nodded.

"Now, Jim, I can call you Jim right? This here act that we've just passed today, well it's revolutionary, in fact, it's more than revolutionary, we're talking a whole new paradigm here, but hell I don't have to tell you that, you practically wrote the thing didn't you?"

Jim tried to choke out an answer, but the President spoke so fast that Jim was mentally still trying to answer the question about his name. He opened his mouth, but it didn't matter, the President had already moved on. "Now this bill is going to call for a new executive branch agency to deal with these human-alien issues. That's the part where you come in. I've discussed this with my staff and we all feel that you would be the best person to handle this task. We're talking cabinet post here, Secretary of Alien Affairs. That's a great title isn't it? Don't like it? We'll change it, it's up to you."

"Well, this is a great honor sir, I'm not sure that I'm up to the..." Jim was cut off.

"Sure you are son, hell, you've been a thorn in the side of the federal government going on seven years now. If you can be that much of a pain in the ass from the outside, think of how much you can do from the inside. That's why I want you on my team son. You see, I figure that group of yours is going to be criticizing the hell out of this new Secretary now matter what he does. I'm going to deflect that by putting you in charge. Brilliant huh? You'll have to deal with the pro-alien lobby, you'll have to deal with the anti-alien lobby. You'll have to give input on our foreign relations, that sort of thing. Hell, I don't have to tell you. You get the picture. You probably know what you need to do even better than me, I've never even read that thing I signed this morning. No time you know? So how about it, do we have a deal?" He leaned back over the table and stuck out his hand.

Jim was stupefied by the offer. For the last ten years, he had been an outsider, someone who fought against government policies. To now become part of that government was something he had never considered. While waiting he had been thinking that the President wanted his advice on how to interpret the new Act, he didn't imagine that he was going to be offered a cabinet position. He struggled to put forth an intelligent sounding answer. "Mr. President, I'd be honored to help you in your efforts to..." Again the President cut him off.

"Great great great. That's exactly what I wanted to hear. Have a cigar," he opened a cedar box on his desk and handed a giant cigar to the alien. "Phil, you know what to do, go!"

"I've got the press release right here," he held up a piece of paper and then rushed out of the room.

"This is one hell of a day ain't it? Welcome to the team son." The phone on the President's desk rang. "I got to answer that, we'll talk later." A staffer walked over to Jim and helped him out of the chair. The two walked towards the exit. As the staffer opened the door to let Jim out, the President shouted, "Hey Jim!" He covered the receiver with his hand. "Of course, anything you can do to help with this re-election campaign would be greatly appreciated. Give me some ideas." He then went back to his conversation.

Jim found himself on the other side of the door as it slammed behind him. The secretary turned from her book and gave him a dirty look that said, 'I hope you don't need anything else.' Jim wasn't sure what he needed. He just stood in the hallway, cigar-in-mouth, dumbfounded. He had no idea what to do next.

Presidential Palace, Abidjan, Cote d'Ivorie, four months after James Miller became the first Secretary of Alien-American Affairs.

The sound of gunfire is in the air, but not the gunfire of war, the gunfire of celebration. Armed troops run through the streets of the capital. Cheers sound from their throats and they wave their weapons wildly over their heads. The populace runs through the streets as well, cheering their liberators, their brothers. Not the entire population of course, just the aliens, just the young. The human inhabitants of this town are either hiding in their cellars or have fled, taking what they could carry. Of course, even those are the lucky ones, the vast majority of the humans in this part of Africa now lie in makeshift graves or strewn across bloody battlefields and muddied streets. The revolution has come.

A faceless soldier scrawls a symbol on the wall of the Presidential Palace in blue spray paint. It is a simple symbol, three stars, arranged in a linear pattern. It is a representation of the Pliedian Cluster, not a particularly accurate representation mind you, but it will suffice for this day. Other soldiers rampage and loot abandoned store fronts looking for food or salable items. Some of these fighters were liberated from concentration camps only a few days ago. They had spent the entirety of their short lives behind rusty barbed wire. Spearhead guerilla units had been storming barracks and murdering guards around Africa for several months now. Most of those liberated from the camps were too weak or meek to fend for themselves, but a few took up the flag of the New Order. In each place the Pliedian army gained more warriors. It grew bolder and stronger and more experienced, until they were ready to unleash the coordinated master stroke. As if on cue, they transformed from a rag-tag bunch of rebels into a ten million man army overnight.

Several dead bodies lie unburied in the main courtyard of the Presidential Palace. Their blood has congealed and separated into a yellow ooze in the main driveway. Eventually they will be disposed of, but not now. Now is the time for celebrating, the revolution has come.

A van with a satellite uplink on its roof is waved past the guard post. International news agencies have been rushing to this area looking for official statements and dramatic footage for the evening broadcasts. On this day, eighteen African countries have erupted into flames. Coup attempts by the oppressed alien populations have occurred almost simultaneously. Countries in the Middle East and South America have also experienced similar events. Most European countries have experienced bombings and other guerrilla attacks in the past twenty-four hours. Rioting masses of aliens have stormed the parliament buildings of several dozen countries. Their success has been varied. In some places they are in full control, in others they have been beaten back. The battle for power still rages in hundreds of places around the globe. Worldwide communication lines have been cut, making detailed reports from many locations spotty at best.

A cameraman exits the news truck and is guided at gunpoint past the dead bodies into the main foyer of the palace. He tries to film as he walks, but the guards discourage him. Up the stairs and to the left is what used to be the office of the President. As the cameraman enters he is shocked to see the order that exists here. In a way directly opposite to the chaos and revelry of the streets, the people here, leaders of the coup, plan and plot with cell phones, satellite maps, and modern computers. Clearly these are not the same people as the main fighting force, which composed mostly of refugees and villagers.

Through the double doors the cameraman is guided to the private office. There are only three people in here. One alien, taller than the rest and arguably noble in appearance, sits behind the main desk, which would be comically too big for him if the situation wasn't so dire as to make laughter impossible. He glances at another alien who checks his watch and nods. The leader turns to the cameraman. "Are you ready to go? Is that on? Can you get a live feed? We need a live feed, trust us, the effect will be much better if there is a live feed."

The cameraman nods. He is the lucky one, if you consider this luck. While revolution is occurring in many places, this is the heart, this is the center. There are a lot of journalists who would kill to have this opportunity. Of course, once actually here, most would kill just to get as far away from this place as possible.

"Ok, are you ready? Give me a signal." The cameraman switches on and presents a shaky thumbs up. A red light begins to blink just above the lens.

"Greetings. My name is Franklin Trinity, and I am the leader of the Pliedian Spearhead. As you may know by now we have just stepped up our operations. While before we were content with random hit and run tactics and some symbolic gestures, we now have the manpower required to make our presence known on a more... global basis. Humans, your time on this planet has ended. We are now in control. Today, the Spearhead has smashed the governments of almost a dozen countries. In the next few days we will begin attacks on a dozen more. I call on all Pliedians to follow my banner, to join in the cause to liberate yourselves from the domination of these doomed apes. To the remnants of the human race, I warn you that today is *our* day, now is *our* time. Your oppression of my species is over. We are your enemy. We are here to prepare the way for the day when our true parents come and guide us to our destiny in the stars. You can't stop us, every day we grow stronger. Even by your own estimates, eighty percent of all births are now of our race. Our numbers grow as yours weaken. This war is over before it has even begun. Today, we drive the final nail in the coffin of your species' evolution. Not with bullets, but with the sword of your own creation. Now is the time to reap what you have sown. Today, your final chance for salvation dies in a brilliant white fire. There is no hope left."

Franklin stared into the camera with the disconcerting eyes of a zealot as Enoch reached behind the cameraman and switched off the feed.

That moment. Niue, South Pacific.

The plane had left Vladivostok nearly three weeks ago. These things can't be rushed after all. No suspicions could be aroused. There was only one hope, one opportunity. If this failed there would be no chance for a second try. The small plane meandered past various islands, always staying to the prepared flight paths, always landing where friends waited. The package was precious. There had been some concern that it wouldn't arrive in time, that it would get here too late and the place would be too well protected, but the fears were unfounded. The package arrived in time for the event.

Everything had been timed. Franklin wanted it like that. He knew the value of spectacle, he knew how to draw people to his cause. Failing to achieve objectives in front of a worldwide audience was not acceptable. The crew of the plane had been chosen carefully. There were so many to choose from, so many willing to do the job, so many willing to die for their species.

The pilot listened to a small radio as the aircraft flew through the trade winds. It had short-wave on it. He knew exactly what time he needed to arrive. He checked his watch as he saw the faint outline of the island rise over the horizon. For the last hour he worried that the revolution in Africa had failed, that Franklin would not be in a position to make his declaration on cue. The pilot was supposed to proceed anyway, but he wanted to hear how his brothers were doing before....

A newscaster broke into the music. He spoke for a few seconds in an unfamiliar language, and then cut to the live broadcast of Trinity's declaration of war. The pilot listened, smiling as be began his decent. He looked over to the passenger's seat where the device was strapped in like a child. As the small plane came downward towards the center of the island, he reached over and pulled the red safety switch, just like he had been taught. He turned the key. A small beep sounded, almost inaudible over the engines. As the speech ended the pilot kept an eye on the altimeter. He watched it read lower and lower– 1300 feet, 1200 feet, 1100 feet, 1000 feet. He waits for the barometric fuse to kick in.

Below, in the courtyard where she had tried to calm the nerves of young Benji Lawson, Nancy Collins was walking with Dr. Mensen. The two were talking about recent progress that had been made in understanding HS-virus protein coats. They heard the sound of a plane descending fast. Planes make a much different noise when they are about to crash then when they are landing. Nancy looked up, but the aircraft was lost in the bright sun. "I didn't think that a plane was coming in til this afternoon," said Dr. Mensen, shielding his wrinkled eyes from the sunlight.

In a burst of atomic fire, seven thousand scientists, two thousand islanders, and the last, best hope for the HS vaccine were lost.

That evening, the E-Ring of the Pentagon, Arlington, VA

The only sound that could be heard was the timid footsteps of the Air Force captain who silently went around the table filling water glasses. Each of the generals sat absorbed with the latest reports that were streaming in from overseas. In typical fashion the normally sleepy intelligence community had gone from not having a clue about the Pliedian Spearhead to producing thousand page reports about them in under twenty-four hours. Actually, it would be unfair to say that the 'community' was totally unaware of Franklin Trinity. He had a file at the FBI, filed deep in a vault. A half-written biography of him had gone unfinished for several weeks because the analyst had been taking a mid-career training class. Trinity had mostly fallen through the cracks. At the Central Intelligence Agency there are multiple, separate organizations to handle different types of threats. The Counterterrorism department considered his movement to fall under the domain of 'Cult Activities.' The Cult Activities department figured that he was more of an international terrorist. Since Trinity was a U.S. citizen, the CIA felt that the FBI was handling it. Since he was operating mostly overseas, FBI felt that CIA was handling it. No one in the Counterproliferation department was consulted about the rumors coming from Russia that someone had stolen one of the suitcase-sized nuclear bombs that were intended for special operations missions.

But whatever the excuse for not exposing the threat beforehand, government analysts began pouring out report after report, examining every piece of data they could find again and again in hopes of being the first to break the story and prove that their agency was the only one not caught with their pants down. Careers would be made tonight. All of these hastily written reports have made their way to the War Room of the Pentagon, where the generals, who were just getting ready to go home for the weekend, are furiously reading them so as to not look stupid and uninformed in front of their commander-in-chief.

"Well?" said President Talbot. There was no answer. "I said, 'Well?'" Again no answer. "You, what's our situation." He pointed to General Landon, the Air Force Chief of Staff.

"Well Sir," she flipped though some more pages, "It seems that this organization, the Pliedian Spearhead they call themselves, is fully in control of about fourteen countries, mostly in Africa and the Middle East, they have considerable power in about ten other countries where it seems fighting is still going on." She smiled nervously and turned her eyes away. She handed a map to the nameless captain, who presented it to the President.

"What's our domestic situation? You, talk," he pointed to General Abrams.

The Army General responded, "It seems that there have been some acts of terrorism in several states, rioting and looting here and there, but it's mostly low key, isolated stuff. We can't confirm that any of it came directly on his orders. But one thing's for certain, it seems that aliens in the U.S. aren't heeding his call to arms en masse. There is no major revolution to speak of. At least not yet."

"And Europe? Asia?"

"Again sir, random acts of terrorism, revolts and rioting in certain countries, they burned down the new parliament building in Berlin. But for the most part, it's under control. Who knows how long that will stay that way though? The more this kook broadcasts, and the more victories he wins, the more people will start to follow him."

The President sat back in his chair and looked up at the ceiling contemplatively for a few seconds. "General Hudson, what do we do about it?"

"Well sir, this is war. This is the war I've been talking about for almost ten years now. The balloon's gone up sir. I've already got a basic contingency plan." He tapped a large pile of reports on the table in front of him. He dealt them out across the table to all but one person. "You can read it if you like, but I'll give you the gist of it. First we organize what we've got left of the military, and along with what we can salvage from NATO, we go after that son of a bitch and slaughter him. They've got antiquated third world equipment for the most part. On the other hand we've developed all sorts of nifty gadgets in the last decade, I don't think that victory will be a problem as long as we can keep our troops loyal. In order to do that we're gonna have to kick all those bug-eyed freaks out of sensitive government positions and military service which, as I told you last year, was a bad idea in the first place. Then we..."

"President Talbot I have to disagree. General Hudson is only going to create divis..." Jim Miller was cut off by the General.

"That's the first guy to go sir," he pointed at Jim. "We're in a war here, and we've got one of the enemy sitting at our table. That is unacceptable. How do we know he hasn't been in cahoots with Trinity all along? They're wily, those little bastards."

The President cut him off. "Secretary Miller is here because I want him here. Go ahead Jim."

"Well sir, Trinity's power base comes from those aliens who feel disaffected. If you look at the countries that he is strongest in, it's the same list that have the worst rights records. There hasn't been an uprising in the U.S. because we've almost got parity between aliens and humans. Trinity is feeding off their hate for humankind. We've got to counter that. We've got to show that it isn't Alien versus Human, but order versus insanity. I suggest that we open negotiations, make it look as if we're willing to talk. We need to be reasonable. Win their hearts."

General Hudson broke in. "That's just the kind of crap I'd expect from one of them sir, we've got to hit 'em and hit 'em hard. If we come in with overwhelming force I'm sure that we can smash their will to fight within a few weeks. I say nuke every city he's got."

General Fitzhue of the Marines chimed in, "That's our philosophy Mr. President, overwhelming force."

President Talbot dismissed him, "I'm not going to be the President who blew up half the planet. I need a better solution. How about embargo, conventional forces, what else do we got? I've got to talk to the press and we need a plan that's going to work. There's an election coming up for god's sakes."

"Sir let me suggest that if we do send in troops, let's use alien troops in the front lines. Again, we can't make it look like an alien versus human war. We can't win a conflict on those terms," said Jim.

General Talbot stood up from his chair, "That's it, I'm not going to have this traitor in our ranks any longer." He pulled out his sidearm and leveled it at the young secretary. The two military police that guarded the room from prying eyes looked at each other for guidance. They were unsure what to do. Jim's eyes opened wide and a look of shock came over his face. He instinctively started backing his chair from the table.

"General Hudson, what the hell are you doing? Have you lost your mind?" screamed the President. General Talbot was sweating profusely. With his arm straight out and his weapon cocked, he looked at the President. Then he looked at the alien. Then he looked at his fellow generals. Then back at the President.

"I gotta get some air. Excuse me sir," he said. He uncocked his gun and proceeded toward the door, which the MPs opened for him. The last thing that people inside could see of General Hudson was his pulling out a cell phone. The door closed.

"Ok, what are we going to do about this? I want answers people. I've got to go to the press in ten minutes. People are going to want a plan. I can't afford to come off looking indecisive."

Various ideas were proposed and discarded for several desperate minutes as the President's staff tried to come up with something that wouldn't make the situation worse. All of a sudden, General Hudson barged back into the room, looking refreshed and smiling. "Gentlemen, the problem has been solved."

President Talbot gave a dirty look to the MPs who let Hudson back in the room. "And by that you mean?" he said.

"Project Zephyr-Alpha sir." He looked directly at Jim. "It's codeword sir, but I guess everyone's going to know about it soon anyway, so I'll spill the beans."

"Project Zephyr-Alpha?" The President looked at the puzzled meeting members. None gave a signal of recognition.

"Project Zephyr-Alpha sir. It's a Cold War legacy project that I've been revamping. Very close hold sir. I believe you were briefed on it when you took office." His eyes were fixed on Jim the way a wolf stares at a sheep.

President Talbot looked over at his Chief of Staff, who said, "must have been that day when the intel folks came over and briefed you on all the codeword programs sir."

"There were like 500 of those things, I lost track halfway through," complained the President. The Chief of Staff shrugged. Talbot leaned across the table. "Talk to me like I'm stupid Hudson."

"Sir, when we shelved our bio-weapons program back in the '70s, some in the military felt that we had made significant progress in certain areas, and there was no reason to lose what we had accomplished. So, we moved those projects to an abandoned tunnel outside of Area-51 and kept going. You wouldn't believe what those guys achieved." He beamed as if he himself had done the research. "It all started when somebody got the bright idea that we could tailor a virus to just kill a certain race. Can you believe that sir? If we had used it in Vietnam, we'd have wiped out half the continent without losing a man! We made anti-Russian, anti-Negro, anti-Chinamen, all of it sir. It's all there, waiting in big drums for your authorization. The idea was to use it in case of a sneak attack, but that never happened, so no one ever bothered to inform anybody. But they've been out there in the desert sir, slaving away."

"That's barbarous!" said General Landon.

"Yeah, ain't it? Perfection! Way cleaner than a nuke. Safer too." He shook his head, "But that's not the point, I'm getting off the subject. The deal is that when Johnston put me in charge of this alien invasion task-force, I went to Zephyr-Alpha and gave them a new mission, and they did it, sir they did it." He pounded his hand on the table for emphasis. "We've got a virus that'll just kill aliens. We used all the data that was collected from the kids in the orphanages. I've been sitting on the news for months now. Just kills aliens, totally harmless to humans. Perfect."

"Hudson, did it ever occur to you that without a vaccine, there aren't going to be any humans left on this planet pretty soon?" said the President. Jim was in too much shock to give his opinion.

"Already thought of that sir. Those Z-A boys have collected about half a million unused frozen human embryos from fertility clinics. They're sitting in freezers just awaiting transplantation. If we can't breed normally, we'll do it artificially, until we get a vaccine of course. Meanwhile, if those bastards from outer space ever try to come down here they'll be dead within hours."

The President put his head in his hands. "Somebody, how many aliens are on this planet?"

Jim regained his composure enough to answer. "Approximately three point five billion sir."

"Three point five billion. Three point five billion," President Talbot repeated over and over, "Three point five billion. General, I won't be responsible for killing three point five billion people. I will not authorize release of that virus. General Hudson, I want you to call those Zephyr-Alpha people and tell them to stand down and begin destroying whatever virus stocks you've got. Then I want your resignation letter."

"Too late sir."

"What do you mean too late?"

"I told you, Zephyr-Alpha is a Cold War legacy project, and a lot of those projects were exempted from the requirement for an executive order to deploy the weapon. Had to do with loss of command and control during a nuclear strike I suppose. I'm the only authority that needs to give the go ahead, and I gave the order a few minutes ago. Right now a plane is being loaded with spray tanks. Within twenty minutes the virus will be nicely distributed."

"Hudson, order your men to stand down. I want that command rescinded!"

"No can do sir. Z-A has strict instructions to cut all communications once the GO order is given. It's been policy from back in the Cold War days. They didn't want some commie impersonator giving false orders. Face it gentlemen, within a week, all alien life on this planet will be over. The only thing left to discuss is the future." He leaned back in his chair and pulled a large cigar from his jacket pocket. "Sorry kid," he said in Jim's direction.

Inside of a mesa, just south of Groom Lake, NV

A blue light silently spins round and round. That's all. One would think that there would be more fanfare for the harbinger of three billion deaths. Shouldn't there be some sort of siren, or wail or noise? Even the people in the project are subdued. No one is rushing around completing last minute checks, no one is screaming "Let's move people, on the double!" or any of the inspirational military phrases you might hear at the movies. These soldiers are all professionals. They have been at their jobs long enough to know what to do and how fast it needs to be done. Calmly and methodically, pilots are checking their instruments, loaders are placing munitions under the wings, commanders are opening sealed envelopes containing classified flight plans. Project Zephyr-Alpha was designed to function even after a catastrophic loss of the chain of command. They know just how much time they have to launch, and they'll take every minute of it. It takes exactly forty-seven minutes between the detection of a Soviet strike and the time the first missile could reach Nevada. The crews have drilled and drilled in order to go from complete unreadiness to launch in forty-five. No need to rush, all motion is ingrained.

1st Lt. Tom Jacobs lies in his bunk, mesmerized by the blue light spinning above his bed. He knows what it means. He has only been with Z-A for ten months, but he knows what the light means. Deep down in his soul he knows what the light means.

He checks his watch, there are twenty-three minutes left before launch. He'd hoped that he would never have to make this decision. He'd hoped that all the training he had been doing in preparation of his mission would be a waste of time. He'd hoped that the leaders of this world wouldn't be so stupid as to activate his squadron. He has played this scenario over and over in his head, not sure of which way he'd go. He'd fantasized about being on both sides of the coin, at least until she came along. Now there was only one thing that he could do, only one path to travel. He hugged the pillow to his chest and stared up at the light. There were still twenty-two minutes to go, he could afford another five minutes of apprehension.

Elsewhere in the facility, the planes were preparing for launch. The anti-alien virus, code-named 'backbreaker' had been pre-positioned in spray tanks. As soon as the blue light began to flash and the confirmation code was given, flight crews began moving the tanks from their cold storage locations in the bio-containment area to the runway. A full-scale runway existed here, underground. It was impregnable to all but the strongest nuclear blast, and virtually invisible to any satellite that happened to be snapping pictures overhead. You couldn't land a plane here, but that was never the plan. Once the virus had been released, the planes could land anywhere, the need for secrecy would be over.

Lt. Jacobs picked up the phone near his bed and called his mother. He barely moved. The pillow was still clutched to his chest, his eyes were still on the rotating blue light. "Hello Mom? Don't talk," he said, "I don't have much time." His mother didn't know where he was of course. The phone he was using had been sanitized, and no trace anywhere could locate the source of the call. "Mom, I know that you've always wanted to know what I've been doing on this secret project. Well, I'm pretty sure that you're gonna find out real soon now. I just wanted to let you know that I love you, and that when people ask what happened here, I want you to know that I did it for Leilana. I can't say more Mom. I know that doesn't make any sense right now, but it will soon enough. Just tell the papers that if they ask. I just figure that people'll... that people'll want to know that's all. Bye Mom." He dropped the receiver on the floor. He looked at his watch again. Sixteen minutes to go. They'd be looking for him soon. He needed to report. The time for reflection was over.

The base housed eight B-1 stealth bombers. They didn't officially exist of course. There was no record of their purchase on any Department of Defense manifests. The pilots had received no official training on their operation, and no shipments of jet fuel had ever officially been shipped to this base. In each of the eight non-existent airplanes, the non-trained crews finalized their detailed flight paths. The B-1 was capable of extended flight, and the eight planes were to follow eight distinct patterns that would allow them to drop their cargo over the widest possible range. Depending on weather, and if their refueling sites survived, they would be able to achieve 94% coverage of all land areas within three days. A much more efficient delivery system than the silver cylinders employed by the alien invaders.

Lt. Jacobs opened his footlocker. It was the one place he had all to himself, his one inviolate secret place within this most secret of places. Inside were magazine cut-outs, pasted to the lid. They had been lovingly cut out and carefully placed to form a collage of images. He looked at the face of the girl he loved. Leilana Banks, the first Alien-American pop singer to hit it big. He ran his hand over the worn paper, and touched the image of her cheek. She was smiling back at him. She was always smiling, and that's what made him fall in love with her in the first place. He shed a quick tear. There was no time to listen to the music he had stashed away beneath his uniforms. He would have to hear her voice in his head. He checked his watch one last time. Thirteen minutes to go.

"Where the hell is Jacobs?" said Major Boone. He sat in the cockpit of his plane. The status checks had been completed and they were just awaiting final confirmation from the loaders that the spray tanks had been properly attached. Of course, they were missing their bombardier, an essential component for this mission.

"Here he comes now," shouted the co-pilot. Jacobs ran across the staging area, still zipping up his flight suit. He dodged his way through the crowd of support personnel and entered the airplane.

"Glad you made it Lieutenant," said the Captain, "Would hate for you to miss the big show. Hope we didn't get you off the can or nothing." There was some chuckling in the cockpit. Tom smiled in mock amusement.

The next four minutes were spent in final flight checks. Everything was ready as far as the pilot was concerned. As the bombardier, it was Tom's job to ensure that the plane was prepared to not only fly, but to deliver its payload. Their plane was scheduled third for takeoff. Tom watched the line of planes in front as they taxied towards the beginning of the runway. Once they were all lined up, and the arm-codes were given, operation Zephyr-Alpha would be underway.

Zephyr-Alpha was a holdover from Cold War paranoia, and some of their procedures were designed for a different time. Not only were the wings of the planes outfitted with spray tanks containing deadly virus, but they were each armed with two nuclear weapons as well. With the loss of command and control possible in a large-scale conflict, the battle plans of Zephyr-Alpha called for the use of nuclear weapons as a backup. Even though their mission had changed completely, their procedures had never been updated. So each bomber still carried four nuclear-tipped cruise missiles. Since the weapons had never officially existed, it was just easier to leave them in service than to figure out a way to dispose of them. Weapons-grade plutonium is a carefully monitored substance, and having a few hundred extra pounds show up somewhere would generate a lot of questions that the Z-A administrators didn't want to answer.

Tom listened as the arm-codes were given over the radio. In almost every case, the bombardier is not given the codes to arm the payload until after the plane has taken off and is proceeding towards its target. This was a safety check to stop anyone who somehow got their hands on a nuclear or biological weapon from being able to use it. But Z-A was a holdover from the Cold War, and their procedures had never been subjected to the kind of review that most battle plans were given. In this case, the codes to arm the weapons were provided just before lift-off. This would allow the planes to still deliver their payloads in the event that the command and control system was knocked out just after takeoff. Tom listened as the codes for his spray tanks were given. They were quickly followed by the codes for the nuclear bombs. No one expected that the bombs would be used for anything, they had long ago been taken out of the target deck, but the codes were given anyway. It was just procedure.

Tom watched as the first aircraft began to rev its engines in anticipation of flight. The blast doors that normally sealed the runway from the world opened, and a glint of sunlight began to shine in on the flat black surfaces of the planes. Tom looked at the rest of his crew. The two pilots were flipping switches. Major Boone had his hand on the throttle, ready to go as soon as the first two planes were out of the way. The co-pilot was chuckling in anticipation. Everyone here was a professional, everyone here knew what their mission was and they knew how to do it. Everyone here believed that they were only a weapon– that they had no control over who or why they killed. They had been conditioned to simply follow orders and not worry about consequences. Tom had been like that once. He had gone through the Personnel Reliability Program, he had gone through the psyche testing and the background checking that determined that he could be used as a unquestioning living weapon for his government. He was ready to do his job, that is until he first heard Leilana sing. He didn't know who she was at first, just an angelic voice coming over the radio. He hadn't known any aliens, at least not personally. He never did have anything against them, but he had never given a second thought to his mission until he heard his angel singing. He couldn't allow this to happen. He didn't care about humanity, he didn't care about the three billion other aliens that would die, he didn't care about his place in history or what people would think of what he did here today. He only knew one thing, and that was that he couldn't let Leilana down. He had to save her.

Calmly and quietly he began entering the arm codes for the nuclear weapon into his console. He flipped up the covering that protected the red launch button. He watched as the first jet began its takeoff down the runway. A nuclear blast in this cavern would undoubtedly destroy all eight bombers and vaporize the entire store of backbreaker virus. He waited until the last possible second before he committed, in the vain hope this turned out to be a drill or that a rescind order would be given in time. Her song played in his head and he closed his eyes. In the end it wasn't the thought of the world ending that forced his hand so much as the thought of the silencing of one person's angelic voice.

Lancaster, PA. Thanksgiving Day, six years after the death of Neil Hayes.

The smell of fireplace smoke was in the air. It was cold here in Pennsylvania already, and as the people walked outside on their errands, wispy, white clouds of breath were visible. It hadn't snowed yet this season, although it looked like it might later in the afternoon. The doorbell rings on a non-descript, brick brownstone on Chestnut Street. It can only mean one thing. Rosemarie puts down her whisk and after checking to make certain nothing on the stove was about to boil over, heads to the door to meet her sister.

"Janice, I'm so happy to see you. Come on in." She opens the door and a downtrodden but joyful woman enters.

"Rosie, thanks for inviting me. I've brought pie." She holds up a disc-shaped package covered with tin foil. Rosemarie takes it.

"You'll have to excuse me Jannie, I've got to keep an eye on the cooking." She turns and heads to the kitchen. Janice unwinds her red scarf and removes her coat, and both end up slumped in the corner of the couch. She then follows her host into the kitchen.

"Where's Jerry?"

Rosemarie continued stirring as she talked. "Oh, I've sent him out on an errand. I needed more milk. Daddy should be arriving in an hour or so. They're not going to want to miss the game, so I'll expect them all here pretty soon."

"Great. Great." Janice filled the teapot with water and found the last available burner. She then sat at the table quietly staring at the brown and white checkerboard wallpaper.

"Jannie? How've you been doing? I mean really."

"I don't know Rosie, I'm doing ok I guess. Normally I'm fine. It's been six years and all. But around the holidays it

301

gets a little lonely you know. I'm just glad that I've got you guys to be with."

"I keep telling you Jannie, you should move back here to Lancaster. It'd be so great to have my big sis back in town again."

Janice poured the steaming water into a plain, yellow mug and sat back down. "I don't know Rosie, I've got a house and all, and a job now. Maybe in the spring."

"We're all worried about you all alone down there."

"I'm fine really," she sat up straight in her chair and smiled, "...really. Nothing to worry about." She tried to change the subject. "So what's new with you and Jerry?"

Rosemarie squinched herself up as if she was about to burst. "Oh Jannie, I've been dying to tell you. I can't hold it in any longer." She rushed to the table and sat next to her sister. She leaned way over and took both of Janice's hand into her own. "I'm pregnant!" She sat hesitantly trying to gauge her sister's reaction. Under most conditions she would have been sure that Janice would be ecstatic, but with all the ugliness and all, she thought that her sister might be a little sad to hear that someone else's family was growing.

Janice sat puzzled for several seconds, trying to process the information. "That's fantastic!" she shouted. "I'm going to be an aunt. Have you told Mom and Dad?"

"No, I haven't told anybody. We were waiting for Thanksgiving to break the news. I wanted everyone to be here together. But I couldn't help myself, I'm so excited."

"That's great news Rosie, I'm so happy for you. Is it natural, or did you go embryo?"

"Natural. We thought about getting an embryo pretty seriously for a while. But I guess that in the end we decided that we wanted our child to fit in. The Lancaster school district is now over 80% alien, and it'll probably be more in five years. We decided not to give our kid a disadvantage."

"Well, he's already got to grow up with Jerry as a Dad, so he's going to be disadvantaged enough," she said with a smile.

"Jannie stop."

"You know, I've got boxes and boxes of old baby clothes in my basement if you want them."

"I'd appreciate that Jannie."

A tear formed in Janice's eye, but not even she was certain if it was because of happiness for her sister or because the news brought her loss into contrast. She took another sip of tea and tried to smile.

Text of a handwritten letter addressed to Mrs. Maggie Watson of Reginald, AL. Delivered four years, eight months after the nuclear explosion in Nevada

Dear Mom,

I know I haven't written in a while like you told me I should. Its been pretty messed up here on the front. But we've quieted down some and the Sergeant sent me back to base camp for some rest. Of course the first thing I'm gonna do is write to you and tell you that I'm ok. I know that you may have heard a lot of stuff about what's going on out here, but I want to tell you that mostly there's no truth to it. It's scary some of the time, especially at night, but we're doing good out here Mom, we're making a difference, and all the guys in my unit are great. There's this one Indian dude who can twist himself all up in a knot for fun. You should see it! He ain't no Indian like the one's we got in America, he's actually from India and all. They all talk funny too. I've been learning a few words of Indian for when I get back, but I can't hardly pronounce anything. They're all good about it though. We got guys from all over Europe too. I woulda thought that they'd all be speaking different languages, but most of 'em speak pretty good English. It's a NATO thing I guess. Or maybe it's from watching tv.

I'm in Lagos right now. That's in Nigeria. I don't know if the censors will let that through, but I hope they do because I wanted you to know were I was. You can look it up on a map. Didn't you say that our family is from round here? It's funny Mom, you always taught me that I was black, but here, everybody's the same, you can't tell black guys from white guys on account of us all being aliens. Even that Indian guy too. It's funny ya know. All that stuff about civil rights and all that you went through, and here we are, nobody can tell who's black or white or nothin.

Mama, you should see them new tanks we got out here. The ones made from that alien ship. They actually float in the air Mama! I'm hoping that by the time I get home they'll have cars floating around. I wanted to drive one of them floating tanks, but they told me I was just infantry. I can still watch em go though. Man thay's cool.

Well Ma, that's about all the time I've got right now. We're pulling out of town pretty soon. I don't like fightin out here. Every day we go on patrol, but you never know whos happy your here and whos gonna shoot at ya. I don't know where they'll be sending me next. I hope

Dominic Peloso

that I can see more of Africa while I'm here, it being like my homeland and all that. I want to take some pictures for you ma, so's you can see how beautiful it is (at least some parts), but the corps won't let me have no camera. So I'll have to just tell you all about it when I get home. It shouldn't be long now ma, I'll be home soon. Say hello to Uncle Curtis and the twins for me. gotta go! Semper Fi!

Your son,
Lance Corporal Andre Watson

Six weeks after Lt. Tom Jacobs saved the world, The White House, Washington, DC

"Welcome to the 6 o'clock news, I'm Toby Phillips. In headlines today, President Talbot presented a posthumous Congressional Medal of Honor to the mother of Lt. Thomas Jacobs at a White House ceremony this morning."

Switch from video of the anchorwoman to footage from the Rose Garden. President Talbot is presenting an older woman with a small black box. She is overcome with emotion.

Voiceover: President Talbot proclaimed Lt. Jacobs a 'national hero' for destroying himself along with the top secret Zephyr Alpha base in Nevada, mere minutes before base personnel were set to release a virus capable of killing all alien life on the planet.

Switch to footage of the press conference immediately following the award presentation.

Pres. Talbot: There is only one time when doing the right thing matters, and that's at the end. Lt. Jacobs may have been tainted by his association with Zephyr Alpha in the first place, but in the final moments, in the time it really counted, he became a hero.

Switch to close-up of singer Leilana Banks.

Voiceover: Also on hand was pop singer Leilana Banks, who praised Lt. Jacobs, saying quote, "I wish I could have met him."

Switch back to anchor desk.

Phillips: Also on hand was Secretary of Alien Affairs James Miller.

A small, static picture of Secretary Miller appears over the anchor's left shoulder.

Phillips: Secretary Miller used this occasion to announce his new "United Earth Campaign."

Switch to footage of Secretary Miller.

Miller: Let this be a lesson to all those out there, human and alien, that life, in whatever form, is sacred, and that we must all work together. Let us stop using divisive terms such as 'human' or 'alien.' We need to get past our backgrounds, past our origins, to understand that we're all 'earthlings.' If Lt. Jacobs' sacrifice teaches us anything, it should be that love of life, love of our planet, supercedes all divisions between human and alien populations. Lt. Jacobs died for all of us, let's use this opportunity he gave us to make a better world for all earthlings.

Switch to anchor desk.

Phillips: In other news, NATO bombers kept up a relentless assault on the Pliedian stronghold of Lagos, Nigeria today. Casualties were reported on both sides. A NATO spokesman said that battle lines have stabilized and that the first priority will be to take back the massive oil fields under Saudi Arabia.

Switch to footage of a news conference. A general stands in front of a large world map. Most of Africa, the Middle East, South East Asia, and China are colored red.

Gen. Abrams: NATO and Indian ground troops are being deployed to the Central Asian Republics to reinforce control of the oil resources located there. The Pliedians are using guerrilla hit and run tactics that are proving to be quite effective against our tank columns in rough terrain. But headway is being made in large, open areas such as the Arabian Peninsula. We expect to launch a full-scale assault against several key cities within a few weeks. However, it's going to be difficult to retake some of the larger population centers without civilian casualties, which obviously we're working hard to avoid.

Reporter: What is the refugee situation General?

Gen. Abrams: I can't comment on that other to say that refugees are complicating the situation, but they are being handled in a manner consistent with international laws.

2nd Reporter: General, is there any truth to the reports that NATO plans to use only alien troops in their front lines, so as to psychologically weaken the separatists' claim that this is a war between aliens and human?

Gen. Abrams: I can't comment on that at this time.

Switch to anchor desk.

Phillips: The General went on to say that barring further problems, he hoped that the Pliedian Separatists would be eliminated by Spring. As a note to our viewers, we remind you to watch the encore of Channel 7's special report on the background, motivations, and goals of the separatist leader, Franklin Trinity, tonight at nine pm. Now let's take a look at our weather, Ken...

A living room in Peoria, IL. Three years after the first NATO assault on Lagos.

"Hold it steady, hold it steady." The camera comes into focus. An older man switches his gaze from the TV playback to the lens. "Good, good, that's good." His gives the cameraman a thumbs up. A long, gray arm reaches forward into the shot to mimic to the gesture. "OK Karen, go ahead," he says.

A middle-aged woman comes into view next to the man. The pair stands in front of a red brick fireplace. The mantle is covered with cards, and stockings hang waving slightly in the breeze generated from the heat of the fire. To either side of the fireplace bare, beige wall is visible. A small end table barely sneaks into the frame at the left. It has a small bowl of nuts on it. "I'm so nervous," says the woman to her husband.

"Just look at the camera." He points to the lens, "Not me, the camera." She giggles.

"They're going to think their grandparents are a bunch of ditzes," says the voice behind the lens. "You're not making a very good impression." The cameraman chuckles.

"Ok, ok." Karen shakes her head vigorously as if to shrug off her nervousness. She stares into the camera. "Hello, my name is Karen Turner, and this is my husband Jake Turner." He gives the camera a wave. "We're your grandparents, or great grandparents, or whatever. I guess it depends on how far this tape gets passed down." She bows. "um... I don't know where to begin."

"Why don't you tell them why we're making the tape Karen," says Jake.

She turns to her husband. "Ok, good idea." She faces the camera again. "Why are we making this tape? Well, we're not going to be around forever, and we wanted you to know us, who we are. We wanted you to see us, to experience a little bit of our lives, sort of as a keepsake. That's why we're making this tape."

Jake continued, "We're figuring that you'll have a lot of questions about your ancestors, now that we're not around anymore. You'll probably be bugging your parents to tell you what we looked like and how we lived and all. You are so different than we are, and you won't be able to see us in your own face, so I guess that this is the next best thing isn't it?"

Karen rolled up the sleeves of her thick red sweater. She spread her fingers and rotated her arms around. "Well, for one thing, we're all pink, or is it peach? I guess it doesn't matter, we're this color."

"And we've got this stuff on our heads, it's called hair. Just like a dog has, or sort of," said Jake. "It doesn't smell bad when it gets wet." He rubbed the hair on his head. Karen followed suit, pulling the bobby pins out of her bun and letting her long hair fall freely around her face.

"We're pretty sure you would have had brown hair, even though Jake's is now mostly white. It's kind of fun to have hair, it's too bad that you guys are missing out."

"Please," says the voice behind the lens, "and spend $50 a month on shampoo and haircuts? Trust me Mom, you're better off without it. I can jump right out of bed without looking like a mess."

Karen moved out of the frame. Jake continued, "Well, I mean, I don't know what else I can tell you about how we look." He spun around slowly. "You've pretty much seen it all I guess. Hopefully you don't find us too ugly you know."

"Show them this, show them this," said Karen returning to view. She held up a small, black box with a hinged lid.

"Oh yeah. Hopefully you'll know what this is anyway, but maybe seeing us with it can provide you with a stronger link. This is a remembrance box."

"They're the latest thing," interrupted Karen, "Everybody's got them now." Jake looked at her. "Oh I'm sorry, you tell them."

Jake opened the lid. "Inside there's a picture of us, a few actually, plus older photos of our parents. We've also got a little family tree. We want you to know where you came from. That'll help you become a strong adult.

"Yeah, everybody's got to know where they came from. You've got to remember your roots."

"We've also got a few locks of hair, just so you can see. Plus there's two blood samples, one from me and one from your grandmother. They're for... they're for..." he choked up a little.

"They're for... 'just in case,'" finished Karen. "I mean you never know about the future right? Maybe we can't pass our genes along in the regular way, but maybe they'll be some new way someday."

Jake recovered. "Well, at least you'll always be able to say you've got your grandparents' genes," he chuckled. "Even if you just keep them in a box." He closed the lid and placed it on the table besides the nuts. "I hope that you guys will keep us in mind as you get older, and try to live right you know?"

"Yeah, remember, we love you dearly. No matter where you go and what you do, we'll always be looking down on you, remember that. You'll never be alone." Karen started sniffling.

As she wiped a tear from her eye with a tissue, Jake said, "I guess that's it. Keep the Turner name in good standing son. You're the guardian of it now. It's up to you. We're counting on you. And remember, whatever Todd tells you about how he was a good kid, don't believe it, he was a hellion. I hope you're as big a pain in the neck to him as he was to us."

"Oh stop Jake." She addresses the camera, "He's just kidding really. We know you'll be good and you'll do great things in life," sobbed Karen, "We love you very much, you'll always have a part of us inside you. Make us proud." She grabs her husband and hugs him tightly, burying her face in his chest.

"Ok, I guess that's it. Todd, turn off the tape." The camera flips over, showing mostly floor.

"Where's the button Dad?" says the voice.

"It's on the side, gimme that thing." The camera shakes violently a few times, then the tape ends.

Five years, three months after the Pliedian Spearhead declared war on humanity. Abidjan, Cote d'Ivorie

Franklin sat in the garden and waited calmly. He liked coming to the garden. The trees here were beautiful, the flowers constantly grew and bloomed, occasionally a lizard would run across the flagstone path. It was peaceful here. There was no war in the garden, there was no death or logistics or reporters in the garden. There was only peace. He occasionally brought work out here with him, if some order needed to be reviewed, if some secret mission needed to be assigned. But not today. Today Franklin sat and waited and prayed.

The air over the city was quiet at this hour. The relentless bombing had ceased for now. No one in the capital city would die on this day. The sound of anti-aircraft fire would not be heard. It was a beautiful morning, a little humid, but not too hot just yet. The sky was clear. Franklin took a deep breath and waited.

A helicopter flew overhead. It came to a landing on the pad outside of the compound. "It wouldn't be long now," he thought. He looked up at the sky and tried to stare through the blue atmosphere to see the stars. "Why haven't you come?" he thought. "Why have you left us here like this?"

A few minutes later the door to the garden opened. Franklin stood up from his stone bench to greet the envoy. Enoch came through first, dapper in his dress uniform. "Franklin?" he said, "The envoy is here." Behind him, still partially lost in the darkness of the hallway stood a figure.

"Thank you Enoch. Please leave us," he said. He had noticed a slight stammer in Enoch's voice, perhaps a small tear was in the corner of his eye. Franklin felt the same way, but he couldn't show it. He had to be brave, he had to be strong; for his army, for his species, for himself. Enoch stepped aside and allowed the envoy to enter the garden. He then stepped back into the corridor and closed the banded wooden door behind him. The sound of the door creaking echoed noisily in the enclosed courtyard.

At first, Franklin didn't know what to make of the envoy. She appeared to be wearing a hood of some sort. As she came into the light, Franklin could see that it was a habit. The woman was a nun. She stepped forward briskly and lifted the fabric to reveal her face. It was one that Franklin recognized immediately despite the extra years chiseled into it.

"Sister Mary Helen?" he said apprehensively, as if unsure of his own eyes.

"Franklin my dear. I'm so happy to see you again." She held out her hands to hug her former ward. The leader didn't know how to respond exactly, but he eventually fell into her arms and gave the diminutive nun a strong hug.

"Sister, what are you doing here? This place isn't safe. I had no idea you were still alive." He tried to maintain a formal posture befitting to a head of state, but it was difficult. The nun was the closest thing he had to a mother.

"Oh don't worry about me Franklin, I know I'm perfectly safe with you. Let's sit." The two sat on the stone bench overlooking the fountain in the middle of the garden.

They sat partially facing each other. The nun held Franklin's hands in her lap. "You're the envoy they sent?" he said.

"It seems that way, doesn't it Franklin?" she giggled.

"Because they figured that you are the only one who I would trust."

"Oh I don't know, maybe that's part of it dear. But it was my idea really. I've never been to Africa before you know. I wanted to see it before I die."

"Don't say things like that Sister."

"No point in denying in Franklin, I'm almost ninety. I'll be kicking off pretty soon. I've got cancer."

"Say it isn't so Sister."

"Oh I'm afraid it is. But don't worry about me, I've led a good life. I'm not worried about what happens next. I'm glad I have this chance to see you once again though. You were always one of my favorites you know, Father Blythe's too. He used to always talk about you. He hoped that you would follow in his footsteps."

"Don't talk about Father Blythe Sister. I don't want to talk about him. You've come to negotiate terms of surrender."

"Well, I suppose, I mean... that's what they told me. Of course I've never been much of a politician or anything, so I don't know why they wanted to send little old me for this task. Mostly I just wanted to see you again." She stood up and walked over to the fountain. "There aren't any coins in the fountain. Don't you ever make wishes?"

"I used to Sister, but not any more. Wishes don't come true. At least none of my ever did."

"I'm sure that's not the case."

"Listen Sister, I am happy to see you again, I really am, but I can't concentrate on catching up with you. We're here to talk about the terms of the Spearhead's surrender."

"*Your* surrender!" the nun said with shock, "You've got it wrong son, I came to talk about *our* surrender. You've won."

Franklin stood up violently. "Stop kidding around."

"I'm not kidding around," replied the nun gently. "I'm here to tell you that you've won. We give up."

"How can you say that Sister. My army lies in ruins. There are only pockets of resistance left. We've got no food, no weapons, no air support, nothing left. We've steadily lost popular support. The NATO force is only days away from capturing Abidjan. The war is over. How can you say we've won?"

She walked over to him and took his hands. "Franklin dear, look at your goals. What have you been fighting for all these years? You wanted equality, you wanted freedom from

317

persecution, you wanted a place that you and your alien friends could call their own. You've got all that. You've won the war. I mean, look at the world these days. It's what, eighty-five percent alien? And how long has it been since there was a natural human birth? We're done for as a species. It's your planet now. Who do you think you've been fighting? There aren't any humans left in NATO. It's over. Tell your men to put down their arms and celebrate your victory."

"But it's still a human world, with human values."

"Maybe for now, but remember Franklin, all civilizations are built on the ruins of their predecessors. We've passed the torch on to you. It's your world now. As time goes by we'll be more and more forgotten and our values will be replaced by your children's. It's the way of the world."

"Why come to me with this Sister? Why are you negotiating anything? We can't stop the NATO army. Why're they coming to me like this now? Why not just finish it."

She took his hands. "They don't want you dead Franklin. In fact, they want you very much alive. They want you to be part of their government. They want you to work with them, not against them. They need you, they need your strength, they need your guidance. They want you to stand with them when the real Pliedians come."

Franklin threw down Mary Helen's hands and walked away. "What the hell are you talking about? After all I fought for? After all I've done and all I've believed in, they want me to switch sides and support the humans against the Pliedians? Are they crazy? Go back and tell them to resume their bombing." He turned away from her and stared at the vine-covered wall, suppressing a sniffle.

She followed him and put her hand on his shoulder. "No, Franklin, you've got it wrong. You're not Pliedian, you're an Earthling. That's what they want you to understand. That's what they sent me to tell you. Don't you understand you've been building a world for these extra-terrestrials without even knowing who or what they are? You don't share their values. You share ours. You're not an alien, you are a son of Earth. Even if you are at odds with the human species, and God knows that you have plenty of reasons for that, you share our core values about life. You believe in a God, you appreciate our standards of beauty. Look at this garden of yours Franklin. It isn't a Pliedian garden, it is an Earth garden, filled with the things that make Earth beautiful. Whose language do you speak? Whose clothes do you wear? Who taught you about art, morality, culture? You aren't an alien my child, you are one of us. What do you think will happen when the Pliedians get here? They'll try to instill their civilization on you, they'll try to make you believe the things they believe, worship the things that they worship, love the things that they love. And that's not you, that's none of us, be it human or alien. We're all the same." He turned to her.

"Franklin, we need you. You've fought for Earth for so long, you've fought for freedom for your people. Now your people need you most of all. We need you to stand with us against some foreign race from a planet far, far away that's going to do who knows what when they get here. You think that you've been oppressed by humans? You think that you've been denied your freedom to choose to live the life you want? Well wait until the real aliens come. Then you'll see that you share so much more with us then you do with them. It's your planet now Franklin, and I know you, you'll never let anyone take it away from you, no matter what they look like. I've spoken to the President about this at length. We know that when the time comes, you'll fight with us, not against us. I was just sent to make you believe that now, before one more earthling gets hurt in our stupid civil war. We're both fighting for the same side. Let's end it now and start working together for a new world, a world for *earthlings*, not for 'humans' or 'aliens,' or even Pliedians. You have a choice Franklin. You can help shape that world, or you can die, here in the jungle and it'll happen anyway. Hasn't half of your army already defected?"

"Yes Sister."

"Well, they know it, why don't you? Don't be so stubborn about it. You were always a stubborn child, now is the time to learn and grow up."

"I... I don't know Sister, there's so much hurt inside, so much pain that cries out for vengeance." He wanted to collapse into her arms, bury his head into her chest, and quietly sob. But he had to keep up appearances. He was still the leader of millions of people. He balled his fists and turned from her.

"I know my child, I know. But today the healing begins. Today is the first day of a world united." She held him for a long time.

One hundred and forty two years after the alien missiles first fell. Brittany, France

There would be no milking of cows today. The chickens wouldn't get fed, the pigs wouldn't get slopped. Today was her last day. It wasn't that she had been doing those things recently anyway. Once she had become old and ill, some of the local boys stopped by her farm to help her. She was alone on the damp fields far outside of town. Alone both literally and figuratively. Her husband had died many years ago, and she had since become a bit of a recluse. It was strange for her to go to town these last few years. Everything was so different. The people looked different, the world was filled with wonders that she could have never understood, even if she hadn't been almost a hundred. Sometimes she wondered where the other people were. Not those little elf-like things that constantly ran around and drove in silent flying machines, but the people. Ones like her– pink and tall with a mane of dark brown hair. They didn't appear on television anymore, none of the advertisements that made their way to her mailbox featured pictures of people like her. Only a few of these elf-people spoke any Brittany at all, so she was isolated by language as well as appearance. "It was ok," she thought to herself, snuggled under a wool blanket at night, "they scare me anyway."

She had no idea of course that she was the last human on Earth. She wasn't the last one born; that honor went to Emmanuel DeHocha of Lima, Peru, who was almost twelve years her junior. But Mr. DeHocha died of dysentery in his teens, and over the years the few remaining humans quietly lived their lives and died unobserved and unnoticed in a world that had passed them by. Veronique St. Germain had been born in a small fishing community on the northern coast of France. She grew up outside of town, on her parents' farm. She had been a pensive child, who never played with others. It was difficult for her to go to school in those days. The people were mostly farmers and fishermen with little contact with the big cities. She was one of the few humans left in her village. There were no human children born in that part of France after her, and she was looked at as a curiosity by her schoolmates. It made her nervous, and she would spend hours just sitting in her room, playing with her dolls, imagining a world in which she wasn't such a freak of nature, a world where everybody looked like her.

In her teens she met Henri Delacroix who was a sheep farmer in the nearby town of Fougéres. Although he was almost ten years her senior, she fell for him immediately, and he felt likewise. The loose tongues in town claimed that it was just because they were the only humans left in the area, but there was a deeper bond between the two lovers, and they spent almost fifty years together, in comfort and happiness until Henri finally succumbed to a long illness. The two never had any children, although they had tried in earnest for many years. Through a cruel twist of fate, Veronique was barren due to a bout of scarlet fever in her teens. It was too bad, because she carried the same immunity gene that was carried by the population of that tropical island, although she never had any inkling, and was never tested.

Not well educated, she worked on the farm her entire life, selling her produce in town or to the occasional merchant. Nights she spent knitting, and her shawls and bedspreads were highly regarded amongst the people who like that sort of thing. The house was far from the main road, and for many years, they had no electricity, never mind television. By the time they were hooked up, most of the world had stopped speaking the Brittany language, and she never bothered to learn more than a smattering of French. She never really understood why all the people had changed into these elf-things. She never heard about the First

Interplanetary War or what happened afterwards. She never really benefited from the new technologies that were developed once Earth joined the interstellar community. She had been told about the Earthling colonies on Mars, Europa, the moon, but she dismissed the tales as nothing more than fantasy. She was a practical, God-fearing woman after all who didn't have time for fancy.

In her later days, as she toiled in the fields, she often had young people come around to stare at her from the road. They were quite curious to see this 'throwback' to another day and time. She was always polite to the elf-people, if not overtly friendly. She never said a bad word about anybody, and when her husband became ill, she allowed elf-doctors to treat him, even if she wasn't comfortable with the idea.

As she grew older and older, and the number of humans alive fell to a mere handful, she had attained a bit of legendary status in the region. People came from all over to visit her. She never quite understood her popularity, or why she was so special. When told by onlookers that she was probably the last human on Earth, she scoffed and said that there had to be more somewhere. But in her mind she knew. She saw the writing on the wall. She understood that a new era had been dawning for some time now, and that her time on Earth was almost up.

In the last decade of her life, dementia and forgetfulness began to set in, and she became too infirm to look after her garden and her livestock. Village teens stepped in and helped her with her daily activities. It was such a thrill for them to experience the way life used to be, when farmers still tended to their garden by hand, and knitted their own sweaters. Anthropology students from the local college came to study her, although they never called it 'studying' to her face. She thought that they were just interested in her wisdom and stories as an elder member of the community. With her deteriorating mental state she never quite grasped the fact that she had done no farm work in years. She maintained until the end that she was a vigorous and independent woman.

No one knew for certain that she was the last human on Earth. Most suspected though, and as she lay on her deathbed, many, many visitors from all over Brittany came to have one last glimpse of this newly extinct species. But on her last day, only one person was with her, the local priest who maintained a vigil as he did for all of the people in his parish. He reported to the local paper that her last words were, "So, this is how the world ends," but he was unable to say for certain if she was referring to the extinction of her species or simply her own impending death.

The day Ray Johnston revealed the secrets of Hangar 18. Stuttgart, Germany

Johannes Handel was only fourteen then, barely a man. He was frightened. As the first of his species, he had always lived in fear, he had always hidden in the shadows. Unlike those who came after him, he had no one to turn to. He had no support system. His parents tried to keep him happy. They tried to provide a good social structure for him. They sent him to a special school for the disabled, where he formed friendships with other children who had visually unpleasant deformities. As long as he thought he was just a disabled freak he could live with himself. He was the same as all the others in his school, and despite their differences, they could all bond because they all had similar social issues.

But, as information began to leak out about the canisters from space and alien plots to pollute the human gene pool, the other children at the school started to look at him differently. Parents of even the most deformed children warned against playing with the alien invader. Rumors grew about how Johannes would eat them with this sharp pointed teeth, how he had a laser gun hidden underneath his bed, that he had dangerous psychic powers. It seemed that the more implausible the rumor, the more easily it was believed. Over time, Johannes spent more and more time alone, confused as to what was happening, and how he was a freak even amongst freaks.

There were more like him of course, younger, smaller. Every year the Handels heard more reports about how so-and-so just gave birth to a baby that looked exactly like him. But instead of bringing him closer to the community, it made him more of a pariah. The locals somehow considered him to be the contagion. They figured that he was somehow responsible for this plague, as opposed to recognizing his status as its first victim. Before long his entire family were social outcasts. It was generally believed that whatever little Johannes had, it was contagious, and that just being near him could cause you to produce a deformed, alien child. Several times, windows in his home were broken by vandals hoping to scare the family into leaving town. Johannes' father, a banker, couldn't believe that in this day and age people still acted this way, that they still could be swayed by outrageous rumors and mob mentality. He refused to leave the city of his birth, he refused to go into hiding, to run from the uneducated boors that were increasingly more threatening. In retrospect, this turned out to be a tragic mistake.

When the news broke that the Americans had found an alien spacecraft, and that the plans for an alien invasion had been confirmed, friends called the Handel household and pleaded with Johannes' father to take the family to safety. The father refused, "This will all blow over in a few days," he said. "We still live in a country of laws after all. They are all fearful cowards, all they do is shout and bluster. They have no bite to match their bark." He was concerned though, and as news reports that evening began to show scenes of escalating violence throughout the world, he began to feel that leaving the city for his mother's house might be prudent. As the family went to sleep that night, he lay in bed awake for some time, eventually deciding to begin packing in the morning.

That time never came though. At about midnight, the fear and hatred in the community boiled over. A large mob made their way to the Handel residence. This time they threw no rocks or shouted angry slogans. The first sign that the Handel family had that something was about to go horribly wrong was the sound of several bullets shattering the downstairs glass. Johannes' father awoke immediately and descended the steps in his dark crimson bathrobe. He walked straight out of the front door and told the mob to go home, to leave him be. He threatened to call the police. From the crowd a rifle was leveled and he was shot in the chest. As he lay on the ground dying his fading eyes could see the mob rush forward and with Molotov cocktails set fire to his beloved home.

By this time the rest of the family was awake and watching from the windows. Johannes' older brother rushed to the front door to assess the situation. The fire was spreading rapidly. His mother would die that night, overcome by smoke as she tried to rescue his little brother from his crib. Johannes' older brother would also be shot that night, trying to get the crowd away from the house. Johannes's older sister took him down the back stairs, and through the dark, black smoke to what she hoped was safety in the backyard. She was wrong. The leaders of the crowd had set the fire in hopes of forcing the alien out, and they were ready. As soon as the children cleared the choking smoke, he was grabbed by the crowd. His sister never saw him alive again.

Many conflicting reports of that night's activities surfaced in later years. A parliamentary commission looked into the events almost two decades later and formally apologized to his surviving relatives. To most accounts, the child was taken, still in his pajamas, and put on a mock trial for his so-called crimes against humanity. To a screaming crowd of onlookers the cold, scared boy was accused of horrible crimes, accused of genocide against the human race, accused of sneaking into sleeping women's bedrooms at night to impregnate them with his vile seed. He was quickly sentenced by the crowd to death for his crimes. From the large oak tree that grew in the park two blocks from his home, from the very branches that he had climbed not a week ago, Johannes Handel was lynched. His head was removed from his body and paraded through the streets of Stuttgart along with the heads of whatever other alien children that hadn't been able to escape the violence. By the next morning, sanity had returned to the city, but neither the body nor head of Johannes Handel was ever found.

Fifty years to the day after the alien missiles first fell. The communications room of the White House, Washington, DC

"Contact has been confirmed Mr. President."

"Astronomers at Berkeley are estimating almost a dozen primary vessels, all just outside of Saturn's orbit. There may be smaller, secondary vessels as well, but our telescopes can't resolve that level of detail until they get closer."

"At their present speed and heading they should rendezvous in Earth orbit in about two months."

The voices of his advisors circled around him. Everybody seemed to have something to say.

"The Vice President is on television right now breaking the news to the American people. In six minutes they'll switch to you for your statement."

"You're sure that the Pliedians will hear what I have to say?" he said to his science advisor.

"Well Sir, we can't be sure that they'll have their radios on, but if they do they'll hear. We'll be broadcasting from the most powerful telescopes we have, right at them, at the same frequency they called us on twenty-five years ago."

"Plus, they're probably expecting a statement from us," added the National Security Advisor.

"Good. Let's synch up with the Vice President." A monitor was switched on. They heard what all of America was hearing, what all of the world was hearing. That positive evidence of an alien interstellar fleet had been detected in our solar system, headed towards Earth; purpose unknown.

As the advisors listened, and the makeup artists put the finishing touches on his face, President Miller tried to go over his speech. It had been written years ago, ready to be pulled out for this eventuality. He tried to go over the words, to ensure that it was still accurate, that it still reflected the will of his constituency, but it wasn't the words that worried him, it was his attitude. He knew that this contact would set the tone for all future relations. He knew that the world's people would be looking to him to provide the courage, the moral foundation to survive the coming days. He knew that his father, old and frail in Tyler, Texas, would be watching. Jim didn't want to disappoint him. He didn't want to disappoint any of the people who had helped him on his way, any of the people who were counting on him.

The Vice President was finishing up his statement. "...But we must stand together as a people in the face of what will undoubtedly be a big change in our world, our culture, our sense of selves. I now cede the floor to our President, who is making a statement directly to the Pliedian fleet. Mr. President, I turn to you..."

The director quietly held up a hand with three fingers. Bright lights glared in Jim's eyes. The fingers counted down, three...two...one...go.

"This statement is addressed to you, the interstellar travelers now barreling down towards our world. My name is James Miller, and I am the President of the United States of America and appointed Commander in Chief of the joint United Earth Alliance forces. I make this statement to you as the designated spokesman of Earth's myriad peoples, and with the full backing of all nations and all our citizens. Know that we stand united in this."

"Fifty years ago, your predecessors contaminated our planet with a virus. It was an insidious thing apparently designed to turn us into beings like yourselves. One can only speculate that the purpose of your attack was to make us lose our sense of history and ancestry, and to make us more willing to submit to your culture and leadership."

"I am here to tell you that your strategy has failed. It has failed miserably. No one on this planet considers you to be more than invaders. On Earth, we hold that there is much more to ancestry than mere genetics. We cannot and do not identify with a race of creatures so cowardly, so evil, that they would resort to using a biological attack against a peaceful and innocent civilization. We identify with our true parents, the original human species of this Earth. We identify with our fathers and mothers who raised us, who gave us a sense of value and a sense of self. We honor the memories of our true ancestors, the people who made our civilization, the *Earthling* civilization, regardless of our genetic links."

"We, the adopted sons and daughters of Earth, reject you, and we will fight you to the last man if you attempt to use force against us. You may have removed our ethnicities, but you have not removed our essential humanity. Your strategy has worked against you. Before your arrival, we were many. We were black and white, Chinese and African, Catholic and Muslim. Before your arrival we fought amongst ourselves, but now that is over. Your cowardly attack has shown us that we are truly one. We are truly the same. We are no longer many different races and nationalities, we are now simply 'Earthlings.'"

"Yes, Earthlings. This is our planet, willed to us by our ancestors, ours by right of primogeniture. We honor our lineage as the children of Earth. We will not submit to any external force attempting to take what is ours by birthright. We love this planet. We love our civilization, our *human* civilization. If you come in peace, you are welcome. If you come otherwise, you will face the mighty force of a combined four billion beings, all of whom will fight for our blue sky, our green trees, and our clear rivers. We will fight for our arts, for our sciences, for our cities and farms, for our children and in our parents' names. Know that Earth will always remain a place for Earthlings, for our culture, for our descendants, and no force, however powerful, will ever defeat our love for the glory and wonder of the planet of our birth."

The transmission ends.

Epilogue

The Heinrich Mensen Memorial Clinic for Genetic Reclamation, Toronto, Canada. Three hundred and twenty seven years after the birth of Johannes Handel.

"Push!"

The young girl strained her stomach muscles. Her heart pounded, her feet pressed against the stirrups. "Push!" the doctor yelled again. The geneticists looked down on their patient from the gallery above. Sweat poured from her face. She breathed, in out in out, it didn't help. The doctor said that this would be a difficult birth owing to the baby's size, but she hadn't expected so much pain. She was about to rip apart.

"I see the head," said the doctor, all crouched down between her legs like a catcher waiting for a pitch. "Give me one more big push, just one more." The doctor had his hands on the baby's skull. The girl let out a groan. The doctor guided the newborn out of the birth canal. The spectators who had been holding their breath in anticipation were relieved to hear a tiny cough, then another, then a child's cry. The experiment had been a success. Their decades of research had paid off. A nurse dropped a tool on the floor in shock.

The doctor looked down at the small bloody thing he cradled in his arms. The first difference that you could see was the color. The child's skin wasn't the traditional gray, but instead a ruddy pink. Its head was smaller, far smaller than normal. The rest of its body seemed large and overdeveloped in comparison. The thing looked up at him with its two small, mammal-like, blue eyes. Several of the scientists burst into the room for a first glance. They looked over the doctor's shoulder and got their first glimpse of the child as it reached out and squeezed the doctor's thumb with its tiny hand.

"The first of many!" exclaimed one of the scientists. A cheer was sounded by all.

About the Author

Dominic Peloso worked for over ten years as a bioterrorism and policy analyst for the U.S. government. He no longer does this.

Adopted Son is his second prose novel. His first novel is entitled, City of Pillars, and is probably available in the same place you found this novel.

He is also the author of the webcomic, Tiny Ghosts. (www.tinyghosts.com).

Also Available from The Invisible College Press